ESCAPE TO FLORENCE

ESCAPE

to

FLORENCE

a novel

Kat Devereaux

HARPER

NEW YORK ■ LONDON ■ TORONTO ■ SYDNEY

HARPER

ESCAPE TO FLORENCE. Copyright © 2023 by Kat Devereaux. All rights reserved. Printed in the United States of America. No part of this book may be used or reproduced in any manner whatsoever without written permission except in the case of brief quotations embodied in critical articles and reviews. For information, address HarperCollins Publishers, 195 Broadway, New York, NY 10007.

HarperCollins books may be purchased for educational, business, or sales promotional use. For information, please email the Special Markets Department at SPsales@harpercollins.com.

FIRST US EDITION

Designed by Jamie Lynn Kerner

Library of Congress Cataloging-in-Publication Data has been applied for.

ISBN 978-0-06-332131-1 (pbk.)

23 24 25 26 27 LBC 6 5 4 3 2

Your Magnificence:

I don't have any horses, cloth of gold, splendid jewels, armaments, etc.

This book will have to do.

1

Tori

"FOR I AM SURE THAT NEITHER DEATH, NOR LIFE, NOR ANGELS, NOR principalities, nor powers, nor things present, nor things to come, nor might, nor height, nor depth, nor any other creature shall be able to separate us from the love of God, which is in Christ Jesus our Lord." The vicar's voice rings out in the near-empty church. She's a pleasant middle-aged woman with cotton candy-pink hair and a West Country accent, and she told us straight away to call her Angie. I like her immensely.

"Margaret came to our village twenty-five years ago, after the death of her beloved husband Hugo," Angie continues. "Her dignity, her grace, her Christian faith and her strong sense of fairness endeared her to all who knew her. Today, in a private service with Margaret's closest family, we gather to celebrate her life and commend her soul to God. Let us pray."

Next to me, my mother folds her black-gloved hands in her black-clad lap. She's perfectly rigid, radiating disapproval of everything around her: the squat stone church, the colorful Victorian stained glass, the appliquéd banners with their fat white doves and wonky crosses. I can only imagine what she thinks of Angie's hair. Not for the first time, I wonder how Granny and Grandad—whom I remember as a vague, gentle presence, all frayed wool and pipe tobacco—managed to produce such an appalling social conformist.

There's a muffled sound somewhere behind me, and I look round to see a little group of women lurking at the back of the church by the noticeboards. I recognize some of them as Granny's friends from the local Women's Institute. I smile and nod, motioning them to sit down, and Mummy kicks me in the ankle. I've broken the rules, you see. This is strictly family only, even though Daddy died when I was little, and my sister Charlie's kids are sick with something violently contagious, and my husband Duncan was simply too busy to come, so that only left Mummy and me. We're supposed to bury my brilliant, generous, loving grandmother quietly and without making a fuss. It isn't right. It isn't fair.

Angie's reading a psalm now, the one about the Lord being our shepherd. I glance over my shoulder and see the WI ladies massed in the back pews, silk-scarved heads bowed in prayer. A sob rises in my throat and I press my hand to my mouth to stifle it, but it bursts out as an ugly, strangled hiccup.

My mother stiffens. She puts her gloved hand on my arm and lets it rest there for a second. Then she returns it to her lap and goes on looking ahead, back straight, perfectly rigid.

⁓

AS MUMMY STALKS OFF ACROSS THE CHURCH CAR PARK TOWARDS her elderly Jag, Angie approaches me. "Tori, are you rushing off? Or have you got time for a quick word?"

"Yes, of course," I say. "My train doesn't go for ages."

She beams at me. "Great. Then we could have a cup of tea and a proper chat, if you like. And I can tell you all about the vigil. It really was a lovely event—I was so sorry you couldn't be there, but I know you were with us in spirit."

I blink at her. I didn't hear anything about a vigil, and I can't imagine Mummy condoning such a thing. It sounds distinctly like making a fuss. "Sorry?"

"The vigil, last night, at the Chapel of Rest. We had ever such a good turnout. Mostly locals, obviously, but word must have spread because a few of your grandmother's friends came from London and beyond. We even had one or two Italians—because your granny had friends over there, didn't she? She told me all about how you two used to go there together."

"She did," I say. "We did."

"That must have been wonderful," Angie says. "Anyway, I know it was too much for you, the vigil, but I thought you'd like to hear about it." She's starting to look puzzled herself now. "You don't know what I'm talking about, do you?"

"I don't," I say.

"Right," Angie says. "Right. Yes, we'd better have a cup of tea. The vicarage is just over the road. Come on." She takes my arm and guides me through the lychgate and across the narrow lane to a pretty, low-slung cottage in Cotswold stone. I'm starting to feel a bit odd, if I'm honest: shaky and unreal. I feel like I might break down and cry properly for the first time since Charlie called me to tell me that Granny had been taken to hospital and then again, just a short while later, to say that she was gone.

"In here." Angie opens a side door and ushers me into a homely kitchen painted in gentle blues and greens, with cacti ranged along the windowsill and an elderly cat dozing in front of a big cast-iron stove. Once I'm seated at the scrubbed-pine table with a plate of biscuits and a clay mug of tea with a peace sign painted on the side, Angie sits down opposite with her own tea.

"The first thing to say," she begins, "is that anything we discuss here is completely confidential. The second is that if you need a bit of a weep, go ahead and have one. I won't judge you." She nods towards the box of tissues by my elbow. "And you can swear all you want—it doesn't shock me, nothing does. Understood?"

She looks so serious. She looks, in fact, really concerned and I have a feeling, a nasty, creeping feeling deep down in my gut, about what she's going to say. "Understood."

"Good," Angie says. "Now, the vigil. You really didn't know about it?"

"I didn't. If I'm honest, I'm not totally sure what one of those is."

"I see. Well, it's not necessarily common practice in the Church of England, but our parish has a tradition of holding a vigil the night before a funeral—a bit like a wake, you know, in the Catholic tradition. It's something we do for people who were really important to our church community. And since the funeral was going to be family only . . . well, it was a chance for all of us to say goodbye, especially as she died so suddenly. So we asked your mother if we could hold one for Margaret, and she gave us her permission."

"What, really?" Mummy finds the C of E a bit infra dig. I can't see her giving the go-ahead to anything that smells even slightly of Rome.

"Well, not right away," Angie admits. "I think she was concerned it would create more work and stress at a difficult time. Which is totally understandable, of course, but in this case we'd planned to organize everything ourselves and she wasn't expected to do anything or even to attend. So once I'd made that clear, she agreed. And obviously our first thought was to invite you. I know you're not a churchgoer . . ."

"Sorry," I say.

"No, no, it's fine. But I know you and Margaret had a special bond. She talked about you all the time. And my own mum died of a stroke—I know what a horrible shock it is, and how painful when you don't get to say goodbye. So I phoned you up."

I put my mug down. "You phoned me?"

"Yes. I couldn't get through to your mobile—it wouldn't even connect. I suppose the signal isn't great up there in the Highlands."

"No," I say. "The house is in a bit of a dead spot."

Angie nods. "I can imagine. Anyway, I phoned your landline and your husband answered. Duncan, is it? I told him all about the vigil, and he said that he was sure you'd love to be there, and that he'd ask you about it and get back to me. Then he phoned about half an hour later and said that you'd talked about it and you weren't feeling up to coming. Losing your granny had been a terrible shock and you wouldn't be able to cope. He sounded completely convincing." She grimaces. "From the way he talked, I didn't expect to see you at the funeral, either."

For a moment I don't know how to respond. All I can think about is how I had to argue with Duncan to be allowed to come here at all. He said that funerals were for the living, and attending wouldn't bring Granny back. He said the train tickets would be extortionate, the plane too much of a fiddle, a hotel room an indulgence we couldn't afford. He said the estate couldn't spare me and I'd be selfish to go. He said I'd only get angry with my mother and come back and take it out on him. He said I'd only get upset. He said I wouldn't cope. He said I wouldn't cope.

"Tori?" Angie prompts me.

I stare at her. "That bastard," I say. "That absolute fucking *bastard*."

⤲

ANGIE DOESN'T TELL ME WHAT TO DO. SHE DOESN'T TELL ME WHAT Jesus would do, either. She just listens as I rant and cry and try to piece things together, supplying more tea and biscuits and, finally, a large whisky from the bottle she keeps in her study. Only when she's giving me a lift to the station in her ancient Range Rover does she finally say: "Tori, if you're ever in a situation where you need somewhere to stay, there's a room at the vicarage for however long you need it. Okay?"

"Okay," I say. "That's really kind, thank you."

"It's no problem. And here we are." She pulls to a stop in front of the station building. It's picturesque like the rest of the village, with immaculate whitewash and pots of purple cyclamen. "Now, before you go—I meant to give you this earlier, but we had more urgent things to discuss." She rummages in her bag and passes me an envelope in thick, heavy cream paper, with *To Victoria* written on it in Granny's perfect copperplate.

For a moment I just look at it, there in my hands. This last thing from Granny. "Is this . . ." I have to clear my throat. "Did she write it in hospital?"

"No. She gave it to me last year, when she was updating her will. She said . . ." Angie gives a sort of choked half laugh. "You know, I didn't really understand at the time. She was worried that if she took ill, she wouldn't get to say goodbye to you before she died. Not your sister or your mother, specifically you. I remember thinking that she was probably just having a fuss, like people do when they think about mortality. Fixating on something to take away the really big fear." She shakes her head. "But now . . . look, she never talked about your husband, or not badly. But I've got to wonder if she had him figured out."

Now I laugh—hiccupy, tearful laughter. "Maybe," I say, wiping my eyes. "It wouldn't surprise me. Granny's bullshit-o-meter was always better than mine. I mean, she only met him, what, a handful of times? But maybe . . ." I trail off as it dawns on me just how rarely Granny and Duncan had actually met—how often I'd had to choose between him and her. How many trips south got cancelled because of some last-minute problem on the farm? How many times did I cut short one of our phone calls because Duncan needed something?

"I think you've got a lot of processing ahead," Angie says gently. "If there's anything you need to talk over . . ."

There's the distant, tinny sound of a voiceover announcement and I look up to see a train—my train—already approaching the station. "Oh God," I say. "I've got to go. Thanks so much again." I'm half-panicked, half-relieved. I lean over and give Angie a quick hug before getting out of the car and grabbing my overnight bag from the back seat.

"No problem," she calls after me as I bolt for the entrance. "Here any time!"

I make it onto the train just in time. I flop into my seat, put my bag at my feet and look at the envelope, wondering what to do. Of course, I'm desperately curious to know what's inside. But once I open the envelope, once I read whatever Granny has to say to me, I'll never have that moment of discovery again. All the words will be finished.

Curiosity wins out as the train approaches Bristol Temple Meads. I rip open the envelope and find a single sheet of paper.

> *Dearest Tori,*
>
>   *In case I don't see you, I want to tell you that I have left you and your sister a gift of £30,000 each. You may use it for whatever purpose you think best. My only condition is that you do not spend any part of it on anyone else. This money is for you and you alone. What you do with it isn't up to me.*
>
>   *But if it were up to me, my darling, I should tell you to go*

back to Florence. I have such wonderful memories of my time there. With you, of course—but also as a young woman, quite free, with the means to do as I pleased. I can't give you that freedom, though I've often wished you'd take it for yourself. Perhaps I can give you the means.

I love you.
Nonna

2

Stella

MY FRIEND BERTA GALLURÌ WAS A HERO OF THE RESISTANCE. IF SHE had lived, I think she would have been one of those great twentieth-century women, an intellectual and a fighter—like Lidia Menapace, Ada Gobetti, Tina Anselmi, Carla Capponi, Rossana Rossanda. If she had lived.

Berta was nineteen when the Nazi occupation began in September 1943. She was a bright young woman from a family of anti-Fascists, the daughter of our local pharmacist, and she was studying literature at the University of Florence. The day she opened her shutters and saw a column of German soldiers marching up the via Romana, her first thought was to find a way home, to Romituzzo, because she knew that we would need her. Not as a courier like me, or a combatant like her brother Davide—although there were women combatants, more than you think—but as an organizer.

Organization was Berta's great gift. Within weeks of her arrival, our little town had a growing network of girls and women who carried messages, smuggled illegal publications and false papers, and took essential supplies to the various partisan groups that were forming in the hills south of Florence. Our partisans were young and old, communist and socialist, monarchist and liberal, Catholic and Trotskyist and anarchist. Many were completely new to combat, while some had served in the military or the police. If all these different people were going to work together, and do so effectively, then they needed all the help they could get.

Berta understood this perfectly. The women in her network belonged to no party, espoused no faction. We went where we were asked, when we were asked; we worked for anyone who needed us, and we never quibbled. This was my Resistance: the everyday routine of messages on cigarette paper and guns in shopping bags, of delivery runs fitted in around school and church and home. If I have no spectacular stories to tell you, it's because my Resistance was unspectacular, necessary, quiet. But it was dangerous, too.

On the evening of 15 February 1944, Berta was returning from Florence, where she had collected copies of the clandestine newsletter *The Workers' Struggle* to distribute in Romituzzo. As she often did, she'd sewn the newsletters into the lining of her handbag. When she got off the train, she was stopped by a German soldier who checked her papers and looked in her bag. A routine check and one she'd passed so many times, but this soldier had a sharp eye. Perhaps the worn old lining, unpicked and restitched so many times, had begun to give way; perhaps the stark black newsprint peeked through a rent in the silk. He took the bag from her, tore open the lining and found the newsletters hidden there.

Berta didn't go easily. That's what people tell me, people who were there. She fought like a cat, screaming and clawing as the Germans bundled her into their truck. The next day, her broken and violated body was left at dawn outside her father's shop on piazza Garibaldi, in the very center of town, as a warning to those who dared resist.

My friend Berta Gallurì was a strong woman, stronger than you can imagine. She died without giving up a single name. I know that because our little network went on existing. I know because the Germans didn't come for me.

⌘

I DIDN'T SEE POOR BERTA THAT MORNING, THANK GOD. I DIDN'T even know that she had been caught. But when I came downstairs to make myself breakfast before school, I found my father sitting at the kitchen table with his face in his hands and I knew that something was wrong.

"Papà," I said, "what's happened? Why aren't you at work?"

My father raised his head. He was a big man, an impressive man—rather like Peppone in the *Don Camillo* stories—but that day he looked tired and old. "Achille has gone to open up the garage," he said, in a voice quite unlike his usual one. "Your mother is having a lie-in."

If my mother was still in bed, something must have been *very* wrong. I sat down next to him and watched as he rubbed a hand over his face. I didn't know what to do, and I'm not sure he did, either. Eventually I put my hand on his arm, and he briefly held it in his own rough hand before letting go again. He took a clean rag from his pocket and pressed it to his eyes.

"Stella," he said, "promise me you won't get involved with the partisans. It's enough that we have to worry about your brother. Promise me."

"I promise I won't get involved," I said. And it wasn't a lie, technically, because I was already involved. I'd been part of Berta's network for months by that stage.

"Good," my father said. For a moment he looked as if he were going to say something else—as if he were looking for the words—but then he cleared his throat and repeated: "Good." He got to his feet and went to the stove, moving a little painfully as he always did in the mornings. Back in the 1920s, my mother once told me, he had refused to fix the car of a local Fascist leader. The Fascist and his henchmen had shattered both his kneecaps. My father never told that story, or not in my hearing.

"I'll make the coffee," I said. "I have time before school."

He was already spooning the chicory powder—nasty stuff—into the coffee pot. "I'm making it. And you're not going to school."

Now I was really alarmed. My father never made anything for me, and he never let me have a day off unless I was very sick. And I had to go to school, because I was supposed to drop something off on my way there. I often managed my work that way. Since I was clever and wanted to be a teacher, my parents allowed me to keep studying even though the nearest high school was at Castelmedici, twenty minutes or so along the train line towards Florence. And since I was small and plain and looked young for fourteen, and I took the same train at the same time six days a week, I could smuggle all kinds of useful stuff without attracting the attention of either the Fascists or the Germans. Or my parents, for that matter.

"Papà, what's wrong?" I asked. "Please tell me. Is Mamma sick? Is that it?"

My father shook his head. He was staring at the coffee pot, watching it as it started to hiss and bubble. I know now that he was fighting with himself, caught between telling me what he had heard—and perhaps even seen—and keeping it from me, keeping me innocent for as long as he could. "There are Germans at the station," he said at last. "More than usual, and they're checking everyone."

"But that's all right," I said, though my heart was beating fast. "I don't have anything to hide."

"I still don't like it." His voice was grim. "I don't like to send you there alone."

"Then get Achille to walk with me, or Enzo. Please, Papà. I have to hand in a Latin composition, a really important one. I've been working on it for days. Please."

My father grunted to himself. He poured out a cup of chicory and put it in front of me with a piece of bread. "I suppose Enzo could take you along, if you absolutely must go," he said. "He's working today."

I was relieved, though I didn't dare show it. Enzo was a friend of my brother Achille, and he helped out at the garage whenever there was spare work to be done. Both boys were ardent communists, although—unlike my brother—Enzo had the good sense to keep his clandestine work a secret from my father. Papà thought he was a good influence. I thought he was wonderful, but, more to the point, I knew he had my orders for that day's run. How simple it would be, how much easier if we could do the handover somewhere quiet, well away from the garage and my father's tiresome vigilance.

"And if he sees me on to the train and meets me when I come back, then there's really nothing to worry about," I went on. "Honestly, Papà, I'll be quite all right. You'll see." I knew that I was on the point of being insolent, that I had already pushed my father much harder than he would usually permit, but he didn't seem to notice. "Please," I said again.

For a long moment he seemed sunk in thought, and then he nodded, just once. "Very well. Finish your breakfast, and I'll go across the road and tell Enzo to get ready." He went out before I could thank him, his hands in his pockets, defeated.

When I went out into the cold hazy morning, Enzo was waiting for me at the gate. He looked serious, but I didn't think anything of it because Enzo was always serious. His father had died in an accident before the war and he'd lost his mother recently, too, when a stray bomb destroyed the factory where she worked just outside Castelmedici. Enzo's parents had moved to Romituzzo when they were newly married, and they had no family in the area. So he had been taken in by the Frati family, who lived in the next street to us on the very outskirts of town. It made perfect sense for him to live there because he was practically part of their household already. Sandro Frati, Achille and Enzo had ganged up together on their first ever day at the local school and now, at fifteen, they were still the best of mates.

"*Ciao*, Stellina," Enzo said, and kissed me on each cheek. It was the most innocent thing in the world, but I still remember how it thrilled me. "Come on—let's get you to the station."

"And make sure she gets on the train," Achille's voice rang out. He was standing in the garage forecourt in his greasy overalls, his cap pulled down over his curly black hair and a thick woollen scarf around his neck. "Don't just leave her there and piss off."

Enzo rolled his eyes. "*Ma dai!*"

We set off together along the road towards the station. As soon as we were out of sight of the garage, Enzo pulled me into a narrow side alley. He took hold of my shoulders and looked at me with that serious expression of his. For just a second, I thought he was going to kiss me for real.

"Are you all right, Stellina?" he asked in a low voice. "If you don't think you can face it today, I'll make some excuse to your father and go instead of you."

"Of course I can face it," I said. I was insulted, and more than a little disappointed. "Do you think I'm going to back out just because of a few Germans?"

"No, no. It's just that, well, after what happened . . ." He was frowning now. "Don't you know?"

"What? What should I know? Everyone's acting so strangely this morning. I don't understand what the problem is."

Enzo took my hands in his and he told me, in simple and terrible words, what had happened to Berta. And then he held me as I cried.

⸎

THE SQUARE OUTSIDE THE STATION—BACK THEN, IT WAS CALLED piazza Burresi—was even busier than usual. I don't know if Papà actually knew about the Germans but, whether he meant to or not, he'd told the truth. The square was lined with armored cars and there were soldiers stopping people on the way into the station and checking their papers. I realized then that I had put Enzo in danger by wanting him to come with me; a young man, a worker, was always going to be more suspicious in the eyes of the Germans than a schoolgirl in uniform. They might think he was a partisan, which he was, or a draft dodger, which he wasn't—but only because he wasn't old enough to be drafted.

"You don't have to come in with me," I said in my brightest voice. With the Germans around, it was best not to sound fearful. "I can manage by myself."

"Don't be silly," Enzo said. "I want to see you off." He spoke lightly, too, but his arm was tight around my shoulders.

As it turned out, the soldiers didn't bother with us. They took a cursory look at Enzo's identity card and waved mine away. Enzo waited with me until the train arrived and then he did kiss me, just softly, on the lips.

"Have a good day, Stellina. I'll be here when you get back."

I got into the train carriage with my cheeks burning and fought my way through the crowd to find somewhere to stand, finally contriving to wedge myself into a corner with my satchel between my hip and the wall. In the satchel were my schoolbooks, my jotter and a little paperback copy of Machiavelli's comedy *The Mandrake*, which Enzo had given me to carry. It might have contained some kind of message in code, likely written in vinegar or some other form of invisible ink, or perhaps it had a compartment cut into the leaves. I didn't open it and I certainly didn't ask for details. The more I knew, the more danger I would bring upon others if I was caught. It was my responsibility to know as little as possible.

When I got to Castelmedici, I was to walk to school as I always did, except that this time I should pause at the gates of the municipal park to shift my satchel from my right shoulder to my left. My contact would find me then. I was used to this kind of arrangement by now, but I still preferred the mornings when I simply went to school and didn't have to rehearse that day's signal in my head and hope, the whole time, that the right person would approach me.

The train was running slower even than usual, stopping and starting. I was hot and uncomfortable, both from the stifling air of the packed carriage and from fear that I would miss my connection and fail to hand over the book.

"No doubt the communists have blown up the line again," a woman in a fur coat said rather loudly, looking around the carriage as if to rally us to her aid. "As if it does anything but make life harder for the rest of us." But she was met with satisfying silence, and one or two people shook their heads.

Eventually the train juddered to yet another stop, and we were in Castelmedici. Now I had to fight to get out of the doors, because hardly anyone else was getting off, but I managed it, and I was outside in the cold air and already ten minutes late for school. I wanted to run, but I forced myself to walk slowly and look confidently ahead, just as if it were any other day. There were fewer Germans at Castelmedici than there had been at Romituzzo—I never could figure out their patterns—and I was able to walk right past a little group of soldiers who were poring over an elderly man's papers, and out into the square. I picked up my pace as I walked, so absorbed in my task that I almost missed the gates of the park altogether. But I caught myself in time and, feigning discomfort, I stopped just long enough to take my heavy satchel off one shoulder and move it to the other. Then I kept walking, because the whole point of these "flying rendezvous," as we called them, was not to look as if you were waiting for someone.

"Mimma!" someone called behind me: a female voice, cheerful and light. Mimma was the code name I used for my work. "Mimma, wait for me!"

I slowed down a little and a woman appeared alongside me, pushing a bicycle with a little boy riding happily in the basket. She was wearing a rather shabby overcoat and her hair was covered with a scarf. She looked just like any young mother out running errands.

"How lovely to see you," she said, smiling at me as if we were old friends. The child, obliging, smiled at me, too. "You're off to school, I suppose. Tonino and I will accompany you some of the way, if that's all right. I should like to catch up."

Her eyes were fixed on me, her manner determinedly bright. I glanced over her shoulder and saw two black-capped gendarmes on the street corner a little way behind us, apparently deep in conversation. These were Fascists, members of Mussolini's National Republican Guard, and their task was to root out and crush those who helped the partisans.

"Of course," I said. "Let's walk together."

We set off, and she began chattering away about people and places that meant nothing to me in the slightest. For all I know, it was completely made up. We walked together in that way for a couple of blocks—the Fascists, thank God, made no move to follow us—and then she made a regretful face, gave me a quick hug and said that she ought to go.

"I'm glad we could catch up for a few minutes," I said. "Oh, and I forgot! Thank you for the loan of the book." I took *The Mandrake* out of my satchel and handed it to her, and she tucked it into her bicycle basket, next to Tonino.

"*Ciao*, Mimma," she said, and cycled off with a wave. I waved back and hurried towards school.

⊷

WHEN I GOT BACK TO ROMITUZZO, ENZO WAS WAITING FOR ME ON the platform just as he promised. I had spent the whole school day with the news of Berta's death going round and round in my head, and I wanted to collapse into his arms, but I didn't. We made our way past the Germans, who didn't even look at us this time, and began to walk home.

"Good day at school?" Enzo asked once we were safely away from piazza Burresi.

"What do you think?"

Enzo laughed. He knew, of course—knew how it sickened me to spend my days pretending to be an obedient girl and a good Fascist. "You could have left last summer," he reminded me.

I sighed. "I know. But then I couldn't train to be a teacher and, well . . ."

He took my hand. "Just think, Stellina," he said quietly. "Just think of the lessons you'll teach one day in the future."

It's miraculous, really. I was scared and sad; there was danger everywhere and yet I could still marvel at the touch of his skin. I suppose that's youth.

"Achille's out on a job," Enzo said. "Been called out to fix a broken bicycle."

"Where? Santa Marta?" This was our shorthand for the old farmhouse, high up in the hills, that had been taken over by the independent communist brigade to which Enzo and Achille belonged. They were both couriers, but Achille was also the brigade's unofficial mechanic, fixing bikes and motorcycles and getting hold of valuable fuel and parts.

Enzo shook his head. "Other way. Sant'Appiano."

Sant'Appiano was a hill village north of Romituzzo, towards Florence. I knew that there was a little knot of partisans operating near there, not communists but monarchists. "A new client, then," I said, trying to keep my voice casual. "How did they hear about Achille?"

Enzo grimaced. "I suppose word's got around."

As we turned into my street, I slipped my hand out of his. My father was waiting, standing in the forecourt with his arms crossed. He nodded as we approached.

"Bye," Enzo muttered, and hurried across the road towards the garage.

My mother was where I knew she'd be: in the back room that served as a laundry and storage space. It was cold in there, but it was the only place where she could see the little road that led from the back of our row of houses up into the hills. Achille always took that route home if he could, to avoid the checkpoints. She was sitting by the window, swaddled inadequately in an old blanket, working through a basketful of socks for darning. She looked so small, so fragile, that I suddenly felt very sorry for her.

"Mamma, won't you go and do that by the stove? I can keep watch."

She looked at me with dull, distracted eyes. "What? No. He shouldn't be long."

"Can I bring you a coffee, at least?"

My mother shook her head. "No," she said, as I knew she would. She never ate or drank anything while Achille was out on a run—it was her bargain with God. "No, thank you. There's some soup in the pantry," she added.

My stomach was tight and acidic. The idea of soup, those bland soups we lived off during the war, was revolting. "Thanks, Mamma," I said, and went to the kitchen to warm myself up.

I was sitting in the big chair by the stove, trying to read the portion of Manzoni I had been assigned for my literature class—and if you have read *The Betrothed* from beginning to end, then you have done better than I have—when I heard the sound of an engine and then, a moment later, a cry of joy from my mother.

"Achille! Achille, *tesoro*, there you are. How you made me worry!"

The door of the kitchen opened, letting in a whisper of frigid air, and Achille strode in. His overalls were smeared with mud and he was chafing his hands together, but his eyes were bright. He always looked so happy when he came back from a run, as if he'd won a race—which I suppose he had.

My mother bustled in after him. "Stella, lazy girl, get up and let your brother sit down. Do you want some soup, Achille? Get him some soup," she instructed me, without waiting for his reply. "I'll go and let your father know you're back." And she hurried out again, pulling the door shut behind her.

"For Christ's sake, don't move," Achille said as I made to get up. "You need the heat more than I do. You look half-dead."

"Do you want some soup?" I asked, though I knew what the answer would be.

Achille made a face. "God, no. I had to force down a bowl of the stuff at lunchtime." He pulled out one of the kitchen chairs and sat on it backwards, resting his arms on the back and his chin on his arms, and grinned at me.

"Enzo says you went out to help the monarchists," I said. "Why on earth did they send for you?"

"Because I'm the best mechanic in the Valdana," Achille said. "And theirs was taken out by the Germans."

I closed my book and held it tight in my lap. "What happened? Was he arrested?"

"Shot. They were planning to ambush a convoy heading to Florence, carrying prisoners for deportation." Achille spoke as if this were the most everyday occurrence—which it was, back then. "They were lying in wait by the roadside when this guy lost his nerve. He broke cover and ran out into the road just as the Germans were approaching." He mimed firing a rifle.

"So they didn't manage to free the prisoners," I said.

"No, they did not, thanks to that *coglione*. And now they're down a mechanic, too. Good thing I could assist."

"You showed up in your red kerchief, of course."

"Of course." Achille fished it out of his pocket and waved it at me. "You think I'd let them forget that a godless communist helped them out?"

The kitchen door opened. Achille stuffed the kerchief back into his pocket.

"Stella!" my mother scolded. "What are you doing still hogging the stove? Where is your brother's soup?"

"It's all right, Mamma." Achille got up and went over to her, put an arm around her shoulders. "I'm fine. I'm not hungry. And Stella should stay in the warm. Look at her, she's shivering."

And I was. I was shivering, and not from the cold—although I was cold—but because the events of that day were crowding in on me.

I couldn't stop thinking about that convoy rolling on unimpeded, the trucks full of frightened people being carried to their deaths.

My mother looked at me with blank disdain. I could see it in her face, how little she thought of me in that moment—and not in the sense that she despised me, although perhaps she did, but in the sense that I scarcely figured in her world. She turned back to Achille.

"You shall have a bath, then, before your father comes home. I'll heat up the water. Stella, go and fetch the tub, and then you can start on the potatoes for dinner."

Achille opened his mouth to protest, but there was no point. I got up and went to do as I was told.

3

Tori

THE FLAT IS BEAUTIFUL. I CAN SEE THAT REALLY. WHITE WALLS AND green shutters, the floor a green-brown-cream tile that might be ugly elsewhere, but this is Florence. It's very small—probably someone's old living room carved in two, with a bedroom only just big enough for a double bed and a chest of drawers. I don't need more space, though. I don't want more space.

The agent, Chiara, throws open a window and beckons me over. Leaning out, she points up and to the right, and there—crowning above a row of uneven terracotta-tile roofs—is the great orange dome of the cathedral.

"See?" She beams at me, and I know she's expecting me to smile back. I know she wants me to be excited about this. It is exciting, of course, and I'll be excited at some point if I ever stop being tired.

"Lovely," I say, and step back from the window. It's cool in this living-room-kitchen-hallway thing, sheltered from the fierce afternoon sun that's scorching the building opposite. That I can appreciate.

"Three hundred and fifty euros per week," Chiara says. She's tiny and slim and immaculately dressed, probably around my age—so early thirties—and she speaks perfect English with a slightly American accent. She is the first agent I tried, because she was at the top of the search results for *florence flat rental estate agent*, and this is the first flat she's shown me. 350 a week. I try to do the math in my head, but it's foggy.

"What's that a month?"

"Now, here there's a deal." Chiara beams again. "If you want it for a whole month, you can have it for 1300. All bills included, of course."

It's a nice flat and this is a nice street and I want to lie down. There's a voice in my mind, Duncan's voice, saying: *Thirteen hundred euros a month for two rooms? You do know you're being taken for a fool?*

"How about for longer?" I say.

"Longer? Like two months?"

"I don't know yet. A year, maybe more?"

"Right," Chiara says. "I see. So you want to stay in Italy long-term?"

"I don't know. Maybe. I thought I should give it a shot while I can—you know, with Brexit coming and no deal yet. It feels kind of urgent."

"And what are you going to be doing here? Do you have a job lined up in Florence?"

"I'm a freelancer," I say. "A writer. I can work where I like."

Chiara is studying me now. I see myself through her eyes: ancient cotton shirt, jeans, long blonde hair in need of a trim. Grayish, just-off-the-plane skin. Shoes, good shoes but definitely countrified, possibly smelling of damp because, after five years on a farm in the West Highlands, everything I own smells of damp. But then her eyes reach the handbag, the faithful old Fendi given to me by Granny.

"You're a writer," she says, with a distinct note of *really?*

"Yes. Well, I do a bit of everything. Bit of journalism, bit of copywriting, bit of editorial stuff—whatever people need."

This doesn't have the reassuring effect I'd hoped for. Chiara looks positively alarmed. "And you'll be looking for freelance work here in Italy? Because I have to warn you, the economy . . ."

"Oh no. I've got a pretty good client network back in the UK. I'm actually taking a bit of time for my own work at the moment, finishing up a book for Swithin and Sons—non-fiction. Under contract, of course." I say it with all the confidence I can muster.

Chiara's smile switches back on. Oh, thank God. "Right," she says. "Well, this could work out nicely. I happen to know the landlady is thinking about looking for a longer-term tenant—at least, she was the last time we spoke. This could save us all a lot of trouble. Let me just call her now." She whips a phone out of her oversized bag and paces off into the tiny bedroom, talking in rapid Italian. My Italian is reasonable enough—I've just about kept it alive with reading and music and sneaking bits of Italian Netflix while Duncan's in bed—but my brain can't handle the switch, not today. I stare out of the window at the vivid-yellow houses opposite until she comes back in.

"The landlady is happy to rent it for longer," she says, phone still to ear. "It would be 1100 a month and the bills in your name. That means some paperwork, but I can help you with that. Does that work?"

"Great."

"Four plus four or three plus two?"

Oh God, not math again. "Sorry?"

"The contract," she says, and I can see that she's wondering if I did any research at all before I turned up in Florence looking for a flat. And the answer is no, not really. "There are two kinds of long-term contract in Italy. Four years renewable for another four, and three years renewable for another two. There's a shorter contract too, the *transitorio*, but I'm not sure whether you can get residency with one of those."

"Whichever works," I say.

"And when do you want to move in?"

"Whenever I can. I've got a hotel for now, but . . ."

"Right," she says, and resumes speaking into the phone in Italian. I look out of the window again and wait for her to address me.

"Okay," Chiara says after a while. "If you decide you want to go ahead, then I can draft the contract and we can fix an appointment with Federica—that's the landlady—to meet here in a few days' time for the handover. Do you have a lawyer?"

"No. Do I need one?"

"I can explain the contract to you, but you might want someone to look it over. And then there's the residency stuff, and the bank, and . . ." She waves a vague hand. "There's a lot of bureaucracy—put it that way."

"I'll be honest," I say, "I don't want to do more than I absolutely have to do."

"Then you definitely want a lawyer. I can send you some names if you like."

"Thank you."

"My pleasure," Chiara says. "Do you want to ask anything else about the apartment?"

I look around again. It's clean and anonymous, furnished in white and slate-gray and plum like the holiday rental it is. There's a mocha pot sitting on the hob and a selection of glossy travel magazines is fanned out on the low glass coffee table. I can't remember and I can't be bothered to look, but I'm half-sure there are fat rolled towels tied in ribbon at the end of the bed. I think of the house I've left behind, the sprawling perma-damp pile with the moth-eaten stags' heads and the green carpet and the portraits of MacNair ancestors, row upon row, stern and reproachful.

"No," I say, "it's perfect."

Chiara hesitates. She picks up the keys from the occasional table where she dropped them when we came in and dangles them from her finger. "You're sure? You definitely want to do this?"

"Definitely," I say. And somewhere deep down, under the layers of grief and pain and cotton-woolly exhaustion, I know it's true.

❧

WHEN CHIARA HAS WAVED GOODBYE AND DASHED OFF DOWN THE street in her sparkly designer trainers, I turn the other way and wander towards piazza del Duomo, the huge irregular-shaped square around the cathedral, in search of a drink. It's only half past three, but the pavement seats are already filling with people cradling big round glasses of luminous-orange Aperol spritz. Granny would think it irredeemably touristy. She knew all the places, the hidden little angular piazzas and the chic bars in the courtyards of apparently private houses, but I want to be touristy today. I want to be in the sun and around people.

I sit down at a table outside a bar facing the side entrance of the cathedral and order a negroni, which arrives in a heavy etched-glass tumbler with a little ramekin of peanuts and some olives and a bowl of crisps. I stretch out my legs, feeling the sun warm them, and take a long sip of my drink. It's pure alcohol, gin and vermouth and Campari, orangey-bitter and ferocious. I take a long sip and stuff a handful of crisps in my mouth and think about ordering a second one.

"Enjoying your trip?"

I turn my head. The man at the next table is watching me. He looks to be in his forties, with a friendly, rather lived-in face and dark hair scattered with silver. He smiles, his eyes crinkling, and for just a moment I want to tell him everything.

This isn't a holiday. I've left my husband. I've left my husband and fucked off to Italy because I couldn't stand it anymore.

"Yes, thanks," I say and almost add: "You?" But then I think, no, he's Italian, isn't he? He's probably a local—though surely locals don't come and sit here. But then a group of people arrive, three men and a woman—all beautifully dressed—and descend on him, hugging and kissing and exclaiming. He gives me a rueful look, and I pick up my drink and stare at the green-striped marble of the cathedral. I'm relieved, I think.

I don't have the second negroni. The first one almost does me in. I didn't sleep last night, didn't sleep the night before; I don't remember the last time I really felt like I slept. I get to my feet, a little bit unsteady, and walk down via del Proconsolo towards the embankment and my hotel. By the time I get to my room, exhaustion is pulling at me. I'll just have a nap, I think, before I go for dinner. Just an hour or so and then I'll shower and change and wander across the river, try and find one of those little places Granny liked so much and have a bowl of pasta. I curl up on the bed and fall instantly asleep.

4

MY PHONE WAKES ME UP. I PEER AT THE SCREEN. IT'S ALMOST SEVEN in the morning and my sister Charlie is calling. I'm groggy and parched and I don't want to talk to her, but I know I'll have to eventually, so why not now? I accept the call and put the phone to my ear, roll onto my back and stare at the painted wooden ceiling.

"Tori," Charlie shrieks. "Tori, what the f... what on earth are you doing? Where are you?"

"Florence." In the background I can hear Charlie's twin boys crashing around and Ben, her husband, grumbling.

"Well, that's rich! That's bloody rich, going off on a jaunt when the Cheviots are still lambing."

"You spoke to Duncan, then."

"Of course I spoke to Duncan," she says. "He phoned me yesterday. Really, Tori, you are appallingly selfish."

There are roses on the ceiling. They look like Tudor roses, but they can't be, can they? "He hasn't phoned me," I say.

"I should think not. He doesn't know what to do with himself, poor bloke. He's in pieces."

"How?"

Charlie sighs. "What do you mean, how?"

"How is he in pieces? I've never seen it happen. I mean, he got a bit irate once about fishing permits, but I don't think that counts."

"I don't know how you can joke at a time like this," Charlie says.

Tears are rising, hot and itchy. I rub at my eyes with the heel of my hand. I don't want to cry, not now, not again.

"Look," Charlie says in that irritating tone of supreme patience, the one she affects when one of the twins makes a Poor Choice like peeing on the floor, or exposing himself to the next-door neighbors. "I see what's going on. Farm life is stressful and you're tired, and obviously the whole misunderstanding about Granny's funeral just tipped you over the edge."

"It wasn't a misunderstanding," I say. "He tried to stop me going! And he lied about the vigil. I could have been there with Granny's friends. I could have said goodbye to her properly with people who loved her, rather than on my own, in a cold empty church, with bloody Mummy doing her Iron Lady act. Thanks for abandoning me, by the way."

"Now, that's not fair. You know perfectly well—"

"Why would he do that?" I burst out. "I hardly got to see Granny when she was alive. And Duncan must have known how much I missed her—what she meant to me. Why would he do this now that she's dead? Why would he lie?"

"I don't know," Charlie says. "Maybe he really did think you wouldn't cope. And you're not coping, are you? Maybe he felt justified in telling just one lie for the sake of a quiet life."

"But that's it. How can you know?"

"What?"

"How can you know it was just one lie? How can I know?" The tears are spilling over, rolling down my face. "I only found out about the vigil because Angie told me. What else has he lied about? What if Granny tried to call me from the hospital? What if I could have . . ." My voice chokes in my throat and I break into sobs.

"Tori, take a deep breath and listen. You're grieving." Charlie's voice is firm. "You're grieving, and grief warps our perception. It makes us irrational, and that's exactly what you're being. Irrational and paranoid. So why don't you have a proper break, process some of those feelings, and then you and Duncan can talk it all over. I'm sure he'll understand why you needed some space. I can speak to him if you like."

"Don't," I manage to say.

"No, no, it's no trouble. I mean, life's hectic here with the children and the community development project and oh yes, I volunteered us all for this red kite preservation thing although God knows they hardly need preserving anymore—I'm forever shooing the bloody things out of my garden but anyway, it's so important for the children to see us *making an effort* and oh yes, what was I saying? Of course I can phone Duncan for you and explain that you're not yourself right now. And then I'm sure he'll be happy for you to go back and sort it all out when you've finished looking at paintings, or whatever. I never really got the Florence thing myself," she adds, with unnecessary sanctimony. "I know you love it and I know Granny did, too. But let's be honest, it's just Disneyland for people who think they're cultured. Still, if you need a few days there to get your head together, who am I to judge?"

"I'm staying here," I say.

"Of course you are. I expect you've found some overpriced room with a view so you can recreate all those marvelous trips with Granny."

"No!" It comes out like a strangled shout. I take a deep breath and clear my throat. "I mean, I'm staying here. I'm not going back. What Duncan did—what I know he did—it was the last straw. I can't live like that anymore. I can't."

"You're overreacting, Tori," Charlie says. "He made a judgment call. It wasn't a good one, but we all mess up from time to time. Surely he deserves a bit of compassion?"

"And that," I say, "is the *fucking problem*. There was never any compassion for me. He's been treating me like shit for years before this—years. I don't think he even sees me as a person."

"But how does he treat you like shit?" Charlie sounds genuinely baffled. "I'm sorry, but it just doesn't sound like him."

"Well, it is. Do you really need more proof?"

"Yes," she says. "Yes, actually, I do."

"Right." I close my eyes for a moment, sorting through the horrible memories that are raging to the surface. "Right, okay. Remember when you and Ben and the boys came to us for Christmas? And Duncan's auntie Rhoda was there, and a couple of his cousins, and an old college friend as well—I don't remember his name, only that he had BO and kept calling me Vicky."

"Well, how could I forget that? We had a lovely time."

I mustn't scream at her. I mustn't. "All right, then. Remember after dinner? When I had a little too much wine and tripped over the rug while I was carrying in the Christmas pudding? And I ended up on the floor with pudding all over me and my underwear on display, and everybody laughed and laughed."

"Of course we did! It was *hilarious*."

"Well, Duncan thought it was hilarious, too," I say. "He told everyone that story. He told the whole village. He told the farrier and the vet and the man who came to clean the chimneys. He told the minister of the local church when he came round for a cup of tea. He's probably still telling it."

"Tori—"

"And why did I have too much wine?" I plough on. "Why was I drinking like that in the first place? Maybe it's because Duncan had been in my ear all day, doling out poison every chance he got. I had on that red dress with the circular skirt, remember, and the necklace Granny gave me. I bloody loved that dress."

"You looked very nice," Charlie says. There's a note of caution in her voice, as if she's talking to someone unstable.

"That's not what Duncan said. He said I shouldn't have worn red because it matched my face. He pointed out the rolls around my waist, the damp patches under my arms, the way everyone could see my tits when I bent over. And just before I brought that bloody pudding in, when he was in the kitchen supposedly helping me with the brandy butter and the cream and all the rest of it, he leaned in and put his mouth right against my ear and told me that I should be ashamed. That I was an embarrassment—that you were all laughing at me behind my back. And no wonder, he said, because in that low-cut dress and big gaudy necklace I looked like a fat old worn-out society whore."

There's silence at the other end of the line. Surely, I think, Charlie must understand now. Surely my sister of all people—my fierce, fair, impeccably right-on sister—*has* to understand.

"We'd all had quite a bit to drink," she says finally. "And drink makes people say regretful things. I hate that kind of language as much as you do, possibly more, but Duncan is a decent man and I just can't believe that he actually meant to—"

"I have to go," I say. It isn't true, but the tears are welling up again.

"Wait!" She sounds desperate. "Tori, please. I just . . ."

"What?"

"I don't understand," Charlie says. "I just don't. I'm sorry, it's obvious that Granny's death has hit you very hard and I'm sure Duncan can be a little insensitive at times, but to throw out a ten-year relationship over a couple of minor incidents . . . I mean, really. He didn't hit you or cheat on you." She says that with total confidence. "What do you want?"

"Something more than, you know, not being hit or cheated on. And these aren't just incidents. That's what he's like, Charlie, when other people aren't watching. He's cruel. You just don't want to believe me."

"Well, *really*," she begins, and I hang up on her.

I have so many difficult conversations ahead. I should really get them over with, but instead I lie there—not sleeping, not quite awake but in a kind of stupor. It's almost eleven when my phone pings with an email from Chiara.

> Ciao, Tori. Attached is the draft of the contract—I've made some notes in English—and a list of some lawyers in Florence you might want to check out. They're all good but the first one, Marco, is the one I know best. He's worked for a few of my foreign clients and they've all been very happy with him. A presto, Chiara

"Marco it is then," I mutter. My eyes hurt and my throat feels raw, and my head's developing that warning throb that tells me I'm overdue for some caffeine. I'm not ringing anyone before I fix that.

❦

I WANT TO BE AUTHENTIC. I DO. I SAIL OUT OF THE HOTEL INTO THE spring sunshine wearing my best and least crumpled linen—all the

Italians are in shiny padded jackets and scarves, but still—and I walk along the embankment before diving into the tangle of streets behind the Uffizi, determined to find a little bar where I can have an espresso and one of those massive pastries glazed with sugar. But as I'm dodging people with suitcases and people holding hands and people who suddenly stop to check their phones, I spot a sign, a cutesy blackboard sign advertising brunch. I peer through the big plate-glass window and see people being served with eggs and bacon and huge mugs of coffee and, oh God, that's a pot of tea. That will do.

It's pleasantly busy inside. I'd say the population is about fifty percent hipsters, twenty-five percent fashion influencers in weird ecru clothing, and twenty-five percent athleisure-clad American exchange students. I manage to get a table by the window and, by the time I've had bacon and fried eggs and some toast (sourdough, naturally), and a large pressed orange juice and half a pot of English Breakfast, I'm starting to feel like I can call Marco.

He answers right away. "Of course," he says when I tell him about the flat, and the residency, and the bank. "I have some time this morning, as it happens. Can you meet?"

"I'm free all day."

"Where are you now? I can come and meet you in around . . . half an hour?"

"I'm in a place called Ditta Artigianale," I say.

"Which one? Via de' Neri or via dello Sprone?"

"Um . . ."

"Are you north of the river or south?"

"North," I say.

"Great. My office is close by. Do you mind waiting for a little while?"

"No problem." I eye my half-empty teapot—yes, I can definitely have another one of those. "I have some writing to do," I say, and then the hot shame hits, because I really do. That bloody book.

"Okay, then. *A presto*, Tori."

I drink the rest of the tea, order another, drink half of that and eat an immense sugary doughnut before I feel brave enough to take my tablet out of my bag and open that document. There it is: my first ever book, due for delivery . . . oh shit, three months from now. Sixty thousand words down and thirty thousand to go. *The Laird's Lady's Guide to Highland Living.*

What a fucking stupid title.

It was my agent, Richenda's, idea. Well, the actual book was my idea because, after a few years of writing various things including a sort-of-funny column for *Modern Country Lifestyles*—confessions of an ex-townie, pheasant plucking for beginners, the best green wellies on the market for under £75—I'd wanted to do something really substantial. Wanted to have a book on the shelf, an ISBN to my name, something I could wave at people who said oh yes, but you're not a *proper* writer, are you? I mean, you're not really *published*, ha ha, am I right? So the year before last, after a particularly vile shooting party had rolled off to their beds after having a good laugh at my expense all evening, I'd put together a book proposal—not a good one, necessarily, but fired by a certain amount of righteous fury—assembled a few of my recent columns into a file, and emailed it all off to a few agents.

The very next day, Richenda had got back and asked if we could talk on the phone. And from there it had all rather snowballed, because Richenda is a dynamic personality, to put it politely, and had very firm ideas about what The Market would and would not accept.

"Posh country satire is out," she drawled in her husky, rather Sloaney voice. "It died with Jilly Cooper."

"Jilly Cooper isn't dead," I said.

"No, darling, thank God. But you'd actually have to be her to pull it off these days, more's the pity. I mean, what you've sent me here is good, and a few years ago I daresay I could have sold it. But for today's market? No, no, what you have to offer is your *story*. The decaying aristocratic family, the rebellious younger daughter defying her toxic mother—"

"Mummy isn't toxic," I put in. "She's just a bit old-school."

"Defying her toxic mother," Richenda repeated, "and running off to marry her old college sweetheart who—oh, joy of joys!—just happens to be the hard-working laird of a Highland estate. It's aspirational and relatable all at once and that, darling, is exactly what the market wants. What does your father make of the match, incidentally?"

"He's dead."

"Even better," Richenda said.

And so *The Laird's Lady's Guide* was born. I'd been doing well with it—had been on track to submit it, via Richenda, to Swithin and Sons: the impressively big publisher she'd somehow managed to land me. For the first months it had been a sustaining thing. Writing it meant reminding myself why, when Duncan's allocated time at Oxford was up and the running of the estate fell to him—being left fatherless at an early age was one of the things he and I had in common—I followed him up to Scotland without a thought. It meant remembering, over and over again, why it was that I'd abandoned a hard-won journalism internship and left my lovely cozy flat and all my friends to move to a place where I had no ties at all apart from Duncan. How much I had loved him; how willing I had been to give up my world and become part of his.

And then at some point last winter, between the lashing rain and the boiler crapping out again and the badly behaved brides and the gangs of stockbrokers arriving, weekend after endless weekend, to shoot badly at fat, stupid pheasant, it started to feel less like creative nonfiction and more like lying through my teeth. I tried to struggle on, but eventually I stopped and stayed stopped. Hardly likely to finish it now, am I?

I didn't tell Richenda when I fell behind, but I should really, really tell her about this. I open my email and start a new message.

Dear Richenda, I

"Tori?"

I look up. There's a man standing in front of my table. He's thin and nervy-looking and he's wearing a sleek navy suit and a crisp shirt without a tie, which might look a bit dickish on some men but, on him, looks perfectly right. "That's me," I say.

"Marco," he says, and holds out his hand. I stand and shake it, and then I gesture to say *sit down* and he gestures to say *just going to the bar* and we both smile awkwardly at one another.

"Do you want anything?" he asks.

"No, I'm fine."

"If you're sure. You've got the contract, right?"

I sit down, gratefully close my unfinished email to Richenda and bring the contract up on the screen. When Marco sits down with his espresso, I turn the tablet to face him.

"Thanks," he says. Stirring sugar into his coffee, he starts reading. "This looks fine," he says after a while. "Three plus two, three months' notice, two months' deposit, one month's rent for Chiara's fee . . . okay. How's your Italian?"

"Rusty. Chiara made some notes for me, though."

"Good. Did you have any questions?"

"Not really, no. But then again, I don't know what questions I'm supposed to have."

"Right. Well, obviously I'll review this properly and go through it with you before you sign anything. You can't sign anyway until your details are complete. You have your Italian tax code?"

"I only got here yesterday," I say.

A lopsided grin. He's attractive when he grins. "You're working fast."

"I don't see any sense in hanging around."

"Quite right. Italian bureaucracy is slow enough without adding on more delays. Well, the tax code is the easiest thing, but you'll need it for absolutely everything: bank account, rental contract, phone, residency, healthcare—tax as well, of course. Do you have a work contract here?"

"I'm a writer. Freelance."

"Okay, so you'll need an accountant," Marco says. "If you don't have one yet, I'm happy to recommend a few. Anyway, the tax code. I can apply for that on your behalf, but you could easily pick it up yourself. All you have to do is go to the tax office with your passport, probably wait around for a while, and fill out a basic form. They'll issue the code on the spot."

The very idea is tiring. "But you can get it for me?"

"If you like. But you might not want to pay me to do something you can do on your own."

"It's all right," I say. "My grandmother left me an inheritance, and she loved Florence. She'd have liked me to use it to make moving here a bit easier."

"A smart woman, your grandmother." Marco takes out his phone. "Do you have your passport with you? I can make a copy now, get the process started."

My passport is in the inner pocket of my bag. I take it out and pass it over.

"Victoria Catherine Anne Desirée MacNair," he says. "Four names and a surname. That's going to mess with people."

"Why? Don't you have middle names in Italy?"

"We do, but not like that." Marco flattens out the passport and takes a series of pictures. "But in your case the tax code will be based on just your first and last names, so that will be straightforward."

A horrible thought occurs to me. "My first name and last name? But if my last name changes . . ."

He grimaces. "Are you planning to change it?"

"No. Well, yes, I mean . . . I'm getting divorced," I say, and I think: that's the first time I've said it. Oh God.

Marco leans back in his chair. "I'm sorry to hear that. Is it . . . look, I have to ask. Is it nearly over? Just beginning?"

"I haven't really . . ." I swallow, hard. "Just beginning."

"So it's going to be a while before it's final." He pushes a hand through his hair. "I guess you don't want to wait?"

I think of my friends who've divorced, how it dragged on and on even when both parties were in agreement to start with. How it's still dragging on for some of them. "There's a real risk that Brexit will happen before this does," I say. "And then . . ."

". . . it would be far, far harder for you to move here. Yes. How easy is it to change your name in the UK? Can you do it before your divorce is actually final?"

I rack my brain. "I think so. I mean, you can fill out a deed poll, apply for a new passport, and so on. It's probably a pain, but not difficult as such. Is it really so much worse here?"

"You have no idea," Marco says. "The Italian system assumes you keep the same name from cradle to grave. You *can* change, if you're really determined, but . . ."

"It's a bastard?"

He laughs. "Accurate. If you're set on it, go home for a few weeks and do everything there. Then you can come back and start your life in Florence with the right name. So long as your paperwork's consistent, it won't be a problem."

Home. Where is home, anyway? I can't go back to Duncan, and staying with Charlie—or, worse, Mummy—is out of the question. I could book a flight, find somewhere to rent for a short while, keep my head down. But I don't want to, I realize. I came to Florence to start again, and even though I'm tired and sad and far, far more nervous than I used to be, I don't want to go back on my decision even for a moment. I don't want to bend.

"No," I say. "Let's go ahead. If I do want to change my name further down the line . . . well, then I'll call you and we'll figure it out. It's just more bureaucracy, right?"

"That's the spirit," Marco says, and gives me an encouraging smile. I smile back, but my heart is hammering. "Out of interest, what was your name before you married?"

"Fanshawe-Carew."

Marco looks at me for a moment. "As your lawyer," he says at last, "I feel obliged to give you a very serious piece of advice."

"Oh? What's that?"

He pushes my passport back across the table. "Stick with Mac-Nair."

❧

BY THE TIME OUR MEETING IS OVER, MY HEAD'S SPINNING WITH THE details of everything I need to do. "Try not to feel overwhelmed," Marco reassures me. "I'll call you when I have your tax code and we'll fix a time to go to the bank and set up your account. Once we have those things, you can sign your lease, and once that's done and you're settled in . . . look, there's going to be a lot of paperwork in your life for the next few weeks. That's the price you pay for living in Italy. But it's worth it, I promise."

"I believe you," I say, and he smiles and pushes back his chair, ready to stand up. "Wait," I blurt out. "Can I ask you something?"

Marco pulls his chair back in. "Of course."

"I think I told you that I have an inheritance from my grandmother." I'm sweating even talking about it—it feels crass some-how, but I have to ask. "I know you're not a divorce lawyer, but I was wondering . . . under Italian law, does that money belong to me? I mean, would my husband be able to . . ."

I trail off and stare at my empty cup. I'm sure Marco's judging me for bringing this up, for wanting to keep Duncan's hands off my money. But when he speaks, his voice is kind.

"No, I'm not a divorce lawyer, so I can't give you any advice on this. For what it's worth, though—and again, I'm not speaking as your lawyer here—I seem to recall that Italian law would treat your inheritance as your own separate property. So in that case, your husband wouldn't get any of it. But you won't be divorcing under Italian law, will you?"

"I don't know," I say miserably. "I'm here and Duncan's in Scotland, so I don't know how it works."

Marco touches my wrist, just the briefest friendly touch. "Look, don't worry about this now. If you like, I can have a look through my address book and see if I know someone who can actually advise you. Would that help?"

"Yes, please," I say. I'm blushing.

"All right, then," he says. He stands, and I stand, and we shake hands. "I'll leave you to finish your work. I'll get in touch soon, but call me if you think of anything in the meantime. *Ciao*, Tori." He slings his bag over his shoulder—rather a smart attaché case thing, very Italian—and goes out.

When I emerge onto via de' Neri. I pull out my sunglasses and put them on, muting Florence into shades of sepia like an old photo-graph. I could do anything this afternoon. I could go to a museum, or see a film, or buy some clothes that don't smell of damp and never will. I could just wander around, take a few pictures, stop for the oc-casional spritz and think about where to go for dinner. I *should* send that email to Richenda. But what I want to do is sleep. It's dragging at me again, that sudden bone-deep tiredness, and I don't even have the strength to wonder at it.

5

WHEN I GET BACK TO THE HOTEL, THE SUN IS STREAMING THROUGH
the window, painting a broad, bright stripe across the white bedcover.
I close the shutters, kick off my shoes—the cold tiles feel wonderful against my overheated feet—and think about doing this properly,
undressing and taking a shower and getting into bed. But even the
thought is too much effort, so I lie down as I am and wait for sleep.

But it doesn't come. Once my head actually hits the pillow, I'm
wide awake. All I can think about is the book, and what Richenda
will say, and whether I'll have to pay back the first half of my advance
if I can't deliver. And that's long spent. That £5,000 installment had
no sooner hit the marital bank account than the roof sprung a leak,
and once that was fixed there were the sheep pens to repair, and then
there was a bit left so Duncan bought a set of vintage golf clubs "for
the house," so that the visiting stockbrokers would have something to
admire. And, just like that, it was gone.

It's not that I can't pay it back. If I have to, I can take it out of
Granny's gift. But the thing about £30,000 is that it seems like a huge
amount of money—and, of course, it is. It's far more than I've ever had
in my bank account all at once. At the same time, I don't know yet how
much it actually costs to live in Florence, except that it's already more
than I thought. I don't know how much work I'll have over the next
year, or when it will come in, or if I'll be in a fit state to take it. I don't
have a pension, or savings, or life insurance, or any of the stuff I'm supposed to have by now. I don't even know how much I'll have left after

the divorce. What if the inheritance isn't even mine under Scots law? What if I'm doing something wrong by trying to keep it all for myself?

I should have thought of all this before I came here and started throwing money around on flats and lawyers. I should have realized that I couldn't just run off and get away with it. Oh God, I feel sick.

I try to banish the thoughts, to bargain with them. There's no sense in looking for trouble. I'll write to Richenda when I'm absolutely certain that I'm definitely not going back. When I've moved into the flat, maybe. When my residency comes through. When I've talked to a divorce lawyer and found out how much *that's* going to cost me. But the thoughts nag and nag, and eventually I sit up and pull my tablet out of my bag and write the first thing that comes into my head.

> Dear Richenda, I'm sorry but things have gone a bit wrong with *The Laird's Lady's Guide*. I've split up with Duncan and moved to Florence to start again, and I'm not sure if I can finish the book as it is. I'm really sorry and I hope we can find some kind of solution. T xxx

I press send before I can think about it, and I lie back again and shut my eyes tight. Surely Richenda won't get back to me before tomorrow at the very earliest. Monday, more likely. Tuesday, even, if she's taking one of her long weekends. I have lots of time to think about what to say next.

The tablet bursts into life. *Trr-trr-trr*, it goes, and a notification pops up:

> Richenda Haughton is calling you.

Shit. I haul myself up again, switch on the bedside light and answer the call. There's a momentary delay, and then Richenda's face blinks into view. She's in her office, with the bookshelf behind her full of colorful paperbacks, and she looks . . . worried, actually. I thought she'd be hopping.

"Tori," she cries, "what on earth is going on? Oh, darling, you look simply *awful*."

"I'm sorry," I blurt out.

"What have you got to be sorry for?"

"The book—"

"Fuck the book," Richenda says. "Fuck it. We'll sort something out. Now, what happened with you and Duncan? You must tell me all about it. Did he have an affair?"

"No."

"Did you? Oh, I wouldn't blame you, darling, nobody would. A young thing like you, rattling around in that big house in the middle of nowhere. It was bound to happen."

"I didn't have an affair, either. Nobody did. It wasn't like that, it just . . . it all just went so wrong," I say, feeling despair well up. "And I tried, I did, but—"

"Say no more." Richenda waves a hand and I realize she's holding a cigarette. "Not. Another. Word. I understand completely."

"You do?" I'm crying. But this time it's from relief, because someone's being nice to me.

"Of course I do, darling, I've been there. You'll never have to justify yourself to me. Oh, you poor thing," Richenda says as I root around in my bag for a handkerchief. "It must have been absolute hell."

"It was," I say, mopping my eyes. The words rush out of me, snotty and undignified. "I just felt so alone and over time it just *got* to me and not even my sister believes me and then . . . oh God, sorry." My mouth is trembling and so is my voice.

"Listen." Richenda takes a drag, blows out a leisurely cloud of smoke. "You can go round and round about what happened. But I've been married three . . . no, four times, and the awful truth is that sometimes it's just bad and you have to leave. It really is that simple. And people are inevitably put out, of course, when you do that—as if it's their bloody business—and they'll say: Oh, but are you sure you can't work it out? Haven't you tried therapy, or swinging, or whatever ghastly remedy's in at the time? Because they don't *know*. They don't know about the efforts you've already made, and the horrible arguments, and all the things that have been eating away at you over time. And quite right, because you don't wash your dirty linen in public. You'd be a colossal pain in the arse if you actually told your friends and family every little detail of your marriage. So it's a shock to them when it actually comes apart. But above all they're scared because, if your relationship can end, then theirs might, too. If anyone's being a pill to you about this, darling, it's really about them."

"Uh-huh." I blow my nose and make an unholy noise.

"What I'm trying to say here is trust your judgment. You were unhappy, you couldn't fix it, so you left. That's fine. The only question is what to do next."

"The book," I say.

"The book, yes, that's part of it. Look, I have to go to this awful industry bash this week, but hopefully Tim Swithin will be there and he's a nice enough chap. I'll have a discreet word with him, just informally, and see how we stand. I'll be frank though, Tori, publishers hate this kind of thing. And so do I. It looks very bad for everyone involved when a writer can't deliver a book. But it does happen, and sometimes there's a way around it."

"Like what?"

Richenda sighs. "Well, that depends on what we can offer them. How much have you actually written? Tell me honestly."

"About sixty thousand words," I say. "It's in draft, but it's there."

"Right, so that's one option: the same book, but shorter. They may not go for it—sixty K is very short—but if they do, I'm pretty sure I can buy you some more time to work it up into something viable. I imagine it's all too raw at the moment. Otherwise . . . let's see. I hate to ask this while it *is* still raw, but is there any chance you could write something about what you're doing right now?"

"You mean in Florence?"

"Absolutely." She grinds out her cigarette and lights another. "Rebellious aristo leaves college sweetheart, begins exciting new life in the city of Michelangelo and the Medici. It could be another *Eat, Pray, Love*."

The idea makes me uneasy. "I'm not sure. It feels a bit . . ."

"A bit what, darling?"

"A bit wrong," I say. "Like I'd be exploiting something really painful."

"Of course you would. That's what writers do. Anyway, you'll find a way to make it as personal or impersonal as you like. It's your story."

"But—"

"We don't know whether Swithins will even want it," Richenda says. "Not least because writing a whole new book will take even longer than tarting up a partial one. Let me talk to Tim, and then we can see. All right?"

"All right," I say.

"But promise me one thing in the meantime. Whatever happens to you, whatever conversations you have or people you meet, write it down. Don't stress yourself out trying to do something with it—not yet. Keep a note of it all as you go, and observe, darling, just observe. Engage that wonderful, inquisitive drive of yours—and I know you've still got it, even if that arsehole did rather leach it out of you. Will you do that?"

It could be helpful, I suppose. It could be a way to find myself again. "I'll do that."

Richenda smiles. "Good. Now, go and enjoy Florence, you lucky thing. I'll update you as soon as I have news."

6

Stella

BERTA'S MURDER, THE PUBLIC DISPLAY OF HER MUTILATED BODY—
all this was meant as a deterrent. It was supposed to cow the people
of Romituzzo into withdrawing all support for the partisans, but it
didn't work. If anything, our movement gained more supporters. If
they weren't fit enough or bold enough to join up and fight, then they
helped in other ways. They gave food and medicine, clothes, whatever they could spare. Above all, they stayed silent. If the Germans
expected us all to inform on our neighbours in the hope of saving our
own skins, then they were sorely disappointed.

Their vile actions didn't intimidate our community. I'd be lying, though, if I said they didn't scare me. I suppose I was always
aware that my work was dangerous, but somehow that danger always
seemed theoretical. Now it was very real and it took a little while before I felt strong on my feet again. During that time, I had a near miss
I never forgot.

It was a Saturday morning and I had to cycle out to one of the partisan encampments near San Damiano, a pretty medieval hill town
about forty minutes' ride away. I remember that my bicycle basket was
full of woollen vests and pairs of socks, which some of the women in
Romituzzo had knitted to be distributed among the partisans. They
had been clever about it—rolled it all up into little bundles to look like
baby clothes, and tied them tightly with any scraps of ribbon or lace
they could find in their sewing boxes. One of them had even found
and repaired an old, chewed-up knitted rabbit belonging to her son,

who was now a partisan himself. If anyone asked, I would say that I was going to visit a cousin who had a new baby. But under my winter cloak I had the really valuable stuff: two bags slung crosswise across my body, one filled with handguns, the other with ammunition.

To get there in good time, the best way was to take the main road south: the via Senese. There was a small checkpoint there, just a hundred metres or so beyond St. Christopher's church and its cemetery, and it was usually manned by a couple of German soldiers. Romituzzo wasn't important—it wasn't a heritage site like San Damiano, or a local hub like Castelmedici—but the Resistance was active all over the valley, so the Germans wanted to know who was entering and leaving. In the early days I made a point of going through often, to visit a friend or go mushroom-hunting or some such harmless errand. They stopped me a few times to look at my papers, and then after a while they didn't anymore. But that day was different.

I was coming up to the checkpoint when I realized that the soldiers weren't wearing Wehrmacht field gray. These were two men with red insignia and red tabs on their collars: volunteer members of the Waffen-SS. These weren't foreigners posted on guard duty in an unfamiliar backwater. They were Italians, perhaps even Tuscans. They knew our landscape, and if they didn't already know us, they had ways to find out.

I don't know what was stronger, my revulsion or my fear. For just a moment I had the urge to turn back, but of course I didn't. That would have been as good as an admission of guilt and, besides, the partisans needed those guns I was carrying. There was a shortage of weapons everywhere. So I cycled steadily on and, when one of the SS men raised a hand to stop me, I showed him the bundles and explained all about my supposed cousin. I was unusually nervous, so I talked too much and even invented names for the baby and its siblings, which I immediately forgot again. And all the time I could feel his eyes boring into me. I didn't dare look at him in case I knew his face.

He clearly wasn't convinced by my story, and no wonder. He frowned and started picking through the tight little bundles of wool, turning them over in his hands. Perhaps he thought I had hidden something in them. I began to feel sick now, and I was praying that he wouldn't start untying the ribbons because, if he did, he would see that this was clothing for full-grown men rather than anything fit for a child. I could feel the straps of those two bags cutting into my shoulders and the handle of one of the guns poking into my side, and all I could think about was what had happened to Berta and how that could now easily, so easily, happen to me.

And then there was the *ding* of a bicycle bell, and I looked up and saw our parish priest approaching the other way, from the direction of Siena. He was little and old and round, and his name was don Anselmo. I didn't like him one bit. From the way he preached, you'd think that communism was a bigger threat to Italy than the Nazi occupation, and if I was not a communist, I knew where my loyalty lay. I'd heard plenty of his homilies because my mother insisted I go with her to Mass every Sunday. That wasn't a problem for me since—unlike Achille—I believed in God. But I didn't want to go to St. Christopher's, to don Anselmo's church. I wanted to go to St. Catherine's, where the dynamic young priest, don Mauro, preached about God's boundless love and our duty to care for the widow, the orphan and the alien.

"I don't like don Anselmo, either," Mamma said when I told her this. "But don Mauro's too subversive, and he's bound to run into trouble. St. Christopher's is the far safer choice."

I hated my mother's logic, but I understood it. More than anything, I knew that obeying her would win me a little more freedom to do my work. So I listened to don Anselmo inveigh against communism every Sunday, and every Sunday I disliked him more. When I saw him approaching that checkpoint with his silly round-brimmed hat and his cassock flapping around, I suppose I hoped that my mother was right and my attendance at St. Christopher's would protect me even a little now. I had no idea.

The SS men must have seen don Anselmo already on his way out of town. Perhaps they knew him, or even simply trusted him because he was a priest. At any rate, one of them waved him on, but he simply waved back with a smile and halted his bicycle right next to mine.

"Why, it's Stella Infuriati," he exclaimed, just as if we'd bumped into one another in the market square. "And where are you off to in this nasty cold weather?"

"I'm taking some presents to my cousin who's just had a baby," I said automatically, and then I regretted it because don Anselmo knew everything about everyone. He would know that I was lying.

Don Anselmo stretched his hand out to touch one of the little bundles. "How lovely. Please give her my best wishes. It's Teresa, isn't it, who was expecting the baby? Your cousin Teresa?"

"That's right," I said. "My cousin Teresa."

"I remember when she came to visit. Charming girl. Well, Godspeed, my child." He smiled up at the SS man, who glowered at him and motioned for me to pass through.

I didn't hesitate. I pedaled off and kept going smartly all the way to San Damiano, but the whole time I was wondering why don Anselmo had gone along with my lie and, more than that, had actually compounded it. He'd lied so easily, too. But if he was a good Christian, if he was any kind of human being at all, then surely he wouldn't want to let me die like Berta did. That was the best explanation I could come up with, and it satisfied me for the moment.

❧

WHEN I CAME BACK TO TOWN, I SAW DON ANSELMO POTTERING around at the gates of St. Christopher's cemetery. I waved to him and kept pedaling, but he called out to me.

"Stella! There you are. You have kept me waiting, haven't you?"

I didn't really want to stop. I was hungry and tired and I still didn't like don Anselmo very much, even if he had helped me this once. But I could sense the SS men at my back, watching me, and I knew how much better it would look if I really did show myself to be on good terms with him. So I got off my bike and propped it up in the church porch, next to his own rather elderly machine.

Don Anselmo opened the door of the church and ushered me in. I barely had time to dip my fingers in the holy water before he was ushering me up one of the side aisles and into the sacristy.

"We shall have some coffee," he was saying as he hurried me along. "Real coffee—none of that foul barley or chicory stuff. I had a birthday recently, and some dear friends in Turin managed to find me a little packet of good coffee and get it to me, although by rather an elaborate route. Of course, I'm assuming you like coffee, too. Do you?"

"Yes," I said. I couldn't understand why we were in the sacristy if we were going to drink coffee together. Surely we should be across the road in the parochial house.

Don Anselmo was rooting around in a cupboard. "Ah!" he said, and pulled out a flashlight. It was a big metal torch of the kind the Germans carried, and I wondered where he had got it. He switched it on and threw open another cupboard, revealing a heavy wooden door built into the wall behind.

"I thought we could take this route to the house," he said. "I should like you to see it." Fishing a key from somewhere in the breast of his cassock, he unlocked the door and beckoned me forward. He shone the torch through the doorway and I saw a narrow landing with a flight of stone steps leading off it. After a few meters, they vanished into pitch darkness.

Don Anselmo gave me the torch. "You take this," he said, "and I shall go ahead of you."

The torch was solid and heavy in my hands. I believe that's why he gave it to me, so that I would feel that I was armed—although I was blissfully naïve in those days, quite unaware of the dangers of going into cellars with strange men. Don Anselmo stepped through the doorway and began to go carefully down the steps, one hand holding up the skirt of his cassock, the other on the flimsy iron rail set into the wall.

"Mind yourself," he called back to me. "There's a sharp bend up ahead. And shut the door after you."

The steps were steep and slightly uneven, and I didn't look up until I had reached the bottom. And then I did look up, and I gasped. Stretching out ahead of me was an arched stone tunnel, and in the light cast by the torch I could see that it was stacked along both sides with rifles and machine guns and boxes of ammunition.

Don Anselmo was already some way into the tunnel before I could even move my feet. "That's the via Senese above us," he said, pointing upwards. "Do watch where you step, by the way. Some of this stuff is rather precariously stacked."

I picked my way along the tunnel, almost holding my breath. Thankfully, the ceiling was just high enough that I didn't need to crouch, although Achille would have found it cramped and I don't think my father could have managed at all. After an agonising few minutes, we emerged into a cellar with another flight of steps and an open door at the top.

"Ah, I see that Assunta has left it unlocked for us," don Anselmo said. "Perhaps she has started the coffee, too." And he bounded up the steps like a little fat gazelle.

Once I was sitting in the parlor by the fire, surrounded by holy pictures and faded old photographs of unsmiling people in formal clothes, the dark, weapon-lined tunnel began to feel like a dream. But I knew it couldn't be a dream, because don Anselmo kept talking about it while I sat there in stunned silence. Perhaps because I was silent, he seemed intent on telling me the history of the tunnel, which had been dug out some time in the early sixteenth century.

"Apparently the incumbent at the time was a devotee of Fra Girolamo Savonarola. You have heard of Savonarola?"

I nodded. Everyone had heard of him. Savonarola was the fanatical Dominican friar, the strange, wild prophet who had briefly ruled Florence and who burned books and paintings on his great fires. I didn't see how he mattered now.

"Well, he had quite a following around here," don Anselmo said. "I believe he even preached in this church once or twice. The story goes that, some years after Savonarola was executed, this don Bernardo— who wasn't a Dominican, by the way, just an ordinary parish priest— used to hold secret meetings with his fellow true believers here in Romituzzo. Of course, they had to be careful. Savonarola had been a great threat to the tyrants in Florence and Rome, and so his followers were also held to be very dangerous. So they would all go to the church for Mass and then, when everyone else had left, they would go down into the tunnel and come here, to the house. That's the story, anyway, and it's entertaining whether it's true or not. Don't you think?"

I was saved from answering by the housekeeper Assunta, who

came in carrying a tray with two cups of coffee and two plates of sliced apple. She put it down on the little table between us, and don Anselmo crossed himself and then popped one of the apple slices into his mouth. I'd forgotten how hungry I was, and I did the same. It was a wonderful apple, sweet and fresh and slightly tart.

"From my garden," he said. "I like to pretend these apples are as good as a piece of cake, but I think we both know that's a lie. I shall be glad when we can have cake every day."

"Me too," I managed to say, and don Anselmo beamed at me. He waited until I'd finished my coffee and devoured the apple slices—all of mine, and half of his, too—and then he leaned forward with his pudgy little hands on his knees and said: "My dear, do you know how to fire a gun? A handgun, I mean."

At that point, my brain abruptly caught up with the rest of me. "Why are you asking me this?" I burst out—and I'm afraid my tone was far from polite. "Why are you keeping machine guns in the cellar? Are you with the partisans?"

"Of course I am, my child," he said. "Had you not realized?"

"But I thought you hated communism. You preach against it all the time."

"I do hate communism. I think it's a terrible ideology, a false prophecy, a perversion of the teachings of Christ that takes that message of His, that wonderful message of justice and care for one's neighbor, and strips it of all its redemptive power. A hollow secular cult that denies every prospect of an afterlife, the very existence of a personal God who loves us and is ready to forgive our every sin if we will only turn to Him. Of course I hate communism. But communists? I know some very fine communists who are doing great work. If I can help them, then I do so to the best of my rather feeble abilities. You still haven't told me whether you know how to shoot, my child."

"Oh," I said. "Yes. My brother taught me."

"Then I have something for you. Wait here."

He rose and went out and left me sitting by the fire, feeling foolish. I suppose a few minutes went by before he returned, but it seemed longer. When he came back in, he shut the parlor door behind him.

"Here you are. It took me a few moments to find the right ammunition." He drew a small gun from the pocket of his cassock and held it out to me.

It really was a silly-looking gun. A funny little snub-nosed thing—the sort of weapon a nineteenth-century lady might carry in her purse.

"It's ridiculous, I know," don Anselmo said. "But I'm reliably informed it's better than nothing. And you should easily be able to hide it somewhere, ah, about your person. I believe I should feel easier if you had it."

I almost laughed. I almost said that I didn't see how I could possibly shoot anyone with such a sweet little toy, not unless he was almost under my nose, and then what kind of mess would I be in? And then it dawned on me exactly what kind of mess it would be, and I put out my hand and let him place the gun in my palm.

Don Anselmo reached into his pocket again and took out a leather pouch of ammunition, which he put into my other hand. The cartridges inside were tiny.

"Thank you," I said, because I could find nothing better. "Thank you for this. And thank you for . . ." For trusting me, I wanted to say. For treating me like an adult, like a comrade. "For your hospitality," I said at last.

"In my Father's house there are many mansions," don Anselmo said. And I could swear that, at that moment, I heard footsteps just above us. Perhaps I've invented that detail in retrospect, because I found out later—much later—that this courageous old priest would open his home to anyone who needed it. Allied servicemen, wounded partisans, Jews fleeing deportation had all passed through Romituzzo, staying in one of those upper rooms until they could safely be moved on.

That night I sat on the edge of my bed and looked at that silly little gun. I believe to this day that don Anselmo meant me to have it for self-defence. He was a good man and a good priest, and in those days suicide was seen as an unforgivable sin. He would never have told me to do it. But I knew with an icy clarity that if the Germans captured me, or the Fascists, it would be pointless to try to fight my way out. I would have to use the gun on myself.

From that day until the Liberation, I carried it tucked into my bra. Obviously, I never needed to fire it. I'm here, aren't I? But for years afterwards, even when my children were grown, I used to wonder what I would have done if I'd been caught. Would I have been quick enough to act before I could give anything away, before I could lead the Gestapo to don Anselmo's door? I like to think I'd have done it. I like to think God would have understood.

7

Tori

"MA NON HA NESSUNO A FIRENZE?" FEDERICA, THE LANDLADY, shoots me a sideways look. She is dressed head to foot in black, with bobbed iron-gray hair, red lipstick and even sparklier designer trainers, and she's been talking to Chiara for about twenty minutes while I lurk at the window with Marco, pretending not to eavesdrop. What was meant to be a simple contract signing seems to have turned into an entire negotiation. "*Niente fidanzato, niente parenti, niente amici?*"

"She's asking Chiara if you really don't have anyone in Florence," Marco says. "No partner, no family, no friends . . ."

"I heard," I say. Chiara is talking to Federica in a low, rapid murmur. "Is it a problem?"

"No, no," Marco says. "She's just worried about you. I think."

"*Ma non parla neanche italiano, lei,*" Federica says.

I can't let that stand—I bloody well do speak Italian—so I clear my throat and say: "*Il mio italiano è un po*" arrugginito, ma sto reimparando.*" My Italian's a bit rusty but I'm learning again. Everyone smiles at me, though Federica looks a little put out.

"*Tori è brava,*" Chiara says, very brightly, for my benefit. "*Fa la scrittrice.*"

The temperature in the room seems to drop. "*Scrittrice?*" Federica says in a tone of quiet horror, and she eyes the folder on the kitchen counter—the one containing several years of invoices, a bank statement and my last tax return—as if it might vanish into smoke.

"*Giornalista,*" Marco puts in, but Federica and Chiara are already deep in conference. The folder is opened again, the papers spread out. I look at Marco in alarm.

"What's wrong with being a writer?" I hiss at him.

"Nothing. We love writers in Florence."

"Then why the reaction?"

"Because we know what writers get paid. And it's incredibly hard to evict a tenant under Italian law." He raises an eyebrow. I can't quite tell whether he's joking.

I glance over to the two women. They're talking animatedly now, apparently bickering over something. I start to feel real panic. Marco puts a hand on my arm.

"It's a dance," he says. "Sometimes signing a contract is completely undramatic, and sometimes it's like this. It really isn't personal."

"I've checked out of the hotel," I say. "I've brought my suitcases."

"It's going to be fine. Trust me."

And then, somehow, it is. The deposit is counted and counted again. Federica and I sign three copies of the contract, a signature on each page, and I'm given my folder back and another one on top, with copies of all the utility bills so I can change them into my name ("I'll take those," Chiara says), the Wi-Fi password, a wad of electronics manuals and a long list of where, how and when to dispose of every kind of rubbish. I'm shown the slight ding on the bedroom window frame and the spot in a corner of the bathroom where the tiles have cracked and been resealed. I'm given two sets of keys and shown how to operate the deadbolt; the thermostat is explained to me, though I don't understand it, and then Federica kisses me on each cheek, welcomes me to Florence, issues a stream of instructions to Chiara and sweeps out with a cry of *Arrivederci*.

"Oh my God," Chiara cries, "the time! I have to run. Tori, I'll register the contract and then I just need you to come in and sign a few things, for the utilities. I'll call you, okay? And if there's anything, anything at all, you call me. *Ciao*, Tori; *ciao*, Marco; *ciao!*" And then she too is off, hurrying down the stairs, and it's just me and Marco and this strange new flat that is, somehow, now mine.

"Right," I say. "What's next? What do we have to do?"

"For now? Nothing."

I look helplessly at Marco. "But there's so much left to sort out. Residency, healthcare . . ."

He spreads his hands. "I don't know what to tell you. I called the Anagrafe this morning—that's the civil registry office, for your residency application—and they don't have any free appointments before next month. And you can't do the rest until you're officially a resident."

"But you made an appointment, right?"

"Yes. I emailed you the details."

Of course—my phone's on silent. Between Charlie calling to hector me and my jumping out of my skin every time an email comes in, in case it's Richenda with some news about the book, I thought it was best to give myself a little peace. I fish it out of my bag.

12 missed calls
36 messages
7 emails
5 missed video chats

"Right," I say, stuffing it back in again. "Oh, did you manage to ask whether my temporary health insurance is all right? Or should I look at another provider?"

"The lady on the phone said it sounded fine. Of course, it really depends on who we get on the day. Relax," he says, and I realize that I'm clenching all over. "You have the right to live here. The worst that happens is some kind of annoying administrative setback, and we can fix those. Believe me, you don't want to know what my non-EU clients have to go through."

"I'm sure," I say. "It's just so weird to have nothing to do."

"Enjoy it. Unpack your stuff, explore the city, work on your book . . ." Because he knows there's a book, of course, just as he knows there's an ex-husband and a mother and a sister. He just doesn't know the details. "We'll be back in bureaucratic hell before you know it."

"Oh no," I say, and smile—but, to my surprise, I'm a little sad. I've spent a lot of time with Marco over the last days, going over paperwork or sitting companionably in waiting rooms or listening while he banters with officials and bank staff and shop personnel. He's the closest I have to a friend here, even if he does bill by the hour. "Look," I hear myself say, "can I buy you a coffee?"

He looks at his watch. "That would be nice, thanks. I have a few minutes."

We go downstairs, cross the road to the nearest bar—my local bar, now—and stand at the counter. "*Due caffè*," I tell the young woman behind the bar, and she says "*Certo*," and starts up the espresso machine.

"You didn't even say please," Marco says.

"Oh no, didn't I? Sorry."

"No, it's good. You say please and thank you way too often by Italian standards. And sorry."

"Sorry," I say reflexively.

"Politeness is a bit different here, that's all. It's more about your attitude, how you speak to people."

"I don't think I'll ever fit in. *Grazie*," I say as the coffees are placed in front of us. I pick up a little packet of cane sugar and try to open it without spilling any, which is a skill that tends to abandon me at nervous moments.

Marco picks up the glass pot on the counter and pours a long stream of white sugar into his cup. "Well, okay, it's unlikely anyone's going to mistake you for Italian any time soon—especially if you keep apologising for everything. But just because you're English, that doesn't mean you can't be a real Florentine."

"Like the old ladies in *Tea with Mussolini*?"

"Ha!" Marco drains his coffee in one. I don't know how anyone can do that. "Well, I suppose I was thinking of your grandmother. She sounds like a character."

"She was."

"You must tell me more about her sometime. But, damn, I have a meeting. Thanks so much for the coffee." For a moment I think he's going to kiss me on the cheek, but he sticks out his hand instead. "Don't worry. I know how you Brits are with your personal space."

"I appreciate it," I say, though I'm not totally sure I do.

"*Ciao*, Tori," he says, and with a squeeze of my hand he turns and is gone. I finish my coffee, grimacing at the gritty sludge of sugar at the bottom, and look at my phone.

19 missed calls
55 messages
12 emails
7 missed video chats

Oh God.

⸎

WORD HAS GOT ROUND. I CAN SAFELY SAY THAT. I LIE FLAT ON
my back on my new sofa—it's hard and shiny and not the most
comfortable—and scroll through my messages. Snatches of text leap
out at me.

I had no idea.
Why didn't you say???
Tori, WTF?
I thought we were friends.
Tell. Me. EVERYTHING.
Wow!!!!
This is really hard on me, you know.

That last one lands like a punch to the stomach. For a second I
think it's Duncan; that he's broken his silence. But it isn't. It's Charlie.

Been trying to call you all morning. Why won't you answer?
This is really hard on me, you know.

I'm staring at the message when her name flashes up on the screen.
She's calling again. I accept the call and put the phone to my ear.

"Mummy is livid," she says, before I can even speak. "Absolutely
livid."

"But she hates Duncan. Thinks he's common."

"Doesn't matter. She's been biting my ear for days about how dis-
graceful it is of you to desert your husband and run off abroad like
a . . . well, you know how she is."

"I do," I say. "Sorry."

"Whatever," Charlie says. "Better she should bite my ear than yours."

"Thanks," I say, and I really mean it. Because she's like that, Charlie—she's bossy and annoying and smug, but then she does something so totally generous that you forgive her everything. It's just like her to keep Mummy off me.

"Honestly, though, between her and Duncan I'm never off the phone. Ben had to take the boys to forest school the other day *and* bring them back. Ben! I'm amazed he managed to collect the right children."

There's a nasty cold feeling in the pit of my stomach. "What do you mean?"

"Oh, you know how hopeless he is. The other day—"

"No," I cut in before she can go off on one of her Ben diatribes. "What do you mean about Duncan?"

"Oh. Well, Tori, you can hardly be surprised that he's upset. We speak, what, two or three times a day sometimes? I suppose I've become his shoulder to cry on."

"Right," I say. "Right."

"Don't start," Charlie says. "He's having a really tough time. It's a very stressful life up there, you know."

"I know, believe me."

"And then with you just leaving like that, out of nowhere, and flinging around these accusations . . ."

"Charlie," I say, "what do you mean? Are you talking about the stuff I told you the other day, when you asked me specifically to prove myself? Because I don't call that 'flinging around accusations.'"

"Well, maybe *you* don't, but—"

"And did he really say I left out of nowhere? Because I told him I was going, and he didn't seem to care."

"That's not what he says." Charlie sounds defensive.

"Well, it's what happened." They're flooding back again, the memories. Hauling my suitcase out from under the bed. Duncan staring at me, just staring, his expression scornful. "I told him I'd had enough, that I couldn't trust him anymore and that unless something really changed, unless he could assure me that he understood why I was hurt and that he'd never lie to me like that again, then I would have to leave. And he said . . ." My throat is clogged—I have to swallow. "He said, 'Do what you want. Makes no difference to me.'"

"Well, maybe he wanted to give you some space," Charlie says. "He was probably scared you'd overreact."

"Overreact?" I squeak. "You weren't *there*."

"See? Overreacting."

"Please stop." I haul myself into a sitting position. "Talk to him if you want. Be his shoulder to cry on. But please, Charlie, don't talk to him and then phone me up and tell me off about it. Please."

Charlie sighs. "Look, obviously I don't know what happened and, in a sense, it isn't my business . . ."

"Then why do you keep asking?"

Charlie's quiet for a moment and I start to think—foolish me— that maybe I really have got through to her this time. But then she heaves another sigh and says, in her best Mummy-Is-Disappointed voice: "Look, all I can say is that your version of events is *very* different to what Duncan is telling me. I'm not making any judgments, Tori. I'm just letting you know."

"I understand."

"Good. Because I really do want the best for you, you know. For both of you."

"Don't call me again," I say. "Bye, Charlie."

"What? Tori, don't you dare hang up on me. After everything I've done in the last few days, don't you dare—"

"Goodbye," I say, and I end the call.

❧

SHE CALLS ABOUT HALF AN HOUR LATER, WHILE I'M HANGING UP MY clothes. I don't answer, obviously, so she leaves me a voice message.

"Tori, listen." She actually sounds a bit contrite. "I got carried away. I . . . I don't know what to do in these situations. It's confusing, and I suppose I wade in and try to sort it out because that's what I'm used to doing. I won't bother you again, but will you phone me if you want to talk? Please? I promise I'll try to do better."

I listen to the message about ten times before I delete it. Then I

pour myself a glass of wine, sit down with the laptop, open my document for Richenda and start to write. It's almost midnight when my
phone rings again.

"Tori, can you hear me?" Richenda says in a loud stage whisper.
Somewhere in the background, a toilet flushes. "Sorry. I'm in the ladies' at the Harper Random Penguin party."

Suddenly I'm nervous. "I can hear you," I say, and take a swig of
wine.

"Okay," Richenda says. "I've talked to Tim and he's very sympathetic. Totally gets it. Now, he's got to talk to sales and marketing, but
the feeling is that the shorter book is out. Doesn't really fit the brief.
Besides, you can't exactly go round promoting a book about married
life in the Highlands when you've left your husband and fucked off to
the Continent."

"Oh," I say. "No, I suppose not."

"But he's intrigued by the Florence thing. Listen, I know you've
been writing, so do you think you can send me some pages? Doesn't
have to be much—just enough to give him a flavor. Ten K or so?"

Oh God. "When do you need them?"

"I don't know, darling. Can you get them to me . . . oh, Monday
after next?"

"Um, I suppose—"

"You're a star," Richenda says. There's a loud banging. "Yes, yes,"
she barks, "I'll be out in a minute. Some of us have *bladder issues*, you
know. Tori, darling, I have to go. Give my love to Florence." And she's
gone.

I look at the document in front of me. I have about three thousand words. Some of it's fairly coherent—and by that I mean actual
sentences—but then quite a lot of it is random notes, like "dogs in
restaurants" and "sparkly trainers—Florentine thing?" And the last
thousand is just me ranting about Charlie being a dick.

Well, all right, I have some work to do.

8

CHIARA PUTS A STACK OF FORMS IN FRONT OF ME. IT'S ABOUT AN inch high and bristles with tiny Post-it notes. "I've filled these out," she says, "so I just need you to double-check all the information and then sign wherever I've put a yellow marker."

"Are these just for the utilities?" I ask.

She nods. "Gas, electricity, water, internet, TARI—that's waste disposal. Do you want a coffee?"

"Please."

"Something more robust, or smooth? Or do you prefer decaf?"

"Smooth, I think. And definitely caffeinated."

She goes to the fancy machine in the corner of her office, picks out a coffee pod and snaps it in. I'd never thought the Italians would be so into pod coffee, but those machines are everywhere. I saw an entire shop dedicated to coffee pods the other day. "Take your time," she says over her shoulder. "Those forms are horrible even for us."

"It says *tariffa non residente* here." I point at the top page. "Is that right?"

"Yes. You're considered non-resident until you register with the Anagrafe. Once you do, just let me know and we'll sort that out. You get a cheaper rate that way."

"Is it going to be as complicated as this?"

"Oh no," Chiara says. She puts a little tray next to me with a paper cup of espresso, a packet of sugar, a stirrer and a tiny madeleine on a napkin. "This bit's the worst."

Fuelled by caffeine and sugar, I work through the pages, checking the details over and over again: name, tax code, birthdate, birthplace, nationality, address, phone number, email, IBAN. After a while, Chiara removes the empty coffee cup and brings me another.

"Thanks."

"No problem." She watches while I go through the TARI form and then set it aside. "All done?"

"Yes, thank God."

"Any questions?"

"I wouldn't know what to ask," I say.

She laughs. "Don't worry. In another year, you'll be fluent in Italian bureaucracy. That reminds me, how are you getting on with Marco?"

"Oh, he's great," I say, and she beams at me.

"Isn't he? He's a really serious guy—I mean, he takes his work seriously. I love that I can send people to him and know they're in safe hands. And he's available." She furrows her brow. "No, sorry, that's an Italian thing to say. I guess the word I want is 'helpful,' but it's a bit more than that. We say that people like him are *disponibile*."

"I know what you mean," I say, and I do. Despite his busy schedule, he's always managed to check in with me, return my calls, fit me in. But my heart's racing just a little, and I find that I desperately want to ask Chiara if she knows whether Marco actually *is* available. Which is ridiculous, of course, because I've only just got away from Duncan. I'm enjoying being alone and free, and doing whatever I like, and eating whenever I want, and not having to think about anyone else. The last thing I want to do is start obsessing about some man who's being nice to me because it's his job. "He's very professional," I say.

"That's it. And he's kind, too." Chiara laughs. "I think all his clients fall in love with him."

See? Ridiculous. "Well, thanks again for recommending him," I say. "Is there anything else I need to do today?"

"No, but I'll give you this." Chiara opens a drawer and takes out a white envelope, which she hands to me. "Here's your registered contract. Keep it safe—you'll need it for the Anagrafe."

I tuck the envelope into my bag. "Thanks."

"No trouble at all. And I know I've said it before, but if you need anything, just call me. I say that to all my English clients and they never believe me, but I'm not just being polite. That's not how we do things here. Okay?"

"Okay," I say. We say goodbye, and I go downstairs and out into the midday sunshine.

❧

CHIARA'S OFFICE IS SOUTH OF THE RIVER, ON VIA DEI SERRAGLI IN the Oltrarno quarter. When Granny first started bringing me here, when I'd just turned eleven, the street still had mostly old-fashioned shops, little bars and traditional restaurants. We'd go to one of the bars and I'd sit next to her drinking sweet-bitter Sicilian orangeade while she chatted with a stream of people who came and went, kissing and embracing her and exclaiming over me. I never really understood the conversations. My language skills were developing fast thanks to Granny's tutelage, but they were no match for a bunch of Italians in full flow.

I wish I'd worked at it harder. I wish I'd listened instead of just letting it all wash over me and wondering when we could go for ice cream. And then when I got older, old enough to safely entertain myself for an hour or so, she'd leave me to look at the shops near the Ponte Vecchio while she came here to catch up with her friends. I remember how pleased I was to be treated like a grown-up, how savoured every new freedom I was given as we returned to Florence year after year. But that whole side of Granny's life—the place she kept going back to, the people she must have loved—that was closed off to me from that moment onwards. Now I've lost her, that's starting to haunt me in a way it never did before.

I walk up the long narrow street towards the river, watching as I go for anything that looks familiar. There are still a few old-fashioned shopfronts, but they're mixed in with tattoo parlours and cocktail bars and funky restaurants with exposed piping and abstract art on the walls. At first sight, I can't see any sign of Granny's bar, and I wonder if I've misremembered. Maybe it wasn't in via dei Serragli after all. But the sun is beating down on my head and I'm hungry, I realize—

properly hungry for the first time in I don't know how long. That in itself is a good feeling. Like the germ of my old self, the girl who loved pasta and would walk from one side of Florence to the other if there was a really good pistachio gelato at the end of it.

There's a trattoria on my right, like a little room open onto the street. It has plain wooden tables and white walls with the occasional black-and-white photograph on display, and it's bustling. Must be the start of the lunchtime rush. I linger for a moment, trying to see if there's any space at all, and the owner—I presume—catches my eye and hurries over.

"*Buongiorno, signora,*" he says.

"*Buongiorno.* Do you have a table for one?"

"*Certo,*" the man says, and extends an arm to show me a little table tucked away by the door. I hadn't even seen it. "Sit down and I'll bring you the menu. Water?"

"Still, please."

"Right away."

I've scarcely settled in when he returns with my bottle of water and a menu that's no more than a short list of dishes, handwritten, on one side of an A4 sheet. I order bruschetta, spaghetti carbonara and a glass of house red, and then whip out my tablet and start typing. I've been making myself do this since Richenda's call: write down a full account of everything that happens to me, as soon as possible after it happens. What I should have been doing all along, in other words. It's dross. But I already have almost four thousand words of dross and, the more I can write, the more material I have to edit into something worth sending her. That's my logic, anyway.

I've managed to write about a page when the bruschetta arrives, two pieces on a plate drizzled with translucent greenish oil. It looks amazing: chunks of slick, bright-red tomato on a thin crisp base that's almost more holes than bread. I pick up a piece and try to bite into it, but the bread breaks and bits of tomato fall off and go everywhere. I cram the rest in my mouth, knowing how undignified it is but not caring—because the tomato is fresh and the oil is peppery and I'm in Florence, on a beautiful sunny day, being a writer. I take a sip of rough, tannin-y wine and devour the other piece of bruschetta whole.

Via dei Serragli is filling up now with the lunchtime crowd. I watch them pass, singly or hand in hand: young hipster couples with matching sleeve tattoos, corporate people in suits, fashionable tourists in cream linen and wide, cropped trousers, this season's statement red lip and huge sunglasses much in evidence. And then, just as the carbonara is put in front of me, I spot him on the other side of the street. Marco in the dark blue suit, his jacket slung over his shoulder—and, next to him, Chiara. She's holding his arm and looking up at him as they walk along, obviously deep into some very intense conversation.

I mean, it makes sense, doesn't it? They've probably known each other for years, they're close, she clearly adores him. Why wouldn't they be together? It's none of my business anyway. I'm a client, and soon enough I won't even be that anymore. What Marco gets up to in his free time has nothing, absolutely nothing to do with me.

"*Signora?*"

I must have zoned out. The carbonara is cooling in its bowl, and the restaurant owner is standing by my table looking concerned.

"What's the matter?" he asks. "Don't you like it? Is there something wrong? I can make you a different dish, if you prefer."

"No, no." My Italian has scattered to the four winds. "I'm just . . . I don't feel, I'm not feeling very . . ."

His eyes widen in alarm. "Are you ill?"

"No, I'm not ill and don't worry, the pasta is very good and I want to eat it but . . ." Oh God, I'm babbling. "I saw something," I say, and feel foolish—because I didn't see anything worth being upset about and yet here I am, upset. "Someone. I have . . . troubles. I'm sorry."

He nods and puts his hand on my shoulder. It's such a kind gesture that I mist up a little, although I haven't cried for, oh, a couple of days now. "Don't worry," he says. "Take your time. I'll bring you something else when you're ready. Carbonara isn't good when it's cold."

He gives my shoulder a little squeeze, picks up the untouched bowl and walks away. I take a few deep breaths and drain my glass of wine, then open my laptop. If I'm going to have irrational feelings, I might as well get a bit of literary mileage out of them. As I start to type, a waitress appears and tops up my wineglass.

God, I love Italy.

9

DUNCAN'S CALVINIST FOREBEARS HAD IT RIGHT: WORK *IS* GOOD FOR the soul. Just as well, because it's all I've been doing. With three days to go before Richenda's deadline, I've managed to write very nearly nine thousand words. It needs a lot of editing, but it isn't complete bollocks. In fact, I'm starting to get excited about it. I've decided to write about Granny: about our connection, our trips to Florence and the experience of coming back here, without her, to try and start again. After all, Richenda said that what I have to offer is my story—and this, right now, is it.

I've taken to crossing the river and spending the afternoon at the other branch of Ditta Artigianale, the one on via dello Sprone. Apart from the tea—which is a major plus, because I can only drink so much coffee—it has an immense window looking out onto the narrow little street, with bar stools and a counter so you can people-watch while you work. Today I've been here since half past two. It's now five o'clock, and I've written . . . oh, three hundred words. Not my best day. I've spent most of the time trying to remember that bar on via dei Serragli, the one Granny used to visit without me. Maybe because of that, it feels more important than any of the other places I associate with her. But my memories are fuzzy and jumbled with time. I can't make sense of them.

My phone buzzes. It's Charlie, sending a photo of her little old dog, Chomsky. He's lying upside down in an armchair, wearing a tiny T-shirt that says MADE IN DOGGENHAM. Gorgeous! I write back, and snap a picture of my teapot framed against the view of the street. The moment I send it, my phone buzzes again. Marco.

Ciao, come va? Did you get in touch with the accountant?

Yes, thanks, I reply. We met yesterday. He's very serious! I was there for hours.

Good. You want your accountant to be serious, believe me. How's it going otherwise?

On an impulse, I send him the photo of the teapot. Working hard, as you can see.

He starts typing, then stops, then starts again. This goes on for what feels like ages, and my stomach starts to feel a bit fluttery, a bit nervous in a way I don't like at all. Just as I pick up my phone to put it safely away in my bag, the message comes through.

Hey, you're at Ditta Artigianale! I'm just round the corner. Fancy a break from writing? I'll buy the drinks.

I'm still staring at the screen when a second one comes in.

I've got some information for you, too.

Oh, well, if it's official business.

(Tori) OK, great.
(Marco) I'll come to you. *A prestissimo* ☺

I put my phone face down and concentrate determinedly on my laptop. I can't bear to look at the street—the idea of seeing him, of watching him walk towards me, is excruciating for reasons I don't really understand and definitely, definitely don't want to examine. I mean, it's awkward, isn't it? Having a drink with your lawyer. Anyone would feel a bit weird about it.

The minutes stretch on and then, quite suddenly, he's there. He settles into the seat next to mine and kisses me on the cheek, just as if he's always done it.

"Oh God," he says, "was that okay? Sorry—I'm on automatic."

"It's fine," I say, going hot. "Really."

"Phew. I try to remember not to go kissing my Anglo friends

but, you know, it's so normal here." He takes off his jacket and I get a whiff of limes and soap and just a hint of fresh sweat. The fluttering starts up again. Fucksake.

"Busy at work?" I say, with a kind of strained nonchalance.

"Every time the BBC mentions No Deal, I get twenty new emails."

"*Qualcos' altro?*" Gianni, one of the baristas, is gathering my teapot and cup onto a tray.

"I'll have a gin and tonic," I say, switching into Italian with the minimal grinding of gears. I'm quietly pleased to have managed that in front of Marco.

"What gin would you like?" Gianni extends a tattooed arm towards the wall of gin behind the bar.

"Oh God, that's too much choice. I'll have whatever you recommend. I trust you," I add, before he can start asking me about botanicals and so on.

"Sure. And for you, sir?"

"Double Talisker, thanks," Marco says. He looks a bit stunned. "Your Italian's improving fast," he says as Gianni walks away. "I almost feel silly speaking English."

"That's down to Granny. Whenever we came to Florence, she made me speak Italian the whole time. We weren't able to make it here for the last few years—it was too hard for me to get away, so I was worried I'd forgotten everything. But it seems to be returning all right."

"I'd say so. Your accent is fantastic."

"Thanks," I say. "I mean, I can make myself understood, and I can understand most things, too. But I can't really have a proper conversation, not like I want to. People are very patient with me but I just know I'm not expressing myself well."

"How do you know? Maybe you're being hard on yourself."

"I know because they keep complimenting me. Granny always told me that you've only really arrived when people stop telling you how good your Italian is and talk to you normally instead." He's watching me intently. I can feel heat creeping up my neck and around my ears, and I pray I'm not blushing. "That's how it was for her. Everywhere she went, people just . . . welcomed her."

Gianni puts the drinks down in front of us. "*Grazie*," Marco says, and raises his glass of whisky in my direction. "We should toast your grandmother. *Cin cin*."

"*Cin cin*." I take a long sip of my drink. It's floral and aniseedy and good.

"You should write about her."

"I am. Well, I'm writing about all this—about coming to Florence, but it's really about her. She's why I decided to come here, though I wasn't thinking clearly at the time. She taught me to love this city."

"That's wonderful," Marco says.

"Yes. It's frustrating, though. There's so much I can't remember, no matter how much I try."

Marco's still watching me. I can't bring myself to meet his eye, so I look out at the street where a tiny dog, a Chihuahua, is barking at a girl on a Vespa. Its owner scoops it up and puts it into her quilted bucket handbag, where it snarls and bristles like an angry puppet.

"There was this bar I used to go to with her, years and years ago," I say. "We went to a lot of places, of course, but I know this one meant something special to her. I've been trying to remember it all day—where it was, what it was like—but it was so long ago now. I've looked for it, but it seems to have vanished."

"Where was it?"

"Via dei Serragli. Or I suppose it could have been via Romana. It was a long street and it was definitely near here."

Marco takes out his phone and starts tapping at the screen. "Okay, so one of those two. Did it have a name?"

"It just said BAR over the door."

"Oh, well. So far, so standard. What can you remember about it?"

"It was quite small, with a long counter and metal tables and chairs. They sold cigarettes, as well, and lotto tickets and so on. There was a TV in one corner, usually showing news or sports."

"A typical Italian *bar tabaccheria*," Marco says.

"Yes. It wasn't Granny's usual kind of place, not really. We'd have breakfast or an aperitivo or a plate of pasta for lunch. She knew all the regulars. They loved her and she must have loved them. They called her Rita, which I thought was hilarious because nobody else was ever allowed to call her anything but Margaret. Not even my grandfather, apparently." My throat is tight. "I didn't really understand at the time, and I didn't ask questions. I just accepted that this was part of her world. And now I can't ask her about it because she's dead. I know that's a stupid thing to say. But I keep wanting to phone her up, and I keep having to remember that I can't. It's like there's some part of my brain that hasn't caught up yet."

Marco takes my hand. He does it so naturally that for a brief, wild moment I imagine turning to him, kissing him, breathing in the scent of limes and soap and warm skin.

"It's all right," he says. "It's hard when you've lost someone."

"It is." I fix my eyes on the stone crest over the door of the house opposite. I'm lonely, I tell myself. Just that.

"Can you remember anything else? What about the people who ran it?"

I take a deep breath. "There was a couple—they must have been about her age, so I thought they were ancient, of course. He was called Giuseppe and she was Maria."

Marco snorts. "Really?"

"I know. But those were their names. Mary and Joseph."

"Don't tell me. They had a son."

"Ha! I'm not sure, actually," I say. "Their children were grown up. They did have a grandson called Niccolò, who used to help out sometimes. He was a student. I thought he was the most beautiful thing I had ever seen."

"I'm starting to see why you can't remember much else." Marco squeezes my hand. Oh God.

"Hey, I was a teenager. I had priorities. Anyway, Maria and Giuseppe were lovely people, I remember that. Otherwise . . . well, it was such an anonymous place. Like you say, just a typical Italian bar. There really wasn't anything to tell it apart from a million other places." An image flashes into my mind of Niccolò standing at the till, his fringe flopping into his eyes, and a framed photograph behind him. "Well, there was one thing. But it's probably standard, too."

"Tell me," Marco says.

"There was a picture on the wall. A framed photograph of a car."

"A car?"

"Yes. I think it was a racing car."

"A racing car?" He lets go of my hand. I try not to look bereft. "Like a Formula One car?" He's typing on his phone, looking really quite excited about it.

"I suppose it must have been."

"Was it like this?" Marco leans over and shows me a picture. One of those terrifying, low-slung, high-tech cars, red and black and alien-looking.

"Definitely not. It was old-fashioned, nothing like that at all."

"Okay, classic models." He's scrolling now. "How about this?"

This time it's a shiny car with leather seats and a big, arched radiator at the front. It looks like it belonged to a 1920s gangster. "No, a bit more modern than that. I don't know how to explain it, but it looked . . . really weird, actually. Made-up. Like something out of *Wacky Races*."

"*Wacky Races*?"

"You know, the cartoon with the racing cars and the laughing dog. Maybe you didn't get it over here."

"*La corsa più pazza del mondo*! I used to love that." He's scrolling again. "Okay, what about this?"

And he shows me the car. The exact car. It's vivid blue, and it looks like a melted cigar tube. "That's it," I say. "It looked just like that."

"Seriously? I only picked it as a joke. That's the Bugatti 251," he says, as if this should all be perfectly obvious.

"You'll have to enlighten me."

"It was the last racing car Bugatti ever made. Well, in their original incarnation. It was a total failure. You're sure it was this one?"

"I think so. Or something that looked very like it."

"Believe me, nothing looks like a Bugatti 251. Damn." Marco switches the screen off and puts his phone in his pocket. "There goes my theory."

"You had a theory?"

"Maybe that's overstating it. But when you mentioned the car, I thought they might be Formula One people. I suppose I had this fantasy that it would turn out to be the picture of a specific car—and if I could identify it then maybe I could find out who drove it, and whether they had relatives in Florence and—" He breaks off, shaking his head. "You know, it's silly now I say it out loud. Like a story for little boys."

He's smiling, but he's clearly crestfallen. It would be so easy to reach out, to take his hand like he took mine, but I don't. I drink the last of my gin and tonic and watch him drain his whisky glass. *Lucky bloody Chiara*, I think.

"Look," he says, "that was a dead end. But maybe you can find out some more about your grandmother's life in Florence. Do you have anything of hers? Letters, diaries?"

I've been so absorbed in meeting Richenda's deadline that the thought hadn't occurred to me. "I don't have anything with me, but I suppose . . . well, she must have left things behind. My mother would know. She's in charge of dealing with the house." I imagine Granny's beautiful Arts and Crafts cottage as I always knew it, full of books and paintings and folders of Grandad's terrible watercolors. God only knows what Mummy will do with it all—though hopefully, knowing Granny, she left the most important pieces to people who'll actually like them.

"Maybe your mother can help you with the story," Marco says.

I laugh, and rather more harshly than I meant to. "Sorry. No, she wasn't close to Granny. She's not that fond of me, come to think of it. But there must be some papers somewhere, and if anyone has access to them, it's her."

"I guess you don't want to call her up for a chat," Marco says.

"No, I do not. But I'll figure something out," I say, fighting down my rising anxiety. "It's a good idea."

He smiles at me. "I'm sure you'll find what you need. But if I can help, just call me. Off the clock, of course. This is friend stuff, not lawyer stuff. *Capito?*"

"I understand," I say. "Thank you. Uh . . . speaking of lawyer stuff, I think you had something to tell me?"

"To tell you? Oh, yes. I had a look to see if I could find you some-one to advise on your divorce, and I actually found a solicitor who trained in Milan and Edinburgh. Funny thing, she's the ex-wife of an old law school classmate of mine."

"I hope she got a decent settlement," I say.

"Ha! Well, I've only met her a couple of times, but I remember that she was pretty impressive. I think you'd be in good hands with her. Let me send you her contact card." Marco fiddles with his phone. "There."

The name Ambra Kurti flashes up on my phone, along with an email address and an Edinburgh telephone number. "Wow," I say. "Thanks. This is really helpful."

"Any time. And listen, if you don't feel comfortable with her or you want to look at more options, just let me know. Okay?"

"Okay," I say.

Marco shrugs on his jacket without looking—no fishing around for the sleeve holes with this man—and gets to his feet. "Which way are you headed?"

"I think I'm going to stay here for a while," I say. "Get a bit more work done."

"Serious. I like it. I'll get these on the way out." He kisses me on each cheek, light whisky-smelling kisses. I'm aware I should kiss him, too, but I don't react in time. "Work well. I'll see you soon." And he's off, heading to the till with an air of purpose.

I've just opened my laptop again when Gianni appears with another gin and tonic. "Your boyfriend got you this," he says, and sort of twinkles at me. "Enjoy."

"He's not—" I begin, and then stop because Gianni's already walking away and, besides, he doesn't care, does he? The only one who's that wound up about who Marco may or may not be to me is, well, me. Besides, he's already told me exactly what he is—he's my friend, nothing more and nothing less than that. It's just that Italians are a bit more . . . expressive than emotionally constipated Anglo types like me.

I remember the restaurant owner's hand on my shoulder; Chiara telling me to call her if I needed help. I remember Granny hugging Giuseppe and Maria like long-lost relatives. Come to think of it, Granny was the most upright Englishwoman I ever met in my life, but she knew how Italy worked. When she was in Florence, she was a Florentine, and she hugged people and kissed them and let them call her Rita and never—I am mortally sure of it—never, ever took any of it as a sign that someone was interested in her when it was perfectly obvious that they weren't.

❧

I DRINK THE REST OF MY GIN AND TONIC WHILE STARING OUT INTO the street. I'm starting to feel a bit tipsy, slightly otherworldly in a way that isn't totally unpleasant but not quite welcome, either. Once I've finished, I pack up my things, say *ciao* to Gianni and head out towards via de' Guicciardini and the Ponte Vecchio. It's not even summer yet, not remotely near high season, but the bridge is already packed with people. By the stern-looking bust of Benvenuto Cellini, a busker is belting out "Lay, Lady, Lay." I walk swiftly, carving my route through the strolling couples and the groups of students posing for selfies. Once I'm across the bridge, I swerve off into a quiet side alley, pull out my phone and call Charlie.

She answers on the first ring. "Tori," she says. "Is everything all right?"

"Did Granny leave any papers?" I'm being abrupt, I know, but it feels urgent. "Diaries or letters, or whatever?"

"Oh." Charlie sounds let down, somehow. "I don't know. Mummy's in charge of the house, and obviously I haven't had time to go down and help. You'd have to ask her, I'm afraid."

"Fuck," I say, and a group of American tourists shake their heads and cross to the other side of the street. "I fucking knew it."

"What's this about, anyway?"

"Nothing, really. I mean, it's a book thing. For the book."

"But I thought your book was about the Highlands," Charlie says. "Oh, Tori, don't tell me that's off, too."

"It's not *off*." I'm aware of sounding ridiculously defensive. God, Charlie always does put me on the back foot. "But obviously it has to be changed now, and Richenda wants me to write about Florence."

"So Richenda knows about all this, then."

"Of course she does. I had to tell her."

There's a brief silence, and I just know that Charlie's holding back some snippy remark. "Right," she says at last. "I mean, I get it. It makes sense you'd write about Florence. It was always your special thing, yours and Granny's."

She sounds hurt. I want to say: *But you could have come with us. I want to say: Look, it's not my fault you filled your holidays with tennis competitions and rowing and cross-country and cleaning up riverbanks.* But I don't, because she's right—it was our special thing. I was close to Granny in a way Charlie never quite got to be.

"Yes," I say inadequately.

"You should really deal with this yourself," Charlie says. "This is the outcome of your decision, you know. I shouldn't have to deal with Mummy for you—I mean, more than I already am." Her voice is already softer, though. I can tell she's relenting.

"I know. I know, and I'm so grateful for everything you're doing. I really am."

"Yeah, yeah." She sighs. "I have to talk to Mummy tomorrow anyway. I suppose I can ask her then. I'll tell her the twins are doing a family history project at school."

"They're only four, though. Don't you think she'll realize?"

"Oh, please."

"Fair point," I say. Mummy never was the most involved parent, and she was clearly never going to step up as a grandmother. "Thanks so much, Charlie. You can't imagine how much I appreciate this."

"It's okay," Charlie says. "But honestly, Tori, I don't know how you'd manage without me. You're going to have to learn to run your own life one of these days. Oh God, the kasha's boiling over. Ben! Ben!" And she's gone.

10

Stella

WHEN I LIVED WITH MY PARENTS, I NEVER GOT TO LIE IN BED IN the morning. In term time I had to go to school six days a week, and there was Mass on Sunday. And when I didn't have school, I had to make breakfast for everyone else and then work through a long list of household chores. I was only allowed to sleep late if I was ill, and I was as strong as an ox back then. I remember being ill only once in the whole of 1944, and it was really providential that I was.

I'd come home from school one day in late March with that horrible dizzy feeling you get when you're about to come down with something. Mamma had sent me to bed straightaway, and I hadn't argued. By the morning I had a fever and a cough, and she took one look at me and told me not to move; she would tell my father I was to stay at home today. I wasn't even cogent enough to be grateful to her. I just sank back into sleep, and woke again soon after to the sound of raised voices downstairs: Mamma, Papà and Achille.

At first I lay there and tried not to listen. I assumed it was just one of their fights, and I resented them for disturbing me. And then I heard the word *rastrellamento*, and I was wide awake. *Rastrellamento* is what we called the kind of sweep the Nazis did periodically, descending on a town and searching every house. Sometimes they'd simply round up all the men of serviceable age, even as young as fourteen or fifteen, and deport them all to Germany for forced labor.

Suddenly my mind was quite clear. I got up, dressed hastily and went down to the kitchen, where I found the dispute in full flow. Papà was the first to see me. He held up a hand to silence my mother and Achille. "Stella, you silly girl, what are you doing? Go back to bed."

I shook my head, making it hurt. "I want to know what's happening."

"The SS are at San Damiano," Achille said before my father could interrupt. "Apparently they've been working their way along the valley."

"Then we're next," I said, and my mother crossed herself.

Achille nodded. "I'm just getting a few things together, then I'll go up to Santa Marta."

"Why would you do that?" my mother burst out. "Why would you put yourself in more danger? You should go to Mercatale with your father." My aunt Giovanna, my father's sister, had a small farm near Mercatale, a little way away in the Val di Pesa.

"Because I'm not a coward," Achille said. "If I have to run, I'll run to where I'm useful. I can serve the cause better at Santa Marta than I can hiding in a hayloft."

My father thumped his fist down on the table. "Are you calling me a coward?"

"You said it, not me," Achille retorted. And then Papà was roaring, and Mamma was clutching at his shoulders, trying to restrain him. I slipped out of the kitchen and ran towards the back door, pausing only to take an old coat of my mother's and shove my feet into shoes. There was something urgent I needed to do.

At the back of the house was a lean-to where Achille kept his motorbike and I stored my bicycle. There was a bit of clutter in there, too, wooden crates and so on. I'd used one of the crates to hide a few donations that had come in to our network, meaning to take them along on my next munitions run. There was an old service revolver that had belonged to someone's father, a handful of cartridges, a length of detonating cord—nothing big, thankfully. I managed to shove it all into my coat pockets and then, tiptoeing around the side of the house with my bike, I pedaled off towards St. Christopher's church.

There was hardly anyone on the streets. It might have been my imagination—or my fever—but the whole town seemed to be holding its breath. Even the Germans at the checkpoint on the via Senese looked tense, scanning the road as if in anticipation. Perhaps they were worried that the SS would find their vigilance lacking. They looked at me as I approached, but I ignored them and propped my bicycle in the church porch. I saw that don Anselmo's bicycle was there, too, and I was relieved.

When I went into the church, I found him praying in one of the pews. I hesitated, wondering whether I ought to clear my throat, or shuffle my feet, or make some other subtle sign. But he knew I was there. He crossed himself and rose to his feet, turning to me with that same benign smile he always wore. Anyone who didn't know him would have thought him unworldly, foolish.

"Stella, my dear child. What can I do for you?"

"Can we talk somewhere private?" I asked, although we were alone already.

He nodded. "Of course. Let's go to the sacristy."

Once we'd gone in and he'd shut the door behind us, I took the gun, cartridges and detonating cord from my pockets and placed them on the table, next to the cruets of wine and holy water. Don Anselmo nodded again.

"Very good. Yes. I shall put these downstairs with the other things."

"You know the Germans are coming," I said. "Will it be safe? I mean, what if they find the tunnel?"

"Oh, I don't mind about that," don Anselmo said. "It's not myself I'm worried about—I mean to say, I can take my chances. But you, Stella, are you quite all right? You don't look very well."

"Yes. No, I'm . . . I'm all right." But I wasn't, not really. The adrenaline was draining away and I was beginning to feel ill again. And it was coming to me, rushing in like a cold flood, that I didn't know where Enzo was. Did he know about the *rastrellamento*? Would he get to safety in time? Nausea washed over me and black dots crowded my vision.

"Oh dear," don Anselmo said. He ushered me over to one of the chairs lined up against the wall and gestured for me to sit down. "Lean forward and put your head between your knees. Yes, that's right. Now breathe as slowly as you can."

He took out a big white handkerchief and handed it to me, and I buried my face in it while the cold, sick feeling rose and then ebbed. When I finally looked up, he was holding out a little silver flask.

"Drink. Just a little at a time, now." He watched me as I took one sip of brandy and then another, and another, and another. The heat of it scorched my throat and made my eyes water. "I think that's about the right dose," he said, gently prying the flask from my fingers. "Now, you have a brother, don't you? And your father is still with you?"

I had to cough before I could speak. "Yes."

"And have they got somewhere to go until it's over?"

Those arguing voices echoed in my ears. "Yes."

"Well, then, that's very good news," don Anselmo said. "And you know, don't you, that word has got around? So if there's anyone in particular you're worried about, I'm sure that person will be fine, too."

I could only nod. I was very tired all of a sudden.

"You did a very good thing coming to me today," don Anselmo said. "Will you get home all right, or shall I walk with you?"

The mortification of almost fainting in front of him was already more than I could bear. "No. No, thank you, Father, I'll manage."

"If you insist, my child." He opened the sacristy door and we went back out into the church.

When I got home, the garage was locked up and Achille's bike was gone. My mother was sitting in the kitchen, sunk in her own private gloom. She didn't look up as I came in, and I knew it would be useless to talk to her. I went into my room, stripped down to my slip and got into bed. I was asleep within moments.

⌘

THE NEXT THING I REMEMBER IS WAKING UP TO HARSH SUNLIGHT. I felt light and weak, washed out, like you do when a fever has broken. Achille was sitting in an armchair by the window, reading Marx's *Eighteenth Brumaire*. I tried to say his name but it ended in a spluttering cough. He dropped the book and came to sit on the bed next to me.

"Hey, little sister. How are you feeling?" He poured out a glass of water from the carafe on my bedside table and handed it to me. I raised it to my lips with shaky hands. It was shockingly cold.

"You're back already," I said once I could speak.

"Got back this morning. Seems like the SS didn't hang around—not much for them to check in a place of this size, and every man under eighty had made himself scarce. And it's the men they want. Mamma says they weren't here more than a few minutes."

"They came into the house?"

"They even came in here to look at you," Achille said. "You were down for the count, Mamma says. Probably just as well."

I pulled the covers up around my neck. I was glad I hadn't had to see the Germans looking at me. "Where's Enzo? And Sandro?" I added hastily. "Did they go to Santa Marta with you?"

"Of course. Not that there was much to do up there, in the end—we just sat tight and waited for word that the Germans had gone. Sandro came back down with me, but Enzo decided to stay on. I thought about it, too, but I'm probably more useful here." Achille shrugged. "Still, I envy him. He's going to see some real action."

I couldn't speak. My throat was clogged and there was a pain deep within me because the boy I cared for—the very first one to hold my hand, to kiss me, to give me cause to dream—had left without saying goodbye. And who knew if I'd see him again?

"I'll have to break it to Papà," Achille went on. "He had no idea Enzo was a communist. Oh, Stellina, don't look so worried. Enzo's a crack shot. Nobody's going to get past him, believe me."

I couldn't bear his kindness. "It isn't that," I said. "I'm glad he's staying. I just . . . I wish I could be useful. I should be out working, not lying in bed."

Achille rubbed my arm. "Don't worry about that. You'll be fit again in no time. In the meantime, I passed a message along to Agnese." Agnese was the woman who had taken over Berta's organizing duties. "She knows you're sick and will have plenty for you to do when you're ready. But you have to recover properly first, all right? We need you to be strong."

"All right," I said.

"Will I let Mamma know you're awake? She probably wants to make you eat soup."

I shook my head. "I don't think I can face it. Not yet."

"Understandable." Achille leaned forward to plant a kiss on my forehead. "Rest well, little sister." He got up and went out, closing the door softly behind him. I buried my face in my pillow and cried in heaving, broken sobs, like a little girl. I couldn't imagine my life without Enzo close at hand. I didn't know how I would manage.

❧

I DID MANAGE, OF COURSE. A FEW DAYS LATER I WAS BACK ON MY feet, and there was so much to do that I simply had to get on and do it. The war was growing more and more intense, and we felt it in Romituzzo, too. Not just in the concrete sense—the train lines blown up and the power cables sabotaged, the troops at the stations, the diktats posted up on walls and doors with their sordid refrain of *will be punished by death*—but in the news that filtered back to our little town by word of mouth and in the clandestine press. A partisan lad captured by Fascists, doused with petrol and burned alive. A pregnant young courier imprisoned and tortured; a woman shot as she tried to pull her husband from the back of a truck. A Jewish family hidden by one neighbor, their location betrayed to the SS by another. These stories were commonplace.

Once, walking out of Castelmedici station with my satchel full of ammunition, I saw bodies hanging from the trees that lined the square. Two men and two women, all of them young, in mismatched and scruffy clothing. Around each of their necks was a handwritten sign that said, in angry black letters, PARTISAN. At their feet, German soldiers held back the mourners who were gathering.

"Just give me my daughter," I heard a woman cry out as I hurried past, my head down. "You've made your point, now let me bury her." One of the soldiers made a jabbing motion with the butt of his rifle and the little knot of women surged together, muttering. If I had not been a partisan already, I would have become one in that moment.

The months that followed were the busiest time of my life so far. Alongside my work with the women's network, I also helped don Anselmo. Sometimes he wanted me to pick up food or medicine from a friendly shopkeeper. Sometimes he would ask me to collect or return a book in Castelmedici or San Damiano, "but only if you happen to be going." Sometimes he'd send me on an errand for don Mauro, or ask me to pass him a note when I next went by St. Catherine's. I always said yes and I never asked to know why. It was enough that I knew about the weapons in the tunnel.

There were days when I stayed out from dawn until curfew, but it never caused a problem at home. I always managed my chores, even if I had to get up in the dark to do them. Enzo was gone and Achille was more in demand than ever before, so my father had to run the garage on his own. My mother haunted the house, waiting for her son to return. She didn't care what I did.

At first, I used to ask Achille for news of Enzo whenever he came back from Santa Marta. Obviously he couldn't give me any details, but he would reassure me that he was alive and well and had asked about me, too—I don't know whether that last part was true every time, or even at all. Achille was a good brother. Sometimes he'd even take a short message to Enzo for me, written on the cigarette paper we all used. Sometimes I'd receive a short message back. But then the replies stopped coming altogether, and I stopped writing. After a while, I no longer asked for news.

II

Tori

"NOW, I'M AFRAID WE HAVE TO TALK ABOUT MONEY," AMBRA KURTI says. She's a young, serious woman in a dark gray suit and pearls, her black hair pulled into a chignon. From her office window I can see a glimpse of the Royal Mile. "Can you give me an idea of how the finances worked in your household?"

I didn't expect to get into this on the first video call, and I haven't prepared. I hesitate and Ambra smiles. "Don't worry about precise details," she says. "If you proceed with the divorce, then you'll both be filling out financial disclosures. But anything you can tell me at this stage is useful, just to get an overview."

"Well, basically we had a joint account for all the day-to-day stuff," I say. "My freelance earnings went in there."

"And how much would that be?" Ambra asks. "Last tax year, what did you earn?"

"Oh. Well, I haven't started doing my tax return yet. But I had a regular writing gig that brought in £250 per month, as a baseline, and of course I took whatever work I could on top of that. I probably earned about . . . fourteen, fifteen thousand last year? Plus the first half of my book advance, which was another five. Obviously that was a bit of an anomaly."

Ambra nods, noting it all down. "Right. And presumably Duncan had some money going into that account, too?"

"He'd put in three hundred pounds each month. We agreed on that number when we got married, back in 2008. It was about equivalent to my writing income at the time," I explain. "That way we'd be contributing equally to costs, at least in theory. Obviously, he still had to cover most of the outgoings for the first couple of years."

"Right. So your contributions to the joint account increased quite substantially from 2008. But his didn't?" I shake my head and she makes a note. "So he's been paying in a lot less than you, even without the advance," she says. "And, of course, the cost of living has gone up considerably."

"Yes, but then it wasn't like Duncan could contribute more. The estate swallowed up every bit of income he managed to bring in. It was always in the red. Some months he couldn't even manage the three hundred."

"Right," Ambra says, still writing. "And approximately how big was that debt? How much money was owed by the time you left?"

"I don't know."

Ambra puts her pencil down and looks at me. "You didn't have sight of the finances?"

"Well, no," I admit. "I did try to get involved when we were first married—you know, take an interest in how the place was run. But the whole situation was so stressful, and Duncan spent all his time trying to keep the estate afloat, so my asking about it only made things worse. I stopped after a while."

"But your income helped pay for the day-to-day expenses?"

"Right," I say.

"And those were just personal—food, clothing and so on? Or did they involve the business, too?"

"Well, of course there was always stuff to do around the estate. Repairs, improvements . . ." Ambra nods at me to continue, and I list the outgoings I can remember over the last few months. When I get to the golf clubs, she frowns and underlines something on her notepad.

"And how much of your income went out on these expenses, would you say?"

"Most of it," I say. "Well, pretty much all of it. I managed to put the tax money aside, just about, but otherwise . . ."

"And did Duncan consult with you on how the money was spent? Did he ask you before he took money from your earnings?"

"At first, yes. But then . . . well, it didn't make sense for him to keep asking. And it wasn't like I did anything around the estate. I grew up in a city and I'm useless with animals, and as for all the technical stuff, like the salmon farm and the forestry side and the shooting . . . really, it was only sensible that Duncan and his estate manager did all that. The money was all I could contribute, not that it even touched the sides."

"Hmmm." Ambra's expression is carefully blank. "Tori, can you think of anything you did that contributed to the life of the estate in some other way? You mentioned a few things earlier—weddings, shooting parties. Were you involved with those?"

"Oh," I say. "Well, yes, there were various events and of course, I did a bit of hostessing."

"Hostessing?"

"Yes, you know the kind of thing. Keeping people's drinks topped up, making sure warring aunts didn't end up at the same table, wrangling nervous brides, dealing with the caterers. Just normal stuff. And of course if people came to look over the place—engaged couples, or whatever—it was easiest for me to show them round since Duncan was usually out somewhere. I suppose my role was mostly decorative."

"Decorative," Ambra echoes. "It sounds pretty demanding to me."

"It definitely could be at moments. Actually, a lot of the time. But it's nothing compared to what Duncan had to do every day."

"It's different," she says firmly. "It's a different kind of work. But, Tori, what you're describing *is* work. Dealing with caterers, managing guests, giving tours—which is a sales role in itself, really—those are all crucial tasks, and they require certain skills. And if you didn't do them, he'd no doubt have had to pay someone else. Unless you did get some kind of compensation?"

"Well, no, I didn't. But that's just being married, isn't it? The least I could do was pitch in, since I wasn't being useful in any other way. That was Duncan's view, anyway."

"Duncan's view isn't relevant," Ambra says. "Tori, what he thinks isn't what matters here. I need you to see that. All the money you've put into the estate, all the work you've done for no pay—these are significant contributions. Exactly how this all works out in terms of a settlement is something we need to establish. But if Duncan made you feel anything less than useful, then he wasn't being fair to you. Do you understand?"

I don't understand, not really. Not yet. But there's something nagging away deep in my gut, a cold, urgent, rage-y feeling. "I think so," I say. "Yes, I think so."

"Good," Ambra says. "Thank you for all this information—it was very helpful. We should wrap up for today, but I'm happy to schedule another meeting now if you like. Or you can take some time, think about it, and contact me when you feel ready to talk about your options going forward."

I'm not ready. The whole conversation has been much, much more than I expected. "I think I'd like to take a little time," I say. "But I'll definitely be in touch soon."

"That's no problem. I do just want to ask a couple of last questions, though, if that's all right."

"Of course," I say.

"The inheritance you mentioned at the start of our meeting," she says. "Which is, as I told you, not considered marital property. Does Duncan have access to that account?"

"No."

"Does he know that you have it?"

"No, actually," I say. "Granny was very strict on that account. The money is for me to use and me alone, so if I'm honest, I didn't even tell him about it. Is that a problem, do you think?"

Ambra shakes her head. "No. No, absolutely not. In fact, I'm very relieved to hear it. And you have enough to live on, for now anyway? Because if some kind of interim maintenance is needed—"

"I'm comfortable. At least for a while."

"That's good. And do you feel safe where you are?"

No.

"Yes," I say. "I mean . . . yes, of course. Actually . . ." I have to clear my throat. "If we go ahead with this—if I'm the one who files for divorce—will I have to see him? Talk to him?"

"No," Ambra says. "You can direct all communication through me, so you won't have to see him or talk to him. Not unless it goes to court."

"I really don't want to go to court," I say.

"I understand. But look, Tori." Ambra taps her pencil against her notepad. "Obviously I can't make any definite statements, certainly not at this stage. But if what you're telling me is anything to go by, Duncan won't want to go to court, either. In fact, he should be very wary of doing so."

❧

WHEN THE CALL ENDS, I PACE AROUND THE LIVING ROOM FROM door to window to sofa to kitchen to door. The rage in my gut is growing and I feel horribly restless. Of course I knew on some level that Duncan wasn't being fair to me when he said all those things about my being useless, a burden, not contributing. But to hear it stated by someone else—to be told in such plain, businesslike terms that I wasn't useless, that I was far from a burden, that I did contribute . . . I stop at the window and lean on the sill, staring out into the sun-baked street as the memories assail me again.

Like the London thing. The year before last, I had a particularly fat royalty payment from the ALCS—apparently lots of people had been photocopying my articles, or something—and I was going to use it to go and visit my best friend from school, Sarah. She and I had barely managed to see each other since I married Duncan and she got a terrifically high-flying PR job. I'd told Duncan I planned to go, and he'd said it was all right. But then when I went to book the train ticket, my card was declined. The ALCS money was gone.

I actually got upset that time. I barreled along to Duncan's office and asked him why he'd withdrawn the money when he knew perfectly well that I had plans for it, and he looked at me like I was stupid and said that the feed barrier in the sheep shed had to be fixed; that I'd have noticed if I ever went near the sheep myself, or did anything other than drift around the house playing at lady of the manor. So then I had to phone Sarah and explain that I couldn't come after all. She listened to me for a bit and then said quite calmly that it was fine. I'd canceled on her so many times that she didn't expect me to make it anyway. And now she doesn't talk to me, not really. We exchange the odd text, if I message first, but that's it.

"Right," I say out loud. "Need to get out."

I grab my bag from the sofa, slip on my sandals and head down the stairs. It's stifling outside and the afternoon sun is beating down. I never usually go out at this time of day. I linger in the shadow of the doorway, unsure of what to do next, until I hear someone calling my name. Elisa, who runs the bar across the road, is waving to me.

"*Ciao*, Tori! Just the person I need to see. Do you have a moment?"

I cross the street, flinching as someone on a bike swerves past me. "*Ciao*, Elisa. What's up?"

"This just arrived," Elisa says, brandishing a copy of *Fiorenza*, one of those glossy English magazines you find in stacks all over the city. "There's an article about the bar—just a short review—Alessio speaks better English than I do, but he's not working today. Would you mind reading and telling me what it says? If you have time."

"Of course," I say.

"Oh, great. Sit down, sit down. Do you want a negroni?"

"If it's not too early."

"Come on," Elisa says. "It's always the right time." I sit down at a table in the shade of an umbrella, and she hands me the magazine before going inside to make my drink.

The review is easy to find. *Ten Hidden Gems in Central Florence*, the headline reads, and then there are ten little mini-reviews of various bars and restaurants. I'm gratified to see that Trattoria dei Serragli is in there, too.

"Well?" Elisa asks when she re-emerges. She places the negroni in front of me along with various dishes of nibbles.

"This is really good," I say. "Listen. *Tucked away in a quiet street near the Duomo, Bar Dianora is a charming little place. Come here for warm hospitality, excellent cocktails and a decent selection of Tuscan wine, all at a more than reasonable price. We especially love the aperitivo with a generous spread of cold cuts and crostini. Our favorite discovery this year.* And look, you're right at the top of the page."

"But that's amazing!" She takes the magazine from my hands and looks at it, beaming. Her joy is so evident that even my spirits lift a little. "Thank you, Tori. This is just wonderful."

"It is," I say. "It really is."

12

THE TEN THOUSAND WORDS ARE FINALLY READY ON THE MORNING of Richenda's deadline day. I polish them as much as I reasonably can and send them off. She replies almost instantly.

> Thanks, darling. Will be in touch ASAP. Now go out and have some fun!

I really should. I've been in Florence for weeks now and I've spent most of it staring at my laptop. But I want to keep going, that's the thing. I'm excited about this project, far more than I ever was about *The Laird's Lady's Guide* or writing articles about the best tweed jackets under £150 or creating website copy for nickel-alloy suppliers. I'm excited in a way I haven't been since I was an undergraduate, churning out tutorial essays by day and sitting up at night to write features for *Cherwell*. God, I hope Richenda gets back quickly so I can forge on with it.

I know, though, that there's no real point in continuing work until I have the official okay. Also, I'm exhausted. I mean, I arrived here exhausted, and what's keeping me upright is mostly adrenaline. If I actually sit down for a moment, if I close my eyes and try to disregard all that productive whirring in my brain, I can feel the tiredness pulling at me, and the grief. Part of me wants to go to bed and not get up for days, and that's something I can't afford to do. There's nobody for me to lean on here; nobody who'll make supper if I don't, or comfort me if I'm too upset to function. I know instinctively that I need to keep moving.

What would Granny do? Or, rather, what would I do if I were here with Granny? Easy: I'll go to a museum. That should keep me occupied, get me a bit of exercise *and* stave off the vague guilt I feel about living in one of the world's most cultured cities without actually doing any, you know, culture. I can't be arsed with the Uffizi, though, or the Duomo, or anywhere that might involve standing in a queue. Fortunately, Florence has dozens of museums that are (inexplicably) left off the standard artsy-linen-clad tourist itinerary.

A quick phone search shows me that the closest one to me is the Bargello, which to my recollection is delightful, insofar as any medieval prison can be delightful. But it has nice bronzes, and I remember being really taken with a group of sculptures—I think they were by Giambologna, or someone else with a name like a brand of cold meat—showing all kinds of birds, from sparrows to owls to one massive peacock. Yes, the Bargello it is.

I'm gathering up my things when the phone buzzes with a message from Charlie.

Mummy has Granny's papers. Do you need me to go through them? Only I can't, really, with so much else on. She attaches a photo showing a stack of archival boxes. My heart leaps. I hoped there might be something, but I didn't realize there would be so much.

Quickly I tap out a reply. Wow, thanks so much for finding these! Would it be all right just to send them all on? I know it's a pain in the arse, and obviously I'll pay you back. I'd be so grateful.

Charlie's reply is lightning fast. Fine, but there's loads. Seems Granny was a bit of a hoarder. It's going to cost an arm and a leg to send them all.

No problem, I reply. I mean, if you're happy to do it. Honestly, it would be so useful to have them.

Charlie types for what seems like an age, and I brace myself for one of her screeds. But the reply, when it comes, is short and snappy. What's your address?

Oh, thank God. My hands are actually shaking a bit. Via Dianora 43, 50122 Firenze, Italy. Thanks so much, C. I'm seriously grateful. xxxxxxx

OK, but don't say I didn't warn you! I hope you have enough space in that tiny flat of yours! x

Typical dramatic Charlie. I'll surely have room for a few boxes if I shove my sofa back a bit. Easy.

My mood now definitely lifted, I saunter downstairs and out in the direction of the Bargello. But just as its grim stone tower comes into view, I'm distracted by one of those shops—the touristy sort you find all over town, crammed with handbags of all shapes and sizes, each one stamped with the Florentine fleur-de-lis. This one has a rack of big leather tote bags in summery pastel colors, pink and yellow and blue and lilac and pistachio green, with a sign saying 50€ in red marker pen. They certainly aren't worth even that. But they look substantial, they're capacious enough to hold a laptop and, above all, they're pretty. I draw closer to take a look and, as I do, the shop owner pops out of the doorway and grins at me.

"Can I help?" he says—in English, of course. I've resigned myself to never, ever passing for Italian, even if the locals did buy from these places, which I'm sure they don't.

"Thanks," I reply. "I'm just looking at these."

"Oh, those are new." He switches instantly into Italian, and I feel a rush of gratitude, as I always do when someone takes my efforts seriously. "They're nice, very useful. Do you want to see?"

I hesitate. I'm not sure I can justify a frivolous purchase while everything's still up in the air. But the shop owner's already unhooking the chain. He takes down the nearest one, in delicate yellow, and holds it open to show me. It's basic: the inner isn't lined and the seams are a bit uneven, but the stitching is good and strong. There's a zippered pocket big enough to hold my purse and another for my phone. The whole thing ties at the top with a thin piece of leather in the same color.

"Try it," he commands, and pushes it into my hands. It might be cheaply made but the leather is soft as butter. I hook the bag over my free shoulder, the one Granny's Fendi isn't on. The straps are long and sturdy and it certainly feels robust enough. Mummy would call it shoddy, of course, and as for Duncan . . .

"Forty-five," the shop owner says. He's mistaken my hesitation for some kind of canny bargaining tactic. "Eighty for two."

I pull the bag off my shoulder and look at it. I like the cheerful yellow, and the pink, too, and the pistachio. They remind me of sugared almonds or Easter eggs.

"How much for three?" I say.

⁂

"LOOK," CHIARA SAYS, "I GET THAT IT'S HARD TO END A MARRIAGE. But I don't really understand why you married Duncan in the first place. Didn't you know what he was like?"

We're sitting outside Procacci on via de' Tornabuoni. Chiara's drunk about half of her spritz and nibbled on one of their famous truffle finger-roll things, while I'm on my second and have put away four truffle rolls and a couple of anchovy ones. I've been enjoying this time, being frivolous for a change. I don't want to talk about Duncan, and I don't want to have to defend myself, but Chiara's wide-eyed not-understanding is getting on my nerves.

"He wasn't always like that," I try to explain. "When we were going out . . . oh, he was charming. And it wasn't superficial charm. We had this amazing, intense bond—I thought he really got me, that nobody else would ever get me like he did. And he was gorgeous, of course," I admit. "I suppose he still is."

Chiara perks up. "Really? Have you got a picture?"

"Actually, I have." I scroll through my phone to find the one, the only photo of Duncan and I that I couldn't bring myself to delete. It's from our wedding at the local kirk. We're wrapped up in each other's arms, him sturdily handsome in a kilt, me flushed and happy in my delicate lace wedding dress. And there, off to one side, is Granny: a lock of silver hair detaching itself from her elegant updo, holding her third glass of champagne and waving her free hand around as she chats animatedly with the pink-faced minister. Inconveniently, it's my favorite picture of her.

"Oh my God, that's him?" Chiara fans herself. "He's like something out of *Outlander*. I'd marry him—well, if he weren't a dick," she adds.

"In fairness, he wasn't one then," I say. "Or he didn't seem to be. It all changed after the wedding, though."

"What, just like that? No more nice, hot, understanding guy?"

"No, that was the whole problem. It crept up on me. At first it seemed like normal stuff, the end of the honeymoon period. One of us would get on the other's nerves—it was usually me annoying him, if I'm honest—we'd argue a bit and then make up again. But then it kept getting worse and worse." I take a gulp of my wine. "It was this constant drip-drip-drip of insults and criticism. Like I couldn't do anything right, no matter how I tried. And then finally he did something so awful I just couldn't stand him anymore."

"The funeral," Chiara says.

"Right. But really, that was the last straw. I was already so worn down and he . . . well, he was just so angry with me all the time. It was completely miserable. But I suppose I was in denial for quite a long while before that. I kept thinking I could fix things—be better, work harder, do more—right up until the moment when I couldn't."

"I see," Chiara says, but I can tell she doesn't see at all. She's looking at me with the baffled pity of someone who's been treated normally all her life, someone who wouldn't think twice about ditching a partner if he attempted to push her around. I try not to think about Marco. "Duncan sounds like an asshole," she says at last.

"He is."

"Your family must have hated him."

"Not really," I say, and bleakness washes over me along with the shame. "I mean, clearly Granny had his number. No doubt that's why he kept me away from her. But the rest of my family . . . no. Actually, pretty much everyone thought he was great. His employees, his friends, my friends—well, the ones who met him. He was lovely to all of them. Kind, fair, hard-working, a real pillar of the community. I thought I was losing my mind, finding him so hateful. I still wonder sometimes."

"I'm sorry." It's obvious that she really is, too. That's why she invited me out and that's why she's been quizzing me about my life for the last half hour. It's kind of her, and I feel like a heel. "We have to find you a nice Italian guy," she says.

Oh shit, I'm blushing. "No, no," I lie, "that's the furthest thing from my mind. Honestly, I'm better off on my own."

"Come on. My mother's French and she always says that the best thing to drive out a nail is another nail." She snorts. "You know, that sounds kind of dirty now I say it."

"I like your mum's style," I say.

"Oh, she thinks she's always right. But she's right about that, you know. There are so many good men out there. It makes no sense to waste your time grieving about the bad ones."

"I'm sure Marco's one of the good ones," I say, because I want to show her that I do know about their relationship and that I'm totally fine with it, even if that's not exactly true. It still nettles me that she said all his clients fall in love with him.

Chiara's face lights up. "Oh, he is. Marco's the best. I mean, maybe he's not everyone's type, but he's so sweet and funny—and loyal, of course. And so smart! He always got the best marks in our class at school. You'd think he'd turn out to be one of these really arrogant guys, you know, but he just isn't."

Jeez, no need to rub it in. "That's great," I say weakly. "I mean, yeah, he seems really nice."

Chiara's phone pings. "I think that's him, actually. I promised I'd meet him for dinner . . . yes, he's already on his way there. Hey, you should join us! We're going to this place that does amazing Florentine steak. You have to try it."

She beams at me, apparently quite genuine. But the idea of spending the evening playing third wheel to Marco and Chiara is more than I can take. "Sorry," I say, and hope to sound convincing. "I'd love to, but I really should get back to work. Maybe another time."

"Of course, your book. You must be under a lot of pressure." She takes out her purse, and I wave for her to put it away. "Are you sure?"

"Absolutely."

"Okay, but I'll pay next time. I insist. And then you can tell me all about how your work is going. I can't wait to read it. *Ciao ciao.*" She grins again and bounces off down via de' Tornabuoni in the direction of the river. No doubt she's deeply relieved not to have a charity case like me eavesdropping on her date with her fabulous childhood sweetheart.

The sun's starting to sink, but it's still warm and I'm beginning to wonder just how I'll survive the coming summer. I'm slathering on SPF 50 ten times a day, but my arms are already sprouting freckles and I'm getting that pinkish tinge around the collarbone, the mark of the pale Englishwoman in a southern climate. Just another reminder that I'll never really fit, I think, and the sadness that's been hovering at the edge of my consciousness starts closing in.

13

RICHENDA DOESN'T GET BACK TO ME FOR ALMOST A WEEK. THE DAYS get hotter and brighter and the urge to go to bed and stay there gets stronger, but I resist. Instead I attack the museums, dragging myself to at least one each day. I stare determinedly at suits of armor and marble busts and paintings of naked people in improbable situations, but my phone is in my hand and my mind is on my phone. Every time it buzzes with a message or an email, I jump.

I'm at the Palazzo Vecchio (again) when a message from Chiara comes in. *Ciao!* A friend of mine has an art show opening tonight—want to come? It should be fun.

My heart sinks. Chiara's been in touch a few times about lunch or coffee or drinks, and every time I've turned her down, pleading work. I feel terrible about it, but I'm a nervous wreck. The last thing I want is to inflict that on anyone else.

Apologies! I write back. I'm on a really tight deadline, but I so appreciate the invitation. Sorry to miss out—I hope it goes well for your friend.

Her reply's almost instant. Sure you can't come by for a few minutes? Marco will be there and I know he'd love to see you.

Ugh. I've heard from Marco once since that evening at Ditta Artigianale. He emailed to ask how I was getting on with Ambra and would I be proceeding under Scots or Italian law, and I said Scots law and she was terrific, and he said well, great, hope it all goes smoothly. Which is fine, of course; it's positively nice, but it doesn't exactly scream "must have your company now." Besides, the more I get to know Chiara—who seems nice enough, if a bit nosy, and is apparently determined to be my friend—the worse I feel about letting myself sit there holding hands with her boyfriend. Even though I'm sure it was a completely innocent action on his part. And if it wasn't—well, that's even worse again. Really, there's no good outcome here.

So sorry, I reply. I'd have loved to come, but I just won't manage it. And then I shove the phone in my pistachio-green bag, right at the bottom where it can't bother me.

Half an hour or so later, I'm in the Hall of Lilies admiring the blue-and-gold wallpaper when I feel a distinct vibration against my leg. A long, sustained vibration like an incoming call. I fish for my phone and see that I have three missed calls, all from Richenda. Shit. I hurry out and down the stairs. By the time I reach the big frescoed courtyard on the ground floor, my heart is racing and I've sweated through my nice summery top. I press redial and close my eyes as the phone rings at the other end.

"Tori! Thanks for calling." She sounds quite upbeat and, for a moment, I'm reassured. "I hope I wasn't interrupting anything fun?"

"No, no," I say. "I was just . . . I was in a museum. Sorry."

"Gosh, you do know how to have a good time. Look," she says, suddenly businesslike, "we need to talk about these pages you sent me. I can't show them to Tim Swithin, darling. I just can't."

"Right." I need to sit down. I cast around for a bench, but can't see one, so I lean faux-casually against one of the big pillars.

"I'm not saying this is *terrible*," Richenda says. "I see the kind of thing you're trying to do. But Tori, darling . . . All this wandering around searching for your grandmother—who I'm sure was completely delightful, if you happened to know her—it's just . . . it's so muted. Low-key. Quiet. Anita Brookner could have written it."

"Oh, thanks," I say, feeling slightly bolstered.

"No, I mean that *Anita Brookner* could have written it. And you know I adore your work, of course I do, but you're no Anita Brookner and if I'm brutally honest, I don't understand why you're trying to be." She sighs. "Come on. You know what Swithins want from you here, and that's a light touch. Something nice and fluffy and sharp and a

tiny bit sexy. Why isn't there any sex in this, by the way? Not that
I want *Fifty Shades* or anything, but it wouldn't hurt to spice it up a
little."

"Because there isn't . . . I'm not having any."

"What, no sex at all? But what about this Marco?"

"Just a friend." My head's starting to thump and there's a tight,
hot feeling in my chest.

"Seriously?" Richenda snorts. "If you're not shagging him, darling, then why do I know what he smells like?"

Argh. "So what happens now?"

"About the pages? Well, obviously they won't do. Even if Swithins
wanted something like this—and I very much doubt it—it's just so
far off being done. I know you only had a few days and, believe me,
nobody expects you to produce anything polished. But it should have
purpose. I should be able to look at it and say: oh, I see where this
is going. And I've read it over and over, and I just can't. I don't know
where you're taking me at all. I don't even think you know."

"I see." I know I sound sullen, but my throat hurts and my eyes
are hot. I don't want to start howling here, in public, among the fres-
coes. I won't.

Richenda's silent for a moment. "I really am sorry," she says, and
her voice is much softer. "I know this is awful, truly I do, and you've
been such a star doing all this work at such a dreadful time. You're
writing about grief and loss and that's so hard, darling, especially
when it's fresh. You're unbelievably brave even to try. I just can't hand
them a reason to ditch you when it would be so bad for both of us. You
do understand?"

"Yes."

"Good. Now, here's what we're going to do. You're going to take
the weekend and have a really good think about the story you want to
tell: about you, about your granny, whatever you really want to write
about. And then try and boil it down as far as you can. Not a page,
not a paragraph, just a sentence. On Monday, you phone me up and
tell me what you've thought of, and then we'll try and lick those pages
into shape."

"But there's no time," I say.

"Not much, no, but there's some. I built in a bit of a margin anyway, and I happen to know Tim's away in the French Alps or the Swiss Alps or whichever Alps until at least next Friday, which really means the following Monday. So I'm not guaranteeing anything, but we might just pull it off. All right?"

"All right," I say. "Thanks, Richenda."

She laughs. "Oh, darling, you sound wrecked. I'm not surprised. Try and get some sleep tonight, drink a negroni or two, do whatever you need to get back to form. Ideas flow better when you're rested. Promise me."

"I promise."

"And do give that nice Marco a call, because you clearly want to shag him. *Ciao ciao.*" She hangs up before I can protest.

❦

I DO GO TO BED, AFTER THAT. I GO STRAIGHT HOME, STRIP OFF MY clothes and sleep like I'm drugged. I don't dream, I don't move, I don't wake until it's almost noon and too hot to stay in bed. I'm making coffee, still half-asleep, when the doorbell rings: loud, obnoxious, repeated. "No," I mutter, willing whoever it is to give up and go away. But the doorbell keeps ringing, and then my phone starts going, too.

"Fucksake," I yell, and I stumble to the intercom. "Yes?"

"*Corriere,*" barks a male voice at the other end.

Courier? Have I been online shopping in my sleep? I stand there for a moment, baffled and groggy, and then the doorbell rings again: a sharp, irritated series of bursts. I press the button and hear the big door swing open downstairs. Gingerly I open the door of the flat and peer down into the staircase.

There are two couriers at the foot of the stairs. Two couriers and an absolute shitload of archive boxes. As I stare down at them, one of the men—a red-faced and stocky type—looks up and catches my eye. "*Arrivo,*" he calls, and he picks up a stack of three boxes and starts stomping and puffing up the stairs towards me.

Oh God—this must be Granny's letters. Oh *God.*

The courier marches in and fixes me with a hard stare. "Where do I put these?"

"There, please," I say, and point to the middle of the floor, next to the coffee table.

He gives me a look that clearly says: you delusional creature. "Then let's move these," he says and, dumping the boxes on the floor, he pushes the sofa to the wall and the coffee table next to it.

"Hey, Carmine." A voice at my shoulder makes me jump. "Where do these go?" The second courier, slightly less stocky but equally red in the face.

"She wants them here," Carmine says, gesturing to the newly cleared bit of floor. The new arrival grimaces.

"But will they all fit?" he says, and looks at me as if I ought to know.

"This is the space there is," I manage to say, and the new chap looks aghast at Carmine, who shrugs. "I'm sorry there isn't a lift," I add, because I really am.

Carmine shakes his head. "It's you I'm sorry for," he says, and then vanishes down the stairs trailing the new chap after him.

It takes several more trips to bring all the boxes up the stairs. By the time they finish, my living room looks like Hampton Court Maze. Carmine and the other courier—his name is Andrea, I discover— each drink a coffee with a ton of sugar and then depart, wishing me good luck.

There's one consolation, I reflect as I stare at the boxes all over my floor. If there is some marketable angle, some irresistibly exciting hook to mine and Granny's story, then it's bound to be in here somewhere. I just have the weekend to find it.

14

THERE'S NO SYSTEM. THAT'S THE PROBLEM. THERE'S NO FUCKING *system.*

The boxes aren't labeled—that's bad enough. But the stuff that's in them, the letters and papers and so on, have all been shoved in willy-nilly so that a handwritten note from 1965 is next to a party invitation from 1997 is next to a dentist's appointment reminder from 1984. Whoever packed these away—Mummy, or someone under her direction—clearly didn't care about the process at all. I suppose I should just be grateful they weren't all put through the shredder.

I shift position on the floor, trying to bring life back into my numbing legs and bum. It's almost evening, and in the time since Carmine and Andrea left I've managed to go through a few of the boxes, pulling out anything that looks vaguely interesting and putting it, roughly in date order, to one side. Nearly all the personal letters I've found are in Italian, which is obviously great, but the problem with personal letters is that they're, well, personal. Every time I stop and look at one I'm confronted with names I don't recognize, signatures I can't read, events I can make no sense of and at least a dozen words I don't know. I've had four large mugs of coffee and far too many chocolate biscuits, I've got a crick in my neck, and I'm rapidly losing all hope in this entire enterprise. Unless I'm very lucky, unless the next thing I turn up is a love letter from the Pope, I'm going to have nothing to show Richenda on Monday. I wish I had someone to help me.

Well, theoretically I do. In fact, I have two people who keep on offering me help and being really quite insistent about it: Marco and Chiara. Obviously Marco is out. Yes, this was all his idea and yes, he seemed genuinely excited about it. But I've been avoiding him, and he hasn't been in touch with me and besides, he and Chiara are a couple. A social unit. I can't just go asking her boyfriend to come round to my flat and look at my grandmother's letters. It even sounds dodgy, like luring someone upstairs to see your etchings.

So that leaves Chiara. But can I really ask her? I've been dodging her invitations all week. Surely I can't just phone her up and say: *look, I know I wasn't available for coffee and a chat the other day, but is there any chance you want to spend your Saturday evening helping me out with a colossal, unmanageable, boring piece of research? I'll buy the pizza!*

I look at the unopened boxes in front of me. I look at the heap of letters on the floor next to me. I think about what happens if I break my first ever book contract, and how much I've loved these last weeks, and whether I'll get to write anything for anyone ever again that isn't about nickel alloys or fishing vests.

I pick up my phone.

❧

"MADONNA," CHIARA BREATHES. SHE'S STANDING IN THE DOORWAY of my flat with a paper deli bag in her hand, and she's staring at the boxes.

"I know," I say. "There's so much. I won't get through all of it in time, but I'd be so grateful if you could have a look at some of the letters I've pulled out and see if anything stands out for you. You can scan them much faster than I can."

"Sure." Chiara deposits the bag on top of the nearest box and comes over to look at the heap of papers, which I've moved onto the sofa. "Is this what you've got so far?"

"Yes. I'm sure most of it isn't relevant, but I keep thinking there might be something in here somewhere, just one detail I can give my publishers." She gives me a puzzled look. "It's a bit complicated," I say and explain, as briefly as I can, about *The Laird's Lady's Guide* and Richenda's attempts to help me keep my contract.

Chiara sits down on the arm of the sofa. She looks taken aback, maybe even a little hurt. "I had no idea," she says. "You must be so stressed out."

"Well, I didn't tell you. I could have told you," I admit.

"Yes. Why didn't you? I don't understand, Tori."

"I'm sorry," I say. "Honestly, I feel like a dick."

"You feel like a dick?" Chiara snorts. "You were going through all this—although, like I say, you really should have said something—and I just kept on trying to set you up. You must have thought I was so annoying!"

"What do you mean, set me up?"

"Oh." Chiara shoves the papers aside and plonks down in their place. "Well, it's silly really, but I got this idea in my head that you'd be perfect for Marco. Clearly you've got way too much to deal with even to be thinking about guys, but . . . look, I don't know. The way he talks about you and the way you talk about him, I guess I thought there was something there."

"What?" I blurt out.

Chiara holds her hands up. "I know, I know. So interfering. I'm as bad as my mother."

"No, I mean . . . you and Marco. Aren't you together?"

"Me and Marco?" Chiara bursts out laughing. "Oh, God, no! He isn't my type at all. I like men who are . . ." She waves her hands around to signal *brick shithouse*. "You know, macho. Not that he isn't . . . I'm sure he can be very . . . Oh God," she squeaks, and is off in another paroxysm of laughter. I'm beginning to feel faintly insulted.

"*Oddio*," she says again, and pulls out a tissue to dab at her eyes. "Shit, my mascara. Look, Tori, it's like this. I've known Marco literally forever. Our mothers were friends long before we were born. He didn't have any brothers or sisters, and I had an older half sister who was way too cool to hang out with a baby like me. So Marco and I played together, we went to school together, we went to university together. I love him, but he's like family. I can't imagine him in a romantic way at all." She gives me a sharp sort of look. "But I think maybe you can."

I grin at her. I can't not grin. I can't stop grinning, in fact.

"Okay," she says, and grins back. "Tori, I don't want to interfere any more than I have already. I'm very happy to look at these papers like you asked. Or . . ."

"Or what?"

"Or you can keep the sandwiches I brought, open a bottle of wine and call the person I think you really wanted to ask in the first place. I won't be offended. If he says no, then of course I'll stay and help you. But I have a feeling he won't say no and, let's face it, I've already been right once today. Surely you won't deny me the chance to be right again?"

❧

MARCO DOESN'T SAY NO. IN FACT, WHEN I TELL HIM THAT I'VE GOT hold of Granny's papers—a lot of them—he immediately asks if I need any help.

"Can you come round this evening?" I ask.

"Of course. I'll be with you right away."

"Right away," I repeat, and Chiara, hovering by the door, punches the air and does a little victory dance. "That's amazing— thanks so much."

I'm going, Chiara mouths. *Good luck*. She slips out through the door before I can thank her, closing it silently behind her.

"Do you want me to bring anything?" Marco asks.

"No. You're doing me such a favour just by coming, honestly. I'm afraid it's all a bit pressured. I've got to speak to my agent on Monday and . . . look, I'll explain it when you get here, but it might be a long session. I've got wine and sandwiches, though, and I'll order some pizza or whatever you want to keep you going."

"Paperwork, fast food and a looming deadline. You're taking me right back to law school." He laughs. "Okay, see you shortly."

I just have time to brush my hair, swap out my sweaty dust-covered T-shirt for a fresh one, open the wine and put Chiara's sandwiches on a plate before Marco arrives. I'd half expected him to be wearing his usual sharp suit, or some kind of GQ-level business-casual weekend outfit, but he's in a plain dark T-shirt and a pair of jeans and the effect is . . . well, it's pretty breathtaking. I've never actually seen his arms before, not properly. They're pleas-antly muscular and have just the right amount of dark hair and, oh my God, he has a tattoo. A stark geometric pattern on his right bicep.

"Shall we eat first?" he says, brandishing a paper bag.

"First?" I echo, a bit dazed.

"Probably best. I know I concentrate better on a full stomach and anyway, we should have these while they're hot." He drops a kiss on my cheek and heads straight for the kitchen corner, where he plonks the bag on the counter and starts lifting out small containers, followed by a wad of paper napkins. "I stopped by my favorite Sicilian place. I've got some arancini, various croquettes, all stuff we can eat with our fingers." He lifts the lids off the containers, releasing a delicious warm fragrance.

"Oh wow," I say, coming closer. "These look amazing."

"They are. But we'd better have some wine to keep our arteries from clogging. Oh, there it is," he says, spotting the bottle with the two glasses I've set out next to the sandwiches. "And you've opened it already. Very organized of you."

"Thanks," I say, feeling rather disappointed in myself. I'd really have liked to see him open a bottle of wine.

Marco pours a glass and hands it to me. I take down a couple of plates and we fill them with a selection of sandwiches and Sicilian fried things before picking our way past the boxes to the sofa.

"So tell me all about it," he says, just as I bite into one of the arancini. "What do you need me to do?"

"Sorry," I mumble through a mouthful of rice, meat and cheese. It's delicious and hotter than the sun. I have to take a swig of wine to cool my mouth. Once I can speak again, I quickly outline the whole business with the old book, and the new book, and so on.

"Ah," he says. "Yeah. That explains why you've been quiet."

"Why *I've* been quiet?" I'm so nervous, so hyperaware of him sitting close to me, that I sound a bit more offended than I meant to.

But he just smiles at me. "I wanted to get in touch and ask how it was going, see if you wanted to meet up, but I knew you were busy and I didn't want to push. And then Chiara kept telling me how much work you had on and that she couldn't even persuade you out for a drink. So I thought it was best to leave you alone. I really hope you didn't think I was ignoring you."

"No," I lie. "No, not at all."

"Anyway, I'm here now and awaiting instructions. Whatever you want me to do, I'll do it."

He's killing me. I think my whole body is blushing. "Well . . ."

"I guess you need a native speaker, right? So maybe you choose the papers that look interesting and I check them over, just to speed things up a bit?"

"Right." I take another gulp of wine, though I'm not sure it helps. "I actually found some already. There's a stack of them next to you."

"Oh yes, I see. And what kind of thing exactly am I looking for?"

"I don't even know, really. Just anything that catches your eye. Anything that makes you say oh, hang on a minute."

"A pretty vague brief, then. I mean nice and open-ended, of course," he corrects himself as I shoot him a look. "Don't worry, Tori. From everything you've told me about your grandmother, I'm sure we'll turn up something interesting in no time."

❧

"YOUR GRANDMOTHER HAD SO MANY FRIENDS," MARCO SAYS.

"I know," I say.

"And they all wrote such long letters, and had such terrible health problems."

"I know."

"And they only ever, ever signed with their first names."

I look up from my seat on the floor. Marco's slouched on the sofa, a hand over his eyes and a letter abandoned in his lap. He looks roughly as knackered as I feel, and who can blame him?

It's past midnight and we've finished all but two of the boxes, and so far it's been a totally pointless exercise. We've found half a dozen letters signed "Maria," but they're in several different hands and none of them mention Giuseppe, or Niccolò, or a bar, or anything that might suggest it's the same Maria I remember. And that's it.

"It's so weird," I say. "I really thought there would be more."

"More than this?" Marco says wearily. "You must be joking."

"No, I mean more about the people I remember. She went back to that specific bar again and again, every time we came to Florence.

I don't understand why we haven't found anything about the family who ran it."

"Maybe they aren't important. For your project, anyway."

"Maybe not," I say. "But it's still weird."

Marco sighs. He puts the letter aside and stretches out his back, reaching his arms over his head. I try not to watch as his sleeves ride down and his muscles flex and move. "Right," he says. "Next box."

"No," I groan. "No more."

"Come on, Tori. We've only got a couple left! That'll take us, what, another hour or so? We can easily manage that."

"Maybe you can. I've been at this all day." I haul myself up onto the sofa and sprawl out, my head lolling on the rigid back. It's too low and makes my neck hurt. "Ow. Hey, can I replace the sofa in a rented flat? What does Italian law say about that?"

"You can, but I think you'd have to store the original one at your own expense. Come on," he says again. "Let's open just one more box. You never know—this could be the one."

"And if it isn't?"

"If it isn't, then I come back bright and early tomorrow and we go through the other one."

I turn my head and look at him. He's clearly exhausted, but there's a spark of real enthusiasm there. "I don't understand you," I say.

"Look, I didn't go into law because I hated a challenge. Or because I was allergic to work."

"Fine," I say, and push myself back off the sofa again. "Fine. But if we don't find anything in this one, you owe me a negroni."

"If we do find something, you owe me two."

"Whatever." I pull one of the remaining two boxes towards me and open the lid. "Wow, that's a change."

This box is packed tight with folders. Old-fashioned, stiff manila folders. I lift out the top one and open it. It's full of handwritten letters, all in Italian.

"For you," I say, and plonk the folder into Marco's lap.

"Great," he says. "Now let's see who owes who a negroni."

I smile and pull another folder from the box. I'm flicking through it when I hear a sharp in-breath from Marco. "Hang on a minute," he says.

"What?"

"This is incredible. This is *incredible*. Look!"

I turn. He's holding a piece of paper in his fingertips, cautiously, as if it were a relic or a bomb. By the look on his face, it could be either. "What is it?" I ask.

He gazes at me. "It's a letter . . . oh God, I can hardly believe it. A letter from Guido Comacchi."

"Sorry, who?"

"Guido Comacchi," he repeats. "Guido *Comacchi*."

"Wait, you mean Comacchi like the car?"

"Like the car manufacturer. Like the racing team. How can you not know who Guido Comacchi was?"

"Never mind that. What does it say?"

"Oh." Marco blinks at the paper in front of him. "Let me see. 'My dear Rita . . .'" He coughs. "Tori, are you sure you want me to read this?"

"Of course I do," I say. "Why wouldn't I?"

"It might be personal. Really personal. Comacchi had a certain reputation as a . . ."

"Serial shagger?"

"Something like that," Marco says, with his lopsided grin. "Okay, exactly that."

"Then I definitely want to know," I say.

"All right, if you insist." He clears his throat. "'My dear Rita, I was devastated to hear of the death of your brave Achilles.' Or Achille— that's the name in Italian, anyway. 'I didn't know him for long, but I saw in him a rare soul and a kindred spirit, and I hoped . . .' Oh, wow. 'I hoped that I could persuade him to race for me one day. I am sorry he won't, but I am sorry above all for you, who have lost a beloved of such extraordinary caliber. We all send our condolences, I most of all, and if there is anything I can do for you then you must only let me know. Your devoted etc. etc.' Sorry," Marco says, and wipes his eyes with the back of his hand.

I'm feeling quite misty myself. "I wonder who he was," I say. "This brave Achilles."

"I think I might know." Marco puts the letter down and takes out his phone. A few taps at the screen, and he turns it to show me a picture. A black-and-white picture of a smiling young man, his dark hair blown back off his face, standing proudly next to an old-fashioned racing car. He's dressed in overalls and he has a certain swagger about him, something irresistibly daring, like a flying ace in an old film. I can practically smell the testosterone.

"Achille Infuriati," Marco says. "The Red Devil of the Valdana. The star driver of the Scuderia Guelfa. And, apparently, someone very important to your grandmother."

15

Stella

IN ALL THE INTENSITY OF THAT EARLY SUMMER, ONE THING STANDS out in my memory: the day Achille killed the German.

It was a warm evening in May. A normal one, by the standards of the time. I had finished my schoolwork and was scrubbing down the kitchen, getting ahead of my chores for the next day. Achille had gone up to Santa Marta on some business or other. My mother was at her usual station in the back room, and my father was at the kitchen table finishing the supper I'd made him. And both he and I were keeping an eye on the clock that hung on the kitchen wall, because curfew was approaching—and being caught out after curfew was punishable by death. Like so many things.

"Should I go through and see how Mamma is?" I asked as the minute hand crept onwards.

Papà shook his head. "Better not disturb her." I reached down to take his empty plate away and, as I did, he briefly took hold of my arm and squeezed it.

And then it came, the sound we were waiting for so anxiously: the nasal whine of the engine and then my mother's cry, but this time it wasn't a cry of joy. It was a cry of horror. The door flew open and Achille came in with my mother close behind. His red kerchief was askew and the front of his shirt was smeared with blood.

"It's not mine," he said. "The blood. It's not mine. Leave me alone!" he snapped as Mamma reached out to him. "I don't want a fuss. Just . . . just let me be, please."

Papà got to his feet. Mamma pushed past Achille and went to him, burrowing under his arm like a frightened child. "You'd better tell me what you did," Papà said in a low, steady voice. You didn't argue with him when he sounded like that.

Achille took a deep breath and the story began to spill out. He had been on his way back from Santa Marta when he'd heard the distinctive sound of a BMW motorcycle engine. He knew that a German dispatch rider was behind him.

"There wasn't much I could do at that point. Obviously his bike was more powerful, and we were on a straightish bit of road—he had a clear shot if he wanted one. I hoped that maybe we just happened to be riding in the same direction. But I took a left at the next crossroads, heading north, to see if he'd do the same. He did. Then I took another left turn and he copied me again. That's when I knew for sure that he was following me."

"What do you expect if you wear that rag around your neck?" my mother cut in.

Achille ignored this. "I knew I had to stay up in the hills, on the back roads," he went on. "I'd have the advantage then, though I'd no idea yet what I'd actually do with it. So I kept twisting and turning, and he kept following—and then I saw the sign for Sant'Appiano, and I knew."

"The Rossi houses," my father said with an air of realization.

Achille nodded. "Exactly." Seeing that Mamma and I were bewildered, he explained. Near the village of Sant'Appiano, on the other side from the monarchists' encampment, was a sort of ghost town: an abandoned farm that had belonged to a local family that went bankrupt back in the twenties. The road that led through it was narrow and lined on one side with cramped terraced houses where the farm workers had lived. There was no pavement, and the houses all opened directly onto the street. "Enzo and Sandro and I used to mess around up there all the time," Achille said. "Anyway, there's a blind corner as you turn into that road, and the first of those little houses sticks out just enough to cause trouble if you don't know to avoid it. Which I did, of course, but *he* didn't. He couldn't."

His face was animated now. Despite his shock, he was starting to enjoy himself. "I wanted to make sure he stayed right on my tail, so I didn't accelerate too much. I even held in the clutch and revved the engine a few times to make it sound like I was having a problem changing gears. He fell for it and followed me, straight into that corner."

"Ha!" Papà barked. "Good lad."

"He came off badly," Achille said. "Ended up across the road with his bike on top of him. He was probably going to die anyway, but I made sure of it." His hand went to the holster at his waist, to the army-issue Beretta he carried. "I made sure of it," he repeated.

For a moment we were all silent. We knew those lists of penalties by heart, you see. For each German killed by a partisan, ten people would be hanged. I thought of what I'd seen at Castelmedici.

"What did you do with the body?" I said.

The three of them looked at me as if I'd sprung from nowhere. I believe they'd forgotten I was there at all. "I managed to roll it off the road and cover it in branches," Achille said. "With any luck, the wild boar will find it soon enough. I took his helmet and dog tags, too."

"And the bike?" my father asked.

"Stashed it in one of the houses along with his rifle. I can go back for them once . . . once it's safe. Papà, you should see that bike," Achille said. "It's really something."

"You're not keeping that thing here," Mamma protested. "If they find it, they'll kill us all."

"Then I'll find somewhere else to keep it. There's an old outbuilding just up the hill—"

"Enough," Papà said. "It's pointless to discuss this now. We have to wait and see whether . . ." He cleared his throat. "Whether there are consequences. For now, son, you need to clean yourself up. And get that blood out of your clothes."

Mamma nodded. "Stella, heat some water for your brother's bath. I'll put that shirt to soak. Give it here." She held out her hand, and Achille obediently took off his shirt and gave it to her. She hurried off, holding it out at arm's length, my father following.

I couldn't look at Achille. I thought I would cry or shout or hit him if I did. I went over to the sink and started filling a big pan with water to heat on the stove. And then I heard a noise behind me—a soft, whimpering noise. I turned around.

"Stella," Achille said. He was as white as paper. "Stellina, I . . . I . . ." His face crumpled and he held his arms out to me, like a child.

Of course I went to him. I went to him and held him, and he cried and trembled and said over and over again that he was sorry, that he hadn't meant to put anyone in danger. But all I could think was: *You stupid boy. You stupid boy, why couldn't you leave him to die on his own?*

❧

THE DAYS THAT FOLLOWED WERE TERRIBLE. ACHILLE WENT OUT ON his runs just as usual, but he came home tired and scared, not exhilarated. I had never seen him scared in my life, and now he started at every noise and moved as if weighed down by some dreadful burden. The first few times, he even refused to carry his gun. I had to plead with him to start taking it again. I didn't like the thought of him out there undefended.

Unlike him, though, I wasn't scared. I don't know whether this makes sense, but knowing that ten innocent people might die—that I myself might die because of something I hadn't done and couldn't control—stripped away the last of my nerves. I went on working with a sort of cold fatalism. What was the point in being afraid now? What would it change? Nothing.

The weeks ticked past, and gradually the atmosphere in the house began to lighten. The German's body had still not been found. I don't know what his regiment thought had happened to him—maybe they believed he'd deserted, as did happen sometimes, or maybe they were simply too harried to keep track of their men—anyway, it scarcely mattered. The SS had not come to enact the death sentence. We had been lucky. Achille began to stand a little straighter, to take some joy in riding out and riding home again, and he put on his red kerchief despite my mother's protests. He was returning to himself, and I was glad.

One Sunday, I came back from Mass to find him at the back door of the house, about to set off. He was tucking his slingshot into his battered and stained old hunting bag, but his motorbike was still in the lean-to. I was surprised. Achille never walked anywhere if he could ride.

"Going to get a couple of rabbits for dinner tonight," he said. And then, lowering his voice: "And I'm going to go and see about that bike. I can't leave it there to rust."

"Then I'll come with you," I said.

"Stellina . . ."

"I want to see it," I said. "This legendary motorcycle that was worth so much danger. Show me."

If Achille wanted to argue with me, he didn't try. Maybe he was glad of the company. He just nodded and we walked silently together up the back road to the hills. It was a hot day and I'd been fasting for Mass, so I soon started to wonder whether I'd done the right thing in coming with him. My feet were aching in my mother's old shoes and I was dreadfully thirsty. But I didn't turn back; there was no question of that.

The woods were thankfully quiet. Most people would be having their Sunday lunch, or what passed for it in those frugal times, and the Germans must have been counting on that. We walked and walked and met nobody, except one old man pottering along with his dog, and a little group of girls who were picking wildflowers at the side of the road. I stopped and picked a few myself, just to have an alibi.

When we reached the turning for Sant'Appiano, Achille gripped my arm. "Not far now," he said. I followed him up a winding little road and there it was: the blind corner, and beyond that, the ghost town with its row of cramped little houses, their shutters decaying and half hanging off, the odd empty doorway like a gaping mouth. There were still faint black marks on the road where the German's bike had skidded.

"It must be in a pretty bad state by now," Achille said. "The body. But I should check." His lips were pale.

"I'll go and look if you want," I offered. A dead body was the least frightening thing I could imagine by that point. "Just tell me where."

Achille shook his head. "No. Wait here." And he was off across the road. I saw him bend to pick up a stick, and then he vanished behind the trees.

When he came back, he was gray-faced and sweating. "Thank God for wild boar." His voice was croaky and his breath sour. "The body's still there—well, parts of it—but what's left barely looks human, let alone German. Have you got a handkerchief?" I handed him mine, and he wiped his mouth and spat.

"Are you all right?" I asked.

"I'm fine. Fine. Now let's go and see about this bike. Come on." And he marched off towards one of the houses a little way along the street. The door had been painted once, and now it was rot-streaked and swollen with damp. Achille put his shoulder to it and managed to push it open on the third or fourth try.

The German bike was standing in the hallway. It was covered with a ragged old sheet, which Achille whisked off like Michelangelo revealing *David*. "There! Just look at that. Isn't it beautiful?"

I looked without understanding. The red MM 125 Achille rode—my father's old machine—was a lightweight racing bike that almost resembled a pushbike. It even had pedals and a narrow triangular seat, just like my own bicycle. But this was another kind of beast: big and low-slung with heavy leather panniers and two broad seats, one behind the other. The BMW mark stood out against the black-painted fuel tank like the badge on an SS officer's cap. I hated it.

Achille was fussing over the bike now, inspecting it, topping up oil and fuel from two canisters he took from his hunting bag. "Looks like it's good to go," he said at last. "I need to do a bit of work on it, but there isn't too much wrong. Hey, look at this." He opened one of the panniers to show me the German's helmet and goggles, a pair of leather gauntlets folded up next to them and a sidearm in its holster, too—a Luger, it must have been. "I'll pass these on to the boys at Santa Marta. They're short on protective gear."

"You're not really taking that . . . thing home with you," I said.

"Ha! No chance." He was already wheeling the bike towards the door. "I'll keep it in that old shed I was telling you about. What Mamma doesn't see won't worry her." He assumed I wouldn't tell her, of course—he knew I wouldn't. It had always been like that, me and

Achille against the grown-ups. "Grab that gun, would you?" he called back over his shoulder.

I turned and saw a rifle propped up at the foot of the stairs. It was new-looking and polished, nothing like the well-used old guns we had. I picked it up and managed to sling it over my shoulder. On the road outside, Achille was already mounted up and ready to go.

"Come on, hop up." He had to raise his voice over the chug-chug-chug of the engine. I shook my head.

"No, thanks. I'll walk home."

"Are you sure? I don't want to leave you to go back all alone." He meant it, I'm certain, but he was already radiating impatience. He wanted to be off.

"I'm sure," I said. "Take the bike across country—see what it can do. I'll meet you back at the house. But you can carry this." I held the rifle out to him and he took it from me, settling it across his back. "Don't forget the rabbits, if you want to keep Mamma happy."

Achille grinned at me. "I won't. See you shortly, little sister." He sped away, accelerator roaring, before I could tell him to be careful.

❦

THE GERMAN BIKE BECAME PART OF ACHILLE'S LEGEND. PEOPLE think it's romantic. I don't see the romance, but I can't deny he made good use of the thing. All that extra capacity meant he could carry plenty of cargo—munitions, food, clothing and the odd passenger—and bring his toolbox, too. And I believe he got a kick out of riding it under the very noses of the Germans, although I wished he wouldn't.

"But if they catch me they'll kill me, no matter what I'm riding," he said when I argued with him. "Anyway, I don't care if I die."

Achille kept on using the BMW even when the war was over. It was no good for racing, much too heavy, but he painted it red to match his MM 125 and rode it for fun on the roads around Romituzzo. When he moved away to Florence, he left it with my parents to look after until he could pick it up. Of course, he never did. Some years later—when my parents were themselves packing up to move—a man came to the house asking about the bike. He was an American: a former GI and trained mechanic who had stayed on in Italy rather than go back and live under segregation.

My father almost chased him away. He didn't understand why someone who had fought against the Nazis now wanted to buy a piece of their military equipment. He didn't understand, until the man told him that he didn't want the bike because it was German. He wanted it because it had belonged to Achille.

"Maybe it feels like I'm trying to buy a piece of your memories," he said, "and if that's the case, I'm very sorry. You just tell me to go and I will. But I have an American client in Florence who's desperate to get hold of that motorbike. If you do want it off your hands, then I promise you he'll pay very well. I can give you a down payment right now." And he took a wad of bills from his wallet and offered them to my father.

Papà didn't even ask what the final price would be. He hated that bike, and he needed the money, too. He was in too much pain by then to work. So he was more than happy to see the BMW go, and I don't think he'd have cared if the deposit was all he got. It was already more than the machine could possibly be worth in his eyes. But the balance came through just a few days later, and it was a spectacular amount of money. Enough to keep my parents for the rest of their lives.

I've often wondered about the identity of that mysterious client. Some friend of Achille's racing sponsor Pierfrancesco, perhaps, or even Pierfrancesco himself. But it's perfectly possible that it had nothing to do with him at all; that some wealthy foreigner simply wanted a piece of Achille's legacy and sent this kind man who spoke Italian to get it for him. He had that effect on people, Achille. He still does.

16

Tori

"AM I TOO LATE?" MARCO SAYS. "MY TEN O'CLOCK MEETING OVERRAN. I'm so sorry."

"Not at all," I say as I open the door to let him into the flat. He's back in his usual sleek-suit no-tie garb, and he's very attractively flustered. "I said I'd call Richenda . . . now, actually. Shit."

"You'll be fine," he says, putting a hand on my shoulder. "You will. We must have gone over this twenty times already."

We really have, too. It's Monday morning and Marco spent most of Sunday here, helping me work through those last boxes. There was far more material than we could actually read but, between what we did manage and a judicious bit of internet research, we put together a pretty compelling presentation. I just have to convince Richenda to listen to the whole thing. I sit down on the sofa and open video chat on my laptop, checking my image on the webcam.

"You look great," Marco says, sitting down next to me. I can feel the blood rise to my cheeks—such a cliché, I know.

"Shove over," I say. "If Richenda sees you, she'll have ten thousand questions and I'll never get round to Achille."

"Okay, okay." He scoots along to the end of the sofa, and I take a deep breath and call Richenda.

"Tori." She's sitting at her desk, looking frazzled and cradling a mug of coffee. Not a great start, I'll admit. "Got your line ready?"

"Yes. But first I have to tell you a story."

Richenda rolls her eyes. "Tori—"

"I know. That's not what you asked for and I can see you're under pressure, but I need you to listen. You'll understand at the end, I promise."

"Can you tell me in less than ten minutes?"

"Absolutely."

"All right then," she says, and leans back in her chair. "Go."

"On the twentieth of February, 1928," I begin, "in the town of Romituzzo in the Valdana region south of Florence, an extraordinary sportsman was born. His name was Achille Infuriati."

"Never heard of him," Richenda says.

I force a smile. "You're not a Formula One fan, are you?"

"Urgh, no. Husband number one was, sadly. Terrible bore. Mind you, I always had a bit of a soft spot for James Hunt. Now *he* . . ."

"Achille Infuriati is a legend in the racing community," I plough on. "He's known—and worshipped—as the greatest Formula One driver Italy never had. Achille was beautiful, talented and fearless, just like his namesake. And, like his namesake, he died young."

It all sounds so artificial to me, so flat and stilted, but Richenda is actually starting to pay attention. I shoot a quick glance at Marco and he gives me a smile.

"He grew up around cars," I say. "His father was a mechanic, and Achille was tinkering with engines as soon as he could hold a spanner. As a teenager, he worked for the Italian Resistance. He routinely risked his life to run errands and fix engines for the partisans in the hills of the Valdana, dashing about on his father's old red motorbike. It wasn't the most discreet method, but he usually kept out of the way of the Nazis. Until, one day, one of their dispatch riders spotted him and gave chase."

"And then what happened?" Richenda asks, right on cue. I smile, and this time it isn't forced.

"We don't know exactly. But we do know that, from then on, Achille made his runs on a stolen Wehrmacht BMW R12."

"Wow."

"That was Achille," I say. "Of course, once the war was won, he had to find his thrills elsewhere. He started out by racing his trusty old red bike—that and his politics earned him the affectionate nickname of the Red Devil. Soon he was raking in the prizes, but that wasn't enough for him. He wanted a new challenge. He wanted to race cars.

"In those days motor racing was the preserve of the rich, dominated by aristocrats and tycoons. Achille was a working-class lad from a little Tuscan town. He didn't have the money for an expensive car, or wealthy friends who could sponsor him. But that wasn't going to stop him. Through his Resistance connections he got hold of a worn-out pre-war Alfa Romeo that had been mouldering in some dead Fascist's garage, and he worked on it every spare minute he had. He got it fixed up, and then he started entering road races and winning those, too."

I pause to catch my breath. To my astonishment, Richenda doesn't chip in. She's just listening, her hands gripping her coffee mug.

"Formula One was in its infancy back then," I continue. "Italy's racing teams were hungry for talented drivers with the nerve and determination to win. It wasn't long before Achille began to attract attention. He was courted by some of the biggest names of the period. The biggest—and most determined—was Guido Comacchi."

Richenda frowns. "Comacchi as in . . ."

"As in the car, right. As in the car manufacturer," I correct myself. "Comacchi was a fierce personality and he usually got what he wanted, but here he met his match. Achille was strong in his communist convictions. He refused to accept money from someone who had, in his eyes, flagrantly collaborated with the Fascist regime. Comacchi pleaded with him—and this was a man who never pleaded. He argued that he'd only played along to survive, that he'd helped the local partisan network by letting them store arms and supplies on his premises. But to Achille that was almost worse. He declared that he would never work with a *doppiogiochista*, a double-dealer.

"Comacchi was furious, but he kept up his onslaught. He so badly wanted Achille on his team that he was even prepared to take his insults. He lost out in the end, though. The Marxist publisher Pierfrancesco Legni, a member of one of Italy's wealthiest families, had a passion for cars and he wanted to support a former partisan. He offered Achille a contract and all the money, resources and support he needed to build a team of his very own."

I take a deep breath. My heart's hammering, and I wonder how I'm going to get through the next part. Richenda leans forward.

"Well?"

"It was a dream deal. Achille signed the contract with Legni in the winter of 1953 and the Scuderia Guelfa, Italy's first and only radical race team, was born. Now he had this opportunity, Achille didn't want to waste any time. He decided that he would start his Formula One career by competing in the 1955 Argentine Grand Prix, which was held in January. That gave him just over a year to prepare. And of course that wasn't all he had to do—Legni had promised him a team, and a team was what he wanted. So while he was competing in every race he could enter and working obsessively to perfect his own performance, he and Legni were scoping out premises, recruiting drivers and engineers, testing and adapting cars, deciding on uniforms. It was incredibly ambitious, even foolhardy. But they had Legni's money and Achille's skill and determination, and I actually think they might have made it."

"I have a bad feeling about this," Richenda says.

"Yes. You have to know that Achille was a proud Tuscan and *romituzzano* to the core. He was preparing to embark on a whole new career, to travel the globe, but there was no way he'd miss the Coppa Valdana. This was a road race that set off from Romituzzo in late September, and this year it would be even more special because he was coming home as a hero. The people of Romituzzo loved Achille, and Achille loved them. It was an emotional day for everyone.

"The morning of the race was sunny, warm and joyous. You can't imagine the rapture when Achille pulled up to the starting line in his much-loved Alfa Romeo with his old schoolfriend and fellow partisan, Enzo Sangallo, as navigator. The route was crowded with people from all over the Valdana and beyond, all desperate to catch a glimpse of the Red Devil. He took a comfortable lead early on, and he maintained that lead until . . ."

I have to take another breath, to steady myself before I go on. Richenda's watching me. "The race route passed through the medieval hill town of San Damiano," I say. "The road to San Damiano is winding and steep, surrounded by trees and the occasional little cluster of houses. If you're coming from Romituzzo, there's an embankment on the right-hand side—that's where the spectators were—and a steep slope on the left. Achille was approaching the gates of the city when a little girl broke free from her parents, slipped under the barricade and wandered out into the road. Achille swerved left."

"Oh." Richenda claps a hand to her mouth.

"His car veered off the road, struck a tree and rolled over several times before crashing into a ditch. The little girl was safe. Enzo survived with a few breaks and bruises, but Achille . . ." Images rise up before me: those grainy newsprint photos of twisted metal and shattered glass. I swallow, hard. "Achille was killed on impact, impaled by the steering column. It was instant. I hope it was instant. He was given a hero's funeral, of course. His former comrades—those who'd made it through the war—walked behind the hearse in their red kerchiefs, heads bowed. His coffin was draped in the red flag and the livery, newly designed, of the Scuderia Guelfa. Visit the cemetery at Romituzzo any day of the year, and you'll find red roses on his grave." I've practiced that bit so many times, but I'm still blinking back tears as I speak. "And now I really should give you that line I promised," I say, relieved.

"Line?" Richenda looks lost. "Oh, yes, the line. Hang on." She takes out a tissue and wipes her eyes, blows her nose. "Right, darling, fire away."

"In December 1953, Achille Infuriati was at a party at Legni's house in Florence when he met a young Englishwoman who was in the city to study drawing. Her name was Margaret Craye, and she was my grandmother."

"Well, fuck," Richenda says. "And I suppose they . . ."

"Yes."

"And then he . . ."

"Yes."

For a moment she just stares at me, and then, suddenly, she's all business. "And what's your angle on all this? What's the point of the book?"

"It's a love story," I say. "Just that. A love story, across class and cultural divides, in the troubled context of postwar Florence."

"Right," Richenda says. "Yes, good. And is it doable? What sources do you have?"

"I have two boxes crammed with all kinds of stuff that belonged to Granny: letters, newspaper clippings, diaries, photographs. There should be material about Achille and his sister Stella in the archives of the ANPI—that's the partisans' association—Stella was a courier for the Resistance. Pierfrancesco Legni died quite a few years ago, but he's bound to have had papers and maybe the family will let me see them."

"Anyone still alive who might remember your chap?"

"Some of his comrades might still be going. The group he belonged to was predominantly young, though Achille was on the young side even so. We do know Stella survived the war, but we don't know much else about her. She was a year younger again, and by all accounts every bit as brave as Achille was, but she kind of vanishes from the sources after 1945. If she's alive, though, I'll find her." I say it with a confidence I don't feel, but Richenda seems convinced.

"And your Italian's up to all this, is it?" she asks.

"My Italian's pretty decent, really. And I may have found a research assistant," I add, with my best innocent face. I daren't look at Marco.

"You are a fast mover. Can you send me a document with all this information?"

"I have it ready to go," I say. "Just a moment." I open a new message and attach the file Marco and I put together in the course of our work, then press send. There's a muffled ping at Richenda's end. "Got it?"

"Got it. Well, I'll send this all on to Tim and make my case, and if he's on board then I'll try to buy you as much time as possible to get it written. Who knows what he'll say, but personally I think it's brilliant. Oh, one thing."

"Yes?"

"When was your mother born? This guy died in 1955, right?"

"Achille died in 1954," I say. "And Mummy was born in 1958."

"So no illegitimacy scandal," Richenda says. "Oh well, can't have it all. I'll let you know as soon as I hear from Tim. Okay, darling?"

"Okay. Thanks," I add, but she's already ended the call. I close the laptop and turn to Marco.

He's looking at me. Just looking at me, with an odd sort of expression on his face. For a moment I think he's horrified, that I've completely cocked up the presentation or that I've got something in my teeth or a booger hanging out of my nose. But then he clears his throat and says: "Wow."

"What?"

"I haven't heard you talk like that before. You seemed so"—he waves a hand—"alive."

His eyes are fixed on mine. I can't quite stand it—I have to look away. "Don't I usually seem alive?"

"Honestly? No. No, you don't. You're always speaking softly, staying calm, looking away. Like you are now. It's almost like you're editing yourself." He pauses, and I can sense that he's choosing his words. "The girl I saw just now—the one who told Achille's story with so much feeling, who was nearly crying when he died—I think maybe that's actually you, unedited. And I like you, Tori. I've liked you from the start and I'll like you whatever you do, however much of yourself you want to show me. But to see that side of you . . . wow."

I look at him now, and he breaks into a grin, that same crooked grin that made my stomach turn over the first time I saw him.

"There you are," he says.

I'm shaky and my heart's pounding and my mind is swirling with doubts, but I want him so badly that, for once, I don't care. I move along the sofa towards him and he takes me in his arms, and then either I kiss him or he kisses me, but it doesn't matter because it makes sense. It makes sense in a way nothing's made sense in years. Marco's kissing me and I can smell soap and warm skin and the scent of limes, and it's just like I imagined, only infinitely better. And then it's like something snaps tight, and all my nerves come surging back.

"Sorry," I gasp, pulling away from him.

"Are you all right?" Marco's eyes search my face. His concern is painful to me—I feel hemmed in, under scrutiny. I get to my feet, smoothing down my top.

"I'm fine. It's just a bit . . . much. Right now, anyway."

"Okay." He nods, like he's making a note. "I'm sorry."

"Not your fault." I'm aware I sound brusque, and I hate myself for it. I try to smile. "Really, it isn't. It's been a stressful few days and I'm on edge. Look, don't you have somewhere to be? I mean, I'm sure you mentioned a lunch meeting."

"Oh." He looks at his watch. "Yeah, I do. I should get going." He stands and picks up his jacket, which is neatly folded over the arm of the sofa. "You'll let me know what Richenda says?"

"Of course. Though Swithins might not go for it."

"They'd be crazy not to." The hint of a smile. "And look, if by some weird chance they don't, your grandmother got letters of condolence from Alberto Ascari, Juan Manuel Fangio, Peter Collins, Stirling Moss . . . You can just sell them all and pay off the publisher. But I don't think it's going to come to that."

"I hope not."

"Let me know," he says again. He kisses me on the cheek, not once but twice—a social kiss, a respectable Italian kiss—and goes out.

17

"SO HOW LONG DO YOU HAVE TO FINISH THE BOOK?" CHIARA ASKS.

We're sailing along in her little Fiat, heading south towards Siena. Hills rise up on either side of the road, scattered with houses and churches and vineyards and olive groves. "Eighteen months," I say. "It's going to be tight. Thanks again for the lift, by the way."

"Oh, please. If I have to drive all the way to San Damiano, I might as well drop you off in Romituzzo. It would be a waste not to."

"I appreciate it, though. I should really get a car myself, now I'm settled."

"Why bother?" Chiara says. "It's so expensive, and it's not like you need one in Florence."

"I know," I say. "But I have a feeling I'm going to spend a lot of time exploring Tuscany. I'd like to drive some of Achille's routes. Within the speed limit, obviously."

"Well, if you do decide to get a car, Marco will be only too happy to advise you. In fact, you might not be able to shut him up."

Oh God, Marco. I don't want to talk about Marco, and I have a feeling that's exactly what Chiara is dying to do. "So what are you doing in San Damiano?"

"Some English clients of mine are looking for a house around there. They've got a house in town—not far from you, actually—and now they want a country villa as well. I've found a few possibilities, so I'm going to go and check them out. Talk to the sellers, take a few photos, scope out the area . . . My clients have a pretty long list of requirements, so it's quicker and easier if I filter the properties first. Saves a lot of awkward visits."

"They sound demanding, your clients."

Chiara shrugs. "They know what they want—put it that way. It makes my job a lot easier when people do, so long as they're realistic about what their budget will actually get them. And what country life involves, obviously. Sure, you get spectacular views and cheap wine and sunshine and friendly people, but there's also bad Wi-Fi and local politics and wild boar wrecking your garden."

"Sounds like the Scottish Highlands. Except for the cheap wine and the sunshine, and it's deer and rabbits rather than boar."

"Do you miss it there?" Chiara asks. "Not Duncan, obviously, but the place?"

"Oh, I loved the place," I say, and I feel a sharp pang of something like homesickness. "We lived in the north-west, up near Fort William, and it was just . . . you know, it was wonderful. Not the actual estate—I'm really not cut out for farm life—but the countryside, the people in our village, the coastline . . . I think I could have felt at home there."

"If not for the guy. And his farm."

"Right."

"And the weather." Chiara gives a theatrical shudder. "I don't think I could cope with the rain."

"The rain isn't great. But it's the price you pay, isn't it? Like the heat and mosquitos in Tuscany." It's already getting uncomfortably hot and I can feel sweat coursing down the back of my neck. I pull out my fan and try to cool myself.

"Nearly there," Chiara says.

Ahead of us, a large sign says ROMITUZZO. I crane my neck, trying to catch a glimpse of the town, but all I can see is what looks like a shopping center.

"It's actually quite a big town these days," Chiara says. "Most of it's new, though."

"So I see," I say. On every side of us are garages, wholesalers, hardware shops and, just ahead on the left, an absolutely massive supermarket. "I don't suppose your clients often ask you to find them something in Romituzzo."

"Literally never. It's too much like normal life." Chiara pulls over at the bus stop in front of the supermarket. Pulling out her phone, she opens the map and shows me the blue dot indicating our position. "Okay, so we're here in the industrial quarter. This was all built in the sixties—it was probably still countryside when Achille was around. You want to head for the *centro storico*, the old town. See the bridge there?" She points past me, out of the passenger window, to a low concrete bridge that spans a sunken riverbed. "And the clocktower on the other side?"

"Yes."

"Cross that bridge and head straight for that clocktower. Walk a few hundred yards, and you'll see the train station directly ahead of you. Just go through the underpass and you'll pop up right in the middle of town. I'll text you when I'm on my way, and we can meet somewhere along the via Senese. That's *the* main street in Romituzzo," she explains as I peer at the map again. "It runs straight through town from north to south. You can't miss it. All clear?"

"All clear. Thanks, Chiara." I open the door and get out into the bright sunshine.

"No problem. And, look, let's go and have lunch when I'm done. Then we can really talk. *Ciao ciao.*" She gives me a cheerful wave and drives off.

⁂

THE WALK TO THE CENTER OF ROMITUZZO IS MOSTLY UPHILL AND mercilessly lacking in shade. By the time I reach the main square in front of the train station, with its war monument and its stone benches and fountains, I'm overheated and tired. I've been sleeping badly these last few nights, caught between anxiety and frustrated desire, and it's really starting to wear me down. I sit down on a bench in the shade of a tree, pull out my phone and open the map of Romituzzo.

The app tells me I'm currently on piazza Achille Infuriati. No surprises there. I zoom out a bit and see that a couple of streets ahead, on piazza Garibaldi, is the church of St. Catherine of Alexandria— that must be the clocktower—and right next to it is the Infuriati cultural center and lending library. To the north, on my right hand, is the Workers' Social Club "A. Infuriati"; to the south, along the via Senese, is the church of St. Christopher with its cemetery, where Achille is buried. A little beyond that, on the very edge of town, is the Achille Infuriati youth club and sports ground.

I put my phone down and look around. The industrial quarter was bustling, the supermarket car park full of vehicles, but here in the old town it's quiet. The clocktower stands at half past ten, and I know I should really get any walking over with before the sun hits its peak. That would be the truly sensible move.

On the other hand, I could really do with a coffee. And some water. Lots of water. In the far corner of the square is the Bar Pasticceria Achille (what else?). I head straight for it and go in, sighing in relief at the cold rush of air conditioning.

"*Buongiorno,*" says the friendly man at the till. He looks to be in his late forties or early fifties, and he's dressed in a black T-shirt and apron.

"*Buongiorno,*" I say, and then I stop short because this place is a shrine to Achille. The wall behind the counter is plastered in photographs and blown-up newspaper headlines, and in the middle of it all is a colossal purple flag with a winged horse and the words SCUDERIA GUELFA.

"What can I get you?" the man asks—in Italian, which still gives me a bit of a boost.

"Coffee, please, and a still water."

He puts a saucer in front of me and a glass next to it. "Would you like a glass of water or a little bottle?"

"Do you have a large bottle? Cold?"

"Of course." He smiles and reaches under the counter to bring out a litre bottle of water, then turns to the coffee machine and starts making my espresso. I pour out a glass and down it, studying the photographs to see whether I can catch sight of Granny. And there she is, a scarf over her blonde hair, bending to kiss Achille as he sits at the wheel of his Alfa Romeo. The headline above it reads "Infuriati's Last Farewell." I shiver.

"That's Achille Infuriati, the racing driver. You've heard of him?" I nod. "And that's his girlfriend Rita," the barman goes on as he puts the espresso cup on its saucer. "She was an English lady. You know, you look a lot like her."

"That's nice of you to say," I say, stirring sugar into my coffee. I don't want to air my family history to this perfectly kind stranger. "Are you *romituzzano* like Achille?"

"No, I'm from Palermo. No Tuscan can make cannoli like these, believe me." He smiles and gestures to a display case full of the little ricotta-stuffed pastries. "My name's Salvatore, Totò for short." He holds out his hand and I shake it.

"Victoria. I go by Tori. Actually, those cannoli do look good. Could I have a chocolate one?"

"Of course. Another coffee?"

"Please."

While I eat the cannolo and drink the coffee, Totò fills me in on his background. It turns out that he only took over the bar recently, though his family moved to Romituzzo in his early teens. "There's just so much more work in the north," he says frankly. "You'll find plenty of Sicilians here, Neapolitans, people from Puglia and Calabria. Anyway, this bar is kind of a local classic. The guy who ran it died a couple of years ago. He was a racing fanatic, but his wife wouldn't have any of his memorabilia in the house, so when I took over I inherited all this stuff. Maybe it's not what I would have chosen myself, but I like racing and I like the regulars, so I kept it."

"I suppose you had to learn a lot about Achille Infuriati very quickly."

"Oh, no, I knew all about him already. Long before I came here," Totò says. "When my dad was a little kid in Palermo, he actually met Achille when he came to town to race in the Targa Florio. Achille knelt down and shook his hand. Dad's still talking about it. Seriously," he adds. "Come here at five o'clock any day of the week, and you'll find him telling his Achille story to anyone who'll listen. Not that you'd necessarily want to be here at five—it's wall-to-wall old guys talking shit about cars. Most of them have an Achille story, too. And if it wasn't Achille Infuriati then it was Achille Varzi, or Tazio Nuvolari, or Giuseppe Farina or Enzo Ferrari. And if they weren't actually there, then they knew someone who was."

He gives me a broad smile and I smile back. "Totò, can I ask you something? A favor?"

"Shoot."

"I'm a writer and I'm working on a book about Achille—well, it's partly about him. Really, it's about my grandmother." My eyes drift to Granny's picture, and Totò turns to follow my line of sight.

"Oh," he says, with the air of a man for whom it's all coming together.

"Look, I don't have time today, but if I came back another day around five, do you think your dad would tell me his story? Maybe his friends would talk to me, too?"

Totò laughs. "Are you serious? Do you really think my father would turn down the chance to tell his Achille Infuriati story to someone who's actually never heard him tell it before? No," he says, "I don't think you're going to have any trouble there. In fact, if you call before you show up, I'll make sure he brings his photo album from home." He takes a business card from the holder next to the till and hands it to me.

"That's wonderful," I say. "Really. I'm so grateful, you can't imagine."

"Let's see how you feel after my dad and his friends talk your ear off for three hours. I'm glad if I can help, though. Anything else I can do?"

"Yes, actually. Could I have another of those chocolate cannoli?"

⟢

BY THE TIME I'VE FINISHED MY WATER, PAID UP, VISITED THE LOO and applied more sunscreen, the sun is high in the sky. Going outside is an unpleasant shock, like when you open the oven to check on your dinner and the heat blasts you in the face. But Chiara should be here soon, and I want to pay my respects to Achille before I go. I turn left down the via Senese and head for the church, clinging to the narrow margin of shadow afforded by the buildings on the eastern side. A little way along the street is a florist, and I stop on a whim and buy six red roses. Even numbers are for mourning—that's what Granny always told me.

"For the cemetery?" the saleswoman asks.

"For Achille."

The woman nods and takes out a roll of *tricolore* ribbon, tying it into an ornate bow around the stems of the roses and curling the ends with a flourish. "There you go," she says, handing me the bouquet.

Just as I step back out into the street, my phone rings. It's Marco. He and I haven't spoken since our aborted kiss, although I did message him to let him know the book was going ahead and he sent a nice message back. I don't know whether I feel more worried or hopeful that he's calling me now.

"*Ciao*, Marco," I say.

"*Ciao*, Tori. Bad news—Chiara just called me in a panic. Something unspecified but, apparently, highly stressful has happened and now she's stuck in San Damiano for at least the next few hours. She knew I'd taken the day off, so she asked if I could come and get you. I don't think she's meddling," he adds. "Well, she might be. But if she is, it isn't because of anything I've told her. Please know that."

Christ, this is awkward. "It's all right," I say. "I can get the train from here."

"Of course you can. I mean, if you want—if it suits you better. But I'd like to see you," he says. "If you want to see me. And we haven't celebrated the book yet."

"We do need to celebrate," I say.

"I think so, too. Great. Where are you right now?"

"I'm, uh, just heading to the cemetery."

"Of course," he says, and I can hear the smile in his voice. My heart gives a small flip. "As it happens, I'm most of the way to Romituzzo already. I had to pick something up in Castelmedici. So I'll be with you in around twenty minutes. Stay in the shade," he adds. "*A dopo*."

The sun's right overhead now and there's no shade, no prospect of shade as far as I can see. Cradling my roses awkwardly, I reach into my bag and bring out the sunhat I've learned to carry since I burned my part sitting outside on a deceptively breezy day. It probably isn't enough, but it's something.

The gate of the little walled cemetery is open, but there's nobody in sight. The graves are neatly packed together, standing in tight rows beneath the high walls covered in memorial plaques. Achille's plot isn't hard to find. A raised slab of white marble hemmed around with flowering plants, a bouquet of roses angled across it like a spray of blood. The blooms are dark purple-red, baked brittle by the sun. I squint at the bronze lettering.

ACHILLE INFURIATI
20.02.1928—25.09.1954
VI VEDRÒ DI BEL NUOVO, E GIOIRÀ IL VOSTRO
CUORE, E NISSUNO VI TORRÀ IL VOSTRO GAUDIO.

I will see you again, and your heart shall rejoice, and your joy none shall take from you. It sounds familiar, somehow, but I can't place it. Dante, maybe, or something from the Bible? I think of looking it up, but it feels disrespectful to take out my phone. Instead, I lean forward and place my roses carefully next to the others.

The silence of the cemetery is so heavy that even the cars on the road outside sound muted. I feel like I should do something, say something. I almost feel like praying, but I don't know how, so I stand before Achille's grave and think, and as I think, I fall into a kind of meditative state or something like it, and I don't notice time passing. I don't even notice Marco approaching until he says: "Communing with your friend?"

His voice startles me back to the present, and I feel tears threaten. I take out my sunglasses and cram them on before he can come too close.

"Something like that."

"It's just like a movie," he says, and smiles. "The mysterious lady with her hat and shades, elegantly sad among the tombs. Oh, look at that." He stops at my side, looks at the grave and its flowers. "I like the inscription."

"Where's that from?" I ask. "Do you know?"

"I think it's from the gospel of . . . John? Yes, John. My mother's very religious," he explains. "When I was a little kid I could have told you the chapter and verse, too, but I've forgotten most of it."

"I can't imagine Achille was terribly religious," I say. "But maybe his parents were." I look at the inscription again, reading the words back. Suddenly they seem very poignant.

"Maybe," Marco says. "But it's a universal hope, isn't it? They lost their son—they wanted him back. Maybe it's that simple."

"Maybe," I say, and then the tears rise and spill over. I scramble for a tissue and wipe my eyes.

"Oh, Tori, I'm sorry," Marco says, and the compassion in his voice only makes it worse.

"Why can't I stop bloody crying? I'm sorry, I'm really sorry, I just cry all the time and it never seems to bloody end."

"Maybe that's just what you have to do," he says gently. "Maybe you have to let some stuff out."

"But I hate it," I burst out. "It hurts, and I hate it. I want it to stop."

"Would a hug help?"

I nod yes and Marco opens his arms. I lean gratefully against him and weep into his shoulder in big, snotty, undignified sobs.

"Sorry," I mumble when the tears have died down a bit. "Embarrassing."

"It isn't. Tori, it really isn't." He's rubbing my back now in firm, slow, soothing circles. "Look," he says, "if you're going to live in Italy, then you might—just might—have to get a little more comfortable with expressing emotion in front of other people. Nobody's judging you. Nobody would."

"Yeah, right."

"No, really. Okay, so we're alone here. But even if we weren't, do you think anyone would care for a single moment that you actually dared show your feelings? You're in Italy, in a cemetery, standing at the graveside of this romantic figure who died this horrible, tragic death. To save the life of a child, if you need me to lay it on any thicker. *And* your grandmother loved this man, and lost him, and ended up having to marry some posh English guy and give birth to your mother who, frankly, seems like a terrible person. If you didn't cry, I'd wonder if you even had a soul."

"Ha," I say. My eyes feel sticky, my hat has fallen off and I'm worried about the state of my nose. But Marco's still hugging me and I can hear his heartbeat, strong and steady. I close my eyes and let it lull me.

"Do you feel better for crying?" he asks after a moment.

"I suppose I feel cleansed, in a power-washer kind of way."

"Then that's good. You must have needed it."

"Maybe," I admit.

"Definitely," Marco says, and kisses my forehead. I think he's going to let go of me, but he doesn't and, oh God, I don't want him to. I just want him to keep holding me. I could cry all over again from how good it feels.

"We should probably get out of the sun," he murmurs.

"Right." I step back, slipping out of his grasp, and retrieve my hat from the ground by my feet. My whole body feels alive, warm and expectant in a way that's really, really inappropriate in a cemetery in the middle of the day. I smooth my hair and breathe in slowly, trying to calm my racing heart, and then I put my hand on the sunstruck marble of Achille's grave.

"Goodbye for now," I say. "I'll be back soon."

Something moves at the edge of my vision. I look up and see a woman, a tiny, desiccated sparrow of a woman standing a few feet away and staring at me. She has a huge canvas shopping bag over one arm and in the other is a bouquet of red roses.

18

I FLINCH FIRST. I SNATCH MY HAND AWAY AND STRAIGHTEN UP, feeling like I've been caught touching something that isn't mine. "*Mi scusi*," I say.

The woman seems to wake up. She shakes her head. "No, no, I'm sorry. I didn't mean to interrupt."

"It's fine. Really, it's fine. We should go."

"If you're sure," the woman says. She's watching me, studying my face with anxious eyes. "You're very kind," she adds.

"No problem," I say. "*Buona giornata.*"

"*Buona giornata.*" She lays the roses carefully on the ground and unzips her canvas bag. I turn and walk quickly to the gate, Marco following. When I look over my shoulder, she's kneeling by the grave, apparently deadheading the plants. I want to run back, to ask her who she was to Achille, who he was to her. But she's so absorbed in her work that I can't bring myself to disturb her.

Marco puts a hand on my shoulder. "You'll be back," he says quietly. "You'll find out more then."

I'm almost dying of curiosity, but I know he's right. Someone in Romituzzo is bound to know something about the woman who tends Achille Infuriati's grave. I can find a way to talk to her, I tell myself. A way that doesn't involve breaking into her private ritual. "I know," I say, and I make myself look away.

In the small car park outside the cemetery, a paunchy man in a baseball cap is leaning against an elderly Fiat, smoking a cigarette and scrolling through something on his phone. He looks up as we pass and then he, too, stares at me.

"*Buongiorno*," Marco says rather pointedly, and the man mumbles a vague *buongiorno* and looks quickly down at his phone. "Asshole," Marco mutters.

The only other car is a long, low, extravagant bright-red thing. Marco takes a set of keys out of his pocket and jingles them, grinning at me.

"Wow," I say, "is that yours?"

He nods. "A 1964 Comacchi Scorpion. That's what I had to pick up in Castelmedici."

"You're a serious car nerd, aren't you?"

"What tipped you off?" He unlocks the passenger door and holds it open. "*Prego*."

"*Grazie*." I lower myself into the seat and swing my legs in, ankles tight together, as Granny taught me. Then the heat of the interior hits me. "Fucking hell," I gasp.

"Sorry about that. The nearest shade was miles away." Marco slides into the driver's seat and rolls his window down and his sleeves up. His shirt is damp and crumpled where I cried all over it—thank God I didn't bother with mascara today. "Where am I taking you?"

"I, uh . . ." My mind's gone blank. "Where do you need to go?"

"Nowhere. Well, somewhere, but I don't care where that is as long as I get to take this one for a spin. Want to find someplace for lunch?"

"Sounds good," I say. My sunglasses are bothering me—they're caked with dried-on tears. I try to polish them on my top, but the salt just smears everywhere and makes the situation worse. I give up and shove them in my bag.

"Are you starving right now, or shall we explore a bit first? We could go to San Damiano if you want," Marco says. "Plenty of nice places to eat there. And you probably want to see what that stretch of road is like, right?"

I shake my head. "I've had enough tragedy for today. Actually, do you know what I want? I want a break from the damn book."

"What, really?"

"Yes, really," I say. "Thanks to Tim Swithin and his twin obsessions with fast cars and World War Two, I get to spend the next year and a half obsessing about Achille Infuriati. Let's celebrate that by going somewhere that has nothing to do with him at all."

Marco thinks for a moment. "We can be in Siena in half an hour."

"And that's not too far?"

He smiles. "I've got nowhere to be today. In fact, I don't have to be anywhere until tomorrow afternoon. We could party all night if we wanted."

For an instant, the words hang there in the air between us. "I've never been to Siena," I say. "It would be nice to go."

Marco switches on the engine. The car roars and then purrs.

"Siena it is," he says.

⁂

"I WONDER WHO SHE WAS," I SAY. "THE WOMAN WITH THE ROSES."

"Fifteen minutes," Marco says.

"Huh?"

He laughs. "I make it fifteen minutes since you said you wanted a break from the damn book."

"Oh, well." I look out the window as the landscape goes by: trees, fields, houses, churches, groves and vineyards, over and over in an ever-varying pattern. I'm quite enjoying the scenic back roads but, after so much time spent contemplating Achille's final moments, the winding bits make me nervous.

"You've done pretty well," Marco says. "I actually thought you'd last five, if that. That was a very weird moment back there in the cemetery. I'd be thinking about it, too."

"I keep replaying it in my mind. She must have been, what, eighty?"

"At the very least," Marco says.

"And there she was with her pruning shears and her red roses. I wondered, actually . . ."

"What?"

"I wondered if she might be Achille's sister, Stella. Okay, she'd be ninety this year, but it's not completely beyond the realms of possibility, is it? Little old Italian women are a force of nature."

"It's true—they are."

"And she seemed, I don't know, possessive of Achille," I say. "She obviously didn't want us there. Besides, why would she be out there in the first place, deadheading plants in eighty-six heat, if she wasn't family?"

"She could be an old ex of his—a really old ex. Or a fellow partisan."

"I suppose so." I sigh. "But wouldn't it be amazing if she were Stella?"

Now Marco sighs. "Look, Tori, I was going to tell you about this later. It's one reason I wanted to see you today. Apart from the pleasure of your company, of course."

"What is it?"

"I hope you don't think I'm interfering. But I did a bit of research and the fact is, the woman you met is very unlikely to be Stella Infuriati. From an official point of view, Stella Infuriati doesn't exist."

I stare at his profile as he looks calmly at the road ahead. "I . . . I . . . what?"

He shrugs. "I know it sounds bizarre, but it's true. Basically, if you're born in Italy or you move here legally, you have a paper trail. Wherever you happen to be living, you're obliged to register with the Anagrafe in your commune—Florence, or Romituzzo, or Siena, or wherever."

"Like I'll be doing shortly."

"Yes," Marco says. "Although it's worse for you because you're new, so you have to get into the system. Once you're in, though, it's pretty straightforward. If you ever leave Florence—God forbid—and move somewhere else, you'll just have to fill out a form and show a couple of documents, and the Anagrafe there will do the rest. They'll even tell your old commune you've moved. So if you want to find out whether someone is alive and living in Italy, you don't even need to know the last place they were resident. You just have to know that they lived in a certain place at some point and then you can trace them from there. We know Stella started out in Romituzzo, so I called the Anagrafe there and asked about her."

"Wait, can you do that? Just ring up and ask for information about a total stranger?"

"Oh, yeah, anyone can. If you wanted to find someone's street address, that would be one thing, and if you wanted to go to the State Archives and get copies of documents, that's another thing again. But the really basic information—name, date and place of birth, commune of residence—that's all public. If you ask the relevant Anagrafe for those details about someone, anyone, they're legally obliged to tell you."

"I don't think I like that," I say.

"It's just the way it is," Marco says. "But yes, now you say it, I don't like it, either. Anyway, I had a good chat with one of the administrative guys in Romituzzo, and—well, this is the situation. Stella Infuriati was born there on the first of May 1929. Obviously, she's then registered as living in the family home with her mother, father and brother. In early 1955, so a few months after Achille's death, her parents both leave Romituzzo and move to Florence. But Stella doesn't go with them. I double-checked with the Anagrafe in Florence, just in case there was some bureaucratic slip-up—after all, this was well before computerized record-keeping. But they had no record of her at all."

"So her parents moved away and she stayed behind?"

"Now, this is where it gets mysterious. If Stella stayed in Romituzzo, there should still be a record of that. She'd move to another address, or become primary resident at her parents' old one. And if she moved to a commune other than Florence, or left Italy altogether, there should be a record of that, too. But there is no record. She doesn't stay, she doesn't leave, she doesn't die, she isn't reported missing. Her file just stops being updated, and there's a new family resident at her parents' address from 1956."

"And there's no way she'd have changed her name at some point, is there?" I ask, remembering our conversation about the tax code. "Even on marriage?"

"Actually, she could still have taken her husband's name. The law we have now didn't come into force until 1975. But to do that she'd have to marry legally—and if she married legally, then it should be in her records. The commune keeps track of anything like that: births, marriages, deaths."

"Maybe she still went abroad," I say. "Wasn't there a huge wave of emigration after the war? I'm sure a few of them fell through the cracks, officially speaking."

"That was my first thought," Marco says. "Fortunately, there's an entire industry in finding people who left Italy. You can search passenger lists, landing lists, all these different records across different databases. Stella doesn't show up in any of them. She's a ghost."

"Bloody hell." I'm dazed by all this new information. "You did all that in a couple of days?"

Marco smiles. "More like a couple of hours. You can't imagine how much time I spend helping American clients track down great-great-uncle Giovanni, who lived somewhere near Naples at some point after 1861. I could do this stuff in my sleep. I just hope I didn't overstep."

"You didn't," I say. "I'd never have figured all this out. You've saved me so much time and stress."

"That's what I hoped, though I should have asked first, and I'm sorry about that. But most of all, I'm sorry I don't have better news. Shit," he says, and laughs. "I'd have felt like a hero if I'd managed to find Stella for you. As it is, all I have is theories, and those are pretty far-fetched. You wouldn't believe some of the ridiculous things I've imagined."

"Please tell me. I'd love to hear some ridiculous imaginings."

But Marco shakes his head. "I don't think they'll hold up to questioning. And you're taking a break from the book, remember?"

"Of course," I say. "Taking a break. Totally. Let's talk about something else."

"Good idea," Marco says, and we both fall silent. He stares at the road and I stare out of the window, trying to process everything he's just told me.

After a few minutes, Marco clears his throat. "I guess I have one theory that's a bit more grounded than the others. Or maybe it's just more hopeful."

I nod vigorously, trying to dispel visions of bodies under floorboards, buried in barns, dissolved in acid. My own imaginings took a dark turn pretty fast. "Hopeful sounds good."

"It's also strictly relative, but okay, here goes. I don't know much about Stella, but I think we can say that she was politically serious. Achille was fifteen when he joined the Resistance—that's already very young. Stella was fourteen, and she wouldn't have been whizzing around on a motorbike like he was. She'd have been going through German checkpoints on foot or by bike. That takes a special kind of guts."

"I'd say so." I've read a few stories about women partisans over the last couple of days, looking for mentions of Stella. They make terrifying reading.

"Of course," Marco goes on, "a lot of the people who took those risks were relieved when it was all over. They just wanted to get back to their lives. But some of them didn't want to stand down. It wasn't enough to get the Nazis out—they wanted to keep fighting, make a global revolution."

"And you think that's what Stella did? Keep fighting?"

"Honestly? I don't know. But she'd be, what, just turning sixteen when the war ended. If her politics were anything like her brother's, I can imagine her getting a set of false papers and running away to join the struggle somewhere else. God knows she'd have had enough choice. Argentina, Abyssinia . . . Yugoslavia, for that matter. That's only just over the border."

"And there wouldn't be any record of her then," I say. "Not as Stella Infuriati, anyway."

"Right. I'm not saying it's the most probable scenario," Marco says. "But I think it's the one I like best."

"Me too. And, look, these things did happen. Granny had an older cousin who ran off to Spain to join the International Brigades. He knew George Orwell. I'm not sure he liked him very much but still, he knew him."

"Wow." Marco sounds genuinely impressed.

"Granny told me the whole story during one of our Florence trips. I was reading *Animal Farm* at school, so I thought it was just amazing, and I felt so grown-up listening to her talk about it all—not that I understood more than half. Then I went home and asked Mummy if she ever met cousin Hector, and wasn't it marvellous how he managed to fight Franco and Stalin all at once? She almost choked on her gin."

"I'm starting to understand why Achille got on so well with your grandmother. And why your mother didn't."

"Mummy always was a status quo sort of person," I say. "And I don't mean the rock band."

Marco snorts. "Sounds like that would have been an improvement. Look, we're almost at Siena. That's Monteriggioni coming up on the right."

I turn my head and see a green hill with a ring of fortifications at the top. It's so perfect, so prettily symmetrical that for a moment I feel unreal, like I've stepped into someone else's Tuscan fantasy. "Is Siena as nice as that?"

"Even nicer," Marco says. "In fact, it's beautiful, but don't tell anyone I said that. We Florentines have to keep up our historic grudges."

The road is rising steadily now, winding upwards, and my spirits rise with it. "Let's make a pledge," I say. "From the time we enter Siena to the time we leave, we're not going to talk about the book. Not a word, not even a thought. Deal?"

"Deal," he says.

19

Stella

IF MY RESISTANCE WAS UNSPECTACULAR, SO WAS MY LIBERATION.

Tucked away in a narrow valley on a minor tributary of the Arno, Romituzzo was protected from the worst effects of the war. We were not all that far from the major strategic points, across the hills in the Elsa valley—San Gimignano, Poggibonsi, Certaldo, Castelfiorentino, Empoli—and of course the fighting there affected us. Enzo's mother and her colleagues were killed by a stray bomb. But we never had to live through bombardment ourselves; never had to rush underground and emerge again into a new, ruined world. Our damage was collateral, marginal by the standards of the time.

And when the Allies pursued the Germans northwards through Tuscany in the late summer of 1944, those same cities took the brunt of the conflict: San Gimignano, Poggibonsi, Certaldo, Castelfiorentino, Empoli. And as the Germans were driven back, destroying and burning and killing as they went, they simply pulled all of their troops out of the Valdana. We didn't have to fight them; in their eyes, our territory wasn't important enough to defend. But that doesn't mean we didn't have to fight at all. There were still plenty of local Fascists who didn't want to cede an inch of ground, who would fight to the death rather than admit themselves defeated. And that's how we got our freedom. Inch by inch, shot by shot.

❧

ON THE MORNING THE FIGHTING BROKE OUT IN SAN DAMIANO, Achille knocked on my door not long after sunrise. "It's kicking off," he said. "Go down to St. Christopher's and get your orders. That's the main assembly point."

I was already digging in my underwear drawer for my gun. "Where will you be?"

"I'm heading up to Santa Marta. I'll get my orders there. Christ, tell me you're not hoping to shoot any Fascists with that daft little thing?"

"It's the best weapon I've got," I said. I felt rather defensive of don Anselmo's gift. "Anyway, I'm sure I'll be given a proper one at St. Christopher's."

Achille grimaced. "I wouldn't count on it. Look, take this." He took the Beretta in its holster from around his waist and held it out to me.

"Achille, no. I can't."

"I've got my German rifle. Please, Stellina, take it. I'll just worry about you if you don't." He was already fastening the belt around my middle, over my nightdress. "You remember how to fire a real gun, don't you? Rotate the safety all the way—squeeze the trigger, don't pull it. Oh, and aim for the belly. Don't try to do anything fancy."

"Right," I said. I must have looked dazed, because Achille smiled and gave me a brief, tight hug.

"Don't worry, little sister. I'll see you out there." He turned and ran down the stairs. The back door slammed, and a moment later I heard the MM 125's engine start up.

"Achille," my mother's voice called. "Achille!"

I knew that I wouldn't get past her without an interrogation. I took the Beretta off again and bundled it up in an old scarf, and I shoved that into my satchel before throwing on the nearest clothes I could find. My mother accosted me the moment I set foot downstairs.

"Where's your brother going at the crack of dawn? Did he tell you?"

"You know he didn't," I said. "Mamma, he can't tell us these things. You know that."

"But it's so early," Mamma said. She was wild-eyed, her hair standing out in wisps around her pale face. "He never usually goes out so early. And it's dangerous out there. I know the Germans have gone, but the Fascists . . ."

"I know. I'm sure he's going to stay somewhere safe until it's all over." I put my arm around Mamma's shoulders and spoke in the calmest, most soothing voice I could, but inside I was bubbling with impatience. "Come and sit down in the warm. I'll make you something for breakfast."

But she was pulling away from me, looking me up and down. "And where are you going? Why have you got your school bag?"

By now I'd got quite used to lying to my parents. I didn't even have to think about it. "I'm going along to the church," I said. "Don Anselmo has an emergency shelter all set up in the crypt. You and Papà can come, too, if you want."

It was a gamble, but it worked, thank God. Mamma shook her head just as I knew she would. "Your father and I will stay here and guard the house. But you should go to don Anselmo." She put out her hand to stroke my face. "Go and be safe."

That was the last tender thing my mother did for me. I kissed her and went out, carrying my schoolbag just as I'd learned to do: carelessly, as if it contained nothing important. The streets were empty and the air was full of expectation, like the day of the *rastrellamento*. Every now and then I saw movement in the corner of my eye, as if someone had looked out of a window or an alleyway and then quickly retreated. I don't know if they were on our side or theirs; whatever the case, I clearly didn't look like a threat.

The doors of the church were closed. I could hear indistinct voices: the tired back-and-forth intonation of morning Mass. At the former German checkpoint, a group of Fascist volunteers loitered in a sullen knot at the side of the road, like schoolboys hoping for a fight. I slipped into the church and knelt in the nearest available pew, shoving my satchel with the Beretta under the seat in front. The Mass was nearly over, and don Anselmo was embarking on the final prayers. I felt strangely disappointed. Mostly because I had imagined something much more exciting than this, but also because I would have liked to take Communion on that day of all days. I closed my eyes and let the words flow over me—don Anselmo's sing-song voice, and the congregation's muttered responses—trying to scrape back what little grace I could.

". . . *et vidimus gloriam eius, gloriam quasi unigeniti a patre plenum gratiae et veritatis,*" don Anselmo concluded.

"*Deo gratias,*" we all said, and the organ burst into a slightly off-tempo, very loud rendition of the "Ave Maria." Don Anselmo raised his hand.

Behind me, there was a muted groan of metal on metal as the bolts on the great doors slid into place. The congregants rose to their feet, pulling out guns and grenades from under their pews, throwing off unseasonal coats to reveal holsters and bullet belts.

A couple of rows ahead, Agnese was issuing orders to a little group of women who were clustered around her. I shouldered my satchel and pushed my way through the crowd until I reached her. "Here I am," I said. "I'm ready."

Agnese looked at me. She was a plump, practical woman who must have been around my mother's age, and I was used to seeing her in drab clothes and carrying her shopping basket. Today she was wearing a baggy old pair of men's trousers and a loose shirt with a *tricolore* armband, and she had a rifle slung over her shoulder. In my cotton dress and scuffed shoes, I felt like the schoolgirl I was.

"Stella," she said. "Good to see you here. Has someone given you a job to do?"

"Well, no." She was looking at me as if my presence were a puzzle she had to solve. I was starting to feel embarrassed. "I've come for my orders," I said.

"Right," Agnese said. "Well, I'm sure we have need for you here. If you go and see don Anselmo—"

"I'm ready to fight," I burst out. "I have a weapon." And I took the Beretta in its holster from my bag.

Agnese's eyes widened. "And you know how to fire that, do you?"

"Yes. I mean, I know how to fire a handgun. I'm sure this one isn't any different."

"Have you ever shot someone?" she asked. "A human being?"

"Well, no," I admitted.

"An animal?"

"No."

"Has anyone ever shot at you?"

"No, but—"

"It's too big a risk." She shook her head. "If you were a little older, or you had any combat experience at all—even hunting—but as it is . . . No, I can't send you out there."

"But I want to fight," I protested. And I really did. I wasn't a risk-taker like Achille, but after everything I'd seen, in that particular moment, I wanted to kill the Fascists with my bare hands.

Agnese patted me on the shoulder. "I know you do. And you're a brave girl—you can't imagine how valuable you are to our movement. We need you safe and well for the future. Now give me the gun and go find don Anselmo." She held out her hand.

Now I felt very small. Obediently I handed Agnese the gun—like it or not, she gave the orders—and went to look for don Anselmo as instructed. I found him in the sacristy, talking earnestly with a young woman in a white kerchief as they counted out rifle cartridges for distribution.

"Excuse me," I said—raising my voice a little to be heard above the organist, who had moved on to "Ave Maris Stella." Clearly he was working his way through the hymnal.

Don Anselmo looked up and saw me. "My dear child," he said, "I'm so glad you're here. Come, come. I have some very important work for you to do here in our command center." Before I could react, he had taken my arm and was hustling me towards the door to the tunnel, which stood open. "Quickly, now. Don Mauro is really more of a pianist than an organist, and I fear he's reaching the end of his capabilities. Besides, our friends outside won't be fooled for much longer."

"What do you need me to do?" I asked as we hurried down the stairs.

"You can assist our medic. Assuming you don't faint at the sight of blood?"

"I don't." Papà and Achille were forever hurting themselves, one way or another—I'd got quite used to dressing scrapes and burns and washing gravel out of wounds.

"Excellent. He'll appreciate your help. And here he is," don An-selmo said as we reached the tunnel, now empty of weaponry and full of blankets and lamps and buckets of water. "Perhaps you two already know each other?"

At the mouth of the tunnel, a slender, bearded man in a red kerchief was rooting through a battered army pack. "We're fine for gauze—well, as fine as we're going to be," he said. "But we could do with more material for tourniquets. Rip up the altar cloth if you have to. And we need windlasses, too, pens or soup spoons or butter knives, anything the right shape that won't break. Oh, hello, Stella."

"Hello," I said. I had no idea who he was.

"Stella's come to give you a hand," don Anselmo said. "I'll see what I can do about tourniquets, but I shall pretend you did not make that suggestion about the altar cloth. Assunta may be able to dig out some old sheets."

"Ask her if she can spare more towels, too," the man said, and don Anselmo nodded and hurried off through the tunnel towards the parochial house, muttering to himself.

The man sat back on his heels and looked at me, clearly amused. "You really don't recognize me, do you?"

But I did, then. Something in his expression, in the tone of his voice, made me see past the long beard and scruffy hair to the neat and tidy medical student I'd often seen helping his father out at the pharmacy. "Of course I do," I said. "You're Davide Galluri."

"That's right. You worked with my sister Berta—I know she re-lied on you a lot. Now take these," he said, holding out a pair of scis-sors and a folded sheet. "I want long strips, ten centimetres or so wide. If in doubt, cut wider than you reckon. Hopefully we'll have some more material soon."

I sat down on a pile of blankets and spread the sheet out over my knees. It was tricky to work like this, but I was glad of the task and I was glad, too, that Davide was the one who had mentioned Berta. It had cleared the air somehow. I cut the sheet in half crosswise and then started to cut the first half into long, wide sections.

"Let me see," Davide said after I'd finished three or four. "Yes, good. We're going to be dealing with gunshots here, maybe the odd knife wound, so we need to have a stock of these. Two for each wound—one above, one below."

"And that stops the bleeding?"

"Yes. Well, assuming it's an arm or a leg that's wounded. For anything else we'll need to use pressure. If I ask you to put pressure on a wound, by the way, I want you to lean on it as hard as you possibly can. Don't worry about causing pain. It's much more important to prevent hemorrhaging."

"And then we can save the person," I said. It was a statement of hope, and it was a naïve one.

"It's not impossible," Davide said kindly. "But what we're really aiming to do is buy some time. Hang on until the Fascists are gone and old Dr. Bianchi won't be too shit-scared to offer help to a partisan."

"Towels!" don Anselmo cried, emerging from the tunnel with his arms full. "Here I am. Towels, and a couple of old sheets, and a whole canteen of cutlery. Will that do?"

"Admirably," Davide said. "Give the sheets to Stella. She's on tourniquet detail. Will you be, uh . . . will you be nearby if anyone asks for you, Father?"

"Oh yes, never fear. Don Mauro has undertaken to be present in the field, so to speak, and I shall stay down here with you." Don Anselmo's voice wavered. "I think you should know," he said, "that the organ music has stopped."

20

Tori

"YOU'RE THINKING ABOUT IT, AREN'T YOU?"

I snap out of my daydream. I'm sitting with Marco on a stone bench in the courtyard of a palazzo in Siena. It's not as stifling as Florence or Romituzzo and there's a pleasant breeze that plays off my skin. But even in the shade it's still hot, that heavy midafternoon heat that drives sensible people indoors. No wonder we have the place to ourselves.

"You're thinking about the book," Marco says. "I can tell. You've got that dreamy look on your face."

"Oh," I say because, for once, I wasn't thinking about the book at all. I was thinking about him. About how it felt when he kissed me; about what might have happened if I hadn't pulled away. "You caught me."

"You writers," Marco teases. "Never happy unless you're working. I don't think anything or anyone could compete with Achille Infuriati right now." He nudges me with his elbow.

"I'm sorry about the other day," I blurt out.

Now Marco looks away, towards the arched colonnade on the opposite side of the courtyard. "What do you mean?"

"The other day, when . . . I got scared. I don't know why," I say. "I can't explain it. You didn't do anything wrong, but—"

"It's okay, Tori." His voice is gentle. "I'm the one who should apologize. I misread the situation and made you uncomfortable. If I could take it back, I would."

"But you didn't." The words break out of me—I can't stop them. "You didn't misread at all. I wanted to kiss you. I was enjoying it."

Marco looks at me now. His expression is wary but he's smiling just a little, just enough. "You were?"

"Yes." My heart's in my throat, but it's good to say it. It feels right. "My reaction had nothing to do with you. You can't imagine how badly I wanted to . . . I just get these moments of panic. Like sudden-onset shame. They come out of nowhere and they ruin anything even slightly fun."

"Is it to do with your ex?"

And just like that, all my new-found courage drains away. The last thing I want to talk about, the last person I want to bring into this beautiful place, is Duncan. "Well . . ."

"You don't have to tell me about it," he says. "I think I might have an idea anyway."

"Really?"

He sighs. "Chiara isn't an indiscreet person. Well, no, let's put it this way—Chiara doesn't set out to be an indiscreet person, but she mentioned a couple of things about that guy that made me think he didn't treat you well."

"He didn't hit me or cheat on me." I echo Charlie's words.

"That doesn't matter," Marco says, suddenly fierce. "I grew up with a cold-hearted asshole for a father and a mother who was always looking over her shoulder. If he did that to you, if he made you feel like you had to be frightened or ashamed, then he's a cruel fucker and I'm glad you got away from him."

His compassion is a wonderful shock. "Then you understand?"

Marco puts his hand to my cheek and it's all I can do not to lean into it, to rub myself against it like a cat. "Of course I understand," he says.

This time there's no question of who makes the first move. I touch my lips to his and he responds, kissing me warmly. It feels so good that I almost tense up, expecting the shame to flood in. But it doesn't come. There's only joy, joy and relief and the marvel of his lips against mine, the rhythm of his breathing and the scent of him. I press myself against him and open my mouth to his and he draws me into his arms; his hand slides across my back just where my top has ridden up, and his fingers brush bare skin. A bolt of lust goes through me and I shiver.

"You okay?" Marco murmurs into my hair. "Just say if it's too much."

"It's good," I say, trying to catch my breath. "Believe me. But maybe . . ."

"What is it?" He's breathing hard, too, and it dawns on me with a thrill of pleasure that he's as excited by this as I am, that he wants me like I want him. "Tell me," he says.

"You said you don't have to be in Florence until tomorrow afternoon, right?"

"Right."

"Then maybe we could stay here until then. In Siena."

For a moment, he studies me. And then he smiles, a slow-spreading smile. "You want to go to a hotel?"

I'm blushing to the tips of my fingers, but I'm long past being coy. "I do. I mean, if you do."

"Oh, I really do." He rubs the back of his neck. "I just wish I could be that guy, you know, that smooth guy who says: *Hey, I know this great little place, let me take you there.* But I don't know Siena that well." He breaks into his familiar grin. "Also, I'm just not that smooth."

"Smooth is overrated," I say. "Anyway, I have a system. What time is it?"

Marco checks his watch. "Half past four."

"Good enough. Take me for a spritz and I'll explain."

⟨❧⟩

"BUT THIS IS MONSTROUS," MARCO SAYS. "YOU HAVE A WHOLE LIST of options and you just pick the first one? What about planning? Feasibility, value for money, pros and cons?"

"That's the point," I say. "This is a system for making quick decisions, not reasoned decisions. Besides, it's how I picked you."

"What, really?"

"Yes. Chiara sent me a list of lawyers and you were at the top, so I called you. Done."

"Oh." He looks thoughtful. "Well, maybe I can loosen up a bit. Tell me again what I have to do."

I push his phone towards him. "Open Google and search for what you want."

"So I just type in *hotel siena?*"

"No, no. Rookie mistake. That's how you end up in a conference center full of German businessmen—unless that's your thing, of course."

"It really isn't." He picks up his phone. "So . . ."

"You've got to be specific," I say. "The more search terms you include, the better the choices."

"Okay. How about *romantic hotel central siena?*"

"You've got the idea. Though personally I'd go for *romantic hotel central siena air conditioning bug screens.*"

"Good point." He starts to type, then pauses. "No, wait. *Romantic hotel central siena air conditioning bug screens free parking.*"

"I think we've cracked it." I take a sip of my spritz. "Okay, what's the first result?"

"Hotel Pandolfo Petrucci," he says.

"Pandolfo who?"

"Petrucci. Lord of Siena in the late fifteenth–early sixteenth century. I think he was involved in the conspiracy to assassinate Cesare Borgia."

"Ooh, the romance."

"The place looks nice, though." He scrolls. "Really nice. Let's see: air conditioning, check, bug screens, free parking, soundproofing . . . oh, but it's right by piazza del Campo," he says, naming Siena's famous fan-shaped central square. "Kind of touristy. Maybe if we look a couple of streets back . . ."

"You're missing the point of the system," I say. "Call them and see if they have a room. And if they don't, then we move on to option number two."

"But . . ."

"No thinking. That's the rule."

"Very well," Marco says. "Let's give it a try." He puts the phone to his ear and reaches for my hand. "Good afternoon. I know this is short notice, but do you happen to have a double room free for to-night? Yes, I'll wait." God, I love hearing him speak Italian. I squeeze his hand and he gives me a wink that makes my toes curl.

"Oh, you have a cancellation?" he says at last. "Double room, courtyard-facing." He raises an eyebrow, and I nod. "Yes, that's fine. When is the room available . . . ? Great. The name's Marco Guadagni. See you shortly."

"What can I say?" I smile as he turns to me. "The system works."

"Let's see what the place is like first," Marco says. "The room's ready when we are. You ready?"

I drain the last of my spritz and get to my feet. I'm nervous and my knees feel a little wobbly, but this isn't fear. It's anticipation.

"Ready," I say.

⊷

THE ROOM AT THE PANDOLFO PETRUCCI IS SIMPLE AND BEAUTIFUL. In fact, it's perfect, with a terracotta floor, beamed wooden ceiling, plain white walls and, at the center of it all, the bed: a plush, white-sheeted double bed, big and comfortable looking. In the far corner of the room, a half-open door shows a glimpse of blue-and-white majolica tiles.

"All right, I'll admit it," Marco says. "The system works."

"Told you."

He takes me by the shoulders and kisses me. "I'm going to go and bring the car round," he says, "and I'll stop and get some toiletries and toothpaste and, uh, other things. If I get back and you tell me that you've changed your mind and want to go home, I'll take you home, no questions asked. You can say that at any time, and we'll just get in the car and go. Understood?"

He's so serious, so worried, that I feel a powerful rush of affection for him. I wrap my arms around his neck, pressing my lips to his cheek. "Understood," I say. "Thank you."

He goes out, and I sit down on the bed and marvel. I can't believe I actually did that. I can't believe that I just propositioned this gorgeous man and he said yes. I've never done anything so bold in my life; not that I've had much opportunity. I had some good times as a freshman, but that was all snogging in the college bar and trying not to fall out of rickety single beds. Not much chance for a dirty overnight in Siena there. And then in my second year I met Duncan, and that was it. And *that* was all the way back in . . . 2006.

Two thousand and fucking *six*.

That's thirteen years ago. I can hardly remember what it's like to have sex with someone for the first time. I can't even remember the last time I actually had sex with Duncan, though I'm pretty sure it wasn't any good. What if I've forgotten how to do it? What if I make a weird noise, or fart at a crucial moment, or accidentally knee poor Marco in the balls? What if I just freeze up from nerves and then he has to drive me back to Florence, which must be *at least* an hour's drive, and then the whole thing's just horribly awkward and I have to decide whether I can ever look him in the eye again? I feel sick at the very idea.

I take a long deep breath and then another, trying to steady myself. I've got to find some distraction before I have a panic attack. I rummage through my bag and pull out my phone. Maybe I can find some silly cat videos or a funny news story to occupy my mind until Marco comes back, and then everything will be fine again.

But I don't even have the chance to look, because I've got five new messages. All sent within the last hour, and all from Charlie.

> Call me when you can x
> I assume you're wrapped up in your new project, but you should know that there are some issues. Call me x
> Just had Mummy on the phone again. She's NOT happy with your new book idea. Call me NOW.
> Tori, this is serious. You need to sort this out. I refuse to do your dirty work anymore.
> CALL ME.

My nerves turn to irritation. I call Charlie and she picks up on the first ring.

"Tori," she says. "It's about time."

"Charlie, what's going on? I'm out of touch for, what, a whole day—and you've gone and told Mummy about the book? You know it's sensitive. I thought you understood that when I asked you to get hold of the papers."

Charlie sniffs. I can practically see her hoicking her bosom. "Well, that was when I thought it was some kind of harmless wanky travelogue thing. I didn't realize you were going to be hauling all Granny's skeletons out of the closet."

"Achille isn't a skeleton," I say. "Well, technically I suppose he is, but not in that sense. He was a good man and Granny loved him. It's a beautiful story and it all happened well before Mummy was even thought of, so what's the problem?"

"She still has the right to know that you're writing about our family. About her mother."

"Of course she has the right to know," I say, exasperated. "And I would have told her, as diplomatically as I could, at the best possible moment. I'd even have let her read the manuscript, not that she has any right of veto. I know she doesn't, by the way, because she isn't even in the bloody thing—and besides, I checked with Richenda and she checked with Tim and he checked with his lawyers. But now I can't even decide when to do that, because you just went ahead and did it for me."

"You shouldn't have told me," Charlie says sententiously, "if you didn't want me to do anything about it."

"I agree. I shouldn't have told you. But then again, if I don't speak to you every single day, you start getting in a froth. Of the two of us, I don't think I'm the one who needs her life sorted out."

There's silence at the other end of the line. And then Charlie says, in a cold, hostile tone I haven't heard since we were both teenagers: "Well, I'm sure there was no need to tell Mummy. You'll never finish the book. Duncan thinks so and I agree."

"You told Duncan about it?"

"Of course I did. He deserves to be kept informed about what you get up to."

"No, he doesn't." I speak as calmly as I can, but my mouth is trembling. "We're not together anymore. What I 'get up to,' as you put it, isn't any of his business. The marriage is over."

"Well, maybe that's how you see it, but he—"

"No, Charlie, it's over. I left him. In fact, I didn't just leave him, I emigrated. It's not like I'm sleeping in the spare room while we work things out. I bought a one-way plane ticket and I left the country." Despite the awfulness of it all, the situation's beginning to strike me as oddly hilarious. "I think that's pretty definitive," I say, and let out an unladylike snort.

"Are you finding this *funny?*" Charlie says, and she sounds so much like a third-rate am-dram Lady Bracknell that it just sets me off. I laugh and laugh until my stomach hurts and my eyes are wet with tears.

"Oh dear," I gasp after a while. "Sorry."

"Well, I hope you feel better for that," Charlie snaps.

"I do, actually," I say. And then I hear footsteps in the hallway, coming closer. "I have to go. Bye, Charlie."

"But—"

"We'll talk another time. If I feel like it." I end the call just as the door opens and Marco comes in.

"Oh," he says, looking a little worried. "You okay?"

"I'm fine." I breathe out slowly, trying to resist the laughter that's still bubbling up. Marco eyes me cautiously.

"Well," he says, "at least you're not crying."

"Stop," I squeak, wiping my eyes. "Oh God."

"What's so funny?"

I shake my head and pat the bed next to me. He puts his bag of purchases on the nightstand and sits down. "It's nothing," I say. "Just some ridiculous family drama."

"I'm sorry to hear that." He puts his arm around me and I lean into him. "Do you want to talk about it?"

His hand is warm on my waist, his thumb stroking my skin through the thin fabric of my top. Something stirs in me then, beneath all the nerves and the agitation—something hot and faintly devilish. "I really don't," I say, and I move even closer and brush my lips against his neck, just below his ear. Marco's breath quickens and he grips me tighter as I trail kisses down towards his collarbone, letting my mouth linger on his skin, tasting him. I put my palm to his chest and feel his heart beating hard and fast.

I think, on the whole, I haven't forgotten how to do it after all.

21

"I SUPPOSE YOU'LL BE BACK HERE SOON," MARCO SAYS AS ROMITUZZO comes into view. "Did you have a good morning yesterday? Somehow I didn't manage to ask."

He shoots me a wicked look and I smile at him. "Well, we had to keep the terms of our deal. And yes, I did, though the heat was unbearable. I swear it was worse than Florence."

"Yeah, it would be. We're right at the bottom of the valley here, so it's like a . . . uh . . ."

"Sauna? Steam cooker? Massive pot of boiling soup with extra mosquitoes?"

"Something like that," Marco says.

The via Senese is busier than yesterday. There's a queue outside the bakery, and people are strolling along the street with shopping bags and those tartan wheely carts that always look so practical. In the shade of the church porch, a little knot of women are chatting. I look to see whether I can spot the lady I saw yesterday, but she isn't among them. There's no car at the cemetery gates and the place itself looks empty.

Marco pats my knee. "You're probably too early. It was well past noon when I came to get you. And she might only visit once a week, or even less."

"Of course." I know he's right, but I'm still disappointed. "I wonder why she was there in the middle of the day? Surely she could visit when it's cooler."

"Definitely," Marco agrees. "In fact, it's dangerous to be working outside in that kind of heat. If I were her son or grandson or whoever that guy was, I'd never let her risk her health like that."

"I know. It makes no sense."

He thinks for a moment. "Unless she doesn't want to be seen. A town like this shuts down for a couple of hours in the middle of the day. Perhaps she wants to visit Achille when she won't be disturbed."

"Maybe." My mind's beginning to work again, churning over possibilities. "I mean, we know she can't be Stella. But maybe you're right and she is an old flame of Achille's, or there's some other reason she wants to keep things private."

"Another mystery. First the Bugatti, then Stella, now this. You're going to need Inspector Montalbano at this rate."

On the corner of piazza Achille Infuriati, Totò's putting up the big canvas umbrellas outside the bar. I wave to him and he raises a hand in reply.

"Friend of yours?" Marco asks.

"We met yesterday." I fill him in on Totò's dad and how he met Achille at the Targa Florio. "If I come back one afternoon, I can hear the story for myself. I wonder if he'll let me record it and use it in the book."

"Somehow I don't think that's going to be a problem."

"That's pretty much what Totò said. Apparently his dad's friends all have stories of their own, too."

Marco laughs. "Well, that seals it. Once word gets around that an attractive young woman author is in town and actually wants to hear a bunch of tall tales about famous racing drivers, you're going to have enough material for a five-volume critical study." In the distance, the clocktower of St. Catherine's church begins striking the hour. "What time is that? Eleven?"

"On the dot," I say.

"Damn, we're going to have to head for the motorway. I've got a meeting at half past one, and God only knows what the traffic in Florence is going to be like. What a shame, though. There are some great roads between here and there."

I open my mouth to say that there will be another time, another opportunity, but then I close it again. Last night was so good—so unbelievably, effortlessly good—that I'm suddenly scared of ruining it. And besides, who's to say that it has to be anything more? It can just be a fling, I tell myself, watching Marco's beautiful hands on the wheel. No pressure. We'll always have Siena.

By the time we reach the Siena-Florence motorway, we're both quiet. Marco seems to be concentrating. *Maybe he's thinking about how to manage the situation*, whispers the chilly little voice in my mind. He's probably wondering how we can go back to being friends without it being awkward, without my clinging on and making a whole drama. Who would want to get involved with me anyway? I'm nervous, damaged, baggage laden. It's amazing he took the risk of going to bed with me in the first place. I sink into my thoughts, feeling colder and gloomier by the second.

When the big South Florence toll gate comes into view fifteen or so minutes later, Marco breaks the silence. "Can you get my wallet? It's in there." He gestures to the glove compartment.

"Of course."

"I'll have to use my bank card for this, if you wouldn't mind taking it out for me. You know, keeping my expenses separate. Thanks," he says as I hand it to him. His eyes are fixed on the car ahead and he seems tense. Maybe he's just preparing to face the city traffic. Or maybe he's got a thing about toll gates, like some perfectly confident drivers have a thing about parallel parking or three-point turns.

As we approach the toll booth, he clears his throat. "Tori?"

Shit, here it comes. He's so desperate to make sure I don't get the wrong idea, he can't even wait until we get to Florence. "Yes?"

"Can I take you to dinner tomorrow night?"

Oh wow. Oh *wow*. "Yes. That would be nice."

"Great," Marco says, and his whole body suddenly seems to relax. He slots his card into the reader and the machine beeps, then gives us a cheery *Arrivederci*. We pass the roundabout and head down a narrow road, and I lean back casually in my seat and do a tiny victory dance in my head.

"Look left," Marco says.

I look and see a massive, ornate monastery in pale stone, looming down on us from the top of a wooded hill. "Oh," I say for want of any-thing better. "Beautiful."

"That's the Carthusian monastery. It's even better inside. We can go and see it sometime, if you like."

"I'd like that," I say, and watch his smile spread. "I'd like that a lot."

22

"LOOK, THERE'S ACHILLE," TOTÒ'S FATHER, CARMELO, SAYS, PUSHING the open photo album across the table towards me. "And that's me." His finger taps the face of the child in the picture.

"That's amazing," I say, but it's more than that. It's haunting. Achille kneeling down, his goggles pushed up on his head, smiling warmly at this little boy who's staring up at him, obviously transfixed. "Can I . . . ?"

"*Prego.*" Carmelo beams at me. I pick up my phone and snap a couple of pictures. "Do you think you'll put it in the book?"

"I'd love to, if it's okay with you. We probably have to do some paperwork." I've been reading up on this kind of thing, image permissions and contracts and copyright, but I don't know how I'd begin to explain it in Italian. "I'll talk to my publisher and find out," I say.

"Whatever you need," Carmelo says. "You just let me know."

Cecco, who's nursing a beer at the next table, leans over. "Let me see that," he says, and I suppress a smile. Cecco's the oldest member of the group and by far the most cantankerous. "My God, Carmelo!" In his strong Tuscan accent, *Carmelo* sounds like *H'armelo.* "You were such a beautiful child. What happened to you?"

"*Cuinnutu,*" Carmelo mutters.

"Language, Dad," Totò says, appearing with a tray. He removes my empty water glass and puts a spritz down in front of me. "I hope these bastards aren't giving you a hard time."

"Oh, no, I'm having great fun." And it's true. In the hour or so since my arrival I've heard any number of funny and scandalous stories about famous drivers, all accompanied by Cecco's acerbic commentary. Very little of it's usable and some probably counts as defamation, but it's all been highly entertaining. And of course Carmelo's Achille story is pure gold. I've made him repeat it three times with my phone on "record" just to make sure I got all the details, though I'm pretty sure he didn't object.

"Well, make sure you get Cecco to talk," Totò says. "Don't let him get away with sitting there sniping at everyone else. He's the only native *romituzzano* here, and he's old enough to remember Achille even if he likes to pretend otherwise." He throws Cecco a warning look and goes back inside.

"Is that true?" I turn to Cecco. "Did you know Achille?"

The old man grimaces and leans back in his chair. "Me? Not really. I was just a kid."

"Come on, Cecco," Vito chips in. Vito's a silver-haired Neapolitan who (he says) once ran over Guido Comacchi's foot when he was a test driver back in the seventies. "You were just a kid when Moses came down from the mountain."

"I tell you, I didn't know him," Cecco says. "My big brother Sandro did, though. He and Achille used to race against each other back in the day."

"You mean after the war?" I ask.

Cecco shakes his head. "No, this must have been right at the start of it. Thirty-nine, forty. Just street racing, you know, local lads on mopeds."

"But Achille can't have been more than twelve," I say. "Surely that wasn't legal?"

A gale of laughter erupts around me. The men hoot and thump and lean on each other as if I've just cracked the world's most hilarious joke. Finally, Carmelo takes pity on me. "It was a different time," he says, leaning forward to pat my arm. "And the likes of Achille—well, he wouldn't worry too much about the law anyway."

"Oh God," Vito wheezes.

"You could have some great times on the roads around here," Ettore, a Florentine, pipes up from the edge of the group. "If I still had my bike, I'd get out there myself."

"Bullshit," Cecco says. "Anyway, Sandro was best pals with Enzo growing up—you know, Enzo Sangallo. He was Achille's co-driver in the . . ."

"In the Coppa Valdana," I say.

"Right. And of course they were both in awe of Achille. Everyone was."

"But . . . ?" I sense there's a *but* here, and I really want to find out what it is.

"I don't know," Cecco says. "Sandro never let me tag along with him. I was too little. But, look . . ." He sighs. "Street racing, getting out with your mates—it's meant to be fun. Everyone wants to win, of course. I know Sandro did, but he didn't mind losing so long as it was a fair competition and he got to blow off some steam. For Achille, though, it was something else."

"He took it seriously," I say.

"*Brava.*" Cecco's mouth is a thin line. "You went up against Achille, you were competing for second. Personally, I wouldn't call that much of a good time."

"Achille was destined for greater things," Carmelo says gently.

"And didn't he know it," Cecco says. "Anyway, that's my Achille story, such as it is. And I never tried to make it in Formula One like some of these bozos, so I don't have any funny anecdotes for you."

"I don't suppose you knew Achille's family at all?" I ask.

Cecco shrugs. "Not well, but it was a small town back then. You couldn't avoid knowing anyone. Why?"

"I was wondering what happened to his sister, Stella."

There's a general murmur, a chorus of sucked teeth. Vito shakes his head, and Carmelo stares into his glass and says *Bedda matri!* which I think is Sicilian for "yikes."

"Now, Cecco," Ettore warns, "mind what you say."

Cecco snorts. "What is there to mind? The facts are the facts."

"And what are the facts?" I ask.

"One fact is," Cecco says, "that Stella Infuriati ran off one day in 1945 and never came back. And the other fact is that my sister's young man Davide went with her."

"Ah," I say. And I'm feeling foolish now because it's so simple.

There wasn't any need for revolution or acid baths. It was just a teen-age love story. "And I suppose nobody knows where she went."

"No," Cecco says. "They didn't leave an address, and quite right. Sandro and Enzo would have beaten that guy to a pulp if they'd managed to track him down."

His voice is stony. I feel bad, but I have to ask—it's nagging at me. "But shouldn't there be some evidence now? My, uh . . . a friend who's helping me with the book tried to trace Stella with the Anagrafe here in Romituzzo, but they didn't have a record of where she went next. And she'd have had to register at her new address, wouldn't she, le-gally?"

There's another wave of amusement, more muted this time. "Such faith in human nature," Vito says. "Such faith in Italian bureaucracy."

Ettore nods. "Even if they followed the law to the letter . . ."

"I doubt that," Cecco snorts.

"Yes, but even so," Ettore says. "Everything was on paper in those days, and things happen to paper records. Fire, flood, earthquake, in-competence. There could be a hundred reasons why that information didn't find its way back to Romituzzo."

"That makes sense," I say—and it does, of course. I don't know why I feel so oddly disappointed about it. "I hope your sister was all right, Cecco."

"Eh. She and Davide were so young, it would never have lasted. And Lucia did eventually meet someone else and marry and have chil-dren, like she wanted, and she was happy then. But it was brutal at the time." He fixes me with a steely eye. "Any other personal questions?"

"No. I think I've ruined the atmosphere enough as it is." I smile to show I'm joking—sort of—and they all smile back except Cecco, who gives a harrumph and drains the last of his beer.

"Don't pay any attention to him," Carmelo says. "He always was a moody bastard and he hasn't improved with age. If there's anything you need to know, just say so. We'll try to help you even if Cecco won't."

"Well, actually . . ." I mean to ask about the lady I saw at the cem-etery, the one who tends Achille's grave. But I remember the shock on her face when she saw me, her obvious desperation to be private and alone, and I can't do it. She probably doesn't want to be found any more than Stella did. "No," I say. "No, really, you've all been so helpful today."

After that, the conversation settles into an easy groove. I fall silent and finish my spritz, listening to them all as they banter back and forth, exchanging comfortable insults. After a little while Vito excuses himself to get home for dinner, and then Ettore gets stiffly to his feet and says goodbye, too. Carmelo, with a press of the hand and a kiss of the cheek, goes back inside the bar to talk to Totò, and then only Cecco and I are left sitting outside in the square.

"I'd better get going," I say. "Thanks so much for today. It was a pleasure."

Cecco harrumphs again. "If you say so."

I smile at him and start packing up my bag. It's about half past six, and if I walk smartly I should make the next Florence train. And then just as I'm getting to my feet, just as I raise my hand to wave goodbye to Totò, Cecco says: "No, wait. I ought to tell you something."

Well, I can get the next train.

23

"SO WHAT DID HE HAVE TO SAY FOR HIMSELF?" MARCO ASKS. HE'S crushing peppercorns with a pestle—or is it a mortar? the grindy thing—for *pici cacio e pepe*. The smell of the pepper tickles my nose. The hand-rolled pici, like fat starchy worms, are ready to be plunged into the salted water; the pecorino cheese is grated and there's a heavy-bottomed pan heating up on the range. I don't think my tiny kitchen has seen this kind of action since . . . ever, probably. Certainly not since I moved in.

"Well, to his credit, he knew he'd been a moody bastard," I say, "and he wanted to explain. Turns out there was a bit more to the story than he'd been prepared to say in front of the others. He never liked Achille, but you don't admit to that in Romituzzo."

"Huh," Marco says. "What would he have against Achille? Was it about the whole history with Stella and his sister's boyfriend?"

"No, not that—or not only that. Remember I said that his big brother Sandro was good friends with Enzo Sangallo?"

"The navigator?"

"That's him. It turns out Enzo was really more like family. He was orphaned during the war and Cecco's mother had lost a child of her own, her oldest boy Tommaso. Tommaso was called up in 1940—he died in North Africa. So when Enzo needed help, she just took him in."

"Very kind of her." Marco tips the pepper into the hot pan and starts toasting it. I eye the smoke detector nervously.

"I think it suited everyone," I say. "But obviously Raffaella—that's the mother—had been through a lot by then. The war had taken one of her sons, and then her daughter got her heart broken. Enzo had fought in the Resistance, too, and that was risky enough. So you can imagine that she didn't want any more pain or fear in her life. She hated it when Enzo got serious about motorbike racing, and she hated it even more when he started joining Achille on road races as his navigator. She couldn't stop him, though I think she tried, but she was permanently on edge in case he came to grief. Then Achille signed the deal with Pierfrancesco Legni and moved away to Florence, and she must have thought the danger was past."

"Poor Raffaella." Marco shakes his head. He's stirring the pepper with one hand and somehow draining the pasta with the other. If I tried that I'd end up calling an ambulance. I lean forward, trying to see how he's managing it. "Come on," he says. "Stop staring and finish the story. This will be ready any second."

"Well, of course Achille came back to town for the Coppa Valdana and wanted Enzo to be his navigator one last time. Raffaella absolutely flipped. Apparently she told Enzo she'd kick him out if he even thought about getting back in a car with 'that devil.' 'He'll get you killed,' she said. 'He doesn't care about anyone.' She only gave in at last because Sandro said that if Enzo didn't do it, he would, and Enzo was by far the safer navigator. So of course Enzo did go in the end, and Achille very nearly did get him killed."

"For a good reason, though," Marco says.

"That's what I said—well, I thought it, anyway. But honestly, I don't think Cecco sees it like that. As far as he's concerned, that little girl needed saving in the first place because her parents wanted to see the famous Achille Infuriati drive too fast in dangerous conditions. I suppose he's got a point."

Marco puts a plate of pici in front of me. It's creamy and glossy and speckled with pepper. "This looks amazing," I say. "I don't know how you do it. When I make any kind of cheesy pasta dish, it turns into wallpaper paste and ruins all my sponges."

"You've got to use the pasta water in the right way." He hands me a fork. "*Buon appetito.*"

We eat the pici in companionable silence. Finally, Marco says: "Are you going to use Cecco's story, do you think?"

I wipe the sauce from my plate with a piece of bread. (It's good manners in Italy, really.) "He said I could. Well, what he actually said was that he didn't give a shit whether I did or not, but he wouldn't mind 'letting a bit of air out of the overblown cult of personality.'"

"He actually said that?"

"Yes. I recorded it and everything. If I'm honest, though, I didn't totally understand until I listened to it a couple of times."

"He's got a fine turn of phrase, this Cecco," Marco says. "I suppose it might not hurt to have a view from the other side."

"I'm starting to feel like that. I mean, look at this." I pull my tablet towards me and open the photo gallery. "I photographed every potentially useful document we found. I've got letters from Achille, letters about Achille, obituaries, race reports, newspaper clippings. This is the first time I've come across something that isn't pure unadulterated heroism. I don't know—it makes him seem more human, somehow, that someone out there thinks he was a bit of a prick."

"What did you do with the rest of it?" Marco asks, eyeing the two archive boxes stacked neatly next to the sofa.

"Oh, I sent all the other boxes back to Charlie. She can bloody well deal with them."

He whistles. "Harsh."

"Not really." I haven't told him the worst of Charlie's behavior—haven't told him much about it at all, in fact. And I've told Charlie absolutely nothing about him. Whatever Marco and I have, it's too new, too fragile and far too enjoyable to subject to that kind of pressure. "You know the most frustrating thing? The whole point of this, originally, was to tell Granny's story. Achille was supposed to be part of that. A really important part, but not the whole thing. But now he's taking over, because I have all this stuff about him and nothing about her at all. She never even told me about him. She had this huge, earth-shattering love affair and I just never knew."

"And you can't reconstruct her side of it," Marco says, "because you don't have anything about her experience. So, really, it's turning into a book about Achille Infuriati that just happens to involve your grandmother."

"Yes, that's it! That's exactly it. If I could only find Maria or Giuseppe or someone, anyone, she might have confided in. Because there must be someone, mustn't there? It doesn't matter how stiff-upper-lipped you are—you can't go through a thing like that without talking about it, can you? She was so young when she lost him. She must have been in so much pain."

"I'm sure she had people to support her." Marco gives my arm a reassuring rub. "Look, you've only been at this for a short time and you've already done a lot of networking. Maybe it will take a bit longer, but eventually you'll run across someone who knows someone who knows someone who can tell you something useful. Like Cecco did."

"I'm sure you're right. I'll just have to keep putting the word out. No, no, I'll deal with those," I say as Marco picks up the plates and takes them to the sink. "You already cooked—I can wash up later."

He shakes his head. "This stuff gets disgusting if you leave it. Besides, it's kind of therapeutic."

"Tough day at work?"

"Tough week, tough month, tough year." He raises his voice above the sound of the running water. "Most of my clients are great. But you'd be amazed how many of your fellow citizens have been living here for years without changing their tax residence or even bothering to register as resident—which is, of course, breaking the law—and it's only dawning on them now that Brexit is actually happening and they're about to lose all their rights. So they call me up in a panic saying it's urgent, which it is, and I spend most of the first meeting calming them down so we can try to sort out whatever mess they're in."

"Bloody hell, I'm sorry. That sounds awful."

"It's okay," Marco says, angling the pan under the tap to blast off the last of the pecorino sauce. "I wouldn't do the job if I didn't enjoy it. And I only want to strangle my clients about ten percent of the time, or maybe it's ten percent of my clients I want to strangle. Either way, I think that's as good as it gets in the legal profession." He stacks the dishes in the drainer above the sink and dries off his hands. Impulsively, I go to him and slip my arms around his waist, resting my cheek against his back.

"Thank you," I say.

He turns around and pulls me close. "I'd say you're welcome," he says, "but I don't know what you're thanking me for."

"It's just . . . you have so much stress, so much worry, so much work. And you're still always there to listen. I don't know how you put up with me when you spend all day helping other people."

"I don't put up with you," Marco says, as if it's perfectly obvious. "I spend time with you because I want to."

"Really?"

"Of course I do. Your project is exciting—your new life is exciting. You're exciting. I want to be involved in all of it." His eyes search mine. "Tori, where's this coming from? Have I done something to make you feel bad?"

I almost tell him, then. I almost tell him about the calls and messages and emails from Charlie, the pleas and the imprecations and the guilt. I almost tell him about the times I've woken in a cold sweat with Duncan's voice ringing in my ears, telling me harsh judgmental things I can't bring myself to repeat even in my mind.

"No," I say. "Not at all. I'm just feeling a bit of pressure about the book. There's so much to do in a year and a half and, well, you know."

"I know." He smiles. "But you'll do a wonderful job—I know you will."

"That's nice of you."

"It's the truth. Who can write this better than you?" He tilts my chin up and kisses me lightly on the lips. "Nobody," he says. "Nobody at all."

He kisses me again, and I close my eyes and let pleasure take over.

⁓

I WAKE AT HALF PAST TWO. MARCO'S SLEEPING PEACEFULLY BESIDE me, one arm flung across my stomach. For a while I lie there listening to his breathing, trying to breathe with him, trying to stop my heart thudding and the cold creeping nausea rising in my throat. But I'm restless and panicky and his arm is like a lead weight. I lift it off me as gently as I can and roll away from him, grabbing my tablet and headphones from the table at my side of the bed.

I'll listen to some music, I tell myself. Or I'll read one of the *Shopaholic* books or watch an episode of *Friends*. Something safe and bright and familiar. What I won't do, what I absolutely won't do, is look at my email. There's going to be nothing in my email, at two-thirty in the morning, that's going to make me feel any better.

I look at my email.

Well, it's not too bad. There's the usual bunch of newsletters I keep meaning to unsubscribe from and haven't got around to yet. There's an email from Richenda titled "Final redraft of Swithin contract." I'll read that tomorrow. And there's an email from Rosa, Pierfrancesco Legni's daughter. I'd written to her just the other day on the only email address I could find, which was her corporate one as head of the Legni publishing house, so I didn't have any expectations about getting a personal reply—certainly not this quickly. I sit up and open the message.

> Dear Ms. MacNair,
> Thank you for your email. I would be pleased to meet with you and will try to help you to the best of my ability. Kindly call my assistant Frida Gattolini at the number below to set up an appointment at our Florence office.
> *Cordiali saluti,*
> Rosa Legni
> *Presidente, Pierfrancesco Legni Editore*

My mind's already starting to race with questions I want to ask, things I need to check. I feel even more awake now, but it's still better than that horrible anxiety. I resolve to call Frida Gattolini first thing in the morning and set up that interview, the sooner the better. And then, just as I go to close the app, I catch sight of an email from Charlie lurking among all the newsletters and other trivia. The subject line reads "Taking a break."

> Tori,
> I've tried my best, but it's becoming obvious to me that you don't want to engage in an open and honest conversation about your issues.

"No shit," I mutter.

> I want to support you, but I no longer have the bandwidth to take on your emotional labor. Perhaps one day you'll be ready to accept the help and advice you so desperately need. In the meantime, I have to disengage from your toxic

drama for my own well-being. I know this may sound harsh, but I need to protect myself and honor my boundaries.

Duncan continues to be greatly distressed by your stubborn refusal to work on yourself and confront the ways in which your behavior has affected him. However, for obvious reasons I am no longer prepared to act as go-between. I have told him to contact you directly from now on and have given him your Italian phone number and current address. No doubt you will hear from him in due course and, when you do, please at least try to listen to his concerns. He is deeply worried about you, as are we all.

My therapist recommended the following books to help me navigate the stress of your situation. Evidently she wants me to understand your perspective "from within." While I'm not quite ready for that challenging task, I'm passing on this list in the hope that some of it might be useful.

Finding the Inner Mirror: Self-Reflection for Self-Centred Personalities by Sherry Amendola
What's Yours is Yours: A Healthy Boundaries Workbook by Dr. Carina Flowers
Wait, What if I'm the Asshole? by Marty Ferrara, PhD
Take care of yourself,
Charlie xxx

The cheek of it. The absolute fucking cheek. Not only does she constantly pester me, not only does she inform Duncan of my every move, but now she's accusing *me* of toxic drama. And she's given him my number and my address, my actual physical address. It's ridiculous, but that feels like a betrayal.

I mean, it's not that I have anything to worry about. Right? Clearly Duncan's not about to abandon his Cheviots and his fishing permits and whatever else and just show up at my door. The worst he can do is call me on the phone and, okay, that won't be pleasant—but it won't be the end of the world, will it? I lived with the man for years in the middle of nowhere, and I survived that. I'm going to be divorcing him, maybe even going to court, and I'll survive that, too. I can deal with a sulky phone call. And if he gets really arsey, then I can talk to Ambra. She already said I could route all communication through her once proceedings start. So as soon as the divorce is actually underway, I can just block his number and let her deal with him. She'll know what to do. She must handle far worse exes than him, abusive exes, exes who hit and cheat and gamble and drink. Duncan's not *bad*, not by those standards, is he? He's not scary.

"Hey."

I flinch. The bedside lamp is on and Marco's awake, propped up on his elbow, watching me. "What's up?" he asks.

"Nothing," I say. "Did the light from the tablet wake you? Sorry."

"No, that didn't wake me." He gives me an odd look. "Tori, you're shaking."

"Oh," I say. "Oh." I am, now he says it. I'm shaking so hard that the mattress is juddering. I take a breath but that's juddery, too.

Marco leans forward and puts a hand on my thigh. "Tell me what's wrong. Please?"

He looks so concerned. More than concerned. There's something in his expression, something tender. It pulls at me. If I start talking now, I'm going to tell him everything, and if I tell him everything, he's going to know how broken I am, and then all he'll feel for me is sorry. And I couldn't bear that, so I take another breath and manage to say: "Nightmare." (Which isn't a lie, not really. It's a fair description of the situation.)

Marco doesn't seem convinced by this. "Okay," he says. "You don't want to talk—you don't have to talk. Can I hug you instead?"

"Yes."

He opens his arms and I sink into them, bury my face in his neck. I can't stop shaking. I can't stop. Marco pulls me into a tight embrace.

"It's all right," he says. "Whatever it is, it's all right. I've got you. I'm here."

24

Stella

IT WAS THE FIRST ONE THAT WAS THE WORST. AGNESE'S SON MAT-
teo carried down the stairs by two of his comrades, his shirt red and
soaked from the knife wound in his belly. I cradled his head as Davide
worked to stop the bleeding, but no amount of pressure could save
him. He bled and bled until he died.

I stayed there stroking his hair, looking into his vacant eyes, until
don Anselmo took my arm and pulled me gently but firmly to my feet.
"I'll take care of him," he said. "You go and clean up."

"Come on, Stella," Davide urged. "Quickly now. We have to be
ready." I took the soap he held out to me and plunged my hands into
the nearest bucket of water. "Get right in between the fingers," he instructed, "and don't forget your thumbs, either. Good, that's good.
Ready for the next one?"

I rubbed my hands briskly with the rough towel as if I could
shock myself back to life. "No," I said.

"It gets easier." Davide's voice was calm and steady. "You had a
rough start there, but in an hour or so you'll feel like you've been doing
this all your life. Really you will."

I wanted to believe him but I didn't know how. I sat down on
the hard floor of the cellar with my back to the wall and stared at my
feet, trying to clear my mind of what I'd just seen and experienced. A
few feet away, don Anselmo knelt over Matteo's body, murmuring his
prayers. Some while later—it could have been ten minutes, it could
have been an hour—there were shouts and clattering feet, and the
whole process began again.

AS IMPOSSIBLE AS IT SEEMED, DAVIDE WAS RIGHT. AFTER THAT FIRST
nauseous shock, a kind of routine set in. Soon I had stopped noticing
blood, stopped seeing faces and become entirely focused on my work.
I remember keeping a cloth clamped to a minor gunshot wound in
someone's leg and watching as Davide deftly tied strips of fabric above
and below and secured the ersatz windlass—a silver soup spoon—
tightly in place. Only when the tourniquet was fastened and the crisis
was over did I realize that the leg belonged to a girl called Giulia,
who'd had a little romance with Achille the summer before. I don't
know whether she recognized me. I rather hope she didn't, because
it had all ended badly between them in the way those adolescent pas-
sions sometimes do. At any rate she was fine, though shocked and in
pain, and was sent off to be looked after by Assunta, who was running
an improvised recovery room at the other end of the tunnel.

I was like an automaton. I sprang into action when every new patient appeared, and the rest of the time I sat against the wall, waiting.
I ate and drank whenever Davide or don Anselmo prompted me, but
I didn't feel thirst or hunger, only a sort of numb determination. And
then eventually it was over. Footsteps thundered down the stairs, but
this time there was no limp helpless body, no wound to treat. There
was only Achille shouting joyfully that we were free.

All around me, celebration broke out. Don Anselmo hugged Davide and they both hugged Achille. At the far end of the tunnel, the
invalids cheered and whooped. Someone began to sing the Internatio-
nale and the others joined in, their voices echoing off the stone walls.
I stood there not really comprehending, not knowing what to do with
all this sudden excitement.

"Stella!" Achille was before me, concern on his face. "Stellina, are
you hurt?"

I looked down. The front of my cotton dress was spattered and
smeared with stiff brown bloodstains. "It isn't mine," I said. "The
blood. It isn't mine. I was helping Davide."

"Thank God," he said, and swept me into a hug. "Come on, sister
liberator, let's get you some fresh air. Enzo's safe, in case you were
wondering. He and Sandro are up at the town hall helping our new

government get settled in." And he began to talk about the wonderful things we would do, and how Romituzzo would be a Red town again just like it was when our parents were very young, before the Fascists took over.

But an awful thought had come to me. "Where's Agnese?"

"Agnese? Right in the middle of it all, just as you'd expect her to be. Why?" His eyes followed mine to the shrouded shape of Matteo's body, which was lying in the corner. Three more blanket-covered figures now lay alongside it. "Oh," he said. "Oh no. I heard he was hurt, but I thought . . . I hoped he'd make it."

We stood there for a moment, quite lost, until don Anselmo rescued us. "I shall break the news to Agnese when the time is right," he said. "I have a few hard conversations ahead—but that, dear children, is for me to worry about. In the meantime, Achille, I should be glad if you would run and fetch Dr. Bianchi. Assuming he'll come, of course."

"He'll come," Achille said, hefting his rifle.

When old Dr. Bianchi arrived a few minutes later with his black bag, he looked around at our makeshift hospital—the bloody towels, the blankets everywhere, the instruments soaking in alcohol—and he shook his head as if we had somehow failed him.

"Very poor conditions, very poor indeed. Do you really lack the manpower to bring these patients of yours to me? I fear there's little I can do for them here."

"I'm not moving them until they've been examined." Davide's voice was cold. "We have three bullet wounds and at least one serious knife injury. They need a proper assessment."

Dr. Bianchi sucked his teeth. "Well, I can only say that this is a highly irregular set-up."

"It's an irregular war," Davide retorted.

But the doctor wasn't listening. His disapproving gaze had landed on me. "And what is this child doing here? Does she need attention, too?"

"Stella is our assistant medic," don Anselmo said, putting his arm around my shoulders. "She's been doing a marvellous job and we are all very grateful to her."

"That's as may be," Dr. Bianchi said, "but she cannot stay here. I have to examine these men. It isn't proper for a girl to be present."

Davide was reaching the end of his tether. "This girl, as you call her, helped save the lives of every single one of those patients. And they are men *and women*, Dr. Bianchi, not just men."

"Is that so?" the doctor muttered, aghast. Don Anselmo took my arm.

"Come on, Stella. I need to go out and make my rounds, and I fear it's going to be sad and difficult work. Will you help me?"

How could I not? I would have done anything for don Anselmo. I followed him upstairs and into the sacristy, where he began to top up the little vials of holy oil and water he kept in his emergency bag along with his stole and breviary and the little gold pyx with the consecrated wafers. "If—when—we find a body," he said, "then we must take note of who and where so that their family can be told. I won't have anyone in this town prevented from burying their loved ones. Do you understand?"

I remembered the desperation of the women in Castelmedici: the bodies hanging from the trees and the German soldiers guarding them. "I understand," I said.

"Very good. Ah, now." He rummaged around in a drawer and brought out a square of white fabric, which he folded diagonally and held out to me. A kerchief: the white kerchief of the Catholic partisans. "Put this on—if you want to, of course. Perhaps you would prefer a red one like your brother's. But as far as I am concerned you are my comrade, no matter your views on earthly rule."

I didn't know what to say. I thanked him and tied the kerchief around my neck, then we went out into the church and I waited while he refilled the pyx with wafers from the tabernacle. "We must be ready to administer last rites if we find anyone close to death," he explained as we headed for the main door. "But I expect don Mauro has done much already. Let's see if we can find him, shall we?"

Outside, the sun was low in the sky and the air was hot and muggy. The checkpoint was now manned by a group of red-kerchiefed lads with machine guns. They saluted with clenched fists as we left the church and began to walk up the via Senese towards the town center.

The street was silent. A little way along we found the body of a young man, in civilian clothes with a *tricolore* armband, lying on the pavement outside the bakery. An elderly woman stood next to him. "He's my great-nephew," she explained when don Anselmo asked. "His mother lives in San Damiano. My husband has gone to find a telephone, to get a message to her. I'm waiting with the boy until she comes."

Don Anselmo reached for her hand and clasped it in both of his. "I'm so sorry," he said. "Wouldn't you like us to bring him inside? It might be a while before his mother can get here."

The woman shook her head. "It doesn't feel right. No, I want to wait for her. But give him a blessing, Father, please."

"Of course," don Anselmo said. He crouched down and, putting a hand on the boy's head, murmured a prayer.

And so we made our sad progress. Every now and then we'd find a broken body in bloodstained fatigues or a black shirt and baggy trousers, and don Anselmo would say: "Ah, this is the son of the blacksmith who lives out towards Sant'Appiano. I believe his name is Daniele." Or: "I don't know this young man, but I see that he's wearing a red-and-black kerchief. When we get to the town hall, we shall see if we can find an anarchist to come and identify him." And then he would kneel down and say a prayer, and I'd help him up again.

By the time we reached the center, there was still no sign of don Mauro. "I'm sure he's around somewhere," I said, feeling the need to be bolstering. "He's probably at the town hall with everyone else."

"Oh, I'm sure he is," don Anselmo said. "He always does want to be at the heart of things." But he didn't sound very sure.

In piazza Garibaldi, the town hall was festooned in red flags and there were armed partisans standing guard outside the door. I scarcely had time to take it in before I heard my name called.

"Stella!" Enzo was striding across the square towards us. Like Davide, he'd grown a beard, if not very much of one. Even though I hadn't seen him in so long—even though I had long since given up on him—I have to admit my heart was beating a little faster. "I'm glad you're safe. Achille said you were, but I'm still relieved." He went to embrace me and then stopped, abruptly, as he saw don Anselmo.

"Good evening, Enzo," don Anselmo said. "Don't worry, I shall let you young people get on with your reunion. But perhaps you could tell me where don Mauro is? I need to speak to him as a matter of urgency."

Enzo turned pale. I could see that he was making an effort to be manly and, for the first time in that whole dreadful day, my heart hurt because I knew what was coming. "I'm afraid that don Mauro . . ." He cleared his throat. "Look, Father, if you would come with me for a moment—"

"Why?" don Anselmo snapped. It was the first time I had ever seen him lose his composure. "Where is he? If you have something to tell me, young man, at least have the courtesy to spit it out."

Enzo bowed his head. For a moment he was silent, and then he said: "Don Mauro died just after three o'clock. It was nearly over by then, but the Fascists still held the town hall. There was a shoot-out just outside and one of theirs was hit. He went down crying to God. Don Mauro ran over to give him the last rites—I tried to stop him—and just as he finished, there was a shot from an upper window and . . . I'm sorry, Father."

At first, don Anselmo just stared. And then he said in a quiet voice: "Where have you taken him?"

"We took him to St. Catherine's," Enzo said. "We thought he should be at home."

"You did right. Thank you." Don Anselmo's eyes were wet. He rubbed them with the heel of his hand, like a child. "My poor friend," he said. "My poor friend."

❧

THE SUN WAS SETTING WHEN I BEGAN MY WALK HOME. I WAS EX-hausted in body and mind, and the shock of the day's events was beginning to give way to a terrible sadness. But I had done everything possible, I told myself. I had looked after don Anselmo the best I could. I had stood with him on doorsteps as he spoke with the newly bereaved, and I had stood with him afterwards as he closed his eyes and spoke silently with God. And even if our freedom didn't feel real just yet, I would wake up tomorrow in a new Romituzzo that was no longer under Fascist control.

As I passed in front of the Frati house where Sandro and Enzo lived, the front door opened and Sandro's sister Lucia called out to me. She was a pleasant young woman of about eighteen, tall and fair, and we all envied her looks. "Stella! You can't go home like that. Quick, come in and I'll find you something to wear."

"Oh," I said. I'd forgotten about the bloodstains. "Oh, yes. Thank you."

"Davide said you were a tremendous help," Lucia said as she ushered me inside and up the stairs. "Just tremendous. I wouldn't have had the guts to manage like you did. I'm so glad you were there with him."

"It was my pleasure," I said. It was a ridiculous thing to say, but it was the best I could come up with.

"He says you'll be a real asset to the revolution. Come on, in here. I share this room with my little sister—she's away staying with our auntie. I'm sure she won't mind me lending you something." She was looking through the wardrobe as she spoke. "How about this?"

I looked at the dress she was holding up. It was pale blue cotton and could easily pass for one of mine. "That looks perfect. If you really don't mind . . ."

"Of course not! It's the least I can do after all your work. Now, take this and I shall fetch you some hot water so you can get cleaned up. And leave your own dress here, all right? I'll wash it and get it back to you." She was really very kind, Lucia. I feel bad to this day for what Davide and I put her through.

Once I was alone, I washed and put on the blue dress, leaving my own one folded over the back of a chair. I picked up the white kerchief to put away in my satchel—I'd taken quite enough of a risk wearing it around town already—and only then realized that I didn't have the satchel with me. In all the confusion, I must have left it at the church. I thought about running back to fetch it, but decided that it would be fine to leave it there overnight. It was more important to get home to my parents before dark. I folded the kerchief and put it in my pocket before I went downstairs.

Lucia was stirring a big pot of something in the kitchen. It must have been as poor and simple as our family's soup, but it smelled rather better. She smiled at me. "Do you want a bite to eat before you go? You must be starving."

"No, thanks. I really should get back."

"All right," she said. "Well, go safely. No doubt I shall see you often now Enzo's back from Santa Marta. You must come and have dinner with all of us some evening soon."

I thanked her again and went out into the warm evening air. Just as I reached the next corner, a strong hand grabbed my shoulder. I spun round, ready to fight, and saw my father looking down at me. In his other hand was my school satchel.

"Papà—"

"Not here," he said. He took my arm and all but pulled me along the street towards home. I had to hurry to keep up with him. When we got back to the house, the kitchen door was closed and I could hear laughter and happy voices—Achille, Enzo, my mother—coming from within. Papà hustled me along the corridor into the back room and shut the door behind us, flinging my satchel onto the floor.

I had seen my father angry, but not like this. "I went to look for you at the church," he said in a terrible quiet voice. "I was worried about you. The fighting was over and you hadn't come home, so I went to the church because you told your mother you'd gone to the shelter there. And what did I find? Not a shelter but a morgue, and a strange young man who tells me you're ever such a help to the cause."

"Papà, I—"

"I told you not to get involved. I told you to stay away, and you lied to me and your mother and got up to God knows what instead. I should lock you up for the rest of your life." He went on and on like that: how I'd brought shame to the family and put everyone in danger; how I'd abused every freedom he and my mother had given me; how my mother would suffer when she knew what I'd done; how there could be no question now of school or friends, and as for books, I could forget it. And all the time he was towering over me, and I knew that I was supposed to be afraid.

But I was beyond being afraid. I'd had enough intimidation from the Germans and the Fascists—I wasn't about to be threatened by my own father. So I waited until he paused for breath, and I told him that he could perfectly well lock me up and stop me going to school, but then I'd be here all the time and he'd have to look at me and know that I'd lied, not once, but every day for almost a year. "And Mamma will know, too," I said, "because I'll tell her. I'll tell her every detail because I won't have anything to lose. How do you think she'll suffer then?"

There was a long silence. My father looked at me with a coldness I'd never seen in him before—a coldness very close to hatred. "Fine," he said at last. "Do what you want." He turned his back on me and went out.

25

Tori

I LOOK AT THE PIECE OF PAPER ON MY DESK, NEXT TO MY LAPTOP. "Can I just check I've noted this down right?"

"Of course," Ambra says. She takes a sip from her mug and sits back, watching me. I drain the rest of my tea and clear my throat.

"Right. So, since Duncan and I will be divorcing under Scots law, then I can petition on the grounds of, let's see . . . unreasonable behavior. One year's separation, if I can get him to agree to the divorce in the first place. Two years' separation, if I can't. Adultery, if I find out he's slept with someone else. Wait, does it count if I have?"

"Only if Duncan's willing to be the petitioner."

"Damn," I say. "Because honestly, that sounds pretty straightforward."

Ambra shrugs. It could be, if you're amicable. Some couples in England actually wait until one of them finds a new partner, then the other one applies for the divorce. But here you only have to wait one year with consent, so there's no need.

"But Duncan probably won't consent. So that leaves two years' separation, or unreasonable behavior." Both options worry me. Ambra has already explained to me that if I choose unreasonable behavior, Duncan will actually receive a copy of the writ containing a list of the things he did to make the marriage intolerable for me. No matter how carefully we phrase that list, I can't imagine him reacting well. But then the idea of waiting two years, of letting this nerve-racking limbo go on and on without doing something about it . . . that's just as bad. Maybe even a bit worse.

"You don't have to make any choices now." Ambra breaks into my thoughts. "There's no custody issue, the two of you don't have to see each other, and you're financially secure—right?"

I force myself to come back to the present, trying to shake off that clammy, sick feeling I always get when I think about Duncan. "Right," I say. "I mean . . . yes, for now, anyway."

"Okay. So there's no pressing need to get this done. You have plenty of time to decide which approach you want to take."

"Which do you think is better?" I know she can't actually tell me what to do, but I'm kind of hoping she will anyway.

"I can't tell you which to choose." Ambra gives me an assessing look. "I can, however, tell you from extensive experience that if someone's already being uncooperative, alleging unreasonable behaviour can aggravate them further—and they may even try to defend themselves in court. It's reasonable to want to avoid that. But then a few of my clients feel that it doesn't matter. Divorce is unpleasant anyway, and you're not going to get through it without some discomfort. For those people, it's easier to brave the backlash and get on with it, especially if they're already living separate lives."

"That does make sense," I say.

"But for many others, waiting out the two years is worth it if it means a simplified divorce. Really, it depends what's at stake. How safe you feel right now, how much conflict you're prepared to tolerate . . . these are very personal things. I tell all my clients to think carefully about the balance of interests and put their own well-being first. Although if you did have a new partner—a serious one—you might find it useful to talk it over with them. It's your decision, though, so don't lose sight of that."

A serious new partner. That's a whole other set of questions, and it's one I try not to think about. "I think that's pretty clear, thank you," I say. "Can I take a bit of time to think about it?"

"Of course. Take all the time you need. Is there anything else today?"

"Nothing you can solve," I say, and Ambra smiles.

"Then just send me an email when you want to talk again. Bye for now, Tori, and good luck."

～

AFTER THE CALL ENDS I MEAN TO MAKE ANOTHER CUP OF TEA AND
get back to work, but I can't concentrate. It's about four in the afternoon and the street outside is blazing with sun. I know that I'll regret
it instantly if I leave my nice air-conditioned flat. I also know that if I
don't put in at least a few hours of work every day, at least six days a
week, I risk falling behind on my deadline. And I cannot, I absolutely
cannot let Swithins down (again).

I suppose that if I went ahead with the divorce now, did the
unreasonable-behavior thing, then I might be in real danger of that.
I've developed a habit of lurking on divorce-related forums recently,
and I've read countless stories of previously reasonable husbands and
wives refusing to accept the petition, pretending not to have received
it, "losing" important paperwork or sending it back incomplete. None
of which can stop the process, of course. But it all slows it down,
consuming time and energy and money and causing endless stress—
which I suppose is the point.

I remember meeting a friend of Charlie's at a party, hollow-eyed
and on her second bottle of wine, raving about how her ex had "forgotten" to sign the financial declaration after weeks of strong-arming
him to fill it out at all. "It's psychological warfare," she declared,
clutching my arm. "The whole bloody process is a war of attrition."
And I felt sorry for her—of course I did, because she was so obviously
distressed and I couldn't imagine, not then, how terrible it must be
to deal with the end of a marriage. But I didn't really see how a bit of
delayed paperwork could cause so much angst. I'm beginning to see
now, and I'm beginning to wonder how well I'd cope if Duncan were
really determined to make my life difficult. Maybe it really is best just
to leave the situation alone, wait it out, spare my nerves.

It might even work. It's been days now since Charlie told me I'd
hear from him, and I haven't. That's got to be a good sign, hasn't it? If
Duncan's not bothering me, and Charlie's not bothering me—though,
frankly, I'm amazed she's kept it up even this long—then maybe this
is just how it's going to be. Maybe I just won't hear from him at all,
and the time will fly past; because it always does, doesn't it, when you

have a deadline? In fact, by the time I deliver the book, most of the wait will be over already. And then I'll just file for a simplified divorce and it will all be sorted. No stress. Well, not as much stress, probably. And even if there is stress, even if Duncan really digs his heels in, I've got loads of time to prepare. Why would I go stirring things up now when I could just live in peace for a while?

My phone buzzes and I start, almost knocking over a table lamp. But it's just Marco, thank God.

> Hey! I've got wall-to-wall Brits today but I should be able to stop work about 8. Trattoria Serragli at 8:30?

See you then, I text back, and he sends me a row of little red pulsing hearts. That doesn't really mean anything, of course. Italians in general tend to be pretty casual in their use of emojis. I learned that the first time my accountant sent me a winky face.

If I'm going to go out this evening with a clear conscience, then I really had better get back to work. I plonk down on the sofa, pick up my tablet and open the document I started before my appointment with Ambra. I've been working through Achille's letters to Granny, reading a bit every day. It was a struggle at first, but I quickly got used to his bold, forward-slanting hand. (Even his writing seemed to be racing to get somewhere.) The vocabulary, though, can be a challenge and I spend a lot of time looking things up.

> *Comacchi continues to pester me, to present me with grandiose visions like Satan in the desert. It won't do him any good. However much money he holds out, however he tempts me with illusions of power, nothing would persuade me to leave Pierfrancesco and work with a [carogna]*

Oh. That literally means "rotting animal carcass." Figurative meanings: lowlife, scum, snake, swine.

> *with a double-dealing scumbag who chose to enrich himself while the partisans he now claims to admire were risking*

everything to overthrow Fascism. I told him as much the last
time we met, and yet he persists in making me insulting offers.
What will it take for him to piss off?

I smile as I imagine Achille, all fire and spit, squaring up to the
patrician Guido Comacchi with his well-cut suit and designer shades.
Perhaps Rosa Legni will have something to tell me about Comacchi's
attempts to lure away her father's star driver. I can ask her tomorrow. I make a note, and then get back to reading. My concentration's
shattered and the words seem to zoom in and out of focus, shifting
before my tired eyes. If I can make it to the end of this letter, I promise
myself, then I can stop for the day. A few more minutes—that's all it's
going to take. Just a few more.

❧

AT TWENTY TO NINE, I'M SPEED-WALKING DOWN VIA DEI SERRAGLI
towards the restaurant, cursing myself for having agreed to meet
somewhere so far from my flat. But Marco's choice was pretty impec-
cable. I've felt a distinct loyalty to the Trattoria dei Serragli ever since
the day they were so kind to me as a lonely new arrival in Florence, the
day I saw Marco and Chiara together. (Marco doesn't know that bit of
the story. I'll tell him someday.)

When I finally get there, the owner Michele gives me a warm hug.
"*Ciao*, Tori. Are you alone this evening, or is someone joining you?"

Ha! So Marco isn't even here yet. "My friend should be joining
me shortly," I say casually, dabbing at my brow. I've got a horrible sus-
picion I'm purple in the face.

"This heat, eh? I've got a nice table for you by the air conditioner.
Shall I bring you a glass of wine?" Michele asks as I settle into my seat.
"Red or white?"

"Red, please."

"*Certo.*" He puts a menu down in front of me—hand-written, as
ever, on a single page—and bustles off.

Marco shows up just as I'm starting on my wine. "Sorry," he says,
leaning down to kiss me before collapsing into the chair opposite.
"Sorry, sorry, sorry. I was on time and then my last client just talked

and talked . . . I almost ran here." He peels off his jacket to reveal practically no sweat stains at all, the smug bastard. I clamp my arms to my sides and try to look nonchalant.

"Sounds like a demanding day," I say, as Michele hoves into view with another menu.

"It was. What's that you're drinking?"

"Just the house wine. I think it's a Sangiovese."

"Great. Could we have a carafe of that?" he asks Michele. "Or better yet, a bottle? And some still water, too. Thanks." He leans back in his chair and makes a face. "Maybe I should have asked him to bring a straw. What's up?"

I realize I'm staring. "Oh, sorry. It's just . . . You switch between languages so easily, even when you're flustered. I think it's amazing."

"Just practice. It's what I do all day, every day. You'll get there."

"We'll see," I say. "I'm sorry you had such a stressful time."

"It's nothing to complain about, not really. But . . ."

"Tell me."

Marco sighs. "Look, I can't give you details of any specific case, but let's put it this way: all my clients are in basically the same situation."

"My situation," I say.

"Right, although they're not all as organized as you. But some of them seem to think they're the only one in the world who wants to move to Italy. And they think I've got no other clients but them. And they want stuff done *yesterday*."

"I know the type," I say.

"Really?"

"God, yes. My mother, for one. Everyone who has to deal with her develops this sort of haunted look. She goes through hairdressers like other people go through toilet paper. In fact, I think the toilet paper has a nicer experience."

Marco snorts. "That just about describes it. Are you ready to order?"

"I think I'm going to have the bruschetta and then the steak and chips."

"Good choice. I'll have that, too. And you can tell me all about your most recent discoveries, take my mind off boring work stuff."

Over the bruschetta, I fill him in on my latest work on Achille's letters. "I'm only about a third of the way in. I'm getting faster, though, so I'm hoping to get through them all in a few more weeks. Then I can start going back and translating the passages that look useful."

"I'm surprised Achille managed to write so many letters," Marco says. "He and your grandmother didn't have all that much time together."

"Well, he was a man with a lot to say. And then he was travelling around to compete in different races, and I suppose Granny couldn't always go with him. But even when she did . . ."

Marco grins at me. "Why do I feel like there's some dramatic detail coming?"

"Hey, don't be mean about Achille. But yes, there is. Every time he took part in a race, he'd write her a letter the night before to tell her that he loved her. I suppose it was a kind of ritual for him."

"Wow. This book is going to break some hearts."

"I hope so," I say. "Just imagine feeling like that, though. Imagine meeting someone and knowing so quickly that this is it for you, this is the person you love. That you want them to know it every single day—that you can't bear the thought of dying without telling them one more time." I've clearly been drinking too fast. I push my glass away and concentrate on lining up my knife and fork in symmetry with the checked pattern on the tablecloth.

"Yes," Marco says. "Imagine that."

The steaks arrive, caramelized around the edges and studded with little crystals of salt. I pick up a chip and bite into it. As ever it's perfect, crispy and fluffy and the right kind of salty. I cut into my steak and find it exactly as I wanted, deep pink in the center and oozing with juices. I've just speared a piece on my fork when Marco says: "How are you doing, anyway?"

"Oh, fine," I say. "I've got the interview with Rosa Legni tomorrow—I think I told you. Otherwise I'm just carrying on with the letters." I put the piece of steak in my mouth and chew it, keeping my eyes fixed on my plate. I can feel Marco watching me.

"Yes," he says, "I'm all up to date with Achille. I'm asking about you."

Me? You want to know how I am? Let's start with that email from my sister, the one that gave me a panic attack in the middle of the night. Or how about the fact I'm preparing to divorce a man I'm fairly sure is going to make my life hell? Oh yeah, that's great romantic-dinner conversation. I bet you'd just love it if I dumped all that on you.

"Tori?"

"Really, there's nothing," I say, and force myself to smile. "Nothing at all to report."

"Okay," he says. "But, look, you know you can tell me if you're stressed about anything. Right?"

"Of course I know that."

"Good," he says, and smiles back. I turn my attention back to my steak, but there's something in his tone—something in his look, in the fact he even asked—that makes me feel . . . I don't know, mulish, somehow. Resentful. It isn't fair of me, I know. It doesn't make any sense, but the more I try to push that mutinous feeling down the stronger it becomes, until I feel like I'm going to cry or throw something if I don't get out. I have to get out.

I put my knife and fork down and push my chair back. "Sorry," I say in the calmest voice I can muster. "I need to go home."

"What's wrong? Aren't you feeling well? I can walk you back, or call you a taxi—"

"It's fine. I want to go alone." I take out my purse, but Marco frowns at me and shakes his head.

"Don't you dare," he says. "I'm getting this."

"Okay. Thanks." My jaw's so tight I can scarcely get the words out. As I squeeze past him, he puts a hand on my arm.

"Are you sure you'll be all right?"

I can only nod. I slip away from him and out into the warm, still air. The street is full of couples, lingering and talking and laughing in the fading light. My throat's burning and there are tears in my eyes, but I can't cry now. This is Italy—if I broke down in public, people wouldn't ignore me politely and hope I'd go away. They'd crowd round and want to look after me, and I can't bear that. I march on, head down and jaw clenched, up via dei Serragli and along the embankment towards the Ponte Santa Trinità. Just as I'm about to turn and cross the bridge, my phone buzzes in my pocket.

I'm sorry I upset you. Can we talk? M
PS: I won't ask any stupid questions.

The tears start to spill over. I wipe them away and carry on, across the bridge—lined, as always, with Florentine youths taking selfies and snogging—towards piazza Santa Trinità with its huge phallic column. I'm starting to feel a bit wobbly now, a bit Bambi-legged and short of breath. I sit down on the wide plinth at the base of the column and plant both my hands on the warm marble, trying to ground myself.

I could call Marco. I could ask him to come and find me and he would. He'd hold me and let me cry—really, properly cry. It's what I want to do. It's what I want, right now, more than anything.

But if I did that, I'd have to explain myself. I can't break down on him *again* and refuse to tell him what's going on. And if I tell him . . . The mutinous feeling rises again and I spread my fingers, pressing down as if I could drive my nails into the marble of the plinth. And then I see Marco.

He's walking from the bridge towards me. His head is down and his hands are shoved in his pockets and I don't think he sees me. I don't think he sees anyone. I expect him to turn right—his right—and head towards the Santa Croce quarter, where he lives in a flat twice the size of mine, with a better sofa and more hair products. But he doesn't turn; he stops and takes out his phone, and his shoulders slump.

"Marco," I call before I can stop myself. "Marco!"

He looks up. "Tori," he says, and he sounds so pleased that my heart gives a painful squeeze. "There you are."

I pat the plinth next to me and he comes over and sits down. I'm oddly nervous, like I used to be in the days when he was just my lawyer. I can't look at him, so I look towards the river and hold out my hand. He takes it and laces his fingers between mine.

"So," he says.

"So." His skin against mine, his warmth, the scent of limes. I breathe in and feel my heart slow just a little. "I'm stressed," I say.

"I gathered that."

"It's really got nothing to do with you."

"Except that you can't bring yourself to tell me about it." He's hurt, I realize. He's trying not to sound it, but he's really hurt.

"Believe me, you wouldn't want to know."

"Try me," he says.

"Marco . . ."

"Really. Try me." His fingers tighten on mine. "Whatever it is, it can't be worse than having you push me away every time something's wrong."

"Okay." I swallow and try to compose myself, to line up the words in my mind. "Okay. Well, you know I'm getting a divorce."

"Yes."

"And you know my ex is . . ."

"An asshole," Marco says.

"Pretty much. Well, he won't accept that it's over."

"What?" Marco turns to me, indignant. "But you left him. You moved to Italy."

"I know that and you know that, but he doesn't seem to get it."

"Is he harassing you? Stalking you? Because the police—"

"No, he isn't doing anything like that. In fact, he isn't contacting me at all. But he and my sister, well . . ." As briefly and as matter-of-factly as I can, I tell Marco about my conversations with Charlie and the email where she told me she'd given Duncan my address. By the time I finish, I'm shaking and the tears are spilling over again.

"Christ, Tori." Marco gathers me into his arms. "I can't believe you didn't tell me any of this. Why on earth didn't you?"

"I didn't want to burden you," I hiccup into his shoulder. "It's been such a short time . . . this is all so new . . ."

"For fuck's sake," Marco says. "Did that matter to your grandmother? Did it matter to Achille?"

"Well, no, but . . ."

"It didn't matter to them. And it doesn't matter to me."

"But it's all so complicated," I say. "I've got to decide whether I file for divorce now, which might make him angrier, or I can wait two years. But if I wait, then . . . I don't know. I don't know what to do. I've been trying to figure it out and I just . . . I don't know," I say again, helpless.

"We can talk it through, you and me," Marco says. "If you want."

"Are you serious?"

"As a heart attack. I know you've got this fixation on being a burden—which is ridiculous, incidentally—but look at it this way. What's a divorce but a whole lot of stressful paperwork? That's kind of my thing," he says, and gives me a squeeze. "You're going to keep working with Ambra, right?"

"Of course." I wipe my eyes. "I've been looking at therapists, too."

"Then there's no problem, is there? You'll have a lawyer to deal with the actual divorce, and a therapist for the crazy family stuff, and for everything else there's me. I don't see any burden there, do you?"

"I suppose not," I say, but I'm not convinced. "Thanks so much, though. This is really kind of you."

Marco snorts. "You're kidding me. Come on, let's get something to eat. I'm still mourning that steak." He stands and holds out his hand to me, and I get up a little shakily.

"Oh God. I'm going to have to apologize to Michele, aren't I? That's the second time I've abandoned a plate of food in his restaurant."

"He's got no problem with you." Marco slips an arm around my shoulders and pulls me into his side. "Me, on the other hand, he hates. I told him you weren't feeling well, but I'm pretty sure he didn't believe me. He clearly thought I was this complete dick who'd invited you out so I could dump you in public."

"I'm sorry," I say.

"It's fine. But maybe you can clarify that with him before we go back again. In the meantime, I know a place."

AS WE FINISH OUR ARANCINI AND ORANGEADE IN THE CORNER OF A little Sicilian place in Santa Croce, Marco gives me a serious look. "I was thinking about asking you something this evening. I thought it might be too early—I didn't want to put you under pressure—but I don't know now."

"What is it?"

"I have to go to Rome for a few days next week. It's not going to be very exciting. I'll be spending most of the time chasing up citizenship applications. But it's a beautiful city and I'd have the evenings free, so I was wondering whether you might take a few days off from Achille and come with me."

I don't know whether the idea makes me happy or scared. My heart's thumping either way. "I'd like to, but I don't think I can. I definitely can't lose time with Achille and, besides, isn't Rome a complete tourist inferno at this time of year?"

"Yeah, unfortunately it is. I'd much rather take you there when it's less touristy and the weather's a bit cooler and we can spend proper time together. But I just don't feel good leaving you here on your own. Not now your ex knows where you are."

I play with my empty drink can, spinning it between my fingers. "I really don't think Duncan's going to come here. He hardly ever leaves the estate. There's always some emergency, and he doesn't trust anyone else to handle things for him."

"Well, you know him, of course. But, Tori, wouldn't it be nice not to have to think about it for a while? To take some proper time out? I know I'd feel better."

"It has been getting to me a bit," I say.

"Then please think about coming with me. You can work in the daytime if you need to. Or, if Rome really seems like too much right now . . . well, suppose you stayed at my place? Look at it as a favor to me," Marco says. "You can, I don't know, water my plants."

"You haven't got any plants."

"Mere details. Anyway, I was thinking about getting some."

"I should warn you," I say, "I kill plants."

"I'll get cacti. They hardly need water at all. Let's not examine the logic too closely here." Marco pushes on before I can interrupt. "I'll feel much happier if I know you're somewhere safe. And you can relax and focus on Achille."

The offer is starting to feel very tempting. The idea of a few days properly off Duncan's radar is like a holiday for my central nervous system. "Your aircon *is* better than mine," I say.

"You know it is. Faster Wi-Fi, too. Do we have a deal?"

He reaches across the table and I put my hands into his. "Deal."

"Great. Oh, great, I'm relieved." He really is, too. He's smiling at me, looking at me as if I matter. As if I matter to him.

Hope spreads through me, warm and irresistible. Maybe I can let myself have this. Maybe I can relax, let go, allow myself simply to like this man who seems to like me.

Maybe it's all going to be okay.

26

THE FLORENCE OFFICES OF PIERFRANCESCO LEGNI EDITORE OCCUPY one of those tall nineteenth-century terraces in Rifredi, a residential area in the north of the city. Inside it's all faded gentility, old-but-good furniture and the odd oil painting. If not for the green shutters and terracotta floors, you'd think you were in some decaying ancestral home in Knightsbridge or St. James. Frida Gattolini, who turns out to be a woman of about sixty with artsy specs, spiky gray-blonde hair and an outfit made of many layers of baggy linen, shows me into a book-lined parlor.

"Have a seat." She gestures to a low, comfortable-looking sofa. "Would you like a coffee? Or are you a tea drinker?"

I got to Rifredi much earlier than I needed to, and have had two coffees from the bar on the corner already. "No, I'm fine, thank you."

"Dr. Legni will be with you as soon as her meeting finishes. Just let me know if you need anything." Frida smiles and withdraws, closing the door after her.

I take out my tablet and quickly run through the questions I'd jotted down—not that I don't already know them by heart. I'm oddly nervous about this interview. Not just because Rosa Legni is a direct, living connection to Achille, but because she's just one of those really impressive people. She's got a degree in PPE from Oxford, a masters in philosophy from Cambridge, and she wrote her PhD at the Sorbonne on some ultra-obscure aspect of Marxist theory. And she's published a ridiculous number of books, all called things like *Towards a Renewed Theory of Permanent Revolution* and *Hunger, Sex and Death: Embodied Struggle and the Challenge of Socialist Art.*

In short, she's terrifying.

I put my tablet away and cast around for something to look at, something that might distract me from the sight of all these fat red-jacketed books—most of which were probably written by Rosa herself. A framed photograph on the far wall catches my eye, and I stand and go over to look at it. It's a black-and-white shot taken in some ornate marble-paved hall, perhaps the lobby of a hotel, with tall columns and potted palms. To the left stands a tall, spare man I recognize as Pierfrancesco Legni, with glasses and wild, curly hair. He's watching indulgently as a skinny teenage girl—I presume, Rosa—holds forth to a scruffy-looking, bearded type in fatigues, with his shirt open to the waist. She seems to be lecturing him, thrusting her finger into the air almost under his nose, and he's looking down in amusement while he lifts a cigar to his lips and oh fuck, it's Che Guevara.

"Ms. MacNair?" says a cut-glass voice behind me.

I turn and see a small, round woman leaning on a stick. Her white hair is in a disheveled bun and she's dressed in a loose floral-patterned top and a shapeless skirt with orthopedic-looking sandals. Like a harmless grandma in a children's book.

"I'm so terribly sorry for the delay," Rosa Legni says. Her English is old-school Oxford-donnish, quite different from Marco and Chiara's vaguely transatlantic tones. "I'm afraid time management has never been my strength. I schedule so many meetings and then end up hurrying from one to the other. Frida tries to keep me in line, of course, but it's impossible. Sit, sit, make yourself comfortable. Don't just hover there, please."

Obediently I sit down in the nearest armchair while Rosa settles onto the couch. "It's very kind of you to make time for me," I say.

"Oh, it's nothing, nothing at all. I like to talk about my father. Now, before we begin, I have something for you—if I can only find it." She's rooting through a huge leather bag. "Ah, here it is," she says, and hands me a slightly crumpled A4 envelope. I open it and pull out two pieces of thin typewritten paper.

"That's the menu for the party," Rosa explains. "The one where your grandmother and Achille first met. And that's the guest list. You might know some of the names."

"Wow." Even from the few I recognize instantly—Roberto Rossellini, Federico Fellini, Anna Magnani—it was obviously quite an event. "I don't suppose you were there, too?"

"In fact, I was. My father had a very liberal attitude to childrearing. My mother died when I was born, so he raised me. I went everywhere with him and did whatever I liked. Of course, you've seen some of the evidence." She nods towards the photograph on the far wall. "I'm afraid I could be rather a pain."

"I'm sure you weren't," I say, not entirely truthfully.

"Oh, I'm quite certain I was, but it was a great education. Sadly, my own children turned out terribly conventional and had no interest in staying up late or talking about politics. Anyway, I was at that party, although I was just eight years old—no, nine—and I shall try to recall everything I can."

"Do you mind if I record this?"

"Of course not. You must do whatever you need." She watches as I fiddle with my phone and put it on the arm of the sofa, pointed towards her. "Is it on?"

"Yes."

Rosa shakes her head. "Marvelous things, these phones. Well, like I say, I was *very* young when that particular party took place. I stayed for a while and then went to bed, not that anyone would have made me. But I remember a few things, and one of those things is Achille."

"He really made such an impression?" I ask.

"I should say so." She smiles. "My father's circle was full of serious, vocational people: writers, artists, actors, musicians. They might have been great performers in public, but they were often quite introverted, and they saw our house as a safe environment. So they were all standing or sitting around, clustered into little groups and having the most horrendously earnest discussions. And then in comes Achille . . . well, how can I describe him? He must have arrived a good two hours after the party started, and he'd come straight from the garage—apparently there had been some emergency he'd had to deal with, some mechanical issue with one of the cars. He'd taken off his overalls, at least. But his clothes were rumpled and his hair was disheveled and he had this streak of black grease . . ." Rosa traces a line with one finger, across her cheekbone. "He was quite something."

"What did you think of him?"

"Oh, I thought he was wonderful. Divine. You know, I had this book of Greek myths that one of my father's friends had given me—I loved that book—and it was just as if Achilles, the real Achilles, had walked into my living room. *Aristos achaiōn.*"

"The best of the Greeks," I say reflexively.

"*Brava.* Of course, you're a classicist," Rosa says. "I google everyone I meet—well, Frida does, and then she tells me the interesting bits. Which college, by the way?"

"I was at St. Gilbert's."

"Oh, lovely. Lankester Hall." Rosa taps herself on the chest. "Of course, it doesn't exist anymore. Anyway, Achille. You know, I've wondered so many times since then whether he knew the effect he was having. I might even suspect him of making an entrance. But I don't know, really. From everything I've heard about him, he was a man who could never be anything other than himself, no matter how much it disconcerted people."

"Maybe he wanted to disconcert them," I say.

Rosa laughs. "You could well be right."

"Was my grandmother already at the party then? Do you remember?"

"Yes, she was," Rosa says. "Now, this is where it gets a little blurry, because that party became a sort of landmark. Especially for my father and for Rita, your grandmother, and really for everyone who cared about Achille. So I can't always tell what I actually remember—what I saw and understood at the time—and what I heard about later. But Rita was certainly there already, she and her young man."

"Really? She had a boyfriend already?"

"Yes. He was one of my father's poets, very promising, very serious. His name was . . . Roberto, that's right. Roberto Borsetti. That's why Rita was there in the first place—she came along with him. But she went home with Achille."

"Wow."

"Are you shocked?" Rosa asks.

"Oh, no," I say. "But my grandmother was always so correct. I can't imagine her just ditching her boyfriend and going off with someone else."

"Well, our circle didn't care much for bourgeois morality. And she was young, and it was Achille, for heaven's sake. I think half the people there would have gone home with him if they had the chance. But they didn't get the chance, because he wanted Rita and she wanted him. From the moment Papà introduced them—and I don't think for a moment that he knew what he was doing, though he always liked to take the credit—your grandmother and Achille were absorbed in one another. It was absolutely obvious. I don't think poor Roberto even tried to put up a fight, though apparently he did get rather drunk and proposition Anna Magnani. Not that he stood a chance with her, either."

Well, I think. Fair enough.

For the next half hour or so, Rosa tells me every detail of the party she can remember: who was there and with whom, the overheard conversations, the fight that erupted between a poet and a critic over the merits of Russian Futurism. ("Ingrid Bergman broke that one up, if I remember rightly.") And in the midst of it all, Granny and Achille: heads together, talking intently in the corner of the room and then slipping out into the night, hand in hand, saying goodbye to no one.

"I was spying on them," Rosa says frankly. "I was too young to understand properly, but I'd read a great number of love stories—Papà never kept me from reading anything, you can imagine—and I knew what I was seeing. It fascinated me."

"And that was the first time Achille came to the house?" I ask.

"The first and only. It wasn't really his element. He spent most of his time with his team and the rest with your grandmother, and that was all he wanted. He didn't need my father to be his friend." Rosa laughs. "Oh, Papà tried, of course. He was a real mother hen, always wanting to keep people around him and tend to their needs, but he got nowhere with Achille. It's not that he was cold, or rude—far from it, he simply wanted to get on with his work and he didn't see the point in wasting his time socializing. The Scuderia Guelfa was a revolutionary project and it was really Achille who drove it, if you'll pardon the pun. My father invested his money, but Achille gave his soul. That's why it couldn't go on after his death."

"What happened to the . . . well, stuff?" I ask. "The cars, the equipment, whatever else?"

"All sold. Papà didn't care about scraping back his costs. He just sent it all to auction, even Achille's beautiful custom-built Formula One car. I think that ended up overseas somewhere. The garage was leased, so that was easy. But there were plans to build a proper installation, track and everything, not far from Romituzzo. I believe they were in the middle of applying for planning permission—and that's no minor process in Italy, with no minor outlay—but the whole thing was dropped. He just didn't want anything to do with the project, ever again."

"I don't suppose . . ." I begin, but Rosa seems to have read my mind. She's already shaking her head.

"There's nothing I can show you, I'm afraid. My father was active in radical politics until the day he died. His papers are subject to the utmost secrecy. There are simply too many people to protect."

Damn. "I understand. Thank you very much for these, anyway," I say, waving the envelope with the guest list and menu.

"I wish I could help more," Rosa says. "As it is, I'm afraid I shall have to wind this up. Frida will be along any minute to shepherd me into another meeting. Do you have any more questions before I go?"

"Yes, actually, if that's all right. Did my grandmother keep in touch with your family after Achille died?"

"To some extent." Rosa smiles. "She was rather like Achille, you know. Self-contained. She and Papà kept in touch, and I know they used to have coffee together whenever she was in town. But that was here at the office, not at home. I don't think she ever came to the house, though I'm sure he invited her. Perhaps it was too painful. She must have had other friends in Florence, though. Or maybe you've found some of them already?"

"Well, sort of," I say.

"What do you mean, sort of?"

I sigh. "Granny used to bring me here all the time, but I was so young and, like you say, she was quite . . . self-contained. I know she had friends here—good friends, even—but there was only one place I really saw her let her guard down, and now I can't find it." And I explain about Giuseppe and Maria and the case of the vanishing bar.

Suddenly, Rosa doesn't seem so friendly. "But that just sounds like a normal Italian bar," she says, and there's a distinct chill in her voice. "Why should it strike you as so unusual?"

"It doesn't, of course." I'm aware I sound defensive. Sitting opposite Rosa with her eyes boring into me, it's all starting to feel like one of my less comfortable college tutorials. "Not in itself. But it wasn't Granny's kind of place, and I suppose that's why it stood out."

Rosa raises an eyebrow. "Not her kind of place. I see. I suppose you think it's demeaning for a woman of your social class to go to an ordinary bar?"

"Of course not, but—"

"Your grandmother was an anti-Fascist," Rosa cuts across me. "And that is not some shallow ideological position, but a fundamental orientation. Everything she did, every connection she forged was founded on a basic commitment to social equality. Had she been any less than a committed anti-Fascist, had she divided the world as you do into rich and poor, acceptable and unacceptable, then my father could never have respected her as he did. And Achille could never have loved her."

I open my mouth to protest, but Rosa's already pulling herself to her feet. She goes to the door and almost flings it open. I get the message. I switch off my phone and make my way out under her censorious gaze.

"Thanks for your time," I say meekly.

"Good luck with your work." *Now fuck off*, she doesn't say—but I definitely hear it.

27

"ROSA LEGNI TOLD YOU TO FUCK OFF?" MARCO SOUNDS AMAZED. HE'S folding shirts, creasing them with military precision before placing them in his expensive-looking black suitcase. I'm sitting at the head of the bed, watching him. It's quite hypnotic.

"She didn't say it, not in words. But she definitely indicated I should."

"You got some good material, though?"

"Yeah, I did. She was very generous right up to the point where she accused me of being a class snob. Again, by implication," I add before he can ask. "It was really startling."

He fastens the elastic straps across the neatly folded clothing and then zips the suitcase shut. "I suppose these old-school Marxist intellectuals can be a bit . . ."

"Arsey?"

"I was going to say doctrinaire, but that works, too." He comes and sits next to me on the bed, puts his arm around me and pulls me in. "It's not too late to come along if you want. I'm sure we can get you a ticket."

The idea's so appealing that I almost say yes. But I need some time alone, I tell myself. No matter how understanding Marco is, I should take this chance to pull myself together. I owe him that. "That's lovely of you. But who would look after Nuvolari?" I point to the spiky little succulent plant sitting on the dresser.

"Ha," Marco says, and gives me a squeeze. "Well, if you change your mind you'll call me, right?"

"Right."

"Okay. And you remember where everything is? Keys, Wi-Fi password, instruction manuals . . ."

"It's all fine, honestly. What I don't know I'll figure out, and if I can't figure it out, I'll call you." He's looking at me so tenderly that I have to fight the urge to say yes actually, please take me with you. "You'd better go."

Marco looks at his watch. "Ah. Yes." Kissing me hastily, he gets up and grabs his suitcase. "Take care, Tori, will you? I'll see you soon."

Don't leave me. The words rise so suddenly, so fiercely that I have to bite them back. "I'll miss you," I say.

A smile and a kiss and he's gone. I curl up and press my face into the pillowcase, hoping for just a little of his scent. But all I can smell is fresh air and washing powder, because he changed the sheets especially for me. He told me that when I came round. It's silly of me to be disappointed.

I lie there until I start to feel that horrible drag of impending sadness, and then I make myself roll off the bed and onto my feet. It's lunchtime, technically, but I'm not hungry. The city outside is like a furnace; the shutters in the living room are all closed, casting it into an odd sort of faux-twilight gloom. My laptop's sitting on the table, and I think about finding the Wi-Fi password—which I'm almost sure Marco said was somewhere in the second bedroom he uses as a study—but decide against it. I'll feel better if I get something written. No distractions, no Netflix, no messing around online. I pick up my phone, connect my headphones and start to transcribe the recording of my conversation with Rosa.

It's long, fiddly work. I haven't done much transcription since my *Cherwell* days—back when I thought I'd get to be a proper journalist—so by the time I've got most of it down, the heat of the day has passed. I open the shutters and see the street already filling up with people. Part of me wants to close the shutters again and get into bed, but that won't do me any good. If I lie down now, all I'll do is think about how I should have gone to Rome. I pick up my bag and head downstairs.

⁓

SANTA CROCE BASILICA IS A HUGE, POINTY, FLAT-FACED EDIFICE IN that green-and-white striped marble the Florentines apparently really loved at some stage. The steps in front are populated with students and tourists and schoolkids sitting in clusters, chatting or scrolling through their phones or indulging in the usual PDA. To one side, a colossal statue of Dante looks scornfully down, snatching his cloak away as if he doesn't want to be associated with such frivolity. The square and the streets around it are lined with bars and cafés and funky little restaurants, but somehow I find it hard to settle on one. They all seem a little too crowded, a little too public—not that I usually mind that. I'm just not in the mood for other people's hilarity.

In a side street a couple of blocks from the basilica I find a small bar with a handful of people sitting outside, on their own or talking quietly in pairs. This I can deal with. I sit down at a spare table in the shade and order a negroni. This arrives with a huge plate of snacks: crisps, nuts, olives, those ring-shaped crackerbread things—taralli, that's it—rice crackers and a little pile of cut-up sandwiches stacked with thin-sliced ham and cheese. I have to remember this place. I sit back and sip my drink, steadily working through the food while I stare out at the street, and fall into a sort of meditative state.

My negroni's almost gone when I become aware that there are people at the table next to mine. And they're clearly on a date. I can never resist eavesdropping on a date. I take my shades out and put them on, picking up my phone as if checking for messages, and take a surreptitious look. He's sitting closest to me: a stocky, bearded man in a tight-fitting T-shirt, his body angled outwards towards the street, legs casually open. She's sitting across the table, nursing a spritz, and her focus is entirely on him—well, on his right ear.

"It's nice, isn't it, this place," she says in a soft Irish accent. "I'm glad we picked it." I can practically hear the plea in her voice.

"Oh yeah," he says. He might be American or Canadian, I can't tell. "Oh yeah. It's a great spot for people watching." He leans back, spreads his legs even further and turns his head away from her, surveying. "That's what I feel like doing this evening," he says. "Just people-watching. Don't take it personally, okay?"

"Okay." Her gaze is fixed on the side of his face. "No, I get it. It's totally fine."

The two of them fall into silence. She picks up a rice cracker and toys with it, taps it absently on the edge of the plate and sets it back down again. She's clearly working up to saying something, some witty retort she hopes will pull his attention back to her. My phone buzzes in my hand.

I open the message and almost burst out laughing. It's Marco, and he's taken a selfie in front of what I guess is the dome of St. Peter's Basilica. He never takes selfies. He's winking and blowing me a kiss, and just over his shoulder an elderly priest in a cassock is turning to look at him, one eyebrow disapprovingly raised. City of love, the caption reads. Wish you were here.

I'm trying to think of a witty comeback when there's movement in the corner of my eye. The woman has risen to her feet and is hoisting her bag onto her shoulder.

"Actually, no," she says. "No, it's not okay. I'm going."

The man leans back further, contemplating her. "You all right?"

She shakes her head. "I liked you," she says. "I liked you, and I thought . . . ever mind. Have a good evening."

"Uh . . . okay. Whatever." There's something in the man's voice, a note of contempt that's horribly familiar. It makes my skin creep.

"Bye," the woman says, and she turns and walks away fast, head down and shoulders stiff. I wonder whether to go after her, but she's already pulling her phone out of her bag. I hope there's some sympathetic friend waiting to listen.

"Crazy bitch," the man says. He looks around as if touting for witnesses and, turning, catches my eye. He gives me a broad, warm smile and nods towards my negroni glass. "Hey, can I get you another one of those?"

"No," I say, perhaps a little more sharply than I meant to, and he shrugs.

"Suit yourself."

I turn back to my phone, try to think of something to send to

Marco. But I can't concentrate, so I pay my bill and start walking back towards the flat. I tell myself I'll take it easy, make some pasta and watch something ridiculous on Netflix. I've worked so hard today—I deserve a break. But once I'm back in Marco's flat, with Marco's things everywhere and no Marco, I find I can't settle. I sit on the couch with a glass of wine in front of me and fiddle with my phone, switching restlessly from message to browser to app until somehow, inevitably, I'm looking up trains from Florence to Rome.

They leave pretty often. Twice an hour, in fact, and the last one's at quarter past ten. If I wanted to, I'd have time to pack, have something to eat, call Marco and let him know I'm coming. I could be in Rome before midnight, if I wanted to.

I really want to.

My finger hovers over the "buy" button. But something's holding me back—multiple things. I should really talk to Ambra again. I should transcribe more letters. I should start hammering out an outline for the book, something I can send to Richenda. I should call Richenda, for that matter, and make sure everything's all right with the contract. What's the point in doing all that from some random hotel room when I'm perfectly well set up here? What's the point in sitting around all day waiting for Marco to be free when he'll be back in a week's time anyway? Am I really so needy, am I really so lacking in backbone that I can't bear being away from him for even a few days? *Pathetic*, whispers Duncan's voice in my mind. *Just pathetic.*

I close the app. Just as I do, my phone starts to ring. Marco, the display says. I quickly end the call.

Sorry, I type. Swamped in work, can't talk. Have a good evening xxx

I don't wait to see his reply. I shut my phone off, pull the shutters closed and start getting ready for bed.

28

Stella

THE MONTHS AFTER THE LIBERATION OF ROMITUZZO WERE HARD and exhilarating. The Allies had pushed the Germans as far as the Apennines and stopped, intending to wait out the winter before resuming the offensive. And so, as before, Italy was split into two zones: free and occupied. The difference was that we were in the free zone.

There was still plenty to do. There were food packages and supplies to distribute; there were meetings to attend and messages to run as the Resistance movements directed their focus north of Florence, towards the Gothic Line. Don Anselmo had work for me, too, and even more than usual since he was filling in for don Mauro at St. Catherine's in addition to his own parish and political work. Soon I was as busy as I had been during the occupation, and when school resumed in September—with a hastily assembled new curriculum, and without the Fascist claptrap—I was back to my old routine of rising before dawn and coming home at nightfall.

My mother never asked where I had been; she spoke to me only to give me my chores or reprimand me when my work didn't meet her standards. My father could not even look at me. Only Achille was his old affectionate self, but I saw him so rarely that it scarcely made a difference. Between the garage, his bikes and his own political activity, he was as busy as I was.

Nevertheless, life was exciting in a way it had never been before. I carried a weapon when I went out on my rounds, and not a dainty little gun in my bra but a Beretta at my hip. Agnese had given me some marksmanship training and pronounced my skills more than satis-factory. I wore my white kerchief and a *tricolore* armband and carried a card declaring me a member of the Romituzzo National Liberation Committee. It scarcely mattered that my parents wouldn't acknowl-edge me. I was becoming my own woman, and every night as I fell into bed I resolved that I'd get out of that house as soon as I possibly could.

~~~

"THE SIN OF PRIDE," DON ANSELMO SAID. "I'M SURE YOUR MOTHER and father are hurt that you betrayed their trust—yes, even for a good cause. But there's pride there too, a whopping great dose, and I'm afraid we can only pray that they get over it."

"What do you mean?" I asked. It was one of those dark chilly evenings in early December and we were sitting in the parlor of the parochial house, going through the clothes we had collected for the refugee shelter run by some Dominican sisters near San Damiano.

Don Anselmo folded a little woolly vest into neat quarters. "Well, to a degree it's understandable. You've been doing this dangerous work right under their noses, and they knew nothing about any of it. They're bound to feel as if they failed to protect you—your father, in particular, will feel that very deeply. That's one form of pride. But this whole business of cutting you out, of treating you as *persona non grata* in your own home . . ." He shrugged and took another vest from the pile on the table between us. "It reminds me of my father's reaction when I decided to go to seminary. He never spoke to me again, though I tried many times to make up with him for my mother's sake. He died without speaking to me."

"Really? I thought he would be proud of you for becoming a priest."

"Oh, plenty of parents are, of course. My mother was. But I was the eldest son, you see, and in my father's view I was supposed to become an important businessman like him. Besides, being a priest wasn't exactly his idea of being a man. Now look at this! What do you think?"

He held a boy's jersey out to me. It was made of coarse gray-brown wool and had been darned and patched so many times that it was thick and misshapen. It had clearly been passed down from sibling to sibling, perhaps even over generations.

"One scarcely knows what to do with such a thing," don Anselmo went on. "Like the widow in the parable, they have given all they have. And yet to give this to some other poor soul . . ."

"Maybe it can be picked apart and knitted into something new," I said.

"Yes, perhaps. I shall put it aside and show it to Assunta later on." Don Anselmo took a shirt from the pile and began to inspect it. "And how is your young man?"

I felt myself turn hot. "If you mean Enzo, he isn't my young man."

"Oh? I am sorry. Have you stopped, ah, seeing one another?"

"No!" I was embarrassed, terribly embarrassed to be telling this to don Anselmo of all people, but indignation spurred me on. "We weren't ever seeing one another, not really. Not like that. But then he came back from Santa Marta and he simply assumed that we would . . . that I would . . ."

"He was presumptuous," don Anselmo said, rather severely.

"Yes. He expected me to do whatever he asked, and he didn't want me to keep up my work. And he didn't want me to wear my kerchief. As far as he's concerned, he was a real fighter and I was nothing but an errand girl. And he said that if I did insist on wearing it, people would think . . ." My jaw was tight, and I realized that I was twisting a woolen sock in my hands as if I were wringing the neck of a goose. I threw it back on the pile. "I don't want to repeat what he said."

Don Anselmo smiled wryly. "I think I can guess. Since you were doing undercover work, and since you are a young woman, and since you happened to survive the occupation and avoided the fate of poor Berta Gallurì—God rest her soul—then he knows that at least some small-minded souls will suspect you of, shall we say, consorting with the enemy? Because I dare say you've heard such fatuous rumors yourself, you and the other women in our movement. And so has Enzo, and it bothers him."

"I don't know why people say these things," I burst out. "I don't know why they even think them. It doesn't make sense."

"No, it doesn't. But, Stella . . . look. When you go home tonight, open your New Testament—I know you have one, for I gave it to you—and look at the passages about Mary Magdalene. You'll see that she was healed by Jesus, and that she went to the tomb and saw the risen Lord. She saw Him before the men did. But you won't see a single thing to indicate that she was a harlot—not that it would make a bit of difference if she were, but anyway. It was the Church that called her that particular name." He leaned forward and looked at me so earnestly that I almost forgot my indignation. "What I'm trying to say, my child, is that those who truly love and understand you will never insult your good character. And you may disregard those who do. I hope you sent Enzo away with a flea in his ear?"

"Yes." I didn't want to repeat exactly what I had said, either.

"Well, that's very pleasing. I expected no less. And I suppose your brother isn't too happy with him?"

"I haven't told Achille," I said. "I don't need him to fight my battles."

"Quite right," don Anselmo said. "Still, you're more restrained than I would be. Shall I ring for Assunta and ask her if she has any of that marvelous chocolate our American friends brought last week?"

We drank coffee and ate chocolate and chatted about nothing until all the clothes were sorted and folded, ready for the sisters. Don Anselmo rose to his feet with some difficulty and accompanied me to the door. He seemed older and smaller since don Mauro had died, and there were shadows under his eyes.

"Now, you will find a moment to come and see me tomorrow evening, won't you?" he said as I stepped outside. "I have one or two matters I'd like your help with."

I was relieved that he'd asked. It meant that I didn't have to invent some reason to look in on him. "Of course. I have a couple of things to do after school, but I'll come round straight afterwards."

Don Anselmo smiled. He seemed relieved, too. "Just whenever you can, my child. I shall be here. Goodnight and God bless you."

⊸≫⊸

I DIDN'T HAVE ANYTHING ELSE TO DO THAT EVENING. THAT WAS unusual—as a rule I scarcely had a minute to myself, but today was an anomaly. After leaving don Anselmo, I had nowhere to go other than home. And I didn't want to go home before I absolutely had to.

I was sitting on a bench in piazza Burresi, swinging my heels and trying not to think about wanting my dinner, when I heard a familiar voice.

"Comrade!" Davide was crossing the square towards me, his shoulders hunched and his hands stuffed in his pockets against the cold. "You can't imagine how happy I am to see you."

I was happy to see him, too. We had scarcely crossed paths since the Liberation. He'd stayed in Romituzzo just long enough to make sure our invalids were healing and our new government was stable before heading to Florence, itself freshly liberated, to work at the hospital there. I knew that he occasionally made it back to visit Lucia, but I'd been avoiding the Frati house. It was bad enough that I had to see Enzo at the garage, to witness him and my father banding together to freeze me out.

Davide sat down next to me and smiled. "I hear you're quite the pillar of our community. Always running here and there with your gun and your kerchief, even if it is the wrong color."

I didn't know what to do with his teasing. It made my throat hurt and I felt suddenly, horribly, like I might cry. "We are all anti-Fascists," I said, sounding rather stiffer than I meant to.

"I know, I know." He nudged me with his shoulder. "I'm sorry. Honestly, I'm relieved Romituzzo has someone like you—someone really serious, someone who's always ready to work and learn and work some more. It gives me hope for our future."

But it was too late. The tears had risen and now they were spilling over, pouring down my face and making me ashamed.

"Oh," Davide said, and put his arms around me. "What's wrong, Stella? Tell me."

And I told him. I couldn't stop myself. I wept it out, all of it, in broken and stuttering words: my parents' cruelty and Enzo's scorn, and how Achille—beloved Achille, my friend, my ally—didn't even notice. "It isn't fair," I sobbed at last, like a hurt child, which I was, really. "It isn't fair!"

Davide pulled me in tight, tight, so that my face was pressed into his lapel. His wool coat smelled of tobacco smoke and fresh air. "No," he said quietly into my ear. "It isn't fair. You don't deserve to be treated like this. But you have me, and I have you, and we'll stick together whatever happens. Even if the whole world's against us. Agreed?"

I couldn't speak. I could only nod.

"Good," Davide said. He shifted his grip on me and planted a brotherly kiss on the top of my head, and I thought he would let me go, but he didn't. For a long time he just held me and I held him, like mourners at a funeral.

We had never held each other before. We never did it again. But nobody in Romituzzo would believe me if I said that now.

❦

ALL THROUGH THAT WINTER, DON ANSELMO GREW OLDER AND frailer almost by the day. He moved slowly and picked at his food, and there was a sadness about him that never quite abated. Really, I should have known what was coming. But it was still a shock when he asked me to the parochial house one evening in early March and told me, after much careful preparation and several squares of precious, hoarded chocolate, that he would be leaving our parish.

"But when?" I asked. "Why?"

"The 'when' isn't quite settled—we don't even have a replacement for don Mauro yet, never mind me. The war has complicated everything in that regard. But I shall go as soon as it's feasible, whenever that may be. And as for why . . ." He was looking at the fire. "Dr. Bianchi says ominous things about my heart and my kidneys and my stomach lining, but the truth is, my dear child, I'm worn out. I have been fighting for a very long time and I'm simply not up to the task anymore. Not physically, and not in here." He tapped a finger against the breast of his cassock. "Besides, I have my orders."

"From God?" I asked, and he looked at me and smiled.

"From the archbishop. Though I rather think he and God are on the same page, as they so often tend to be."

I wanted to argue, to plead with him to stay with us at least until the war was over—but I couldn't. It was simply unarguable. "Where will you go?" I asked.

"Further south, that much I know. Perhaps even very far south, to Sicily. I hear there's a wonderful rest home on the coast near Palermo, and they say the climate is so healing."

As I left him that day, he put a hand on my shoulder. "My child, I must ask you to keep this news of mine to yourself. Until the details are quite certain, it would only cause unrest in our community and that would not be right, especially now. But I wanted to tell you in particular."

"But you'll say goodbye before you go," I said. "You won't just leave."

"Dear Stella," he said, "of course I shall say goodbye, if God lets me. I should hate for you to feel abandoned."

When I got home that night, Achille was out somewhere and my parents had already gone to bed. Dishes were piled up in the kitchen sink, and on the table was a basket full of the clothes I had ironed that morning before school. They looked as if they had been angrily crumpled up and slung back in at random.

Next to the basket was a note in my mother's firm, slanting hand:

> Stella,
>> Wash dishes
>> Scrub floor
>> Clean stove
>> Iron clothes **_properly_**

I sat down at the table and put my face in my hands. My head was throbbing, and don Anselmo's words were going around and around in my mind. *I should hate for you to feel abandoned.*

That was exactly how I felt. Abandoned by my parents, on whom I was helplessly, frustratingly dependent. Abandoned by Achille— abandoned by don Anselmo—abandoned by everyone.

I knew then that I would not stay in Romituzzo when the war was over. Nothing was worth it: not school, not the promise of teaching, not even the safety of a roof over my head. I would find a place where I was wanted, and I would go.

❧

WHEN ACHILLE CAME DOWNSTAIRS THE NEXT MORNING, HE FOUND me at the ironing board. "Morning, little sister," he said. "Hard at work, eh? I don't suppose you've got a clean shirt for me? I'm not sure this one can last another day."

"I ironed all your shirts yesterday," I said. I had not slept in the few hours allowed to me but had lain there seething, rehearsing over and over every slight my parents had dealt out to me in the last months. And then I'd got up, in the dark, and had scrubbed the floor and washed the dishes and cleaned and polished the stove, and all the time I had kept seething. "I even put them all on the end of your bed. But obviously Mamma got to them before you did, so now I have to iron them all again."

Achille frowned. "What do you mean, you have to iron them all again?"

"I mean what I said. My work wasn't good enough yesterday, by Mamma's standards, so today I have to iron all the clothes all over again. Your shirts included, sorry. And then no doubt Mamma will find a streak on the floor or a smudge on the stove, and then I'll have to do that all over again, too. It never ends." I pushed my damp hair back off my forehead and kept on ironing the creases out of my school underskirt, pressing the heavy iron down into the fabric and letting it sit there just a fraction too long so that the smell of singed cotton filled the air. Achille was watching me.

"Oh, sit down," I said. "I'll make your breakfast in a minute."

But Achille didn't move. I set the iron down on its end and looked at him, and he stared back at me with baffled innocence.

"Does she really do that?" he asked. "Mamma. Does she make you redo all your chores?"

"Enough of them."

"It doesn't seem fair," he said. "You already do lots around the house. And you've got school."

"I know."

"And your work."

"I know!" I snapped, and Achille flinched. Of course, I had never shouted at him before. "But this is how it is," I said, forcing myself to speak gently now, trying to mollify him even as another part of me wanted to scream and shake him for being so obtuse. "You know Papà's still angry at me about my courier work. And you know Mamma doesn't love me."

"Stella, don't say that. Of course she—"

"She doesn't love me. Not even the smallest fraction of how she loves you. She's always treated me differently. You know, because you've stood up for me so many times. You know, so stop pretending."

Achille hung his head. For a little while we just stood there in silence with the ironing board between us. My words seemed to linger in the air like fog: those cold, true things I had said and now couldn't take back.

"It isn't right," he said at last. "It isn't fair. I'll talk to her about it—to both of them."

My anger was ebbing now, leaving tiredness and resignation behind. I wished I had never said anything to Achille. I wished I didn't have to deal with his bewilderment now, when my own was so painful. "No, don't," I said. "It won't help."

"But I have to. Someone's got to stand up to them."

"I did. I stood up to Papà. He didn't even want to let me go to school."

"That isn't enough. Stella, they can't keep treating you like this. They just can't. I won't let them."

Achille's face was flushed. He had that determined look about him, the look that said: *I'm going to do this stupid thing, and you can't stop me.*

"No," I said. "Don't antagonize them."

"I won't *antagonize* them. I'll just—"

"Anything you do or say will antagonize them." There was a knot in my chest and I was choosing each word, struggling to keep my voice level. I knew that if I broke down, Achille would want to protect me, and then he'd storm off to confront Mamma and Papà and all hell would break loose. "They're punishing me because they're hurt that I lied to them for so long. That's bad enough, but it's understandable. Maybe they'll even get over it in a while. But if you start arguing with them on my behalf—you, of all people—then they'll punish me even more."

"But—"

"Please believe me," I said. "If you fall out with them because of me, then it will be my fault. That's how they'll see it. And they'll take it out on me, not you. So please, Achille, don't talk to Mamma and Papà about this. Don't make it worse. Please."

29

Tori

THE SADNESS CREEPS UP ON ME. IT COMES ON SO QUIETLY, SO EASILY, that I don't notice for a while. I work and eat and force myself out periodically for a coffee or a drink, and every time I do that the effort required is just a little bit harder until I find myself, on the fifth day, slouched on the sofa at seven in the evening wondering whether I can just go to bed now or whether I really ought to put in another hour of writing first.

I pick up my phone. I put it on silent a while ago, worn down by the *bzz-bzz* of new messages I couldn't be bothered to answer, and now I see that Marco has been in touch. Two hours ago, I realize with a pang of guilt. He's sent a snapshot of a young priest in a cassock and sunglasses straddling a Vespa and smoking what looks like a cheroot, with the caption Achille's clerical cousin. He's sent me so many pictures like this—a cheeky pigeon on the statue of Marcus Aurelius, two elderly ladies chatting up a pair of strapping carabinieri, a Swiss Guard ignoring a curious dog—and I've loved them all, and hated myself for not being able to summon up the energy for a proper reply.

Impressive! I type back. Are all the priests like that? I have this urge to visit the Vatican. ;)

Marco starts typing right away. Maybe he's been waiting for my message. Maybe he's been feeling neglected and oh God, I've gone and sent him a stupid joke about hot priests. I'm such a dick.

Only the Jesuits, I suspect. How are you doing? Is work OK? Nuvolari behaving himself?

I want to hear his voice. On impulse I tap his number and the phone starts to ring. He picks up before I can think twice.

"Tori!" There's so much noise I can hardly hear him. Music, voices, what sounds like a dog yapping. "Hang on," he says. "Hang on, I'll just . . . hey, guys." He's switched into Italian. "I have to take this call. It's my girlfriend."

There's a wave of noise from the other end, the sound of good-natured male derision. "Fuck you guys," Marco says. "Hang on . . ."

The noise dies down. "Sorry," Marco says, his voice suddenly perfectly loud and very clear. "Some old friends of mine . . . we always go for a drink when I'm here. I'd have suggested somewhere quieter if I knew you were going to call. How are you? Is everything all right?"

"You called me your *fidanzata*," I say.

"Oh. Yeah. I mean . . . is that, uh . . ."

"It's fine," I say, though my heart's speeding up and I feel a bit clammy. It could be excitement or panic—I don't know which, and I don't want to think about it now. "Really."

"Good." He sounds happy. "How's it going? There isn't anything wrong, is there? You haven't heard from . . ."

"No. No, it's all very peaceful here. Maybe a little too much," I admit. "I miss you."

"I miss you, too. Not long until I'm back, though. Just two more days."

"Two more days," I echo.

"Two more days." His voice is soft. Somewhere in the background, a siren wails. I imagine him standing in some winding, cobbled side street, maybe leaning against the wall while people stroll past him in chic 1950s clothing, because I mostly know Rome from the old films Granny used to love. "So what are you up to?" he asks.

"Not much," I say honestly. "I've been working a lot. I . . . I'm sorry I wasn't good at being in touch."

"It's fine. I know how it is when you're in Achille mode. Are you feeling all right? Is everything okay with the flat?"

"Yes, everything's fine." It's definitely panic I'm feeling. I want to get off the phone. "You should get back to your friends."

"I don't have to. I can stay here if you want to talk."

"That's lovely of you," I say. "But you should go and have fun, honestly."

"Are you sure?"

"Really. We'll see each other soon."

"You know it." I can hear the smile in his voice. "Okay, but you'll call me if there's anything, won't you? Promise?"

"Promise. *Buonanotte.*"

"*Notte, tesoro.*"

I end the call and look around me. It seems ridiculous that I've been sitting around here feeling sorry for myself when everything's so . . . well, I don't know what it is, but it definitely doesn't call for sitting around.

"Right," I say out loud. "No more."

The next couple of hours are a whirlwind. I gather up the empty pizza boxes from the coffee table, stack and run the dishwasher, make the bed, run the vacuum and collect up all the dirty laundry that's draped all over the bedroom. I hadn't realized how horribly messy the place was; hadn't seen the unwashed mugs and glasses, the hair in the shower drain, the toothpaste clumps in the sink. Isn't that what happens to people with depression? They stop seeing their surroundings. Thank God I called Marco when I did.

By the time I've finished, glowing with sweat and a sense of righteousness, it's just past nine and I'm starving. I could go out and get something to eat. Or I could stay in, actually cook something for myself and put a load of washing on—I should just about manage a rapid cycle before the night-time noise curfew. Or . . .

Or I could go home.

I mean, I *could* go home. There's no really good reason for me to stay here, is there? If Duncan hasn't been in touch by now, he's hardly likely to show up in the next couple of days. And hanging around here, waiting for Marco to come back . . . well, it clearly isn't doing my mood any good.

I don't give myself time to think. I throw my stuff into my overnight bag, pack up my laptop and tablet and check that everything's switched off. Then I head out and down the stairs before I can change my mind.

MY FLAT IS WARM AND STUFFY. I DUMP MY BAG ON THE FLOOR AND
march over to throw the windows open and let the night air in, damn-
ing the mosquitos that will inevitably come in with it. That's something I really like about Marco's flat, actually: all the windows have
bug screens, which ought to be absolutely bog standard in Florence
and yet, somehow, isn't. Maybe I could have screens fitted here. I
probably have to clear it with Federica—I'm sure there's something
about alterations in my contract—but she wouldn't mind, would she?
I'd only be adding to the value of the place. I should ask Chiara about
it. After all, I don't plan to move any time soon.

Unless I move in with Marco.

Not that it's likely in the near future. Or the mid-future. Or
maybe any time. I like living alone, I remind myself as I shove my
clothes in the washing machine and measure out detergent. I came
here to live alone, to have my own space, to put my work first. To put
myself first. I don't need to throw all that over for Marco, even if he
did call me his *fidanzata*. Which is actually quite a major thing to call
someone. I mean, it's not "fiancée"—well, it technically can be—but
it's mostly used in a pretty vague way to mean someone you're serious
about. Someone you might actually want to live with. Someone you
love. It's a big word, especially this early in a . . . well, relationship, evidently. It's a really big word.

I pour out a glass of wine and sink onto the sofa. For a long while
I just sit there, trying to make sense of what I'm feeling. I'm a bit
taken aback, to be honest. I didn't plan to get into anything serious—
certainly not now, maybe not ever. In the abstract, the thing terrifies
me. Actually, it terrifies me in the concrete sense, too. But it's Marco.
It's Marco, and while part of me wants to run away and never come
back, another part keeps thinking about whether we'd live here or I'd
move into his place or maybe we'd look for something else, something
a bit bigger where each of us can have a study. Maybe in Santa Croce,
or maybe south of the river . . . yes, somewhere near the Boboli Gar-
dens. Or even further south, just outside the city gates where there's
that lovely green avenue. Via Machiavelli, that's it. Still in the city, of

course, but it would be so easy just to hop in the car and drive south, to Siena or Arezzo or really anywhere . . .

A church bell shakes me from my reverie. Shit, it's almost half past ten and I still haven't eaten. I pick up the phone and order a pizza from my usual late-night place, then open up Achille's letters. I can't just sit here daydreaming. I need to get at least a few more pages done before I can let myself sleep. My mind's whirling and I keep reading the same sentence over and over again, but I'm finally getting into the rhythm of it when my doorbell buzzes. I press the button to open the main door and quickly head to the kitchen corner to top up my wine and get a couple of napkins from the drawer.

I'm just struggling to shove the cork back in the bottle when there's a knock at the door. "It's open," I call, because I've ordered from that place so many times that we're all long since on familiar terms. But whoever's on duty tonight must be new, because a second later there's another, louder knock.

"Okay, okay, I'm coming." I finally wedge the cork into the neck of the bottle and hurry to open the door. "Sorry about that—" I begin, and then the words die in my throat because it isn't the pizza guy at all. It's Duncan.

30

IT'S DUNCAN. HE'S TALLER THAN I REMEMBER, AND BROADER—HE'S
taking up the whole of the doorway, and he doesn't have any luggage
with him, only the shabby old shooting bag his grandfather owned.
He's let his beard grow in; there are dark patches under his eyes, and
he smells of sweat and airplane. And he's looking at me with something in his expression, something I don't like.

"Well?" he says. "Aren't you going to let me in?"

I step back reflexively and he pushes past me into the flat. "I wasn't
expecting you," I say.

"But you were expecting someone," he says. "You let me in. You
didn't ask who it was."

"A pizza. I ordered a pizza." He looks at me, face stony, as if I've
lied to him. As if he wants me to account for myself here, in my own
flat, months after I left him. "Look," I say, "you can't just show up like
this. This is my home."

He dumps his bag on the sofa and looks around. It's as if I haven't
spoken. "Nice place. I suppose a hotel was too basic for you?"

"This is my home," I say again.

"Fascinating what you'll waste your money on. Or your gran's
money, I should say. Charlie told me all about that, by the way, so
don't bother lying to me."

Of course she fucking did. "Duncan—"

The door buzzes again and I turn away gratefully and press the
intercom. I can feel Duncan's eyes boring into the back of my head.

"*Pizza,*" comes a tinny voice from the speaker, and I can't help but shoot him a look of triumph.

"Come on up."

It's Luigi, the son of the family who own the pizzeria. He hands over the box and asks how my book is going, and I say fine and ask after his new baby, and he whips out his phone to show me a photo of her wearing a ridiculously frilly dress and all the time I can feel Duncan's presence just offstage, glowering. My skin's prickling and I have that nasty cold feeling, the feeling you get when you might be sick. I say goodbye to Luigi and close the door, and only then does it occur to me that I could have asked him to create a distraction somehow, give me some reason to get away. Duncan doesn't speak Italian. He wouldn't have known.

I take the pizza over to the counter, avoiding Duncan's eye. "You can have some if you want," I say.

"What's on it?"

"Buffalo mozzarella and anchovies."

He snorts. "Disgusting."

"I didn't order it for you, I ordered it for me. Glass of wine?"

"No."

"Suit yourself." I take out the pizza-cutter-wheel thing I bought a while ago and busy myself slicing the pizza into manageable pieces, then I sit down at the counter. My hands are shaking, and the harder I try to stop them the more they shake, but I'm strangely determined to act normal. God, I wish I'd stayed at Marco's. I pick up a slice of pizza and take a bite, swallowing convulsively as the salty anchovy taste hits my tongue.

Duncan sighs. I hear it, and I hear the creak of the sofa as he sits down, but I don't look at him. "Tori," he says, "aren't we going to talk about this?"

"About what?"

"About *this,* for fuck's sake!" He pauses and clears his throat. "About our marriage. About you, running off to Italy to play at being a writer without . . . without giving me a chance to fix it. To fix us."

Now I look at him. "I did give you a chance," I say. "I gave you lots of chances. And I'm not playing at—"

"Yeah, yeah, okay, okay." Duncan holds up his hands in an exaggerated show of surrender. "You're a real writer. Fine. I just don't understand why you need to be one here, and not at home."

"But this is my—"

"Charlie thinks you're making a point," he goes on. "She says you're playing up, punishing me for what happened with your gran. And look, I'm sorry I'm not perfect. I made the wrong decision, and I admit it. All right? Can we stop this now?"

"I'm not playing up," I say, keeping my voice as level as I can. I'm clenching my jaw, I realize. "I told you I was leaving. I told you, and you said you didn't care, so I left."

"I didn't think you were *serious*." He looks as incredulous as he sounds. "I thought you were just being dramatic. God, I can't do anything right."

I can feel my blood pressure rising. But some still, cool voice tells me that the only way to deal with this is to stay as calm as I possibly can. I breathe out slowly and take a sip of wine before I speak. "Duncan, why have you come here? Why couldn't we talk on the phone?"

"Because I wanted to give you space," he says, with a distinctly martyred air. "I thought you'd calm down if I left you alone for a while."

"Right. And now you're here because . . . ?"

"Because this needs to end. I've been patient, I've tried to understand, but I've had enough now. You need to stop pissing about and come home."

My head's starting to pound. I close the pizza box and push it away from me. The smell of the anchovies is giving me nausea. "We're not having this conversation."

"But—"

"No," I snap, and then take another breath. "It's the middle of the night. I need to sleep, and I'm sure you do, too. I'll call you a taxi, and then we'll talk about this tomorrow in daylight." In a public place, I think. "Which hotel did you book?"

"I didn't book a hotel."

"What?"

"Of course I didn't. Why would I? I'll stay here until you've packed your things and sorted yourself out, and then we'll go. I've got us plane tickets for the day after tomorrow. I assume that's enough time."

The panic's rising. I put a hand on the counter to steady myself. "No, Duncan," I say. "I'm not going back. I'm sorry if you can't accept that, but it's true. And I want you to stay somewhere else. You can't sleep here."

Duncan gets to his feet. He walks towards me and all I can think about is how big he is, how angry he is, how much stronger he is than me. He comes up to the counter and leans forward just a little, just enough to make me want to lean away, and he says: "I'm not going back home on my own while *my wife* stays here without me. And I'm not going to a hotel. So stop whining and start packing."

Every nerve in my body is shrieking at me to back down. But then I find myself thinking of Stella. Stella, the scrappy little teenager who smuggled guns past big, scary men every day. If she could do that, I tell myself, then I can do this.

"All right, then, you sleep here tonight," I say. "You sleep here and I'll go . . ." I manage to stop myself just before I can mention Marco. "I'll sleep at a friend's place. We can have breakfast in the morning and sort everything out then. I'll text you where to meet." I hop down from the stool, pick up my keys and bag and head to the door.

Duncan's staring at me. "What are you doing?"

I open the door and then turn and give him my best I'm-so-reasonable smile—the one I used to give to obnoxious drunk stock-brokers. "Help yourself to whatever you need," I say. "Just shut the door behind you when you leave in the morning. If you need to go out before that . . . well, don't."

I step out and pull the door shut. As I hurry down the stairs, I half expect to hear his footsteps behind me, but there's only silence. Still, I'm most of the way to Santa Croce before I stop looking over my shoulder.

⁓

I DON'T SLEEP. I LIE IN MARCO'S BED AND REPLAY THAT AWFUL CON-versation over and over in my head. I want to talk to Marco, but it's too late to call him and anyway, I wouldn't know how to start—I don't think I *could* start and, besides, there's no sense in worrying him. I'll get rid of Duncan tomorrow. I'll insist he leaves, like I insisted on leaving him. In just a few hours, it will all be over. And in a few more, Marco will be home.

I smile at the thought. But I'm still shaking.

It isn't even six a.m. when I get a text from Duncan. Are you coming back so we can talk?

I roll my eyes. Meet you at Bar Dianora in an hour.

I don't know where that is, he replies. Just come here.

Right opposite the flat. Can't miss it. See you there. I shove the phone away and get up before I can see any more replies.

When I get to the bar, Duncan's waiting outside. To my shock, he looks terrible. Genuinely terrible: pale and crumpled, like he's been punched in the stomach. I feel a strange mix of relief, irritation and a horrible edge of guilt.

"Morning," I say. I almost ask whether he slept well, but it's obvious he didn't. And I don't want to be asked, either.

"Morning," he mumbles, and follows me in.

Behind the counter, Elisa gives me a cheery hello. I order a cappuccino with a chocolate pastry and turn to Duncan.

"What would you like?" I say as jauntily as I can. "The cappuccino's great here, but the espresso's lovely, too. Properly strong, but not at all rough. And the pastries are super." God, I sound like a primary school teacher.

He stares at me like I've just offered him the choice of death by beheading or disembowelment. "I don't mind."

"All right. He'll have the same," I tell Elisa, and she nods.

"Go and sit down and I'll bring it to you."

"Thanks. Inside or outside?" I ask Duncan, but he just shrugs. "Let's sit outside," I say, and lead the way to a table. I sit down, and Duncan slumps into the seat opposite and fixes me with tragic eyes. We sit there in awkward silence for a few moments, and then he speaks.

"There was hair gel in your bathroom cabinet," he says. "And shaving cream, and aftershave, and deodorant. Men's deodorant. With limes."

My head's starting to throb again. I feel weirdly like I've been caught in a lie, but I haven't lied, have I? "You went through my stuff," I say.

He shrugs again. "I was looking for something."

"Right. What were you looking for, exactly?"

"Can't remember."

"*Ecco a voi*," Elisa says. She puts a tray on the table between us and unloads the coffee and pastries. "Do you need anything else?"

"Oh, thanks, this all looks great." Duncan's watching us, eyes pivoting like he's a spectator at Wimbledon. I've never been more grateful for his staunch refusal to learn so much as a word of Italian.

Elisa raises an eyebrow. "Everything okay? Your friend doesn't look too happy."

"He isn't," I say in my cheery-teacher voice, and gesture to the pastry in front of me as if I'm describing it. "And he isn't my friend, either. He's my ex."

"The guy you told me about?"

"Right. And he just showed up here last night out of nowhere. He's been going through my things and now he's accusing me of cheating on him although I left months ago."

"Oh," Elisa says in the same faux-bright tone. "You mean, with . . ."

"Right," I cut in before she can say Marco's name. "Sorry for the drama, but he wanted to talk and I thought it was best to meet somewhere public."

"You did right. What a prick." Elisa shoots a smile at Duncan, who smiles faintly back. "If he starts to get nasty, just yell and I'll call the carabinieri. *Buon appetito*."

She pats my shoulder and hurries back inside.

Duncan gives me a suspicious look. "Were you talking about me?"

"Of course not," I say, and take a sip of my cappuccino.

"Well, I don't know, do I?" He picks up his spoon and stirs at the foam on his coffee. "I know you don't wear lime-scented aftershave, though," he says.

"I'm sorry," I say. And, oddly enough, I am a little bit sorry. He looks so broken down that, against all sense, I'm actually starting to wonder whether I really did do something wrong. Maybe I *wasn't* clear it was over. Maybe I could have done more and avoided this whole situation.

Duncan drops his spoon with a clatter and pushes his cup away. "I'm such an idiot," he says. "I'm a bloody idiot. Coming all the way here, thinking I could get you back, trying to convince you when all the time you've been . . . oh God!" He slumps forward. "I can't . . . I just . . ."

Oh, fuck. I lean forward and put my hand rather awkwardly on his arm.

"Look, Duncan." I lower my voice in the hope that this will somehow calm him down. "I can see this is a shock, and I am sorry. I wish you hadn't found out like this, but the fact is that . . ."

"I can't believe it!" To my horror, he grabs my hand and pulls it to him, holding it against his cheek. I try to extract it from his grasp, but he only grips it tighter. "I can't believe you'd actually . . . I never thought you'd be s-so . . . I thought you loved me." His voice is an agonized near-whisper. "I thought you loved me like I love you. Because I do love you, Tori. Maybe I don't always show it like you want me to, but I don't want to carry on without you. Don't make me."

"Tori!" someone says just over my shoulder. I turn and am deeply relieved to see Chiara, wearing a sharp suit and holding a takeaway cup of coffee. Oh, thank God, the cavalry's here.

She glances from me to Duncan and back again. "What's going on?" she says in Italian. "Isn't this your ex? The guy from the photo?"

I tug my hand away and this time Duncan lets go, burying his face in his hands in an attitude of abject suffering. "Yes. He just showed up out of nowhere—my awful sister gave him my address. I'm trying to get rid of him and he won't leave. Can you help me? I don't know, have a real estate emergency or something? You can make up any old shit, really. Just so long as I absolutely have to go with you right now."

For a moment I think Chiara's going to leap to it. I think she'll invent some brilliant excuse and whisk me away. After all, she's my friend, and she knows what Duncan did to me. But she's studying me. In fact, I realize, she's got that look again—that same quizzical look she gave me when I tried to explain why I'd married him, why I'd stayed so long. "But you were supposed to be staying at Marco's this week. Weren't you? Or have I missed something?"

"I was. I only came back to my flat to wash some underwear and, er, improve my mood." My Italian's going now, fragmenting under stress. "I didn't know he'd show up and I'd ordered a pizza but it wasn't pizza, it was him, and I can't make him go away and I don't know what to do. That's why I need your help. Please."

Chiara looks at Duncan, who's still hunched over in an attitude of misery, and then at me again. "I don't understand. I thought you broke up with him months ago."

"I did! I did break up with him, he just didn't . . . accept that I had," I finish lamely. Her disbelief is so obvious that even I'm starting to feel this is all a bit far-fetched.

Chiara shakes her head. She looks genuinely regretful, which is somehow even worse. "I'm sorry, Tori, but this is really weird. I can see there's something going on here and that it's distressing for you. I want to believe what you're telling me—I really do. But . . ." She sighs. "Marco's my best friend in the world. You know that. And there's something here that just doesn't add up. I wish I could help, but I can't, not in good conscience. I have to look out for Marco, and I'm going to have to tell him about this. I'm sorry. Good luck."

"Wait," I begin, but she turns on her heel and walks off.

"Sorry," Duncan says. He sits up, rubbing his face. "I embarrassed you in front of your friend."

"It's fine," I say, although it's not. It's not fine at all. I'm hurt, and I'm exhausted. All the broken nights, all the stress and fear and effort seem to be bearing down on me like a wave. "She's not my friend. Well, no, she is. But she's really close friends with, uh . . ."

"With him," Duncan says. "Mr. Lime-Aftershave Guy."

"Yeah."

"I suppose that's over, then."

He says it neutrally enough, but there's a hint of satisfaction in his tone. And, just like that, I lose the last of my tolerance. I reach for my purse and slap a ten-euro note on the table, anchoring it with my pastry plate. "Your flight's tomorrow, isn't it?"

"What?"

"I said, your flight's tomorrow. Right? You did say you'd booked one?" I shove my chair back and stand up. Hoisting my bag on my shoulder, I look Duncan straight in the eye. He goggles back at me.

"Um, yes. Tomorrow morning. I told you, I . . ."

"Right. So you need somewhere for tonight. Have you unpacked?"

"Er . . ."

"Doesn't matter. I'll go and get your things—you can wait here—and then we're finding you a hotel. Shouldn't be difficult around here."

"What do you mean, a hotel?" Duncan frowns. "I'm staying at yours."

"Duncan, no!" I'm beyond caution now, beyond diplomacy. "I want you out of my flat. I shouldn't have let you in to start with. I said *wait here*," I snap as he gets to his feet.

"Tori, you're overreacting." He doesn't raise his voice. But all the hurt is gone and there's that edge to it now, that scornful undertone that always used to make me feel small and ashamed, but it doesn't anymore. Now it just makes me furious. "I'm allowed to go where I want. Okay? There's no need to make a scene."

"Of course there's a fucking need," I say. "And I'm not making a scene. I just want you to leave me alone."

"Tori." He steps forward and puts a hand on my shoulder, and I jerk away. I'm aware of the people at the next table talking in whispers, of passers-by on the pavement opposite slowing down to look. Duncan notices, too, because he makes a face—a wry, exaggerated face that says *sorry, she's with me*. He takes my arm and I will myself to pull back again, but somehow I'm frozen.

"You're being hysterical and you need to calm down." His voice is low, almost caressing. "Now, I'm prepared to forgive you for fucking me around like this. But first we're going to go back upstairs together and sort all this out properly, in private, like reasonable people. Right?"

His eyes are locked on mine, his fingers pressing into my flesh. All I can do is stare up at him. And then there's a yell and Elisa comes rocketing out of the bar, phone held aloft.

"Let go of her," she commands. "Let go of her right now or I'll call the carabinieri."

Duncan's brows draw together. "What's she on about?"

"I call the *police*." Elisa brandishes the phone and he lets go of me, backing quickly away.

"Whoa," he says. "I think there's been a misunderstanding. My wife was upset and I was trying to calm her down. That's all."

"*Ma che stronzate!*" Elisa spits. Duncan looks puzzled.

"She says that's bullshit," pipes up a helpful American from the edge of the crowd that's starting to gather.

Elisa turns to me. "You want me to call?" she says in loud, clear English. "If you say, I call."

I take a long look at Duncan. He's crimson to the ears, and at least three people are clearly filming this on their phones. "No, it's fine," I say. "So long as he stays here while I fetch his stuff, and then fucks off quietly and never bothers me again, I think we can leave the carabinieri out of it."

There's a ripple of amusement. Duncan looks brilliantly disgruntled. "Of course," he says. "Obviously that's fine."

"Sit," Elisa barks, and he plonks down into the nearest chair and stares mutinously at his feet.

"I wasn't doing anything," he mutters, to nobody in particular. "I don't know what the problem is."

⌘

MY NERVES HOLD PRETTY WELL UNTIL DUNCAN'S GONE—PROTESTING, to the last, that I promised to help him find a hotel—and I've drunk a couple of coffees and listened gratefully to Elisa's reassurances that of course Marco will understand; that any decent man would, and that neither Duncan nor Chiara can possibly do anything to hurt my relationship with him but if by some remote chance they do, well then, good riddance. But my legs start to feel a bit wobbly as I'm climbing the stairs to my flat, and by the time I've shut the door behind me, all I can do is slump onto the sofa.

Part of me wants to call Marco right away. Time's ticking, and Chiara might get to him before I can. And if she does call him up and pour out all her concerns . . . well, who will he believe? The friend he's known since childhood, or the newish girlfriend who turned up in Florence a few months ago with a dramatic backstory and nobody to vouch for her? Obviously there's a real chance he'll believe Chiara, and it's pretty clear that, even with the best will in the world, Chiara doesn't understand about Duncan after all. So if I'm going to have any chance of keeping Marco around, whispers that urgent little voice, then I need to call him now, right now, and get my side in first.

Unless that makes me look even more defensive, of course. Which it might. And if he'd believe Chiara anyway, then what earthly difference does it make if I speak to him first? In a way, this is the acid test of our relationship. I don't want a man who *wouldn't* trust me implicitly, I remind myself. If I have to beg and plead and defend myself, then he isn't for me. I had enough of that with Duncan. So the best thing I can do—I know it logically, anyway—is leave the situation alone and see what Marco does when he gets back. He knew there was a chance that Duncan would show up. He must have known, from everything I've told him, that there was an equally strong chance he'd try to pull some kind of manipulative trick. If he doubts that for a moment, then that's his problem, not mine. I've only ever told the truth. I have nothing to hide.

I still want to call him, though. I think. I'm staring at my phone when it lights up with a call from an unknown number. I don't usually answer those—they're spam ninety-five percent of the time, but this time I'm so glad of the distraction that I pick up the call.

"*Pronto.*"

At the other end, someone clears their throat. "*Buongiorno*," says a voice—a hesitant, older female voice. "Am I speaking with Victoria MacNair?"

"Speaking."

"Good." The speaker clears her throat again. "Victoria, my name is Maria Furlan and I was a friend of Rita . . . of your grandmother. I don't suppose you remember me?"

Furlan. The unfamiliar surname throws me, and it takes a moment before I remember that I do know a Maria. A Maria, married to a Giuseppe, who ran an anonymous little bar in the Oltrarno quarter.

"I remember you," Maria says, before I can speak. "And I believe you've been looking for me. You're writing a book, is that right? About your grandmother and Achille Infuriati?"

"Yes, that's right. But how did you—"

"You were at the cemetery when I brought my roses. I had such a shock when I saw you," she adds with something between a laugh and a gasp. "I thought it was Rita back from the dead. I told Rosa Legni all about it the last time I saw her, and she gave me your number. I'm sorry if she was rude to you and tried to put you off. Her father used to look out for me, you see, and now that's her job. But I've been thinking about it and I believe I'd like to talk to you. There isn't really any reason to hide away and stay quiet, not anymore. I'm just so used to it. I've had a lifetime of it."

She sounds so nervous that my stomach twists in sympathy. "Maria," I say, "I'm so glad you got in touch, and that you want to speak to me. But I don't quite understand. You say you've been hiding away?"

"Yes. Because of my old life, you see."

I sit up. Gradually, inexorably, the loose ends are starting to come together.

"In your old life," I say, "did you have another name?"

"Yes," Maria says, and takes a shaky breath. "My name was Stella. Stella Infuriati."

31

NOW I DEFINITELY HAVE TO CALL MARCO. I TAP HIS NUMBER AND listen to it ring as I pace from window to door to kitchen to sofa to window.

"Hey, Tori! Everything okay?"

"I just heard from Stella," I say.

For a moment he doesn't answer. He must be walking somewhere—I can hear the *tap-tap* of footsteps on pavement. "Stella," he says. "Stella. Wait, you mean . . ."

"Yes. Stella Infuriati. And you know the most amazing thing? She's the lady with the flowers. And she's also Maria."

The footsteps stop. "Hang on, what? I don't understand."

"I don't really understand, either," I say. "I'll find out more, but you remember Granny's friend Maria, who ran the bar?"

"With the Bugatti and the hot grandson."

"Right. Well, she's actually Stella. And apparently the Legni family had been hiding her, somehow, but now she doesn't want to hide anymore and she wants to talk to me. For the book," I add, completely unnecessarily. "We're meeting tomorrow."

"Wow," Marco says. "This is . . . wow. Incredible. You found her."

"Well, not really. She found me."

"It's still incredible. We've got to celebrate," he says. "I'm taking you out as soon as I get back this evening. Deal?"

"Deal."

"Great. I can't wait to see you," he adds, in a low voice that brings the blood to my cheeks. "I've missed you."

"I've missed you, too." But that cold, creeping feeling is filtering back in, making me feel guilty, though I've nothing to be guilty about. "Uh . . . I don't suppose you've heard from Chiara?"

"Chiara? No, why? Is there a problem?"

"It's nothing, really—we had a misunderstanding. I'll tell you about it when you get back."

"Are you sure? If something's wrong . . ."

I almost tell him. I almost open my mouth and let it all spill out, but I can't just tell him over the phone that Duncan showed up. I need to do that in person. Maybe Chiara will call him before I can do it—maybe he'll even be as confused as she was, but that's a risk I need to take.

"No, it's fine. Nothing to worry about. I'll see you later, okay? At mine," I say hastily. "I'm back here now sorting things out."

"Okay. I'll come straight round. I can't believe it," he says. "About Stella. It's just fantastic."

"It really is," I say.

✍

BY MIDMORNING I'M FIZZING. I TRY TO WORK, OR REST, OR DO ANY-thing but obsess over what just happened with Duncan. But the fear's subsiding and the anger's rising. I can't think about anything else. I can't rest, and I'm certainly not going to get any work done.

Maybe it's time to do what Marco's been nagging me to do for ages, and take a day off. I could, I suppose. I've been making good progress with Achille's letters, and now I'm actually going to talk to Stella . . . The book's going to be all right, I realize, and a little warm glow sparks up somewhere inside me. It's going to be better than all right.

I suppose I could go to a museum. I haven't been back to the Uffizi yet, and that was one of Granny's favorite places. The Uffizi takes a whole day if you want to do it properly, and for the last weeks I just haven't had a day to spare. I have a day now, though. Marco isn't back until around seven, so I could totally go to the Uffizi.

The idea is quite galvanizing. I chug down some more coffee, put on my most comfortable shoes and practically bounce down the stairs, feeling like a woman with a plan. But then I walk out from my quiet street into via de' Pucci and find it heaving with people dragging suitcases and consulting maps and taking selfies, and my resolve fails. I don't want to stand in line for ages so I can haul myself around a museum. I don't even know what I was thinking. No, what I want is peace. Somewhere I can be alone, but not isolated; somewhere I feel safe and understood.

Suddenly, I know exactly where I need to go.

∾

AS I EMERGE FROM ROMITUZZO STATION INTO PIAZZA ACHILLE IN-furiati, I'm already starting to feel better. The square is quiet—empty, in fact, bar an elderly lady sitting on one of the benches with her little dog. The only other human in sight is Totò, who's cleaning the tables in front of his bar. I wave to him and he beams, setting down the spray bottle and tucking the cloth into the pocket of his apron.

"*Ciao*, Tori." As I approach he advances towards me, pulls me into a brief bear hug and plants a kiss on each cheek. "Come to do more research? Please tell me you have. My dad will be over the moon."

"Not today, though I will, I promise. I've just come to spend some time with Achille."

Totò nods. "Say hello to him from me. Are you heading there now?"

"Yes, I thought I'd go while it's quiet. And then come here for lunch, if you've got a table for me?"

"Of course. I'll see you shortly. Oh, wait a second." Holding up a hand, he vanishes into the bar and returns holding out a little bottle of water. "Take it, please. I know summer's over, but the humidity's a killer today. Don't want you passing out."

He's right, too. By the time I arrive at the cemetery gates, sweat's rolling down my back and I'm regretting wearing jeans. I down half the water straight off and tuck the bottle into my bag.

The roses on Achille's grave are still red, the petals darkening around the edges. When was Stella last here? Yesterday, the day before? *I had such a shock when I saw you*, her voice echoes in my mind. *I thought it was Rita back from the dead.*

"Not Rita, I'm afraid," I murmur out loud, brushing the marble of the tombstone with my fingers. "Sorry, Achille. But then I suppose you're with her now, if that's how the universe works."

It's funny: I thought I'd feel silly talking to Achille, but somehow I don't. There's nobody to hear me, after all. And I've spent so much time reading his personal letters, talking about him, thinking about him, that he feels like . . . like a person in my life. A friend, or a family member—though, come to think of it, he's a bloody sight more reliable than either of those. I feel like I could tell him anything; weirdly, I actually *want* to.

I take a deep breath. "Achille, I'm scared," I say. "Okay, mostly I'm angry. Really, really angry. But deep down I'm scared. Maybe that's even the main issue."

Wow. That actually does feel better. I look around to make sure I'm definitely alone, and go on.

"I'm not scared of Duncan anymore. No, that's not right," I say, as my gut gives an unpleasant squeeze. "I am still scared of him. He terrifies me. But I'm scared for other reasons, too." The words are starting to flow now, coming of their own accord. "What happened this morning was horrible. And on top of that, and I know I shouldn't be, I'm worried about what Marco's going to think. What if he doesn't believe what I tell him? What would that say about him? Honestly, Achille, if I've gone and got involved with *another* arsehole—"

My phone starts ringing at the bottom of my bag. I fish it out and my heart sinks as I see Charlie's name on the screen.

"Sorry about this," I say to Achille. "I know it's rude, but if I have to talk to her then I'd rather have company while I do it." I accept the call and put the phone to my ear. "Yes?"

"Before you start," Charlie says, "I had no idea he was going to show up like that. You have to understand."

Oh God, I'm so tired. "You gave him my address," I say.

"Yes, and why shouldn't I? It's a perfectly normal thing, passing on someone's details. The two of you are married, you know. It's not like I gave your address to some random stranger. And I was just exhausted from absorbing so much negativity—I had to do it for my own well-being. I have a life of my own, Tori. I have to put my needs first occasionally, since nobody else will."

I roll my eyes in Achille's direction. "Charlie, I'm in a cemetery. I can't have this conversation now." *Or ever,* I add silently.

"Well, I just want you to know that I didn't tell Duncan to go to Florence. His decision had nothing to do with me at all."

"Noted. Look—"

"And I couldn't have known," she goes on. "There was no way I could possibly tell what he was going to do. So if you're about to blame me for that on top of everything else, Tori, then you can just—"

She breaks off so abruptly that for a second I think my phone has died. Then I hear a sigh.

"No, that's all wrong." Her voice is flat, matter-of-fact. "I could perfectly well have known. I should have known."

I'm so surprised that it takes me a moment to summon the power of speech. "Uh . . . sorry?"

"Maybe I couldn't have guessed his exact plans. But I might have known something was wrong. I mean, a few years ago the two of you were all loved-up, and then at some point things changed. And then you were sad and stressed and nervous. I just didn't understand it and, frankly, I found it annoying." She sighs again. "If I'd really paid attention, I'd have understood. As it was, I didn't actually realize Duncan was so toxic until I spoke to him just now."

A jolt of nausea. "You spoke to him?"

"He spoke to me. Phoned me up and ranted. According to him—"

"Don't tell me." I close my eyes and feel the world tilt. "I don't want to hear it."

"All right, I won't. Anyway, it doesn't even matter what he said. It was how he said it. He sounded so . . . so . . ."

"Cold? Scornful? Vicious?"

"Yeah, basically." Charlie hesitates. I can almost see her fiddling with her earrings, like she does when she's embarassed and doesn't want to show it. "Tori, did he talk to you like that?"

"Yes."

"And was it . . . I mean, did he only do it when you were arguing? Or was it more . . ."

"Regular. I told you already, that's what he's like."

"Right," Charlie says. "Well, clearly I have to do some serious work on myself. If I couldn't spot a bad relationship dynamic at such close quarters, then I'm obviously out of touch with my own innate sense of healthy boundaries. I've actually been thinking about changing therapist, trying more of a psychodynamic approach. Besides, my current one has seemed quite stressed lately and it's starting to affect my self-esteem. Anyway, if Duncan spoke to you like that all the time, I'm not surprised you were so passive and whiny."

"Thanks," I mutter. But I feel a perverse rush of affection for my bossy big sister, although—or maybe because—I know this is the closest I'll ever get to an apology.

"Emotional abuse is a dreadful problem," she goes on. "Most people don't really understand it. And of course those of us who've been inadequately parented are especially prone to repeating that kind of dynamic. I can recommend some excellent books if you . . . wait. Did you say you were in a *cemetery?*"

"Yes, and I have to go. I'll tell you about it sometime," I say firmly as she starts to protest. "Just not now."

"Okay. But we really do need to talk about your boundaries—"

"Goodbye, Charlie. And good luck with the new therapist."

"Goodbye then. I do love you, you know," she adds, sounding almost aggrieved.

"I love you, too." I end the call, switch my phone off and shove it back into my bag. "Well," I mutter, "so much for peace, quiet and understanding."

I stay with Achille a while longer, letting my heart slow and my mind clear. Then, when the hunger pangs start to assert themselves, I head out and along the via Senese to Totò's bar.

❧

I'M HALFWAY INTO A PLATE OF *PICI CACIO E PEPE*, SCROLLING through BBC News on my phone, when a shadow falls across my table and I look up. Cecco's standing in front of me, looking faintly disapproving and leaning on the back of a chair for support.

"Oh!" I say. "Hello there. That seat's free if you want it."

"I thought you'd never offer," Cecco says. With a certain amount of puffing and muttering, he lowers himself into the chair just as Totò hurries over.

"Leave the poor girl to eat in peace," he says, earning a glare from Cecco. "Tori, just say if this old fart's bothering you and I'll move him on."

"It's fine, really."

"See?" Cecco says. "I'll have the cacio e pepe as well, and a glass of white wine. Bring one for Tori, too. Unless you have important work to do this afternoon, madame writer?"

"None at all," I say. "I'm having a day off."

"Make it a half-liter, then." He gives me a sharp look. "How's the book coming on?"

"Really well," I say. I almost tell him about finding Stella—it's on the tip of my tongue, but of course I can't. I already feel a little guilty about telling Marco. "I'm making good progress. You know, perpetu- ating the overblown cult of personality."

Cecco snorts. "I suppose you know your market. God, we're going to be overrun with tourists."

"And no bad thing," Totò cuts in. He fills my glass and Cecco's before putting the carafe on the table between us. "I need the busi- ness. Your pasta's almost ready," he tells Cecco, "so don't you harangue me about it."

"I wouldn't dare," Cecco retorts. "I'm a very well-mannered per- son. *Cin cin.*" He raises his glass to me, and I toast back.

We sit in silence for a while. I finish my pasta and Cecco starts on his. It's actually quite companionable, but something tells me he's working up to saying something. Finally, he sits back and looks away from me, across the square.

"I think," he begins and clears his throat. "I think perhaps I seemed rather harsh when I spoke to you before. About Achille."

He's so obviously uncomfortable that I could almost laugh. In a nice way, of course. "I see. Do you want to retract your statement? Maybe make another one?"

"Oh no. I meant what I said—I meant every word, and I'll stand by it. It's just . . . well, your grandmother loved him. He was impor-tant to her and of course he's important to you, too." He shrugs. "You must have thought I was a bad-tempered, joy-killing old bastard."

"Nothing could be further from the truth," I say. Cecco turns to look at me, and I quickly clamp my napkin to my mouth to hide my smile.

"I'm being serious," he says, with an air of wounded dignity.

"I know. And look, I appreciate it. It's good to have a different view. In fact, it's going to make the book much better."

"Really?"

"Of course," I say—and I'm not even being diplomatic, because it's true. "Achille was such a big charismatic personality, and he's dead, so people only remember the good stuff. Or that's all they'll admit to remembering. Do you have any idea how refreshing it is to find some-one who says: *well, personally, I didn't like the guy all that much?* Be-sides," I add, "conflict makes great copy. Readers love a bit of drama."

"Oh." Cecco's fiddling with his napkin. He seems to be process-ing. "So it's good that I told you about all that."

"Absolutely. It's great material."

"In a way," he says, puffing up a little, "you could even say that I did you a big favor."

"You did," I say. "Honestly, you did."

❧

BY MY CALCULATION, I GET BACK TO FLORENCE AT LEAST AN HOUR before Marco's train should come in. But as I approach the house, fishing for my keys, I see him sitting at a table outside Bar Dianora and looking towards me. Looking for me. His face lights up, and I feel a rush of joy and anxiety and I don't know what else. He stands and opens his arms and I go to him, burying my face in his shoulder, breathing him in.

"Tori," he says. "Tori, thank God."

"You heard, then," I manage to say.

"Elisa told me all about it. I can't believe that asshole. Thank God you're safe," he says, and his arms tighten around me.

I have to ask. I can't not ask. "And Chiara, did she . . . ?"

"Oh, I heard from Chiara." Marco's voice is dry. "I'm sorry she reacted like she did. She made a few wrong assumptions, to say the least."

Emotion bubbles up in me. I could weep, or laugh—I'm just so bloody relieved. "It's okay," I say, compelled to defend her now I know the threat is past. "She hasn't known me that long, and you're her friend. She's bound to be protective of you. And besides . . ." I stop myself before I can say that he hasn't known me that long either, that he could perfectly well have believed her. But Marco seems to pick up on my thought, because he loosens his grip on me and steps back, fixing me with serious dark eyes.

"I know you," he says. "I know you, and I trust you, and I . . . I'm happy you're here."

"I'm happy, too," I say.

For a long moment we just look at each other, grinning like fools. Then Marco clears his throat. "Well, we have a few things to celebrate. Where shall I take you this evening?"

I wrap my arms around him and reach up to kiss him. "I think," I say, "I'd rather stay in and order pizza."

32

"ACHILLE DIDN'T LISTEN," STELLA SAYS. SHE'S TOLD ME TO CALL HER Stella, because it's her old life we're here to discuss. "I begged him not to interfere. I told him it would only make things worse. But it was impossible. Once Achille saw that something was unfair, he simply couldn't let it stand. And the way my parents were treating me was very unfair. So he went and told some home truths to my father. And, exactly as I predicted, my father didn't shout back at Achille or hit him or punish him. He was angry with me—both he and my mother were. I had ruined their relationship with their darling boy. I was the problem. It was all just as I knew it would be."

She smooths out the blanket across her knees, fiddling with the fringe. My mind's racing with a thousand questions, but something tells me to stay quiet and so I do.

We're sitting on the terrace of Stella's house, which stands alone on a hilltop a little way south of Florence. I took a train and two buses to get here and I still struggled to walk the last stretch: a winding stony path so steep that I wonder how Stella's little Fiat can survive the ascent.

There's a whining, creaking sound and an elderly Chihuahua toddles out through the open French doors towards us, blinking in the sun. "Come on, Diego," Stella coos, her face soft with love, and she leans down and scoops the little dog into her lap. Diego turns a baleful, bug-eyed stare on me and wrinkles his lip in a desultory way.

"My guard dog," Stella says.

"He's lovely," I say, and Diego gives me a filthy look before curling up with his back to me.

"*Maleducato*," Stella says in mock reproach. "Now, what was I talking about?"

"About Achille and your parents," I prompt her.

"Yes. Well, the atmosphere became unbearable after that. My father was openly hostile, and my mother would cry and sulk and say . . . oh, awful things, vicious things. Worse than I'd heard from Enzo—worse than I'd heard from anybody. And Achille wouldn't let it rest. He kept on at both of them like a terrier after a rat—and the more he worried at them, the more they punished me, and so it went on and on. The Germans surrendered, the war ended, and my parents just kept going. I'd already decided that I would leave Romituzzo one day, but now the situation was becoming urgent. I couldn't live in that house any longer. You do understand that?"

Her vehemence takes me aback. "Of course," I say.

"I came to that decision quite alone. I think that I would have run off to a convent, or gone to Florence to try and find work there. Anything, anything to get away. But then, as it happened, I saw Davide in town one day late that summer. We didn't seek each other out, he and I, but if we happened to meet then we would make some time to talk. I expect people think we did much more than talk."

"I suspect so," I say, thinking of Cecco.

"But it wasn't like that. It wasn't a romantic bond Davide and I had. It was something much more important." She's staring out across the valley. "He understood. He was perhaps the only person in my life who treated me like a real comrade, except for don Anselmo. And don Anselmo had left. He managed to hang on until the very end of the war, until the first of May—the very first May Day celebrations of my life, and my sixteenth birthday—and then . . . well, he was gone and there was this rather horse-faced young priest in his place. And he never did say goodbye, even though he promised he would. After a while I came to understand that it was probably the best thing for him. He was so very unwell by then and he needed to look after himself, to do whatever was right. But at the time I didn't understand at all. I felt betrayed."

Stella falls silent again. In her lap, Diego rolls over with a grunt, exposing his belly for her to scratch.

"Little pig," she says distractedly as she ruffles his fur. I watch her, resisting the temptation to reach for my phone and double-check that it's recording. I have a feeling that telling this story is costing her; that she won't tell it again.

"So I saw Davide," she says at last. "And he had this letter from his cousin Giampiero. Giampiero had been in the army, you see, fighting in Yugoslavia when Italy was still on Germany's side. But he'd deserted to join Tito's partisans, and now the war was over he was going to stay there. And Davide told me that he was going to go, too."

"To Yugoslavia?"

"Yes. In a way, it was a natural choice. Davide was a communist but he hated Stalin, and he hated how Togliatti—that was the head of the Italian Communist Party—well, he did what Stalin told him. Davide believed that Marshal Tito was building a new revolution: a revolution from below. It seems strange now, but it's what many people believed at the time. Achille believed it, and Enzo—all the members of their group did. If I had been a communist, I would probably have believed it, too."

"But you weren't a communist," I say.

Stella shakes her head. "I wasn't, no. I had a lot of sympathy with the communists—the good ones, like Achille and Davide—but I didn't have faith in Marshal Tito like they did. And, ultimately, I was right. But in that instant . . ." She breaks off, and for just a moment she looks like that lost, wounded teenage girl. "Davide was so excited about going. And he told me that if I were to come with him, then we could keep working together. There would be plenty for us to do. And I could train to be a teacher if I wanted, or even a doctor. I had a gift for medicine, he said, and I'd have so much more freedom in big, cosmopolitan Belgrade than I would in provincial little Romituzzo. He told me so many things and promised me so much, but all I knew was that this boy—the one person in the whole world who was left to me—was giving me a way out, the chance to build a new life. So I didn't think about it, didn't ask myself if I really wanted to go and work for Tito's revolution. I agreed to go right away.

"The moment I said yes, the wheels were in motion. Davide soon got it all sorted out. He got us false papers that made it look as if we were from Trieste, on the Yugoslav border. We'd have to keep our mouths shut while travelling, of course, because a Tuscan accent sounds like nothing else on earth. It's unmistakable. And we'd have to leave in secret so nobody could hold us back. Davide's family would understand, he said, but Lucia wouldn't. She'd have tried to stop him and blown our cover in the process. As for my parents . . ." She sighs. "They had Achille, and that was all they wanted. They were so hostile to me, why shouldn't I leave? The only person I felt bad for in that moment was Achille himself. I knew he'd be hurt—I knew he'd miss me. But I had to save myself. I couldn't afford to worry about his feelings."

"Maybe you needed to get away from him, too," I say.

Stella nods. "I think so."

"So you and Davide set off."

"At dawn, like two lovers. The journey was . . . well, you can imagine. I kept repeating to myself silently: *My name is Maria Furlan.* It was the blandest, most inoffensive name, which I suppose is why they picked it. I believe Furlan is the commonest surname in Trieste. We travelled from Romituzzo to Florence, from Florence across to Bologna, and from there northwards to Ferrara, and all around us was devastation. I'd never seen anything like it. The fighting, the bombings, the atrocities and the deportations . . . you could see it in the wrecked cities, in the faces of the people. That's when I really understood how sheltered my life had been until that point. I began to feel very small, very small indeed. It was overwhelming." Diego's coiled up asleep now and she's running one of his ears through her fingers, over and over.

"When we got to Ferrara," she continues, "a comrade of a comrade of Davide's cousin picked us up in his car and drove us out of the city and into the countryside. Have you ever been to the Po Valley?"

"No."

"Well, it's flat. Perfectly, horribly, absolutely flat. I had never been outside Tuscany, and so I never knew that anywhere could be so flat. We were taken to a safe house on a farm in the middle of nowhere. The farm belonged to yet another comrade, and there was nobody around for miles except for the family who looked after the house.

A couple and their daughter and son. We were shown to an upstairs room with a view of . . . well, nothing, just flat green fields and the horizon. And then Davide's cousin's comrade's comrade told us to wait there and speak to nobody. Someone would come for us in the morning and take us on to the next stage, to Trieste, where we'd be given our instructions. Then he drove off and left us." She makes a wry face. "That was when I started to get nervous."

"I can imagine," I say.

"I spent a dreadful night in that room," Stella says. "Lying next to Davide, daring myself to ask him to hold me because I was really scared for the first time in years. It was as if all the fear I hadn't allowed myself to feel, that I'd had to suppress just to keep on doing my courier work, had burst in on me all at once. But I didn't ask in the end, because he didn't seem worried at all and I knew he would think I was a coward or, worse, a traitor. When morning came, we were brought breakfast—there were eggs and fresh bread, beautiful stuff—but I couldn't eat. All I could do was stare out of the window. Davide kept talking about the work we'd do in Yugoslavia, how we'd keep building that revolution even if we had to fight a whole new war to do it. I listened and tried to feel the enthusiasm I'd felt when we were at home in Romituzzo, but it just wouldn't come. I hated myself for that. I told myself over and over again that I would be fine once we were underway, that my urge to survive could not and must not overcome the promise I had made. And then at some point Davide went to the washroom, and while he was out of the room I saw it. A car coming along the road to the farm. It was like something gave way inside me."

"So what did you do?"

"I ran," Stella says. "I ran downstairs without any real idea of what I was doing, only that I could not get in that car. And as I was racing into the hallway I collided with the son of the caretaker family. His name was Giuseppe." When she says his name, her face lights up. "He asked if something was wrong, and I said something like: *They're coming to fetch me, they're coming to take me over the border to Yugoslavia and I can't go. I don't want to go.* Giuseppe didn't think twice. He bundled me out of the back door and there, propped up in the yard, was a battered old motorcycle. He got on and I got up behind him, and we were off. He took me a long way away, to this little inn where he persuaded me to eat a big bowl of polenta and drink some wine, and he didn't ask me any questions at all but just let me talk. We stayed there until the sun started to go down, and then we rode back to the house. I was so worried about what was going to happen next—what his family would say, where I would go, what would be done about me. But I already trusted Giuseppe. He was so warm, so kind. And he had listened to me, really listened. I thought that was wonderful."

Stella's smiling now. Diego slides off her lap and toddles to the edge of the terrace, where he flops down on his side with a huff.

"I expect there was a bit of a scene in your absence," I say, rather fatuously.

"I expect there was. But the car had gone and the place was silent. We crept up to the back door and put our ears to it, but nobody stirred. Giuseppe offered to go in first. He said: 'Look, I might have to explain a few things to my mother and father. Can I tell them something of what you told me?' And I said that of course he could, he could tell them whatever he wanted, and off he went. The wait was agonizing, but eventually he returned and told me to come in. It turned out that his parents and his sister were all very relieved and thought he'd done well to get me to safety. They were good comrades, of course, like so many country people—they'd helped the Resistance in every way they could—but they thought I was far, far too young to be running off to a foreign country. I was afraid that they'd send me back to my parents, but there was no question of that, either. I don't know what Giuseppe had told them, but they said that I could stay with them for as long as I wanted. Perhaps they saw that he and I were already falling in love."

Now I'm smiling, too. "And that was it."

"That was it," Stella says. "I stayed with them and I helped with the pigs and chickens, and went to Mass with his mother and sister every Sunday. When Giuseppe and I married, I married him as Maria Furlan, not Stella Infuriati. I was Maria Furlan, after all—that's what it said on my papers. We had a little boy, and then another. The silence and the flatness of the place grew on me and I came to love the Po Valley. How could I not, when it had given me all these gifts?

"And then one day, I was in the kitchen with Giuseppe's mother. She came from Ferrara and she wanted to teach me how to make that pumpkin-stuffed pasta the Ferrarese love so much. I was doing very badly at it, but we were having tremendous fun. The wireless was on, the sun was shining, and then all of a sudden we heard . . ." She shivers, drawing the blanket up and around her. "There was a news report and it said—I can still hear it, that grave voice—it said that Achille had been in an accident. That he was dead and that Italy was in mourning. That was the exact phrase."

"You don't have to talk about this," I say. "Not if you don't want to."

"No, I should talk about it. I need to talk about it. That wonderful, peaceful life I had . . . it was only ever leased to me. I should have known that Achille wouldn't live long, and once he was gone then my parents would be alone. Alone and destroyed, because they loved him more than anything in the world, including themselves, including me." Her expression is grim. "I could have left them to it. That's what Giuseppe said, anyway, but I couldn't. I'd always be thinking about them otherwise, imagining their suffering. The newspapers said that Achille had been in partnership with Pierfrancesco Legni, so I wrote Pierfrancesco a letter and explained the situation as best I could, and asked if he could help. And he did, of course. Pierfrancesco loved Achille, but above all he would do anything to help a fellow partisan."

"So he set you up with the bar," I say.

"Oh, he did more than that. He gave us quite a substantial loan—well, he said it was a loan, but we both knew perfectly well he'd never ask for it back—enough to bring my parents to Florence and Giuseppe's, too, if they ever needed it. And he set up the whole process with his own lawyer, his bank manager, his accountant and so on, so that nobody ever gave my poor little false papers a second look, or asked why I sounded Tuscan when I claimed to be born in Trieste. Pierfrancesco really took care of everything. He even gave us a housewarming gift—this silly photograph to hang up in the bar until we could start to make it our own."

"The Bugatti 251."

Stella gives me a watery smile. "Then you remember. It became kind of a bittersweet joke between us, that picture. Because the Bugatti never raced, you see, and we both wished that Achille had never raced, either."

I want to go over and hug her but I don't dare. She's too dignified, too tense. "You didn't want to go back to being Stella Infuriati?" I ask. "Officially, I mean?"

She shakes her head. "I'd been Maria Furlan for years by then. I'd matured and changed, I'd had two babies—I didn't look like my old self or even feel like her. Maybe I could have changed back and had Pierfrancesco smooth it all over for me somehow, but I liked my new life and I wanted to keep it. I thought my parents might object, might try to insist that I resume my old name or even move us all in with them, but they didn't. After Achille died, they didn't want to stay in Romituzzo or have anything to do with the people there. They couldn't bear to see their son memorialized, couldn't stand how everyone was forever talking about him. It was far too painful for them. They were content to live with us, play with their grandsons—whom they adored—and wait out the rest of their days until they could see Achille in heaven. And that's what they did, more or less. My father lived another five years, my mother rather longer, and if they were never happy again, they were at least comfortable. I couldn't replace Achille for them, but they were pleased to have me back and they didn't care what I called myself. Our relationship was . . . fine."

"Only fine?" I ask.

"That was the best I could expect." The pain in her voice is palpable. "But I didn't need more, not really. I had my own family and I had Pierfrancesco on my side. He was a great friend and the best of allies. And then I met your grandmother, and from that day on I had a sister. There's a whole story attached to that," she says, giving me an assessing look, "but perhaps we should save that for another day? I've been talking for hours, and no doubt you want to get home to that nice young man of yours, the one with the red sports car. He is your young man, isn't he?"

"He is now," I say, feeling a blush spread up my neck. (The reunion with Marco was *very* satisfactory.)

Stella claps her hands. "I knew it! Well, I shall have to disappoint Niccolò. He noticed you that day, you know, but I told him he was too late." She grins at me, obviously not put out in the slightest. "If you want to run along I shall understand. I can tell you the story another day, if God spares me. Or I can make coffee and we can talk a little longer."

I pull my phone towards me and check the time: not even five o'clock. Marco said he'd message after work to see whether I needed to be picked up, and he can't be anywhere near finished yet. And I really, really want to know how Stella met Granny.

"Coffee would be lovely," I say.

❧

THE SUN'S ALREADY SETTING WHEN I SAY GOODBYE TO STELLA. AS I turn to go, she clutches at my wrist. "Wait," she says. "I want to give you something."

She pulls a silver chain from the neck of her blouse and begins to fiddle with the clasp. Her fingers are stiff, and she mutters under her breath.

"No," she snaps as I open my mouth to offer help. "I can do it. *Oddio* . . . there!" She takes off the necklace and presses it into my hand. "Wear it or don't wear it, but it's yours. Take it."

I look at the necklace in my palm. A heavy silver locket tarnished with age and wear; I can just make out an ornate cross engraved into the metal. I pop it open and there's Achille, defiantly facing down the camera. His curly hair is slicked back and he's wearing a kerchief knotted around his neck.

"But . . ."

"Take it, please." She looks as fierce as he does, and for the first time I see the resemblance between them. "My mother wore it every day, and she made me promise to wear it once she was dead. I don't want to carry it—to carry him anymore. He belongs with you."

Her tone brooks no argument. I close my hand over the locket. "Thank you," I say, though it sounds incredibly inadequate.

Stella pats my arm. "Don't thank me. Now go to your young man—I can see him waiting out there in the yard."

And Marco is waiting, sitting patiently in the red Comacchi. "I thought you were meeting me at the bus stop," I say as I open the door and slide in.

He snorts. "And let you break an ankle coming down that damned path in the dark? Not a chance."

"I appreciate it." I'm rooting through my bag, looking for a safe place to put Stella's locket. Marco switches on the overhead light and leans over.

"What's that you've got there?" he asks, and I open my hand and show him the necklace. He takes it from me and runs his thumb over the engraved surface. "Wow. This must be an antique."

"Stella gave it to me. Open it."

"Wow," he says again. "Red kerchief and all. What a face! Are you going to put it on?"

"I don't know. I suppose it's the safest place for it."

"I think so. Lean forward." I gather up my hair and he fastens the chain around my neck, his warm fingers brushing my skin. "There," he says, patting the locket where it rests against my breastbone. "You're Achille's guardian now. Wait, what did I say?"

"Nothing, really. It's just . . . that's what Stella said, pretty much. I didn't realize what a hard time she had." I shiver remembering her words. *I don't want to carry him anymore.* "I'll tell you all about it when we get home."

Home. The word slipped out before I could think about it.

"Home," Marco says, and smiles his dazzling, crooked smile. "I like the sound of that." He turns the key in the ignition of the Comacchi and the engine thrums into life. "Ready to go?" he asks.

I take a deep breath and look ahead. The valley lies before us and in it is Florence, lit up against the night sky. I can just make out the dome of the cathedral.

"Ready," I say.

33

Stella

IT WAS THE SUMMER OF 1955 WHEN I FIRST MET RITA CRAYE. I RE-member that I'd had to go up to Rifredi to see Pierfrancesco about something—some detail about the running of the bar, perhaps, or some other minor issue—and I had my youngest, Carlo, with me. He was two years old, and at a stage where he rebelled against everything but never wanted to be apart from me, either. So we had a long and sticky tram journey and arrived at the Legni Editore offices rather late and disheveled. But Pierfrancesco was running over time as he so often was. His secretary brought a coffee for me and some biscuits and a couple of picture books to keep Carlo occupied, and we settled down to wait in the lobby.

We must have been there for about ten minutes when there was the sound of high heels coming down the stairs, tac-tac-tac, and Rita appeared. I recognized her right away, of course, because her face had been all over the papers when Achille died. She looked much as I thought she would: slender and blonde and so beautifully dressed, wearing the kind of simple clothes I knew even then had to be expensive. But there was a terrible, heavy sadness about her. Haunted, that's the best word I can find. She looked haunted.

I'm ashamed to say I stared. There was something shocking in being confronted with this legendary figure, this foreign socialite who had been the love of my brother's short life. She said a warm goodbye to Pierfrancesco's secretary, who was rushing forward to open the door, and then she smiled at me and Carlo and said *arrivederci* to us, too.

"Go on up," the secretary said as she hurried back to her post.

In his big office upstairs, Pierfrancesco was looking out of the window. He turned as we came in, and his face lit up at the sight of Carlo; he adored children and they adored him. Carlo could be a terror for me, probably because I indulged him—I loved him so much that I had a horror of being too harsh, of treating him like my parents had treated me. But he always behaved for Pierfrancesco. He climbed up into one of the chairs in front of the big desk and looked at him, just looked, as if waiting for his orders.

"Now, comrade Carlo, let me see what I have for you today." Pierfrancesco opened a drawer and brought out a wooden toy: a steam engine, painted all in black with a bright red star on the side and Cyrillic writing underneath. He told me later that it was meant to be Commissar Trotsky's armoured train; a Russian exile friend had made it specially. "What do you think of this?" he asked, holding it out, and Carlo smiled and reached out his fat little hands to grab it.

"Say thank you," I reminded him.

"Fank you," Carlo whispered. Clutching the toy to his chest, he slid off the chair and sat down on the floor, where he ran the engine over the tiles and made chug-chug noises.

Pierfrancesco ran a hand through his hair, making it stick up even more than usual. "I'm sorry, I'm a little distracted today. Remind me what we need to discuss?"

I reminded him about the issue, whatever it was, and we went through the paperwork while Carlo played happily at my feet. It's extraordinary, really—Pierfrancesco was an important man with endless demands on his time, but somehow I never felt like a nuisance when I had to show up with some minor problem for him to fix. He always contrived to make me feel as if I were the one helping him, even when he was doing me some colossal favor like lending me money (or pretending to lend it). Different as they were, he and don Anselmo were cut from the same kind of cloth.

Once we were done, he had coffee brought in and started asking me all the usual questions: how was Giuseppe, how were my parents, how were things at the bar. But I could tell that there was something else on his mind. Pierfrancesco was very transparent. He listened restlessly, folding and refolding a piece of paper that lay on the desk before him, and then finally he said: "Margaret Craye came to see me earlier today. You know, Achille's young lady."

Carlo was getting tired and fretful. He raised his arms to me, the little wooden engine still clutched in one fist. I lifted him and settled him in my lap where he leaned, warm and heavy, against me and stuck his other thumb in his mouth. "Yes," I said. "I saw her on her way out."

"Oh, you did? I suppose you were bound to cross paths. Very elegant, isn't she?" Pierfrancesco leaned back, attempting to be casual. "Of course, she's suffering terribly, poor soul," he said. "Not that she'll talk to me about it. I try and try to draw her out, but . . . well, she's so *English*. She won't open up at all."

"I'm sorry to hear that," I said. Poor Pierfrancesco, he did so hate it when he couldn't fix people.

"I thought . . ." he went on. "Well, maybe she doesn't want to talk to an old man like me." Pierfrancesco was forty-five, fifty at most. "Maybe if she had someone her own age to chat to . . . a woman friend, you know, someone who could really understand . . ."

I was playing with Carlo's hair, stroking his fine dark curls away from his forehead. I knew exactly what Pierfrancesco was driving at—he wanted me to befriend this strange woman, to share stories, to listen to her talk—and I didn't like it. I already had to deal with my parents. I had to live with the grief that seeped from them and poisoned everything. I had to live with Achille the dead hero, picking my way around the gaping rent he'd left in their world.

Pierfrancesco must have seen my hesitation. "I know," he said. "I know I'm asking a lot of you, and it's very likely she won't want to talk anyway. But if you did have a little time, and she did want to meet, just once, and talk for a few minutes . . . would you consider it? For me?"

Damn him. "I'll consider it," I said.

WHEN A WEEK HAD GONE BY WITHOUT WORD FROM EITHER PIER-francesco or Rita, I began to relax. I'd been dreading that she really would get in touch and be eager, horribly eager, to talk all about Achille and make me dig up every childhood memory I had.

"Thank God I don't have to do that," I said to Giuseppe as we lay in bed one night—that was the only private time he and I got in those days, between the children, the bar and my parents. "The last thing I want is a long in-depth conversation about my dead brother. Can you imagine?"

But Giuseppe was looking at me as if I'd said something . . . not wrong exactly, but odd. "Are you sure?" he said. "Don't you think it would feel better if you did talk about him?"

"I talk about him all the time," I said. "He's never not the subject of discussion."

He shook his head. "*Tesoro*, no. I can't remember the last time you mentioned his name—you or your parents. I'm sure you think about him all the time, but you don't talk about him. Really."

"Oh," I said. It was a strange realization, and painful in a way I didn't quite understand. Giuseppe gathered me into his arms.

"It's all right," he said. "Everyone has to mourn in their own way. Whatever you need to do, you'll do it in your own time. I'm sure it's a good thing that this woman has decided to leave you alone."

But she hadn't. A couple of evenings later, just as the last stragglers were paying for their aperitivo, Rita came into the bar. She was alone and wearing a gaily patterned dress that looked like it came from Paris. I pretended not to recognize her. What else could I do? For all I knew, she had no idea who I was. For all I knew, she happened on the bar by accident.

"Good evening," I said. "What can I get you?"

"White wine, please." Her face was serene, a mask, but her hands were clasped tightly together in front of her. I felt very sorry for her in that moment. I also knew that she hadn't just wandered in by chance, that she must have come to find me, to speak to me. My heart sank.

"Sit down and I'll bring it to you," I said. "We have a Trebbiano and a Vernaccia. Which would you like?"

"Just whichever you recommend. Thank you." She sat down at a table by the window, pulled out a little red notebook from her handbag and began to flick through it. I poured out an extra-large measure of Vernaccia—if I could do nothing else for the poor girl, I could do that—and brought it over to her with a bowl of olives.

She barely looked up when I set her glass down. "Thank you so much," she said, her eyes still fixed on her notebook. I thought I'd been given a reprieve. I turned away, fully intending to summon Giuseppe from the back room and let him take over while I went upstairs and stayed there until Rita had gone. I'd got almost as far as the counter when she spoke again.

"Maria?"

I turned back. Rita was looking at me, twisting a ring round and round on her finger. "I hope you don't mind," she said, "but Pierfrancesco told me where to find you. I'll go away if you prefer. But I thought that maybe, if you like—if it would help you, too—then we could talk. I miss your brother very much." She said that last part quietly, with utter simplicity. And that quiet simplicity was like a cry.

"All right," I said. "We can talk. If you want, we can talk."

HISTORICAL NOTE

FLORENCE IS REAL, ALTHOUGH IT DOESN'T ALWAYS SEEM LIKE IT. But the little town of Romituzzo is entirely invented, located in a fictional valley, the Valdana, that's shoehorned in somewhere between Florence and Siena. Readers who know the area may spot some references to the city of Poggibonsi, where I was fortunate enough to live for a while. This is a loving tribute, not a direct parallel. Far from it: Poggibonsi's strategic location meant that it suffered immensely in the course of the war. The city was almost entirely destroyed by the time of its liberation. By comparison, the rural backwater of Romituzzo gets off very lightly.

However, that doesn't mean that the inhabitants of Romituzzo and the Valdana have a safe or peaceful life. The various partisan groupings who fought in the hills and mountains of Italy drew their support from rural communities, and providing that support in any capacity—however marginal or passive—was a seriously dangerous undertaking. The German and the Italian SS, the Wehrmacht, the Fascist National Republican Guard and Fascist volunteer groups such as the Black Brigades waged an intensely violent campaign against partisans, their allies, and those who engaged in strike action. Many were hanged, shot, imprisoned, tortured or deported to concentration camps from which only a few returned.

Violence was also intentionally used as a deterrent. The threat of killing ten Italians for every dead German was not an empty one. There were public executions: Tina Anselmi describes how, as a seventeen-year-old trainee teacher, she and her classmates were made to witness the hanging of thirty-one partisans at Bassano del Grappa. (In her case, as in so many others, the deterrent did not work—her response was to join the Resistance.) And there were times at which the Nazi-Fascist regime exceeded even its own stated policy of brutality, such as the murder of 335 civilians and political prisoners at the Ardeatine Caves outside Rome on 24 March 1944, and the slaughter of around 560 civilians—including more than a hundred children— at Sant'Anna di Stazzema, near Lucca, on 12 August 1944.

My characters are invented, and so are the specific situations in which they find themselves. But their fear is real, and so is their determination.

⤜∽⤛

THERE WERE MANY DETERMINED YOUNG WOMEN LIKE STELLA. PARtisan couriers tended to be female, because it was easier for women to pass unnoticed. They took messages, supplies, literature, weapons, even explosives from point to point, keeping the work of the Resistance moving. They travelled on foot or by bike or on public transport; they wove notes into their hair, stuffed guns into their bras, concealed their contraband in shopping bags and prams and school satchels. It was hard, scary, indispensable work, and those who did it knew that—if captured—they would be tortured for the information they carried.

It's no wonder that some of Italy's foremost women politicians and activists started out as couriers. Lidia Menapace, Tina Anselmi and Rossana Rossanda are just three of the most famous names. But many couriers, like Irma Bandiera, Stefanina Moro, Ines Bedeschi and Clorinda Menguzzato, did not live to see the Liberation. They died defending the secrets they held.

There were also women organizers, like Berta and Agnese in this story. The cross-factional network Berta founds in Romituzzo is a small-scale, local version of the extensive Women's Defence and Assistance network founded by Ada Gobetti, Bianca Guidetti Serra and Frida Malan, which is described in Gobetti's *Partisan Diary*. And there were women combatants, increasing in numbers as the war went on.

They often had to fight for acceptance, but they also proved themselves in battle. Carla Capponi, Norma Pratelli Parenti, Rita Rosani and Iris Versari are just four of the nineteen women awarded the Gold Medal of Military Valour for their exceptional actions in the Resistance.

Like Stella, many women partisans saw their contributions dismissed when the war was won. Only in the last decades has increasing attention been paid to the value—and the valor—of women's participation.

Don Anselmo, too, is a very familiar figure to anyone who knows Resistance history. There were many priests and religious whose faith and humanity compelled them to oppose Fascism and the Nazi occupation, often at the cost of their own lives. The Archbishop of Florence, Cardinal Elia Dalla Costa, worked strenuously to save Italian and foreign Jews from deportation and murder—and he strongly encouraged his clergy to do the same. Don Anselmo would certainly have been part of his network, and he shares the cardinal's anti-communist and anti-Fascist convictions.

Don Anselmo has a number of spiritual brothers, such as don Aldo Mei, don Pietro Pappagallo, don Giovanni Fornasini and don Francesco Foglia (a keen explosives expert, also known as "don Dinamite"). But perhaps his closest real equivalent is don Giuseppe Morosini, a former military chaplain who was active in the Roman resistance, helping the partisans with intelligence and weapons as well as moral and spiritual support, and who was executed on 3 April 1944. Don Giuseppe was also a model for Aldo Fabrizi's heroic and lovable don Pietro in my favourite film, *Roma, Città Aperta*.

Stella, don Anselmo and their comrades are the most clearly recognizable types in this story, but the historical parallels don't end there. Guido Comacchi will be identifiable to fans of classic Formula One, while publishing types will spot a few familiar traits in the character of Pierfrancesco Legni. The secret passage in Romituzzo is a copy of the famous one at Niccolò Machiavelli's country estate in Sant'Andrea in Percussina, although there it connects the manor house with the pub across the road. (You can visit both, and you should.) In general, I've tried to make sure that my inventions are anchored in some kind of reality.

Achille Infuriati has his antecedents, too. There were many brave young men in the Resistance, and there were many gifted racing drivers in the post-war period. And there were some who combined the two spheres. One was the Italian American driver Alfonso Thiele, an OSS captain during the war, who married the extraordinary partisan Walkiria Terradura. Another was Jean Achard, a French Resistance fighter and journalist who died in an accident before his motor racing career really had a chance to flourish.

But if I owe a debt to anyone in particular for the creation of Achille, it's the late James Hunt: a great sportsman and passionate anti-apartheid campaigner who spoke candidly about fear, death and the psychology of calculated risk-taking. I returned to his interviews again and again.

IN WRITING *ESCAPE TO FLORENCE*, AND STELLA'S STORY IN PARTICU-lar, I have tried to do a little bit of justice to all the people I have named here. But the nature of Stella's clandestine work, her young age and her small-town context mean that hers is a small story, not a big one. She isn't privy to the strategic operation of the various factions she's helping, or the work don Anselmo and don Mauro are doing from their respective parochial houses. And for her own safety and that of others, she must remain ignorant. This means that I have touched lightly, for now, on important topics that deserve proper consideration. I will explore these further in future work, beginning with my next novel, set in Genoa and centred on the Jewish-Christian resistance network DELASEM.

In the meantime, I have done my best to make sure that Stella's little world is authentic in feel and believable in detail. I had a tremendous resource in the many first-person accounts by women partisans, both written and recorded. There are too many to name, but the stories of Tina Anselmi, Luciana Romoli, Ada Gobetti and Teresa Vergalli were particularly inspiring.

I also took advice wherever I could. I'll save the most fulsome stuff for the acknowledgments, but Catherine Jones, Hilary Ely and Michael Carley all carefully read my manuscript from their various angles of expertise—guns, bikes, racing drivers, the complex landscape of the Italian Left—and not once, but several times. Mirna Bonazza, Marisa D'Angelo, Enza De Silva, Eliana Nucera and the staff of the Biblioteca Ariostea in Ferrara provided me with a beautiful and peaceful place to work as well as access to valuable material. Nicola Rebagliati was an exceptional consultant in all matters of Italianity, Teresa Vergalli provided invaluable additional details about her courier work over email, police adviser Graham Bartlett answered my questions about corpse decomposition, and Professor Geoffrey Swain kindly talked to me about Yugoslavia.

If, with all this help, I still managed to get something wrong—and I'm sure I did—that's entirely my fault.

ACKNOWLEDGMENTS

FOR THOSE WHO ARE DRAWN TO IT, WRITING IS THE BEST AND MOST satisfying vocation in the world. It's also demanding, often lonely and always precarious. I am deeply grateful to (and for) my writing buddies Catherine Jones, Taylor Cole and Michael Carley, with whom I've been swapping drafts, workshopping ideas and chatting shit for over a decade. April Doyle, Carol Goodall, Hilary Ely, Margaret Kirk, Jenn Strange and my dad, John, all provided valuable input and support on this particular project. I'm also indebted to my mentor, the writer and teacher Emma Darwin, for her ongoing help and guidance.

Since I first arrived in Italy, Michael and Yana at Trattoria Boboli (in Florence) and Betty, Mirko, Carmine and all the wonderful people at Villa Machiavelli (in Sant'Andrea in Percussina) have provided me with comfort food, great conversation, and a warm, welcoming place to write, translate, read and think. Matteo and Libero Saraceni have been extremely generous in allowing me to linger in Machiavelli's study, pace around his garden, and go back and forth through the secret tunnel while I work out sticky plot points. And if the legend is true and Machiavelli haunts the place, then I should thank him, too.

I was very fortunate that my brilliant agent Broo Doherty spotted the potential in this story and encouraged me to work it into something much more substantial. She and her wonderful colleague Helen Edwards got it into the hands of two fantastic editors, Rachel Faulkner-Willcocks at Head of Zeus and Sophia Kaufman at HarperCollins US. Together with copy editor Helena Newton, who worked with great sensitivity to perfect and polish the final manuscript, they were just the right combination of tough and supportive. I am also profoundly thankful to to Amy Baker, Katie Teas, Meredith Dowling, and every else at Harper Paperbacks who has made this book possible. Working with all of these people has been a delight, and I appreciate for their time, faith and insight.

None of this could have happened without the first and best friend I made in my adopted country. This book is dedicated to him.